SECRET DREAMS

By the same author

SWAN DIVE
ARCHANGEL

SECRET DREAMS

Keith Korman

ARCADE PUBLISHING • NEW YORK

FIRST EDITION

This is a work of fiction. Names, characters, places, and incidents are either the product of the author's imagination or used fictitiously.

Library of Congress Cataloging-in-Publication Data

Korman, Keith.
    Secret dreams / Keith Korman. —1st Edition
        p.   cm.
    ISBN 1-55970-288-5
    I. Title.
PS 3561.066S43 1995
813'.54—dc20   94-43026

Published in the United States by Arcade Publishing, Inc., New York
Distributed by Little, Brown and Company

10 9 8 7 6 5 4 3 2 1

BP

Designed by API

For Those Who Stood

With Me

Through the Coldest

Watches of the Night

Homo sum

Humani nihil a me alienum puto

I am a man.

Nothing human is alien to me.

—Publius Terentius

Contents

BOOK I

THE PATIENT
DOES NOT EXIST

Chapter *1*

Frau Direktor

Frau Direktor put down her pen and turned away from the unfinished letter. Beyond her office window, new snow fell onto the street below, muffling the scrape of horse-drawn sledges and the rattle of carts on the icy cobblestones. The pen felt awkward in her hand; her fingers had grown thick and clumsy, as though swollen from the effort of writing. . . . Once more she stared at the stubborn page, damning herself to force a line or two from her tired brain. Just a little further. Anything. Just to finish and be done. Put the thing in an envelope and lick it closed. Find a stamp and take it to the corner. . . . God, how she hated to beg.

> Herr C. G. Jung
> Bollingen Tower
> Bollingen Zee, Schweiz
> January 10, 1933
>
> Dear Beloved,
>   How many years since we have spoken? I've lost count. The time has passed so quickly. Though I never thought I would be able to live without you, I have thrived nonetheless. Now I must beg a favor. But first, rest easy; all is well here at the Clinic. We recently received our quarterly payment from the Ministry of State Medicine, and so our near future is certainly assured. It is gratifying to know we enjoy the confidence and support of those above. . . .

What lies! Nothing could be further from the truth. But how else could she get a letter out of the country without attracting attention? Rumor had it the authorities opened all the international mail. Perhaps they did, perhaps they didn't — how could one know? But if they *did*, they would find no complaint, no grumble of discontent, no hint of trouble in this awful, awful place. Ach, even to address him as her *beloved*. How obscene. Having loved did not make you beloved. No, the rose had died, no petals left upon the stem. He had seen to that. Her one and only — who found her lost in an asylum room, who unlocked the door and led her gently out. Who cast her away in the end . . . So when he read her calculated lies, he'd know at once things had gone from bad to worse and the days of her clinic numbered by those who kept watch in far-off Moscow.

So what should she tell her precious Herr Doktor to make him do what she so needed? To accept one of her children into his care. The one child she would manage to spirit out of the city. The last survivor of all her hope and devotion. And if Herr Doktor's ever watchful Frau Emma should come upon her letter first? Cold, spiteful Emma, keeping a man she never really wanted. Then all would be in vain. . . .

The evening wind played havoc with the papers on Frau Direktor's desk; the unfinished plea turned over by itself. The sound of horses' hooves clattered through the frosted panes of glass. In the black years of her madness, the clippety-clop of hoofbeats would have set her teeth on edge, sent her cowering to some dark, safe place. But Herr Doktor had mended her of that. Or tried to. The window opened easily; she forced herself to look below. Still battling the renegades of bedlam after all these years. Gritting her teeth against the innocent sound of horses' hooves upon a street of stones, simply because once upon a time it used to drive her mad.

Raving.

When other young women sat primly at garden parties, she ranted in empty rooms, shut up in the prison of her mind. But a Frog Prince had laid a kiss upon her brow, turning her into a butterfly that flew between the bars.

And now, incredibly, she stood in an office of her very own. Wastebasket overflowing. Pencil points broken. But hers. All hers . . . Frau Direktor of the Rostov Children's Psychiatric Institute. Rostov-on-

4

Don. U.S.S.R. The house of the last chance when all other doors had closed. The pompous lines she had written reproached her:

> I must confess it still pleases my vanity to hear the Clinic's two interns call me Frau Direktor, pronouncing that imperial title with your erect Germanic K — as I heard it so often in that place where we began. . . .

To one who knew her, that overbearing prose would only show how completely topsy-turvy matters had become. Why bring up "that place where we began" except to reveal her own fear? All the important words in the paragraph lay exposed for him to see like some word-association test they had done a thousand times. Confess. Vanity. Title. Direktor. As if to say: I confess, my title as director is all just vanity. I direct nothing. Not like That Place where we began.

No, not like that great European institution at the turn of the century. Where their exalted Herr Direktor ruled the lives of hundreds of patients and a phalanx of staff. Like a field marshal or a god; where the professors and the doctors were his captains, the nurses and orderlies his soldiers. And the lowly interns, beholden pages, bowing and scraping for the merest nod from on high. The lot of them appearing the very model of proper Swiss behavior. All in the polished marble corridors of a Zurich sanatorium for the mentally diseased in the year 1905, the very walls exuding order and security. Respectability. And permanence.

Nothing like her own clinic. Nearly three decades later, the Rostov Children's Institute, despite its daunting name, was merely a run-down four-story town house in a damp part of town, where people threw stones at their windows just for the hell of it and bargemen stumbled down the street drunk, shouting abuse. Several of the clinic's windows had been broken and still needed mending. The hallways wanted paint too. Her "Institute" had no grand staff — just one orderly, one nurse, two interns — and only a dozen children. Nothing whatsoever like that place *where she began* . . . The pen came to her fingers and flowed across the page:

> And it has always been my hope that what we once started would never really end. But that we would

somehow pass on to others what we had learned. So
in this way we may never die.

There! The key words. End. Die. Pass on. Hope. He'd have to be
stone deaf or stupid not to perceive what had come to pass. For the
Institute had been put on notice. Their pimply orderly had failed to
report to work. Their dining room workers had gone as well, and with
them the food deliveries. That meant someone had to spend long
hours buying food piecemeal in the markets, a tiresome and consuming job. Yesterday a moving van had stopped at the Institute's
front door; the stout driver and a pair of porters in blue jumpers asked
if the furniture and brass fixtures were ready to be removed. Frau Direktor sent them away, saying there must be some mistake. No, she
knew. . . . There was no mistake. Obviously the police were coming
to get her.

The pen moved of its own accord; the lines crawled across the
page. . . .

That is why I am referring a colleague to you. One
of my old Zurich patients is in need of therapy. The
patient is suffering from a troubling relapse and has
begun acting like a child again. You remember, the
kind of behavior we all wish to escape.

What nonsense! She had no "Zurich patients" — when last in
Switzerland, *she* had been the patient, no one else. And once more,
the code words. Trouble. Child. Suffer. Escape. Colleague. Zurich.
Therapy. What could be plainer than that? My colleague is escaping
with a child in need of treatment. . . . But which intern should she
send? And which child?

She addressed an envelope and found a stamp; she took her coat from
the stand and went outside. The snow had thinned; tiny drifts shivered on the clinic's steps. The post box on the corner stood alone under a shaft of light. The metal grate squealed and snapped as the letter
went inside. She scanned the blind windows in the buildings for any
sign of life or watchful eyes, peering closely — but saw nothing. The
lighted windows of her clinic's living room shone into the dark. Beyond the shabby curtains her interns, Maximilian and Madame,

6

waited to begin their regular end-of-day discussion. Frau Direktor and her interns held their meetings in that old dilapidated living room when the children lay in their first lap of sleep. Later they might wake with night terrors and call the adults from their beds, but in the evening the staff seized this first sigh of slumber, when the house was quiet.

She took off her coat and hung it on the stand; the light from the living room spilled redly across the floor. The walls were covered in pink satin wallpaper with a red rose motif, the budding flowers like drops of blood. The pink satin had curled, yellowing like an opium addict's skin. Frau Direktor had come to see her town house as the rotting husk of some mysterious plant, and her helpers as its complex living seeds, waiting only for the gentle rain and warmth to split their shells.

They would have finished putting the children to bed by now; sitting in mismatched chairs, as they always did, heads bowed close as though telling secrets. Maximilian's low voice came down the hall, the words blurred and indistinct. . . . The man was a lanky thirty-five-year-old bachelor, dainty and fastidious, with the scent of witch hazel and solitary meals about him. He was already an accomplished surgeon at the Leningrad Hermitage Hospital when he came to the clinic two years ago. Giving up the lucrative and respected Leningrad practice must have appeared odd to his peers, for by leaving the Surgery Unit of the Hermitage he gave up not only thousands of rubles in "insurance fees" when servicing elite members of the Party or the army, but also the well-laid path to all the better things in life: a larger apartment, quality food, good liquor, fine tobacco, unprocurable books to read — all the gifts an eminent surgeon might expect in return for removing a commissar's gallstones or a Hero of the Revolution's swollen prostate. His patients were those corrupt old men who refused to die, who would pay anything to keep the slender thread spinning out a little longer. And here a young man gave that up in favor of an obscure clinic that specialized in a peculiar branch of psychotherapy? Which few authorities believed in? It made Frau Direktor wonder. Many months passed at the clinic before Maximilian told anyone the real reason for his departure from the Hermitage Surgery Unit.

As a child of ten, he had suddenly been struck down by a repulsive affliction: a purplish growth the size of a ripe plum rose out of his forehead like a rhinoceros's horn. Instantly he became the unpopular freak, a Quasimodo, who was picked on unmercifully throughout his school life. His otherwise prissy appearance, his long, delicate fingers, the way he minced about from place to place — add to these the rhino growth, and inevitably Max's classmates used him in an endless dance of torture. The pleasurable torture of schoolboys, notoriously the most savage of mankind's primitive tribes.

In Maximilian's teens, a moderately competent surgeon removed the plum from the center of his forehead. After the operation his hair partly covered the incision; a coin-sized circle remained, like a burn scar — not so unbecoming for a man. But the damage had been done. Young Max had been touched for life. While surgery saved him from endless years of looking repulsive, the lad still had to carve beauty from the beast within. Though only a mediocre student, Maximilian studied like a madman, eventually becoming a surgeon in his own right. Among the best the Hermitage Hospital had ever seen. Delicate. Precise. And flawless.

Even as surgery and the learning of surgery gave him a chance at a life in the world of men, now Max indulged the ache of his old wound, and a sick fascination blossomed within him. For he learned how to pick unmercifully into the bodies and organs of others. His long fingers probing the moist innards of a helpless body, feeling the yielding forms of the organs within. The power of it! The depravity! Arousal in the very guts of life. Stirring him to an erection. And when, as sometimes happened during a long and difficult operation, Maximilian needed to urinate, the inevitable obliging nurse appeared at his side, ready to help him — that is, by taking him out of his trousers and holding a glass beaker as he passed his water. Those unfamiliar with this odd operating room procedure might find this nurse-to-surgeon encounter either shocking or hilarious, but it had its practical side. The doctor eventually has to urinate; must he leave the patient, hobble down to the lavatory, and stand at a public urinal — perhaps beside an anxious relative, desperate to know how the operation is going? No: far simpler for a nurse to hold the receptacle and resterilize *her* hands. Much simpler than for a sawbones with his fingers in the soup to wash them off after handling his dirty spoon.

To this sensible surgical practice Max added the touchy problem of a spontaneous erection. And though needing to urinate might partially subdue his arousal, his swollen condition was still evident to the nurse handling him under the table. And even when he did go down, the poor fellow nearly always found it impossible to relieve himself. Pee-shy is the vulgar expression. Making the surgeon (once again) the source of high amusement among the Hermitage operating room staff.

For many years Maximilian cultivated an appearance of cool indifference. After all, he saved lives, and not just any lives but those of influential Party members and admirals awarded the Order of Lenin. Yet he was also slowly getting even; now, as a surgeon, *he* could laugh, laugh at his patients on the table as his fingers touched their brains. Laugh so wide his head nearly split at the ears, for his erection was a monstrous howl, roaring, See! I'm *in* you! In you all the way! And that he couldn't urinate was simply a direct message from his hidden better self:

All this nonsense must stop, Max. Stop now!

In the end the young man had three choices. Discredit several nurses to keep them from gossiping. Graft himself to some dangerous functionary as that man's personal physician, insuring a terrified silence in the operating room and far beyond. Or the final choice: leave the practice of surgery at the Hermitage forever.

For indeed, if Maximilian kept on much longer, his secret laughter was bound to slip out and his private monstrous howls of revenge would soon be perceived by people even more dangerous than himself. It had to end somewhere; he heard a rumor about a clinic in Rostov that specialized in the neuroses of children. With considerable difficulty, he resigned his post. He had no clear plan. . . . First travel south, then offer his services as a doctor, and in return — in return, what? In many ways the Hermitage Hospital had been Max's reason for being. For without the critical surgery of his youth and the skills he learned later, Max certainly would have twisted into something malicious. A worse man would have stayed and contrived to hide his secret laughter as he denounced one talkative nurse after another, while saving worthless old men from death. But the hospital's usefulness had come to a close, nearly destroying him. Frau Direktor thought it a mark of good character that Maximilian *did* in fact leave the operating room; a mark of his better self that he heeded the hidden message of his inability to urinate. He had read the message in the nick of time. And chose to try something different.

9

Yet all this thinking had brought her no closer. Perceiving hidden messages was one thing; taking care of crazy children another altogether. Max had youth and strength in his favor: arranging forged papers, negotiating trains and steamships, passing through customs, avoiding the police, all well within his powers. Certainly easier for him to start life again in a strange country, learn a new language, but what of the long haul with *whatever* child? The loneliness and doubts through the endless nights and struggling days? And what of therapy? A mere two years' experience at the clinic was hardly sufficient, and he had never undergone analysis. Max possessed all the raw materials to become the bedrock of a sick child, to help a broken thing build itself from scratch — but had never been refined. And no time was left to do it now. . . .

Frau Direktor's other intern could not have been more different, with all the required skill, experience, and insight, but perhaps she'd been refined too much. Madame Le Boyau, of Paris, had been a practicing analyst longer than Frau Direktor herself; a mangy dowager now, Madame had a ruined face of lines and jowls. A monkey's face, toughened and embattled from years of listening to the ceaseless demands of other people's problems. Troubles she could no longer help them solve.

Too many of her patients had been whiners and shirkers, unfit for analysis: people who expected their problems to be analyzed and enjoyed like the rarest food and wine. . . . Madame Le Boyau had allowed herself to become the maître d'hôtel in the restaurant of their minds, serving up one dish or another for them to taste or reject. And like the *propriétaire* of a chic restaurant, she tried to make their dishes pleasing and palatable. A light, calm soufflé for the widowed Society Neurotic, her furs and lovers both wearing thin. A bracing cocktail for an insecure Writer of Plays, a scribbler spoiled by too much money and easy acclaim, yet suffering gnawing pangs that his talent was a fraud.

In case after case, Madame Le Boyau served up delicacies to people who were under the impression that because they possessed nearly everything important in life, and a few luxuries besides, they had *arrived*. So why were they miserable? Madame Le Boyau's therapy no longer held any answers. She had merely grown accustomed to their fees; protecting them from the ugly struggle of life, taking their good money, but giving nothing in return. She even stimulated their doubts when they showed signs of leaving her, with a word here, a gesture there . . . weakening their will, letting them pay and pay. And as often as required, she promoted the feeling that they were really accomplishing something when they paid Madame the hour-long visit. . . .

In truth, Madame had only really cared for her last and final patient. A pretty, polished young man of twenty-two in a terribly desperate state. She called him her *fleur du mal.* He was the worthless son of a well-to-do manufacturer, who had shown little interest in the family business and little aptitude for anything else. At last he found a position with an elderly and respected art dealer. The situation seemed perfect for a boy of genteel temperament, bred to the better things in life, with exquisite taste and an eye for objets d'art. . . . His father was satisfied; at least the boy had a future. *Bonne chance!*

When the young man appeared in Madame Le Boyau's office he had been employed by the art dealer for about a year. He claimed to be suffering from insomnia and opium addiction. He wrung his ivory hands and hung his head. "Save me!" he begged her. "It'll kill me! For the love of God, please save me!"

What would kill him? Employment? A wealthy art dealer?

At once a curious change came over him. He no longer groveled but became superior, patronizing. "Did you ever wonder," he asked coyly, "what young men are good for? Or how a dilettante with no prospects secures a position? Oh yes, I have some talent, a good eye, but *he* doesn't need that. An old man needs a young man to do what he no longer wishes to do for himself. A personal secretary. A court jester. I provide his distractions, his entertainment. I'm his procurer."

What in heaven's name did the boy mean? And so he indulged her, spinning out his tale a little longer. . . . "In the beginning he had me do simple tasks for him. Run errands, catalog shipments — the busy work of the gallery. Then he drew me in. First we stayed out all night, eating and drinking. Then we tried opium together. . . . We went to a brothel. Soon we became habitués; the proprietress knew us well. She arranged for specialty tastes, boys or girls or both. First in the brothel, then other days bringing them to a private apartment he kept. . . ." The young *fleur* paused for what seemed a long time, then flushed sheepishly and shrugged.

"After a month of this, I knew what he wanted without even

having to ask. And it became clear why he hired me. . . . 'A pretty poppet,' he might murmur when I arrived at the gallery in the morning. But soon it wasn't necessary to say anything. He kept a small icon of baby Jesus on his desk, the same way people keep pictures of their wives. When he wanted his distraction, the icon always faced me as I came in the gallery door. . . . And I knew what to do." Yes, the lad knew his task. To steal out in the black of night into the crumbling corners of the city, where people lived like rats in hovels a few feet above the storm drains. And once there, the young man found a child to purchase. The poor were always willing enough to part with an extra mouth. And so the procurer left the hovels with his pretty poppet, meeting his employer by arrangement in the apartment across town.

"Sometimes after a night of his pleasure, he let the child run home to its parents with an extra wad of francs." The young man's voice darkened. "But sometimes not. And I waited through the long hours of the night until he had done with his possession. Until it was no longer a thing to possess."

"And what happened to the child?" Madame demanded.

"That was my last duty. I took the body down to the Seine. And spent the rest of the week in a friendly brothel I knew, drinking and smoking opium. Trying to forget. . . . He's a charming man, really, if you meet him. This wasn't the first time he's trained a procurer. He's mastered the art of going inch by inch. It seemed like you were hardly moving at all, until you looked over your shoulder and saw how far you'd really come." The young *fleur* fell silent. Madame's eyes had taken on a look of doubt. "I daresay you don't believe me. Well, I suppose I could scrounge up a body for you if you want. I hid one in a rotting boathouse on the river."

Madame was dumbfounded. She hadn't even the presence of mind to ask, How many times? She didn't want to know. This pink-faced boy revolted her.

But would she hand him over to the Prefecture of Police? Madame said nothing. Where was the proof? A body in a boathouse? Perhaps he'd seen it there and woven a fantasy for her. . . .

At once she brought all her old powers to bear on this young *fleur,* helping him to dissect himself. The young man did, in fact, shortly leave the art dealer and soon thereafter cease his opium smoking. But as to his sick story — true or false? Had he invented it for reasons

12

she could not fathom? Should she turn him over to the police or let him delve a little further? She hesitated, letting him explore. . . . One day she felt sure the tale was true — the next, equally sure it was false. And so she let him disassemble himself, allowing his fragments to fall where they would. She led him to the dark, weedy pool where the *fleurs du mal* cluster, and there she bid the boy stare into its still water and drink. . . .

By allowing the young man to go on talking and talking, Madame picked at the scabs of his troubles, forever opening his sores so as never to let them heal. Of course the story of the wicked old art dealer was true! Of course she should have turned him over to the police. Was she *crazy*? No, she was exacting justice of her own making: for when the young Narcissus gazed deeper and deeper into the fetid pool, he saw at last his own dark reflection in its loathsome depths. In the end he saved Madame herself from the Prefecture of Police; he took his own life. They found a note implicating the art dealer. Madame Le Boyau's name did not come up. She was safe.

In a roundabout way Madame Le Boyau had avenged the little possessed poppets, while revenging herself on the hollowness of her own practice. But she had failed miserably in losing the one patient with serious enough troubles to be worth caring about. And she had doubtless added to the crime: the respectable art dealer went on with his perversions as the young man had talked and talked — how many more children had there been? Was not their fate her fault too?

This, then, became her disaster.

She had taken a police matter into her own hands for her own ends and caused more harm than good. In failing to unmask the deepest source of the young man's troubles, she had merely led him to a sour backwater of his mind and left him there to die. But she had unmasked herself as a fraud: so weary of her own life that she thought nothing of watching another destroy his. And just as guilty as the art dealer. Worse, in fact, because all along she knew better.

With the last few shreds of common sense and common decency, Madame Le Boyau took steps to close her practice of thirty years and refer her few remaining patients to the other analysts of Paris. She had some funds, more than she could spend, and cared little for comforts. She wandered across Europe on a slow sightseeing tour to nowhere. Along the way she conceived the idea of writing a monograph on the psychiatric institutions of the Continent. And so she visited place after place, talking with doctors and their staffs and making her notes. In reality she was searching for a place from which to start afresh. A place where she could find once more those qualities she had banished to the attic of her self. And since her chance arrival at the Rostov Institute, Madame had indeed begun to flower again, as though healed by her work with the clinic's children. She had even mentioned her desire to undergo yet another analysis this late in life; perhaps with Maximilian. For his fragile looks appealed to her, strangely reminiscent of that other *fleur*, lying in the ground a continent away. Madame had found her home at last. She deserved another chance.

But in all frankness Frau Direktor had no illusions about these people. One too inexperienced, the other too old to see the process through. The young man a kind of cripple, with the scar of an old wound that could never really heal. And the old woman a kind of dangerous charlatan, whose tricks had nearly done her in. . . . Yet both had shown that one quality essential to their work by amputating their sickly parts — cauterizing their frailties and turning them to strengths. Disarming their follies and taking charge of their fate. Perhaps each could take a child to her precious Herr Doktor in Switzerland?

Ach, Madame would be lucky just to save herself. . . .

Chapter 2

Variations on a Theme of V

No child baffled them more than their Marie.

The clinic's most puzzling charge had come up for discussion nearly every day for countless weeks past. Marie . . . the "promising child" now crippled by an unforeseen madness. Once she had been a bright, intelligent girl of nine, kindly and cheerful. The child's mother told Frau Direktor how Marie had long studied the piano, taken to music as children sometimes do, learning whole pieces at a time. Every day without fail, mother and daughter sat for an hour as Marie practiced her scales or tried to master new phrases. Then one afternoon, while taking the ferry across the Don, she was struck down by an inexplicable fainting fit. When the child revived, she no longer spoke.

Instead she began mindlessly repeating snatches of tunes. She hummed or sang bits for a few bars and then abruptly changed to something else. A few more irritating bars off-key, then off again to a new piece. A chaotic jangle of broken melodies, never singing one long enough to bring out its form, but enough to make one want to hear the rest. Infuriating the way a dripping faucet inevitably drives you mad. Yet occasionally her mother thought she detected snatches of familiar melodies. Was that the first three bars of Beethoven's Fifth Symphony? Or something else, in three-quarter time — a waltz, perhaps?

State physicians hinted darkly at some kind of mental, emotional cause. They prescribed medication, which either put Marie to sleep or made her sing all the more stridently. Travel abroad to seek medical help was out of the question. Though if Marie's father had been alive, he might have had some influence. As a merchant ship's captain, he traveled half the year, but had been lost at sea some months before the child's fit.

The mother was a pretty, pinched woman — prone to melancholy airs. A wan, pale spirit who could go for days without speaking a word. She frankly told Frau Direktor her marriage with the girl's father had been in name only. In the months he sailed the Indian Ocean or the China Sea, she shunted Marie from neighbor to neighbor and back again (staying with her "aunts," they called it), the child spending nights away from home while her mother sought a furtive kind of satisfaction with the men she entertained: men, Marie soon knew, who were not her "uncles."

An unbridgeable chasm grew between husband and wife, yawning wider with each voyage. While Marie's father was away, he was away. And when he returned, well . . . he slept in the house and ate in the house and went about with his daughter. Alone. The marriage became a noose, slowly strangling both parents with each passing year. Still, they made no break, waiting as couples often do. They were still waiting when his ship went down at sea.

After the child's fit, the mother tried to take her daughter in hand. But dealing with a brat who squalls random snatches of melodies went far beyond the mother's powers. Shouting and threats had no effect; they merely changed the frequency and tone of Marie's idiotic rantings: from La-la-la to Li-li-li, from Na-na-na to Ni-ni-ni. Marie's mother was reduced to brute force; she hit on the idea of rationing the amount of water the child drank. Little by little she allowed Marie less and less. No water with meals, no water before bed — just half a glass in the morning. After ten days, Marie drank only the barest minimum required for life. The result: the little girl sang herself hoarse after her half glass in the morning and then went quiet as a church mouse for the rest of the day. At first her mother thought she had succeeded in some way. But soon Marie began starving herself. Her hair fell out, sores appeared on her mouth, her skin went gray. The girl's clothes hung like limp rags. Marie was dying. . . .

The mother grew terrified, seeing her mistake. She tried letting the girl have water again, tried coaxing her to eat — but to no avail. Marie kept on as before, drinking little, eating almost nothing. In desperation her mother cornered the state doctor in his office, screaming shrilly at him, "Cure my baby! Cure her, damn you! Do something!"

The doctor was exhausted from an endless day. Whose crazy mother was this? He had treated dozens of little girls that week already: Marys, Maries, Marinas — *which* little girl? The tirade grew worse, ranting now — they were all witch doctors, ghouls; it was the pills they gave her. "Poison! Filth!"

"Get out of my office," he shouted at her. In moments a pair of meaty orderlies forcibly ejected Marie's mother from the building. But even as she brawled in the street, with her dress ripped, and one orderly clutching a kicked shin, the state doctor remembered *this* Marie and dashed downstairs. He sent the orderlies off and calmed the mother. She must forgive him; he was not such a bad man, "but in our place we see so many children, please understand." He sighed, then in low tones he told her about the Rostov clinic. "I know the director — you can have a letter of introduction. . . ." State doctors weren't encouraged to refer large numbers of cases there, but in view of how badly the girl's condition had deteriorated, perhaps the Children's Psychiatric Institute might do some good.

When Marie first arrived, the staff thought she was mute. Now free of her mother's deprivations, nothing changed immediately. But after a week or so she began to eat a little more. And drink. As for her apparent muteness, they all soon learned better.

Marie was dying of thirst!

The little girl liked nothing better than sitting in a warm tub half the day, drinking the bathwater as she let it soak into her. Drink the bath and pee in the bath. And then drink some more. After an hour Marie's skin was puckered and the water smelled a trifle cloying. But Madame, who supervised the child's bathtimes, solved the problem by opening the drain a crack and letting the tap water flow half a turn. Soon Marie drank from the tap exclusively, the water from her body passing harmlessly into the warm tub and down the drain.

As soon as her parched vocal cords drank their fill, the inane toneless singing began once more. Clearly Marie sang some kind of musical notes, but no one could place them, they were so garbled, so atonal. . . . Max alone thought he detected the first few bars of Beethoven's Fifth Symphony.

And then one night, as Madame tucked the little girl into bed, Marie finally spoke two words, whispering them into an empty corner of the room.

"Go away," she said.

At first Madame thought the child had cruelly dismissed her. But when she withdrew, the girl's off-pitch bleating became frantic; she hacked on till she nearly choked. No, Madame realized . . . Marie didn't want *her* to go away. For when the old woman returned to the child's bedside her frantic stutterings subsided and she let Madame stroke her hair. Snuggling sideways under the covers as she always did when calming down, letting Madame pet her until the toneless singing lapsed into silence and Marie fell into a restless sleep.

The little girl now ate regularly. Her hair no longer fell out but grew in dark and glossy. And Max had become a favorite of hers, reading to her at bedtime. As he read, her toneless singing dropped to a dull hum. She even played with toys: a doll in a periwinkle-blue cotton dress and a small model tugboat that she took into the bath and sometimes even to bed. At the time she spoke those first words, Go away, they all felt the child had *indeed* come a long way. . . . When Frau Direktor went back over her case notes, she saw Marie had been with them a year.

Typically, no one was ready for the child's lapse when it came a month ago. . . . One day Marie reverted to silence. All the old troubles reappeared; she refused water and no longer wanted to bathe. Her eating fell off. Max made the clever suggestion that Marie's silence was in fact a demand for the opposite — that is, noise, sound. Music.

Frau Direktor managed to borrow an old phonograph and a slightly scratched recording of Beethoven's Fifth. Alas, though Maximilian swore he saw a glimmer of pleasure in the girl's eyes — no real response. A clever idea, but wrong. And Marie worsened. . . . But when the girl's case arose for the umpteenth time at yet another end-of-day discussion, it seemed that Madame had finally latched onto something. The old woman had the annoying habit of staring out the window as she talked. Plucking an endless chain of cigarettes from a platinum case and smoking them in a stout, businesslike holder, which she clenched between her teeth, she glanced outside with watery eyes as her words floated across the room on a wretched cloud of Balkan tobacco smoke. . . .

"Let us recall Marie's only words to date. A command: 'Go away!'" Her cigarette glowed as she inhaled. "But is this really a command? What else do we know about Marie? That she was a fine young pianist. That her mother entertained men. That before her father went down with his ship he brought his daughter presents and gifts from foreign lands, lavishing all kinds of attention on her. So much attention the mother admitted growing spiteful and angry. And lastly, that when Marie's father went off to sea, the mother took many of the gifts away — only to return them for show when the father came home again. Given and taken away . . . ," Madame mused to herself. "Given and taken away . . ." Suddenly her eyes narrowed. "Marie's words are not a command but a description. 'Go away' describes the unhappy state of her home life, in which the father was always going off. Yet they also apply to the hard evidence of his affections, the toys and gifts — which vanished and returned. . . . And finally the words 'Go away' apply to her mother, whose secret sexual life entailed that the girl be sent off to strangers, so the woman might be free. In fact, Marie may have wished that all the inconveniences of her life had simply 'gone away.' And now it appears the words also describe what the child managed to accomplish. Like her father before her, she too has gone away from home. Gone away and come to us."

Max sat up sharply, struck. "But in your case, she didn't want to be left alone in bed. She didn't want you to go away!"

Madame Le Boyau opened her hands in agreement, allowing yet a new twist on the child's words. "Ah, well, there now, so you see . . . old Madame has detected a method to the madness." She discarded the stub of a cigarette in an ashtray by her elbow, then coughed gently into a pretty Swiss handkerchief. She glanced into the hankie, but whatever she saw did not surprise her, and she put the frilly thing away.

"Let us consider the child's most striking symptom. The muddled droning. What a stunning signal of her unhappiness. Marie stutters music because she used to *study* it. And as for Beethoven's Fifth, well, it's a very famous piece of music. . . ." Madame touched her throat, massaging it. "Pardon my singing." Then she belted out a fairly credible pounding of the Fifth Symphony's opening bar:

"Dah-dah-dah-*dah!*"

She paused to regain herself. "We've all heard it, no?" A sly smile came into Madame's crinkled eyes; she ruffled her shoulders like a molting bird. "Tell me, what are Marie's favorite toys? Boats. Ships. Vessels. All touching upon her father. And lately she has even played at shipwreck. Is she sailing the sea in her own toy boat, I wonder? And if she finds the *Korkov*, on which her father served, how would she signal him?"

"By radio?" Max tried.

"But if the radio is broken. Or the ship is at war?"

"Then the ship is silent. Mute . . . ," Max answered. "Just like our little girl."

"Bravo!" Madame clapped her hands. "And when ships are silent, how do they signal each other?"

"Morse code!" Maximilian cried at once.

"Morse code," Madame agreed. "Ships at sea flash silent signals across the waves with blinkers. In the chaos of a storm with the radio down, or in a state of war, ships flash signals to each other. Dah-dah-dah-*dah!* In code that's Dot-dot-dot-*dash.* The sign for the letter V . . . Breaking through the storm of Marie's chaotic, stop and go singing, it comes again and again. She is calling out the code sign V . . . V . . . V!"

"Consider the many ways we can read the sign V," Madame went on. "It is the Roman numeral for the number five. As in Beethoven's Fifth. It is the common abbreviation for the Latin word *versus.* As in 'this against that.' It is the first letter in the name of the female love goddess, Venus. And to my mind, the symbol V is the most common pictogram of the female genitals —"

"Oh, really now!" Maximilian growled skeptically. "That's positively absurd. . . . What are you saying? That when Marie was five years old she heard Beethoven's Fifth and talked to her father in Morse code? Then had some mysterious experience with her vagina? Thought her parents were lost souls at sea or, worse, like ships at war? As in mother versus father?" Maximilian leaned back in his chair, slowly stroking the side of his face. "I forgot to include the volcano Vesuvius somewhere."

Madame stared wide-eyed at the surgeon for a moment and then shook with laughter. "No, no, no, my dear Max, but that's a wonderful tale. Who knows? Maybe some of it is true. A mysterious experience with her vagina! I like that, coming from a man. Vaginas are mysterious things by and large. I daresay many men have found them so. . . .Which is unfortunate. For the vaginas, that is. Of all mankind, only Tiresias the Seer was both male and female in his lifetime. And he said:

> If the parts of love's pleasure be counted as ten,
> Thrice three go to women; only one to men!

"The Seer was obviously a blind optimist," — Madame sighed — "more than ready to believe in the best of all possible female worlds. His name in ancient Greek means 'He Who Delights In Signs.' And his remark clearly indicates that at least one mysterious sign of V is more pleasing than others. In the case of vaginas, unquestionably true. But I'm afraid you've got me wrong, Max: what I meant to show was not coherency but coincidence.

"And here I have been a trifle unfair with all of you, for there is still one coincidence, one sign I have not shared. Our sweet chamber-maid, Petra, found a clue in the pocket of Marie's jumper before it went into the wash. Good thorough girl, that Petra — always checks the children's pockets before she accidentally boils some precious artifact which might have been left there on purpose . . . Does anyone recall Marie's mother remarking she heard a waltz in the child's droning?"

Madame opened her cigarette case and took out a slip of worn, red-colored paper. "A concert ticket to the Rostov Orchestra. Notice the seat — one of those secluded boxes above the pit, number five. Notice the program printed on the ticket; it is written in an abbreviated form to save space:

BTHVN V, SATIE VALSE "VEUX."

"What a considerable wealth of information is crammed into that brief line. The first item on the program is clear enough — Beethoven's Fifth Symphony was to be played. But what of the second offering? Valse "Veux"? Easy if you know a little music. A short piano waltz by the composer Erik Satie, his most famous waltz (*valse*, if you will), entitled, 'Je te veux' . . . I want you . . ."

"*Je te veux*," Maximilian said softly, feeling the words on his tongue. "I want you."

"As between intimates." Madame's voice sank. "Lovers." Her last word stood alone. "Yet how many more V's have appeared! One more in the word 'valse.' Another in the word 'veux,' want. A hidden V in the 'First Ring Box Number Five' . . . Artless, did we call the child's ranting? *How eloquent,* I say! Call it, rather, Variations on a Theme of V. Variations hidden from our eyes until we learned to see. From Beethoven's Fifth to the Morse code sign for V to a program of *valses* in a Rostov theater — the Black Water Theater, I think they call it. Ominous, no? Prophetic, even. Was this little red stub the last memento from a father and daughter's final waltz?" She shrugged. "And was Petra's finding the ticket simply an accident? Hardly!" she snorted. "No, Marie saw it as a kind of test. Of *us,* if you will. Would we throw away the ticket in our ignorance? Or discover the precious stub and decipher its message? Yet for its message to be heard, the ticket must pass from hand to hand until someone reads it who understands. The child is saying, 'Petra, here is my ticket. Show it to your cousin Henrietta, who makes the beds; show it to Kurt the orderly, and Hanna the nurse, and Freda the cook. Please, Petra, I want them all to see.'" Madame's eyes went hard, cruel. Raising her voice as though speaking to the deaf and dumb, "Show it to them all! To you! And you! And *me!*" She slapped her chest, exploding into a fit of coughing. Then waved away Maximilian, who rose up in alarm. She lay back weakly in her chair, eyes half shut, pale and sick and altogether wasted. The silky cigarette croup rumbled in her throat. "*Je te veux* . . . I want you. Her father, who else? But as for the child's recent lapse into silence and starvation? And why her fainting fit on the ferry, which started it all — this I do not know."

Sitting with her interns that evening, Frau Direktor could see the Black Water Theater in her mind. She knew it well. The wonderful old place had fallen into ruinous decay — like everything around them now. She'd seen the crossboards nailed to the doors and the broken windows staring down in wide-eyed blindness. The posters plastered around its huge front columns were peeling off like scabs. The management of the Black Water Theater had come under some kind of official cloud. Squatters lived within. They had torn up the seats and used the stuffing for their clothes and the wood for their fires. Now those first ring boxes were like little caves in the side of a cliff. With the electricity shut off, cook fires flickered in all the private boxes, tier after tier.

She remembered statues of gilded plasterwork. Gods and goddesses rising up in an arch over the proscenium, making love until they reached the top. . . . Now the gold paint flecked off in patches, showing them not as gods at all, but merely white plaster underneath. The cherubs nearest the stage had their noses broken. Time had been when people came by carriage, and footmen stood at the door to every box. When box seats in the first ring were lit by candles, and heavy burgundy curtains hung at the back. Sitting there, you were cozy and secluded, and when the orchestra played, the sound flowed everywhere, like the fragrance of roses in winter. Close your eyes, and it filled your head. The warm romance of father and daughter sitting up there alone. Listening as the music swirled into the padded little box. As the waves of sound surged over them like surf pounding a cliff, only to fly apart into a thousand silver drops, white pearls falling back into the seething black . . .

"In many ways Marie and her father were abnormally close," Frau Direktor told her interns. "More and more so each time he came ashore. I believe the father had no other woman. And because Marie was a child, she had no other man. What veiled bonds held them, which no one saw or felt but them *alone?*"

Frau Direktor watched Maximilian's face gradually darken, one particular V crawling into his mind again. Was all this just some lurid incest knot between a lonely evil man and a helpless love-starved girl? Frau Direktor nodded sadly to herself. It could be. Such dark things there were in the world. Hidden wishes. Secret loves. And people make up fairy tales — stories they want to see come true. Wounded children most especially.

Especially Marie.

"Madame's bit of evidence hit closest to the mark," Frau Direktor said at last, "when she saw that V stood for Venus and versus. I now recall that Venus is one of the goddesses portrayed along the arch of the proscenium in the Black Water Theater — and also Neptune, god of the deep, water and seashells streaming from his hair. Father and daughter rising above the multitudes. Was it so hard for the child to see herself in the gold statue? Or see her father in the other, holding his golden hands above the world? If we had listened more closely to Marie, would we have heard Satie's love waltz 'Je te veux' in the frayed snatches of the child's endless songs? The tune itself is halting and slow, with more rests between the notes than notes themselves. A

23

little like the girl herself, singing bits of broken songs, songs that always shift — and therefore never end . . . Unfinished. Unresolved. I hear the song of her stop-and-go. An endless repetition: Stop and go, stop and go.

"Didn't the mother tell us, Marie clamored to be taken for a ferry ride every chance she could? Marie adored the rides. Of course she did! With her father out to sea, she played Venus searching the waves for Neptune. Once on board the ferry, the girl actually traveled upon the water for the man she loved. Yes, a pathetic search, a hopeless search — but while her father lived, a search it was.

"Yet when her father died, do you imagine Marie no longer wished to find him?" Frau Direktor's words rose and twisted into Madame's cigarette smoke. "Of course not! When Marie's father was lost at sea, the child wished to find him more than *ever*!"

Then, in a hush, "But the father no longer sailed the ocean; he had sunk below it . . . and to search for him in the cold black water, Marie must go below the waves herself. To find him, she must drown. . . .

"The father is lost. The mother adulterous. The family a failure. Marie had a bitter choice. To die, searching for her father beneath the waves — or give him up, losing him forever. Is it any wonder the girl had an insane fainting fit on the deck of the ferry? Any wonder she revived hours later unable to speak, ranting bits of V! V! V! Follow her father or lose him forever? When the mother denied the girl drinking water, Marie took starvation as her final path. This, then, is the last hard road to us.

"Strange fate. For in this place she can have as much water as she wants. Gallons and gallons. Endless baths where she can sing the stop-and-go to her heart's content. Indeed, with us Marie is able to *drown* in water if she pleases. And so her search continues — soaking in the water and drinking from the tap. Hoping against hope that one day she'll find her father's body: if not on the seabed, among the sunken wrecks of other families, then perhaps at the bottom of her own bathtub. . . .

"So her fainting fit on the ferry and her current regression to silent starvation are tied together. Marie fears abandonment. Fears we will leave her. For if she gives up her most critical symptoms, silence and starvation, if she becomes better, if she is 'cured,' then her time with us must come to an end. Back to her mother once more. Who took her toys away, who shuttled her off to any available 'aunt.' Marie's current silent starvation is her life rope. While she clings to that, she will never leave. For we have become her family now. And so must never part.

"Never go away . . ."

A worn sigh escaped from them that bygone evening. Not the search and discovery but the final seeing of a thing tired them so. After the effort of holding out, resisting, *refusing* to see the answer for so long. More than enough for one end-of-day discussion. And why not? Only a short week ago, Frau Direktor and the others fully expected many, many more. Always another meeting, another moment for reflection, stretching out in an ocean stream of talk.

Their own endless stop-and-go.

Chapter 3

No More Fairy Tales

And what of this could Frau Direktor put in a cryptic letter to that eons-distant friend? The letter might get there, or it might not. A child might arrive safely with Max or Madame — or might not. . . . For in a few short days their world had changed. Almost overnight, it seemed, the clinic staff had struck camp. No rattle of work in the kitchen or footsteps in the halls. Kurt, their silent giant of an orderly, who for years attended the children in every conceivable way — from discovering the whereabouts of a lost sock to fetching the special glue to mend the broken arm of a doll — simply stopped coming to work. Hanna, their hook-nosed nurse, who could coax a thermometer into a chattering, feverish mouth, cure a case of rampant diarrhea, or find the right salve for a bruised knee — now she was gone. Their cook, with the face of a boiled lobster, and her Serbian dishwasher, with arms mottled from the suds — one who prepared and cleaned up an endless cycle of despoiled meals and the other who always found the special treat each child secretly loved (from a mandarin orange to an anchovy) but never told anyone, placing the dainty on the tray with a wink and a nod — they too were gone.

And the clinic's giggling imp of a chambermaid — good, thorough Petra — who made sixteen beds a day, who washed the wetted sheets and soiled clothes, who swept the floors and straightened the rooms, putting a hundred tin soldiers back in their box without losing the one-legged infantryman under the dresser, and who always placed the stuffed tiger on the pillow just so . . .

All gone.

Flown up into a winter sky like sharp little chimney swifts who feel an earthquake coming in their thin bird bones; hovering over the earth until the tremors subside and it is once more safe to land. Marie's

26

fears were coming true despite all their efforts to understand. Soon to be put in a box and sent home. All the children sensed it. *Where's Kurt? I wanna see Hanna. Petra, are you there?*

And it struck them now, like a slap in the face — that their maid had never been merely a housekeeper, their cook merely a preparer of food, or their nurse the fetcher of clean bedpans, but the nimble fingers and willing backs that allowed the directorial "brains" to float above the daily cares. Abandoned now to the chosen elite, the clinic had become a leaden weight.

Especially when the place was unkempt and there was no time to clean it, with mouths to feed and no hands to cook, when they felt lost and tired and too weak to care.

Even crazy children knew. Their clinic was doomed.

After a few days without support staff, Frau Direktor, Madame, and Max — consumed with cooking and cleaning — faced the brutal fact that three adults could not manage a dozen troubled children (nearly all of them prone to fits and rages) when housekeeping was thrown in too. You could tend to the furies or make the beds. Not both.

Maximilian had missed shaving a spot on his chin several days running, giving him the appearance of someone sporting a new and bizarre style of beard. Bits of food clung to Madame Le Boyau's clothes, and she had torn her dress. In addition to cooking, she'd been changing the sheets of the chronic bed wetters — sometimes more than three times a day — later crawling about on her hands and knees to straighten the rooms.

Then one morning Petra the housekeeper appeared on their front doorstep as if to save them. "I'm back," she said simply. "I missed Marie." And with no further fuss, Petra, that good, thorough girl, went quietly to her tasks as if nothing had happened. But still, the daily routine — wash, cook, clean — was grinding them down. And so the accumulation of their errors began. First casting off one minor chore and then another. Telling themselves it was really much quicker that way. Then giving up cleaning the toilets or preparing every meal; losing their grip one thread at a time. Until it was all they could do just to rise from bed in the morning and face the day . . .

And so who was worse off? A child like Marie, returned to the mother who made her want to drown — or the children with no parents at all? Their fate lay in the hands of the state. A few miles across

27

Rostov stood the new city orphanage, the Home for Children, installed in the altered hulk of a bank. Children surrounded by walls of grieving marble, rows of metal beds with crusty paint flaking off and thin mattresses over the coiled springs. A place of communal showers and lukewarm meals spooned onto dented tin trays. Frau Direktor had seen a notice in the press praising the home for being "modernly efficient" and housing five hundred. Five hundred what? Tons of sausage? The newsmen slurred words together for the sake of rendering complex thoughts into digestible hunks: modernly efficient — as if a Home for Children were some kind of meat-packing plant, where they packed little living sausages onto coil-spring beds and kept them fed and washed and warm enough till the next meal came around.

Frau Direktor ceased squandering her time on dark thoughts; for better or worse she had put her hopes in a cold box on an empty street. No use dwelling on outcomes she could not affect. No, she must stand before her interns. Tell them what she had written and show them what they must do. Run. Fly from this place. They had to try.

Her two interns rose to greet her. "Thank you," she said. "It would have been hopeless here the last few days without your help. Most of all, you, Petra, who came back heaven sent." Their young housekeeper sat shyly on the couch like a wallflower at her first dance, clearly in awe of her sudden admittance to the inner circle of the clinic. Nighttime pressed against the windows; the streetlamps outside shone like yellow coal miners' lanterns in a smoky tunnel. Upstairs the children slept, that whole part of the house breathing as one.

"We have to get out," Frau Direktor said. She waved her hand about the four corners of the dilapidated living room. "It's over."

At first the blank eyes stared dully back. The slaves had adjusted to their extra burdens, to the lack of sleep, the gritty food. They had stopped looking forward — plodding on like yoked oxen, never raising their heads. Their backs about to break, and they didn't even know it.

Madame Le Boyau perceived her exhaustion first, nodding slowly as if she'd finally seen the future. "How much time do we have?"

Frau Direktor could see their minds furiously spinning, tracing paths of flight: quick mental head counts of the children tossed like

28

photographs, snap judgments weighing one child's merits over the next. Which ones would travel well? Which the best in crowds? Easiest to feed? Or in the toilet?

"Do you want me to choose for you?" Frau Direktor asked thickly. "In a few days and with a little luck, you'll be on your way out of the country. You may be lost in an unfamiliar city, or running in a railway station with minutes to catch your train. There'll be a policeman at the end of the platform, checking papers, and a family of fat Slovaks pushing you from behind. You'll have a mentally disturbed child on your hands, threatening to explode. Maybe more than one. So if you have to rely on me for your analytical technique to get you on that train or out of that public rest room, you're in serious trouble. Because I'm not leaving. I'm staying here. For the police."

This left her breathless; she felt a constriction in her chest, a faint whistling. . . . Asthma. Her first attack in years. She tried to ignore it. God, how awful! The choking on her own tubes, the frantic drowning with air all around. Why was she staying behind? To give the authorities their victim? No: to punish herself. Because she had failed. Failed to secure the safety of the clinic and its most precious wards. The subconscious strangling the life out of her body; soon it would strangle her to death. . . .

Madame Le Boyau's cigarette had grown a long dangling ash — precarious, yet intact. Like all of them: so fragile, wanting only the slightest tremor to break and fall.

"It's our fault too," Max said, a note of panic in his voice — as if ready to overlook anything so long as he got the last seat on the train. He forced a smile and gave a little nervous shrug. "We've been sitting under the ax so long, I guess we didn't see it anymore. Just slipped our minds. When what we really needed was a good *Fehlleistung*."

Our minds?

How could a thing like that just slip your mind?

Max had used the German. *Fehlleistung*. *Fehl* meaning faulty. *Leistung* meaning achievement. Not a simple slip but a veiled accomplishment. A hidden gain. Frau Direktor's obvious failure had been to ignore the voice of doom when it cried Beware! But whatever in this mess could be construed as an achievement?

The asthma that strangled her? Perhaps . . . as a timely message. For it forced desperate life to rise inside. Commanding her to take a chance. Throw the dice. Play out the game to the bitter end. And Frau Direktor heard those same urgings in all the other German words for clever mistakes: *versprechen, vergreifen, vertun* . . . misspeak, mistake, misdo.

A mere slip of the tongue was easy to grasp. Easy to say, easy to laugh at, easy to misunderstand. With a simple slip there might be faults but not much achievement. Nowadays people called it a *Freudian* slip, as if the man himself had concocted the thing in a dim, gaslit nineteenth-century laboratory and quietly infected the world. Somehow his "slip" managed to escape its glass test tube, to spread unchecked from city to city like a runaway virus. All mankind catching the same nasty cold, the Freudian flu.

So her stubborn denial of their common danger was more accurately: a *Vergreifung*. A mistaking. But the *greifen* in *Vergreifung* also meant to snatch, to catch hold of, as if by making this error she really tried to grasp the thing that lay just beyond her reach. Frau Direktor began to murmur softly, recalling a passage in a book. She struggled for the air to say the words out loud:

"'When I set myself the task of bringing to light what human beings kept hidden within them . . .'" — and here, she gasped for breath — "'by observing what they say and what they show, I thought the task was harder than it really is. He that has eyes to see and ears to hear may convince himself that no mortal can keep a secret. . . .'" She filled her lungs. "'If his lips are silent he chatters with his fingertips; betrayal oozes out of him at every pore. And this task of revealing the most hidden recesses of the mind is quite possible to accomplish. . . .'"

When she found the air to quote the source, her voice had fallen to a whisper. "'Fragment of an Analysis of a Case of Hysteria,' *Monatsschrift für Psychiatrie und Neurologie,* 1905. Later reprinted in the *Sammlung kleiner Schriften,* 1909. At one time, my friends, the most scandalous piece of prose available to the reading public. When scandal and shame were inseparable. You read your filthy book alone, you stared at your dirty pictures by yourself. . . ." She gasped for air, pawing the armrests of her chair as if that helped. "But a certain Herr Professor Freud had the bad judgment to publish a paper where he claimed his young patient Dora had a goodly knowledge of sexual practices. Some she repressed, others she misunderstood, and some she applied to inappropriate persons. Now, to say that little girls might have sex-

30

ual thoughts hidden under their lace petticoats was evil enough. To publish it as a truth of *nature* — this was unforgivable."

Frau Direktor strained to breathe. Her hands futilely gripped the armrests of her chair. "I doubt the man sold three hundred copies of his work in twenty years."

She clutched her chest, trying to press the tightness to other parts of her body, where it wouldn't matter so much. "Forgive me," she said hoarsely. "I get carried away. . . . But in the matter of our immediate future, this asthma of mine is really a soggy way of shouting: See, you dolts! Achtung! It's not too late!" She brought out a carefully hand-written copy of her miserable letter. Now Frau Direktor unfolded the paper and passed it around for each of them to see.

"However, it has never been my intention to send you out into the void. There's someone you can contact; someone who knows what we do and knows me well. I've written a letter of introduction. Perhaps someone who can help . . ."

Chapter 4

Herr Kinderweise

To her eyes the living room had taken on a yellowish tinge, as though seen through old glass. Everything gone flat and pale, all the blood and color drained off. It seemed too that the people were hardly moving, like life-size dolls sitting placidly in their chairs. Waiting for what? For their Frau Direktor to take them by the hand and lead them out? She had tried to show them there were really *two* men who understood their struggle. The one in Zurich, with food and clothing and shelter and money, a man of connections and influence who could help them work the complicated machinery of life.

And then the other, the older one, in Vienna: too frail now to ease their road, but who had smiled upon her long ago. Whose written words and thoughts would light the way even in the dark. The words of that certain Herr Professor echoed faintly in her head:

He that has eyes to see . . . No mortal can keep a secret . . . Betrayal oozes out at every pore.

But those stiff dolls sitting there like lumps, did they really see the man who wrote those words? Did they know his smile, feel the terror in his growl or the bark in his laugh? And when she said *"Monatsschrift,"* could they feel the thin waxy paper of this publication? Or know his entry was just one among others? Other essays, soberly weighed and gravely discussed. While his at the time — "Fragment of an Analysis of a Case of Hysteria" — was studiously ignored. His and his alone.

Decades passed before the man became a target worthy of abuse. Years in which solitary people studied him in countries far away, applying fragments of his method with untrained hands. Her own imperfect cure had been a product of such times. In the years when his

Wednesday Society grew to fullness, many who knew those sessions knew them by that chance name, given simply because Wednesday was the day chosen for the group to meet. This when the circle was a scant handful of five or six men. Those evenings they talked about what they knew of their own minds and what they guessed of the minds of others, sharing the strange cases they had known, and always, always the dreams. . . . She had gone there herself once, in her first bloom of sanity, gone to touch the hem of his magic robe and thank him. Arriving one Wednesday of the latter days, to give a paper she had written and to be admired. The highly polished dining room table where they sat glowed black . . . and the faces gathered round were reflected back again, as though gazing upward out of a deep pool of dark water. Here the images of speakers mouthed soundlessly from below what was said above. Pale ghosts speaking out of a lagoon, past the ashtrays and aperitif glasses that floated upon its sullen surface.

The conspiracy of sitting around a shadowy hidden pool, and the sudden laughter when someone made a slip of the tongue. For the guilty mishandler, there was no escape. All case discussion ceased: the rest of them examining his faulty achievement, peering into the cracks of his character, while the image of the poor speaker drowned helplessly below in the black depths. . . .

The scent of tobacco smoke preceded him like invisible cherubs, their nakedness garlanding him in the sweet whiffs of a good cigar. She met Herr Professor for the first time in his downstairs hallway. He cleared his throat softly before he spoke, saying, "Mein liebes Fräulein Doktor!"

And she was embarrassed at the title; for she had been Fräulein Doktor only such a little while. He took her hand, covering it in both of his. "At last," he said. "We know each other's face."

But what of his face, then? The portraits taken in the early 1900s were stiff, dead things. He posed for them as though he were sitting for an oil: regal, motionless, dignified. Posing as he wished the world to view him, posing for a public of strangers. But in real life his face fairly rumbled; his eyes roving over you, though without making you feel exposed. He led her up a flight of well-worn stairs, countless feet having rubbed the steps smooth. Climbing one-two-three! Arriving in the parlor out of breath.

33

A rug filled the room, a Persian carpet, colored tiger rose, with cobalt tracery in the pattern of a battlement, with spearheads bristling behind as though hidden men waited for an assault. And then within the battlement, the white crescent moon of Allah and his white scimitar, repeated endlessly like soldiers of the faith. And yet deeper inside the fortress of this Persian carpet there came a line of flowers, blue irises and yellow daffodils: a garden kept inviolate behind the wall of spears and swords. The innermost panel of the carpet was laid out like a royal garden, with tracery walks and azure pools, green grass, more daffodils and fountains. The flowers were very human, for the daffodils' little faces thrust out of the stiff collar of white petals and they half pranced on the twining paths, tipping their heads this way and that like the court princesses of Suleiman the Magnificent, out for a dainty stroll. Making young Fräulein Doktor think suddenly, *Is this where they keep their women? In a garden, safe behind swords and spears?*

"You're wondering what kind of men would keep their women behind battlements and swords," he said.

"I am."

Yes, what kind of men?

If Allah kept his women behind battlements, perhaps God and his Prophet knew better than to trust their men with women. Or perhaps the women were a kind of luscious bait to lure infidels on to a futile assault upon his walls. Enemies of the faith martyred on the altar of their sisters and mothers. Was this why Allah's people cherished the story of a flying carpet — a carpet ready to fly them from the prison of their passions, over the walls of a garden forever under attack?

A beautiful bas-relief hung on the wall of his study: a Roman copy of a Greek temple carving. Small, intricate, perhaps made of yellow stone, not plaster — for in places it was polished smooth and pitted with age. The frieze showed a man riding a chariot, the rider whipping the horses to a gallop.

"Look at the galloping man," he said. And with those words, her host's real name no longer rang the same again. No longer was he Herr Professor Freud of 19 Berggasse; no, no longer just a signature at the end of a handwritten letter, or the coda of the strangely familiar hand that led her up the carpeted parlor stairs. In that moment she found her own name for him. A private name, only for him. Like

34

the taboo names of the South Sea Islanders, which they tell to no one. Only now could young Fräulein Doktor claim a shred of his soul for her very own, like the lock of hair one treasures for a keepsake. For when her host said, "Look at the galloping man," and not, "Look at the galloping horse," he said it as a child might say it, knowing the frieze in its overwhelming entirety. Binding the man and the horse, the chariot and the speed, as one. For it was only dull adult minds that saw things in their separate logical parts, squeezing out the life in crushing correctness. Herr Kinderweise. Herr Childwise.

"Look at the galloping man," he said, "how they both have the speed and the power. He is the horse, and the horse is him. The chariot spokes are his bones, and the horse his muscle. They are the rush of air, the clatter of hooves, a harsh cry on a dusty road. They are the crack of the whip and the sting of a pebble as it shoots from under the screaming wheels. An earthquake. A tempest. A swirling cloud flattening everything in its path. He is the Horse God. And the beast — the God of Horses. Riders of the mighty wind!"

Herr Kinderweise. Herr Childwise. She never spoke that name for him out loud, fearing it might slip off her tongue and lose its magic forever. Yet for the rest of her life, it was carved and pitted in her brain, like the yellowing stone of the man and the horse.

Her interns were moving sluggishly like marine plants, sea anemones swaying gently in deep ocean currents. Yet she felt an invisible wall of glass between herself and everyone else, dividing them in time and place. As in the vastness of space, where the movements of the stars, coming from such great distances, had long since ceased to occur. An ash from Madame's cigarette took many seconds to fall to the floor. Max had risen to close the living room door, which had yawned open, but he walked like a slow drunkard. Petra crossed her legs, but temptingly, luxurious and sexy — not at all what she intended.

Frau Direktor heard the young woman ask, "What — is — the — matter — with — you?"

She tried to touch her own face. The fingers seemed to take an age to move. Finally, after a great effort, her leaden palm came off the chair. What was happening? Was this Newton's world of ordered rules — or was their hollow room but a shabby cardboard box in time, the people stuck within like porcelain dolls, expressions painted on their faces?

No, like stones . . . Like the carefully nurtured stones in a Japanese rock garden. Their bodies weighing them down: planted stones. Silent. Immovable. Stable for a lifetime. Forever, compared to the lightning flash of the mind. There in the garden they sat: the weathered, craggy stone in a smooth sea of raked sand, a scrap of moss quietly thriving in the shade, and nearby a miniature shrub of pine, standing in repose. Fifty years it took the gardener to arrange this garden of stone, as all the while the air around it was vibrating and alive. While rain came and snows. And sun again. An irreverent butterfly lands on a stone pinnacle of their little rock and then flits off into eternity. A wisp of thought on its own wings: gone in a sky of blue and gold . . .

Maximilian had finally managed to reach the door and close it. A new length of ash was beginning to grow on Madame's Balkan cigarette. Petra finished crossing her legs, laying her hands in her lap like dead fish. Everyone moved slower and slower, as though wading through a pool of mire — and Frau Direktor began to feel the heat of their thoughts glowing in their brains: little flickers of flame behind their eyes. . . . Their minds lay open for her.

Inside Maximilian a curl of resentment rose like a tidal wave: what a waste, the clinic, the effort, the children. Did anyone really believe a silly letter to Mister Jung in Zurich would change anything? Then a weak, diabolical stab: what if he, Maximilian, could save the clinic? Just find the right levers of power. The proper official in control. If you just found him and reasoned with him — that would fix it. After all, Maximilian wasn't "political." He could take all the children into his own care and start afresh. It was the *others* who were condemning them to ruin. Frau Direktor obviously had not been in touch with the proper authorities. A series of waxy faces drifted across his mind, colleagues at the Hermitage Hospital, surgeons, administrators, research scientists: they'd vouch for him all right — they'd know the proper steps to take, they'd know the real official in charge!

Then all at once this silliness collapsed with the flat slap of despair. There was no help for it, no mysterious official with the proper levers of influence. Max's silver ball clattered around the roulette wheel, hopping back and forth over the green double zero. As the croupier with the pencil-thin mustache called out, *Messieurs et mesdames, les jeux sont faits! Les jeux sont faits!* What rubbish, him thinking he wasn't part of it. So how the hell were they going to get out?

A hot cinder burned in young Petra's head. Ex-chambermaid! Ex-housekeeper! No more beds, no more laundry. She preened inside. . . . *Intern* Petra. She'd flee the country with Marie. Then a sharp twinge. Alone? With who, then? That old badger, Madame? Ugh. Or the other? The man . . . Why did his Houdini eyes seem so terribly a part of everything now? She imagined her fingers touching his dark hair while he slept upright on a steamer trunk in the baggage coach of a train. She saw herself brush the locks from his forehead, touching the faded purple scar, whispering, Don't leave me, stay and sleep, darling, stay with your Petra and sleep. . . . Then a bitter swallow as she suppressed the whole thing. What the devil was the man to her? She could get on without him. As well as anybody. And with the children too . . .

Madame Le Boyau's mind was the smoky glow of a wick after the candle had been blown out. She had long ago dismissed the idea of fleeing as absurd. She felt too old to go begging at the doors of famous strangers. She would wait with Frau Direktor until the end. Let them take her brittle bones. Better to die dignified, sitting in an old dining room chair, than tremble in a cold, muddy ditch with ice at the bottom, while the whole countryside was out searching high and low. . . . Better to sit it out and wait.

And yet part of her wondered how in heaven she would manage cigarettes in the days and weeks following her arrest. She quickly began to scheme this way and that — which merchant she might pay for an extended period of credit, which jailer she might corrupt to smuggle in her Balkan brand. How to achieve it — seduction or bribery? Ah, you flatter yourself, *ma chère*. Inevitably she'd lose a percentage off the top. From the merchant to the guards, they would all cheat ruthlessly. And what if they sent her to a camp? There must be all kinds of contraband floating about, plenty of thieves and racketeers. What had she to offer any rascal in exchange for the simple creature comforts? Therapy?

*   *   *

The three of them had become transparent. Had Frau Direktor become transparent too . . . ? And they to each other? When the po-
licemen came to take their bodies away, would their minds return to
the dilapidated living room, the familiar hallways of the clinic?
Where was Herr Kinderweise right this very moment? And what of
her remote Herr Doktor in Zurich? Was either of them alone? Reading in his study? Listening to a patient? Or with his wife? No, she
sensed Herr Kinderweise's thoughts turned elsewhere. And her precious Herr Doktor had long ago managed to banish her out of mind.

There came a sinking, the air barely reaching down her trachea.
The asthma very bad. She heard the labor of her breathing.

Maximilian, she thought, said, "What's the matter? Can we get you
something? Look out!"

The room turned on its side. Max's face peered at her, upside down.
He was saying, "Someone, quick! Get me a pillow for her head!"

Chapter 5

The Enduring

The slowness of everything made her think of dandelion puffs floating through the air, lazy specks drifting aimlessly across a summer field. The wall of glass between herself and the others had become thicker and thicker. But now blurring, glazed over as if with frost. Maximilian's head tilted gently from side to side; he looked concerned and puzzled, like a troubled dog who can't understand laughter or tears. Madame Le Boyau flickered through the cigarette smoke. "I'll prepare the bed," she said, and was gone.

She guessed they were planning to carry her upstairs. Why so soon? There was so much left to do, so much to discuss and decide. Frau Direktor wanted to stop them, saying, "Never mind me, let's get on with it," but moving her mouth was such a great effort, her tongue as thick as leather. Her body felt impossibly heavy, arms and thighs like sacks of meal. "Check her pulse," a voice said. Then, "Loosen her clothes!" A harsh light glared into her eyes: Max was holding up an eyelid. His thumb seemed as large as a brick. Get your damn thumb out of my eye! But her tongue was too thick for it. They lifted her, Max on one side, good thorough Petra on the other.

"Can you walk?" Max asked. "Come along now, try to walk. We'll go to bed. You're just tired, that's all. Too much housekeeping."

She tried to smile into Max's face. Beads of sweat stood out on his forehead. They stumbled up a long flight of stairs that went on endlessly into darkness, one weary step after the next. But all the while Max's face stayed right beside her own, the sweat running down his shaven cheek. She felt like telling him what a nice fellow he was to keep her company this way. Just say, You're a nice fellow, Max — but she was simply too tired to make the words come out. . . . Besides,

39

her tongue felt so awfully thick. Lungs all choked. Tubes blocked. Just no extra breath for it.

They carried Frau Direktor into her tiny room. A small electric lamp stood on a nightstand by the bed. It burned, shedding a pale white light.

Did she faint? she wondered stupidly. . . .

Petra's voice now: "Look, look at her hand! It's twitching. Stop it! I can't stand to see it twitch like that!"

Twitching, she called it? No, that was wrong. They used to call it by another word. Twitting. Twiggling. No, wrong. Twiddling. Yes, *twiddling!* What a funny word. Try to tell Petra. Try to say it out loud for her: twid-twid-twid. Oh, Petra, listen carefully and you'll hear it on my breath: twid-twid-twid . . .

The ring of faces around the bed had grown blurry. "She's barely breathing. Is this asthma?" Madame asked. "I've never seen it this bad. Will it go away?"

No answer . . .

After a moment Max said, "There now, Frau Direktor's sleeping." But he was wrong. She was looking straight up at the cracked ceiling through half-shut eyes. She tried to focus on his face, but she saw only a round blur like a rising moon. . . . One by one the faces floating about the bed drew off. Everyone was leaving. Madame, last of all, shuffled stiffly to the door. She tried one last time to call out for her to stop, but she kept on shuffling. Barely picking up her feet; the dry steps fading out the door. Please come back, don't go. Wait for me! I'm coming! Wait!

Frau Direktor rose and went to the door. Glancing back at her bed, she was dimly aware of a snuggled lump, hidden under the covers. The faded light from the bedside lamp seemed to be shining on the huddled form as from a great distance. Illuminating it, faintly, and leaving all else in gloom.

Madame had left the room, closing the door behind her. But that did not matter now; how easy to follow her down the stairs. Frau Direktor could feel the house living all around her. In the handrail she grasped, a family of termites gnawed happily and methodically away. Upon the wall, the wallpaper was becoming more and more brittle, imperceptibly peeling off the plaster. In another part of the house, a

40

toilet flushed. And in yet another, a child cried in its sleep; then a short moment later came the sound of caring footsteps hurrying to the rescue.

She tried not to let the life of the house distract her from following Madame down the dark staircase, but the old woman seemed to be swept beyond her reach. I'm dying, Frau Direktor thought. Look, even the staircase was changing, becoming narrower and narrower and altogether black. She heard the faint sounds of people talking . . . But then this too was gone, as though they had stopped. The air grew hot and stuffy. The house now filmy and transparent: a ghost house, like a stage with paper doors, no glass in the windows, and walls of scrim. Snow lay on the street outside; the streetlamps glowed. A few flakes came down, weaving in and out of the lamplight, settling on the black iron of the lamp cages. A brewer's cart with great casks strapped in place rolled down the street; the horse team snorted in the cold. From the black sky above, snowflakes drifted down in lazy spirals. White coming out of the void . . . And then even the snow ceased to fall.

In the top floor of their town house, she saw the dark little room with the bedside lamp that gave hardly any light. And she saw the huddled lump in the narrow bed. Then the room faded, leaving her alone in the empty night. It was much better when you didn't have to breathe. Was this how you came to an end? With a pause in eternity stretching from one heartbeat to the next, one moment to the next, one age to the next — when nothing moves, in a deep, patient stillness? Was this the life after death? A long silence between living and dying. Yet no oblivion . . . Only a long gray staircase leading up and down from one moment to the next — to walk upon time as though upon a stair — when your lifetime was but a single landing.

And when you died . . . dissolution. An interminable fading while the intricate machine of your existence shut down. All its components taken out and disassembled. One by one each piece crushed, or melted, or rusted away; until nothing stood on the steps of time but the soulless dust of souls. And this, too, to be swept off the gray stairway. No molecules, no atoms. Only the pause in the clock's second hand existed. One duration flowing into another. And when she had endured eternity she was in another time. Another place. Times and places, places in time. Forward or backward. Persisting. Existing.

Enduring in the minds around her . . .

*   *   *

41

A fresh breeze scented with jasmine and gardenia swept into a brightly sunlit morning room. The sound of a fountain pen scratched softly across a paper tablet. But that was all she knew or heard or saw: her enduring had narrowed the senses down to a slim band. As though, when swept off the staircase of eternity, all her senses had been pressed together, only to be handled selectively, and one at a time . . .

A writer's hand wrote with a black fountain pen; the writer's script tilted dramatically forward, as though everything he thought was angled only toward the future. Then, as the enduring faded, a few familiar senses returned as well. She recognized the hand immediately, though it had changed with old age, the script feebler. . . . Herr Kinderweise. As old as a man could be.

But this was not the study in Vienna, the study of the galloping man! Where were they? And even as the last shred of the enduring dissipated and her senses bloomed in all directions, Frau Direktor knew somehow one important fact — she existed no more. She was some years dead. But this did not particularly trouble her, for the police had long ago enacted whatever fate decreed, and for that she was grateful: because it seemed she had been spared the grim pain of punishment. And now her senses were free, to drift upon the wind. She forgot about Herr Kinderweise's new study and raced out to look over the world, listening for a billion heartbeats, for a billion voices; feeling the rain in a backwater Amazon jungle and the raw bite of wind on the Greenland ice pack; brushed by the pungent smell of turmeric and reeling from the caw of parrots in a noisy, crowded Rangoon market stall. Her restored spirit reached out into the world, and then she knew for certain that all of them were gone. Her poor clinic no longer on any person's mind, not even the Russian Special Police; a final closing of the bedroom door . . . not a soul on the planet remembered Frau Direktor at all.

But the motion and the voice of things were open to her: the strips of clouds in the blue sky, leaves rustling in the wind, and the trickle of water running down a gutter in a city — minor things and great things and the confused thoughts of men like the steady roar of the sea over dunes. Chaotic, for she heard the babble of many tongues: a great war was brewing across the continent of Europe, much greater than the one she had known in her youth. She saw the spray of golden showering sparks in arms factories, the shunting of trains, and the flickering needles of a thousand electric sewing machines stitching a million bits of braid on the collars of uniforms. She heard the bark of orders and the answering shouts of men; the sound of marching ants, singing the same marching song, stamping the same billion feet: soldiers' feet in every city, town, and village.

Already in the East an empire from Japan was rising like a great wave to hurl across the Pacific Ocean; and on the mainland of China she felt their single will like a heavy canvas smothering Manchuria: a muffled scream from Shanghai, the feeble voices of people drowned out by shellfire and the moans of those trapped under collapsed buildings. While from within the great landmass of Asia, she sensed a coldly burning coal from the brain of the man who ruled Russia. He still ruled it — alive and plotting — while the ghosts of millions he had sent out of his sight hovered about him in the very bedroom where he slept with a woman. But he was a hard man, who slept soundly despite the wailing throngs beside his bed. They did not trouble him. He dreamed of adding to their millions.

And suddenly her eye lit upon Vienna. The National Socialist flags flew everywhere: the red field, grand white circle, and black swastika. They hung smartly from public buildings, and pairs of smaller flags from lampposts along the avenues; red, black, and white bunting draped from streetfront windows, miles of it in every *Strasse* and *Platz*. The city was all dressed up as though for Easter. Throngs of gray-uniformed soldiers chatted loudly on the sidewalks and shopped in the stores; officers in gleaming boots ordered bottles of champagne in the restaurants. There seemed to be a teeming rally or party in every flat and alley, while bejeweled royalty danced gaily in the crystal-lit ballrooms of the Imperial Palace of the Hofburg.

But no music came from the Freud family house at 19 Berggasse; no electric bulbs burned in the sockets. The Freud family had gone; the upstairs rented out to strangers, who hung their wash in the rooms and never did the dishes. The old study lay empty — no books or pictures — and the furniture had vanished. There were cigarette butts ground into the hall carpet and muddy bootprints on the stairs. Down, down through the house she peered, looking for some clue, some trace of those who had left. Dust and dirt were crammed in every corner; someone had urinated on a wall. The closets ripped open, empty, except for a torn dress hanging limply from a hanger; a pocketful of change tossed on the floor. The stench of human filth

43

grew worse in the basement; on the concrete floor she saw what looked like a few shards of cracked pottery. The chariot frieze she liked so much, now broken junk. Recognizable only by the pitted stone. Off in a corner a fractured piece of the horse's head, ending just behind the jaw. The galloping man had fallen.

And his owner? Driven out? Run away?

How stupid to think she could be omnipotent all in a minute, to think she might swoop over the world without becoming hopelessly lost among the intricacies of a billion minds and their trillion works. Try to picture it: that brightly lit morning room, painted butter-cream yellow with white trim on the window — she only glimpsed it, and then only glimpsed his hand, scratching across a paper tablet with a fountain pen. Where was he? Someplace here in Vienna? She felt the urge to panic, to flee from street to street, shout questions at German soldiers, rip into their brains!

Stop this. Reason coolly. It had been a bright morning but now was midday in Vienna. West, then — she turned her ear, listening hopefully for that hand still scratching on the pad. Trying to shut out all else; the Vienna cellar grew dim and gray, tissuey . . . the pile of yellow rubble from the frieze lay in the dark like a heap of burning coals. How many men were writing now? Where was that hand, among all the hands, where was the one she sought? Just in the city itself, many hands crawled across lined paper, writing all the time: hesitant hands, hands that pressed forward, hands that paused to doodle on an empty page. The small pile of broken stone glowed on the floor — the only thing that mattered — and slowly one by one all those other writing hands put down their pens. . . .

Then she heard his sound; it drew her on, separate from the sound of a thousand squints scratching their squibs across the continent. He was writing a letter, and thinking the words as he wrote:

20 Maresfield Gardens
London N.W. 3
April 1, 1939

Dear (name mumbled, didn't catch it)
It is surprising how little we can foresee the future. If you told me before the war — or twenty years ago — that a society for psychoanalysis would be founded in

44

London, I would never have imagined that a quarter of a century later I might be living next door. And, even more unlikely, that, while living next door, I would *still* not be able to celebrate the occasion with you. Accept these good wishes in lieu of my presence.

Unhappily, people here are trying to lull me into an atmosphere of optimism. I don't believe it, and I don't like being deceived. If only some kind of intervention would cut short this cruel process . . .

The words were hushed, tremulous, so soft they could barely be distinguished from the babble of human noise coming from every corner of the world. His writing mind became a thin thread that never left her hand, and she ran alongside it back to the sunlit room. England. Smoggy, gray London. Steaming taxis, vistas of brick row houses . . . She found his new home quiet and out of the way.

His study was brighter than the old one, with a bit of well-tended garden beyond the French doors. Outside, the leaves of an almond tree stirred in the wind, their color a tender springtime green. She wanted to ask, What happened? To Vienna? To my clinic? Did anyone tell you? But though she might circle the earth a dozen times, or sink to the depths of the sea where the devilfish lit their way in the dark, she couldn't pick up a pebble. Make a sound. Or blow a fleck of lint from his sleeve. Yet she could travel in his mind. And know his thoughts . . . The date on the letter read 1939: six years gone by. A mere six years for all of them in Rostov to be forgotten. Not even a shred of memory fluttering in a passing thought . . . And as she watched his hand crawl across the pad, she could feel the man was sick. Too sick to care about anything else. Perhaps he had a month to live. Perhaps a week.

They had made yet another appointment for him at the London Clinic. A mere formality. Lün, the chow dog, lay under the desk and breathed sleepily. No formality in that. Looking down, he saw that Lün had cracked open one eye, which glanced upward at him. Then she pushed her soft, furry body past his cold legs. She circled once on the rug and sat heavily on the carpet. Often, he could walk only that far himself. A few weak steps in the garden and then back to his desk.

He had seen a picture of himself in the paper last week. It showed him standing outside his new English home, his face clamped and sour, the corner of his mouth drooping to a mushy line. The doctors had removed a section of his jaw as neatly as you'd bone a chicken. They had shown him the bone afterward: black and soft with cancer. In its place they had put a prosthetic implant that fit closely into the hollow they had carved out. Already the muscles were cleaving to it, so that he could talk, even if he slurred.

He had used those jaws — to talk and howl and laugh, to kiss and eat. How he loved meat. Roasts and steak and flanken. Chew the bones and suck the marrow out. Now the thought of all that gnawing and bone-cracking left him weak and slightly nauseous. He fed himself with a spoon at mealtimes, his old man's fingers shoving in a puree of infant's mush. . . .

Lün lifted her head slowly and stared sleepily out into the garden. A thrush had landed on the ground and pecked daintily at the dirt. The thrush looked at the dog and the dog looked at the thrush and they held each other's gaze for what seemed a long time. Then the bird chirped once as if to say, Bye-bye, Lün! and turned tail, hopping off. It flew up into the lower branch of the almond tree and preened. The dog yawned and laid her big head back down on the carpet.

"You're a lazy hound," the old man said. Lün thumped her tail gently on the carpet, agreeing without too much effort.

They had found a new cancer near the prosthetic implant. . . . He knew he smelled, that his whole mouth smelled rotten with decay. That's why the dog chose a spot on the carpet far away. Sometimes he fancied that he could still taste those Canary Island cigars he used to buy by the box. He saw it clearly: a snug balsa wood box, holding twenty Triple-A hand-rolled cigars, each wrapped with a green-and-gold band.

Pope Julius II brand, they were called; the pontiff's profile and Medici nose were embossed on a miniature tinfoil plaque in the center of the box. His Old Jules, he used to call them, and during the long middle years of his practice each box cost twenty florins. That was the combined revenue from three and a third analytic sessions, each at six florins an hour. If he spent three hours in the morning analyzing three patients, they paid for the box of cigars he bought during lunch. But if the slow holiday season of a Vienna summer left his consultation room hideously empty, while the long afternoons slipped idly into evening, then that slim day's work barely covered a nasty indulgence. The smoke of those cigars wafted sweetly in his memory, hanging motionless in the air of the old consulting room . . . shifting as the murmurs of his patients floated through their veils. And even now, at the end of his life, the whiff of Old Jules clung to him as cancer in his jaw.

The old room had been a little like a museum filled with collectibles and cherishables — more like a spinster's curiosity shop than a doctor's office: inlaid marble boxes from the Orient, a print of the Sphinx in the Gizeh Nile Valley, embroidered pillows with worn tassels and book upon book on shelf after shelf . . . While nearby a watchful tribe of miniature antiquities silently guarded three sides of his green blotter.

Some of the statuettes were originals, others copies of copies. Some were gifts, some he had bought himself as the state of his practice and the price allowed. Isis the moon goddess was one of the first miniature statues he bought. He had fallen in love with her name, which meant "She-Who-Weeps." A Roman copy made of soft marble, seven inches high; her lips full, her belly round and navel deep. Her breasts hung separate and alone, and they stared at him kindly. With such a pleasant, giving body, what did she weep for? For whom . . . ?

Next came Marduk, a four-inch god of war: his face had smoothed with years, leaving his beard a few mere scratches. In one hand he once held a weapon no bigger than a matchstick. Yet his mouth was cruelly carved — the insatiable lips of Nebuchadnezzar, the bitter breath of battle fume and death. A tiny battle god like an outrider who precedes the main host. A blot on the horizon, yet the herald of doom. Rapine, ruin, and slaughter. He didn't have to be big, just the right size to swing from your neck as your sword rose and fell and the blood ran down its hilt.

In an alley shop in Siena he had found Astarte. And when he saw her he knew he must possess the little love goddess of fertility. The ancient days had seen so many of them, a score of lusty maids for a score of lovers. So many Astartes had been made from common clay, perhaps in honor of the sacred temple prostitutes of her name. Common clay-feet country girls, serving for a time in the big city, before being sent home pregnant, with a sack of coppers in their belt. This one, so shameless, so blatant — she made him covet her in an instant breath of lust. And yet a figure so old and weathered there was precious little left of her to admire.

But what was left told all. The long-dead maker had concentrated on her woman's parts. They were raised like a lozenge, as though meant to be adored. Swollen, impossible to overlook. And after millenniums his eyes were still drawn to the space between her thighs. So she was meant to be: a wanton, luscious thing, with taunting voluptuous parts and the heavy splayed feet of a barefoot country girl. So a sculptress made her. For it had to be a sculptress — so much self-love, self-adoration in the thing. The maker had to be a woman, and knowledgeable in the ways of men. Maybe a prostitute who thought herself a goddess. One of dozens who lived in a temple of fertility and love. A sacred precinct run by prostitute priestesses in a town full of soldiers and merchants: where outside the town walls the good wives kept their husbands at home, digging out crumbling furrows under the sun of Assyria.

He would never know. . . .

Chapter 6

The Wise Man Dies in Childhood

The sun had shifted along the carpet, a bar of light warming Lün's dark-brown nose. And the thrush had returned from the almond tree. The bird stood in the open garden doorstep, a foot or two from the sleeping chow. The old man looked down at the figures surrounding his green blotter. The blotter had been replaced twenty times since he had begun putting statues on his desk. This one was fresh and untouched. It mocked him, for he would never wear it out, never fray it with thoughtless scribbles and a pointed pen. They had put it on his desk to remind him of the old office. To make him more at home. But in trying to make these strange surroundings more familiar, they only made it more obvious that he had lost forever everything that came before. Another kind of death.

His little tribe of gargoyles would pass into the future without him, as they had done with countless owners since their beginnings. The possessor of life died, and yet the mute stones remained: is that what people meant when they said the gods were immortal?

He had saved them from the sack of Vienna — if a man could save a god. Stowing them about his person, even in his wife's purse, smuggling them across the frontier like forbidden idols from a hostile land. His favorite, Pan, thumped heavily in his overcoat pocket. Keeping his coat on no matter what, in the June heat, in the sweaty waiting rooms and stuffy railway compartments. Even when he had to urinate in the spotless coach toilet; it banged against the locked door as the train rocked him unsteadily from side to side. He missed the swaying toilet and wet his shoes. He didn't care. Pan was with him.

Pan. The bawdy joker, the thief, the horny monster. He drew the statue across the blotter. Five inches of bronze, green with age —

cloven hoofed, his limbs taut and supple. The body of a wrestler, who could wriggle out of the tightest grip or throw you on your back. Stubs of antlers grew from his head. His green eyes lit with mischief; his frisky tail ready for the chase. The artist had captured him lifting one knee in the air as if dancing a jig, his hand held up in a mock salute.

And Pan had an erection. Curving upward like a horn, the monstrous thing reached nearly to his navel. So that's what his naughty smile was about, teasing, "Eh, missy! Is this what you want?"

How easy to imagine the rogue sitting under the shadow of a fig tree, the shadow obscuring his shaggy haunches. Passing for a weary field hand, resting at noon with the glaring sun beating down all around him. His tail leisurely flicking the flies from his legs. And then he saw her — a small black speck across the land.

She was slowly lugging water in a heavy jug to the hands who toiled in the dirt. When they threw back their heads to drink, the water splashed on their faces and on the ground. When the jug ran empty, she trudged back for more. All day . . . up and back, the heavy jug pressing deeper and deeper into her shoulder. And finally, when she'd watered a dozen men's dusty faces and most of the ground at their feet, she set the heavy thing down gratefully. Across the long strip of earth she spied one last man loafing in the shade of a fig tree. Oh, God . . .

With a sigh, she hoisted the jug upon her shoulder once more, pushed one sluggish foot in front of the other. The bottom of the jug dug a red crease in her flesh, aching with every step. She had long since given up switching shoulders, and she tried to put the pain out of her mind by staring at her dusty feet. They were the same color as the earth, toenails cracked, pads of callus harder than the ground. The sun beat down and her eyes began to swim. What a low cur. What a lout. Not even getting up to meet her!

Sweat ran down her sides in long rivulets. It was probably Picus, the headman's son. Lazy Picus. Loudmouthed, good-for-nothing Picus. Never doing a lick of work but always on hand when the wine was being mixed, then coming after his father's women. The headman's older wives were more than idle . . . so he might have some welcome there. But Picus only chased the young pretty ones; and he was a gap-toothed clown, stupid looking when he smiled. Who would want to kiss a face like that? But there he sat, like the headman

50

already, making her come to him. Black despair wrapped her in a cloth; the lone fig tree shimmered in the distance, never seeming to come any closer. The bastard! She would see him dead one day.

Then at last the shade yawned before her like a puddle at her feet. She let the heavy jug down, water sloshing over the rim. Less for him, then.

"Well, if you want some water come and get it, Picus."

"No, you come . . . Come into the cool and rest yourself."

Rest herself! She should go. Leave him sitting there without the water. To spite him, she hefted the jug and drank. Rivulets ran out the corners of her mouth and down her front. It felt delicious and cool, and her rags hung wetly. She knew he was staring. Let him stare. Setting the jug down, she bent farther than she ought, showing herself off. For a slow moment a crawling silence gathered in the shade of the fig tree. He broke it with a low chuckle.

"You drink well, but I'm not very thirsty. . . ."

Damn him, then!

She turned away proudly, showing off her hips. Showing him something he'd never have. And then he laughed. Her wet rags went cold. Picus never laughed like that. She tried to imagine his gap-toothed grin, but now she could not recall his face. Her eyes roved across the fields, but the fields lay empty. Where were the others? The hairs rose on her calves. . . . She took a step back from the jug, shading her eyes against the glare to peer into the gloom under the tree. The figure stirred. Slowly it stood, shaggy haunches unfolding from the long grass at the trunk, hooves crumbling clods of dirt. His tail swished back and forth. He had his man-thing out — coming, coming for her.

She ran, her shout swallowed up in a deaf sky. She noticed a little cloud, all alone in the blue: a tender silky nimbus racing with her. . . . And then another cloud descended down upon it. The dark cloud spread out its gray cloak, gathering in the silky one. Why see this now? Her shoulders no longer ached, her wet front warm as summer rain. And she suddenly felt hungry for a piece of roast meat between her teeth, the juice running over her chin.

She stole a glance over her shoulder. He fell over himself as he came on. Above her, the two clouds were tangled. She stumbled, her body hot and sweaty in the soft dirt. She wasn't fleeing from him any-more. . . . His breath blew against her ear and smelled of mown grass.

She squirmed, struggling in the dirt to make the taking sweeter. To make him want it more. Her rags ripped and shredded; the sun shone on the backs of her thighs. She raised her bottom for him, and he hugged her to the ground. Beside the fig tree her jug had fallen over, and the water from the water jug gurgled into the soft earth. She howled, glad no one could hear her cry. She was open and ready. . . .

Beg me for it, Picus. I'll laugh in your face tonight!

The old man came back to his study; he touched Pan's smooth bronze skin. How much he wished he had that huge manness now, possessing the great swollen heat of it. He remembered it as a separate part of him, an animal, distinctly not human, with its own needs and wants. Then came a stab of burning envy. That horny goat with the smooth green skin had owned his manhood for three thousand years and would own it for another three. But not himself. Not Herr Professor of Maresfield Gardens, not Herr Doktor of 19 Berggasse, not the lover of Martha, the father of his children. Not his mortal, human self who possessed the man-thing for a brief score of years, a poor little tail, withered and flaccid in the end.

How irrelevant an old man's penis was — compared to what it had always been. An old man's stick, no good for women and hardly even good to pee with. Then, last of all, becoming a leaky faucet, a constant drip you couldn't ignore.

Now he bore his wife's kind smiles when she came to him in bed; the last time he had gone to her was almost a year ago. At eighty-two! How cocky he felt that day. A swift year later he had waned for good. While in the darkness of each night he felt her push her warm bottom up against his cold flanks. What did she think of then? His younger days? Then the kindness of her smiles killed him. Much too late now to tell the world that the envy of an old man for his younger self was the last bitter breath of life. That — and your wife drifting off to sleep with an old woman's sigh . . .

In a flicker of torment, he saw her bottom as it looked in her youth, round and firm like a pear that he could split open with his fingers whenever he wanted and devour it. A lump rose in his throat, and he feared he might cry. Cry right there in his sunny morning office, in front of Lün. Dogs understood about crying, whining mournfully or coming over to snuffle your leg. And Lün sensed his mood, nosing it out of the air like a smell. Even his own Lün . . . She shifted her furry

52

head off the carpet and stared at him with great brown watchful eyes. The dull pain in his jaw returned to trouble him. Somehow he had let the statue of Pan fall on its face. He managed a dry chuckle, then stood the god upright and drew Astarte alongside. Pan with his great erection and, beside him, Astarte — showing the world her voluptuous vagina. He turned the figures face-to-face. "You know," he slurred, "you two should think about getting married."

The London Clinic was one of those horribly efficient places only British medicine could run and maintain. As the old man walked unsteadily down the corridor, he spotted a nearly unforgivable oversight. Some nurse or orderly had failed to collect a bedpan, leaving it out in the open on a gurney in the hall. The stainless-steel receptacle contained someone's sickly green feces, the smooth consistency of toothpaste squeezed fresh from the tube. A singularly repulsive sight, with the aura of incontinence and disease and slow wasting. Yet the pan surrounding the excrement was clean and spotless, as if the patient's elimination had been put there by hand and the metal rim polished like a fancy dish served in a smart restaurant. Was this some kind of joke?

"Oh my heavens," came a squeak in the hall. A reedy nurse with blond hair tucked into a starched cap had discovered the offending artifact. She hastily made to carry it off in disgrace. Her body was young and compact, strapped neatly into the white hospital uniform. The old man stopped his shuffling to watch her; she held the scandalous thing with a considerable amount of poise. Yes, a dying man's joke. Here's my sick shit, Nurse; be good enough to take it away.

The reedy nurse cast an accusatory glance at the old man as she marched past, as though silently charging him with complicity in the matter.

"Rest assured," he muttered as she went by, "it was not mine, my dear."

She came to a halt.

"May I help you, sir?"

He noticed she had a bitten face, too tight for her own good. He had read somewhere that these efficient English nurses were so capable they could sweep the curtains around a bed in one of the crowded wards, wrap a dead body, and spirit away the patient's corpse while the rest of the ward took their tea. Faced with this compact creature at ten paces, he was completely prepared to believe it. He didn't want to go like that, not with a frigid young woman's hands the first things to touch him after he was gone, the blood still warm in his veins. . . . No! Not like an eyesore, like a nuisance, like a misplaced stool in a bedpan, requiring nothing but swift removal — all because he had the thoughtlessness to die.

"Thank you anyway," he slurred through his rotten jaw. "I know the way."

The reedy nurse tried to hide a wince at the sight of his sagging face, the recent scar. He wondered if the corner of his mouth was leaking; he touched his fingers to his dead cheek. Dampness. A thin stream of saliva, darkening his white collar. He had long since failed to notice when his mouth leaked. The nurse managed a thin smile.

Everyone smiled at him now.

Professor Praeger was a small, tidy man who looked more like a ferret than anything else. A middle-aged ferret, with a pointy face, quick black eyes, and a small mouth that didn't seem made for kissing. He combed his glossy hair very slick, with a graying band along one side. The sharp pointy face betrayed nothing, yet, like a chunk of dry ice, Praeger's mind let off a chill vapor. A cold mind, of logic and calculation . . . Desk bare, except for a pen set, with two black pens darting up like insect antennae. This was the place dying men came to, to be told the worst. This was the place where the faces stopped smiling.

The quick black eyes saw everything; they knew the condition of the man's jaw and the medical history of the rest of the parts. On the tip of the ferret's tongue you could almost hear the steady clinical catalog, the sad summary of the case. Not my patient's case, not Herr Freud's case — but the Subject's case. The same frank language used for case notes; the cold catalog going something like this:

Subject's mouth cleaned ten days ago; brown crusts removed from upper gums. Crusts histologically negative. Three pits of cancer discovered, which retained bits of food; the area was painful. The diameter of the cancerous pits was five millimeters, coagulated; they have not reappeared. Evidence of puffiness under the right eye. Suspected narcosis in the first nasal tube. Possible tumor developing in the cheek.

Then a decidedly unscientific opinion sneaking in: Subject's eyes losing clarity; suspect film over cornea due to radium treatments.

And finally a touch of pity: Subject complained of headaches.

The ferret spoke: "How's your bladder, Herr Doktor?"

"Fine, Professor Praeger, and yours?"

The ferret grinned a sharp black grin. "And the headaches? Are they still troubling you?"

"No, the morphine did well. I stopped taking the grains after a few days."

The old man felt a slight twinge poke his bladder, a nagging discomfort distracting him from the pressing ache on the side of his face. It hurt to lie to Praeger. The morphine had been useless. Without the narcotic his mind seemed to dull the pain, become used to it, pushing it into the background. But the morphine destroyed all that. The pain ceased to matter, yet when the drug's dulling effect had run its course the pain came back stronger than ever, a claw on the side of his head. And he felt betrayed. Better to deal with each wave of pain as it washed over him . . . only to recover, weak and shaken, facing the truly unbearable thing: the thought of his mind going out like a candle. For when the pain ebbed he remembered how sweet life was. Should he try to tell Professor Praeger any of that? He had long ago grown sick of himself complaining, whining feebly, I have pain, I have pain. . . .

His bladder nudged him again. Soon he would have to find a place to urinate. Professor Praeger's face said something he couldn't catch; how could he interrupt the professor and ask him for a place to go? The pain in his jaw came in a wave that clouded his vision, clogging his head.

He closed his eyes and stopped listening.

There was always the back porch of his parents' house. How grateful he felt to be able to visit there right now. Not much of a porch, just some slats of wood nailed into a deck where people sat on summer evenings as the dusk closed around them.

He was crawling under the big people's legs. Past his father's trousers, past his shoes. They weren't interesting. His father gave off a man's smell: healthy sweat, a touch of tobacco. The smell warm and hard at the same time.

Then his mother's legs; like towers rising up into her skirt, disappearing into the press of her thighs. A different smell, like moist cut flowers and fresh cotton shirts. In the summer heat she had her dress hiked up, so he saw all the way to her knees and the curved undersides of her thighs. She shifted her legs for him as he crept past.

"He's five years old. He can walk, can't he?"

This from his father. The man seemed to expect some kind of answer, but when none came:

"So why doesn't he walk?"

Again, no answer.

Then his mother, finally:

"He likes to crawl." Obviously she didn't mind, really. Maybe even liked him staring up her dress. Admiring her that way.

Again, his father:

"We didn't raise him to crawl. So if he can walk, he should *walk*." This settled it for his father.

At last he crawled to the end of the porch and stood up by the white picket fence that surrounded the deck.

"Thank God," his father said. "He stands."

Then as he stood by the picket fence he unbuttoned his little wool shorts and they fell to his ankles. He peed in a long stream that arched beyond the edge of the deck and through the fence and fell in some disordered clover. The clover bent and trembled as he rained on its leaves. His father barked, "Is that what you teach him?"

Henny, their big-bottomed cook, came out on the porch just in time to see him pee. She was scowling, but with a glint of laughter around her eyes. Then she cackled like an old bird.

"Just like you used to go," she cawed at his father in Slovak. "Only you didn't hold it as nice as he. You used to wave it around." Henny showed how Father used to go, her plump red hands waving about.

His father sat down gruffly, crossing one leg over the other. He fumbled with his pipe. Then frowned darkly at Henny as he got it going. Henny gazed back at the man, nodding serenely like a cow in a meadow.

Mother's eyes were laughing. "Oh, you little Hun!" she cried. "Come here and show Mama how you put your pants back on."

He ran to her, his wool shorts catching around his ankles.

The reedy, bitten-faced nurse accepted the vial of his urine as if it were a glass of wine. A Vouvray with drops of blood. He had a brief fantasy about her. That once upon a time this fine, compact lady had not been a nurse at all but an Irish convent nun who had somehow broken her vow . . . broken it with a handsome, devil-may-care auto mechanic, who took her in a water closet in a pub. Without wooing her, without words, simply ripping open her black habit with his grease-stained hands and plunging into her standing up in the filthy toilet —

Ach!

He wanted her raped because he was a broken wreck while she was complete and alive, the master of her face. Even his bloody urine had not made her wince. She stood with her back to him, calmly writing out a specimen label as easily as you'd check off a grocery list. When she finished marking the vial, she glanced at him. "You needn't put your pants back on."

He had not bothered but remained perched on a tall metal stool like the classroom dunce. Ja, the class dunce, with his skinny legs dangling over the floor like an idiot. No point in dressing, because they always gave him a bath before the X rays. The problem was his limbs trembled, and his head shook — ruining the plate. So instead of endless exposures, they hit upon the idea of a bath. The warm steam and the hot water soothed his limbs to stillness, nearly putting him to sleep. And in the warm afterglow, the clinic technicians always got a good X-ray plate of his jaw.

When the nurse showed no signs of leaving, he slid carefully off the high stool and took off the rest of his clothes. The water enveloped him as he let himself down into the stainless-steel tub. First his ankles, then his legs, then his cold groin. He sucked his breath as the warm water reached his ribs. Lying back, he closed his eyes. . . .

The reedy nurse was still there.

She must have been a substitute for the regular one: a silent old crone, who left him alone.

This new one did not know she was free to go. He felt her fidgeting — at a loss, not knowing what to do. She adjusted the water temperature for him but didn't ask if he liked it. He thanked her anyway. And a brief human smile flitted across her face. She was missing an eyetooth.

She bit her lip as if weighing whether to tell him something. At last she blurted out, "When I knew you were coming here — to the clinic, I mean — I started to read one of your books. My friend

Martha" — the crone — "she said you were a perfect gentleman and spoke English too." The young nurse sighed as if the confession had let a little pressure escape from inside that taut uniform.

"Oh, really!" he replied. He hadn't realized people in the hospital talked about him. A celebrated case, apparently. He felt sorry he didn't know the young woman's name. "Well, what did you think about what you read?"

Her hand hung over the rim of the tub; it dabbled in the bathwater, a gesture both flirtatious and awkward. "I'm afraid I don't understand very much, sir; you see, I never went to university. Though my mum always made me read hard books, mind you — but I guess the truth is I hate looking up all those big words." She said this in a long, gushing spew.

He grumbled to himself, annoyed. He had heard more of this than he cared to think about. His translators had loaded up the English editions with big, obtuse words. But it was too late to do anything about it now.

"Which one?" he asked her gruffly.

"Pardon me?"

"Which one did you read first?"

"*Civilization and Its Malcontents*," she stammered.

He sighed at the mishandling of the title. "It's the wrong one to start with," he mumbled into the bathwater.

"What?" she cried. She seemed terribly dismayed, as if she'd done something wrong *already*, made some false step, something a smart "university girl" wouldn't do. He patted her arm, gripping the edge of the bath.

"That's all right. You broke the ice, you tried. Now try the dream book. The short one if you can get it. If not, read the long one. But if you pick up the long one, you can skip the first hundred pages, where I'm just a smart fellow trying to prove all the sages wrong. Go direct to Chapter Two — then you'll be able to start interpreting your dreams right away."

Her hands went to the hot-water tap, and she turned it up a little. "Oh, thank you! Thank you so much! Your book was so frightfully complicated. I was really afraid" — her voice dropped — "afraid even to talk to you in the hall. I thought you'd see right through me." Then, whispering, "I hate carrying bedpans."

"If you find anyone who likes it, send them to me."

She laughed; the gap from her missing tooth flashed blackly at him. Her finger strayed to the water in the tub; she yanked it away, scalded. "So hot! I'm sorry."

He had gotten used to it.

"Why were you trying to prove all the sages wrong?" she asked.

He had not thought about why, but now he said, "I was unsure of myself. My practice was flagging. I was forty. I was in debt. And yet I had discovered a secret of the universe. The beginning of the dream book is merely an incomplete summary of what others wrote about dreams and how they were wrong. I was showing off. I thought it would help."

"Did it help?"

"No . . ." He smiled.

"But that's all changed now," the nurse said.

He rapped the steel tub with his knuckles for good luck, a hollow empty sound. "It has changed." He laughed. "But I *was* right back then. More right than all the others." He sank back contentedly into the tub, the warm water lapping at his chin. "In a little while there'll be *other* others, more right than me."

He slurred so badly when he talked. It was impossible to tell where one word began and another left off. "How can you understand me?" he asked.

"I'm a mind reader," she replied.

"Of course . . ." He drifted, the warm water doing its work. The pain in his jaw dulled, dispersing like a tendril of steam. He closed his eyes and went back to the bathroom of his parents' house of long ago. There they had a white bathtub with brass claw-and-ball feet. His mother sat behind him in the water. His little self curled into the hollow of her thighs. He put his head back against her breasts and felt the rich contained press of them, and the droplets that ran down over his ears. She was his, and he was hers. . . .

The bathroom door eased open a crack. His father's man-smell stole into the steamy room on a draft of cold air. He stared into the widening doorway, pressing his cheek over his mother's breast; he groped for it, feeling it swell and shift in his hand. It gave and pressed back at him.

Suddenly his father stood in the doorway, his shirt open, his collar clinging by a stud in the back. He rolled his shirtsleeves over his forearms, a dark smile on his face. The man's hair swept wildly apart in the middle, as though two black antler stubs had risen from his skull.

"How long do you think you can hide in there?" his father growled.

He squirmed back against his mother's breasts to capture them again. But when the grown man knelt by the side of the tub, Mother's breasts were no longer his. When they gave and pressed back, they swelled for the new face that hung above. Water dripped from his father's hand; he noticed the soft hairs growing out of the skin. Then the hand stroked the thigh stretched out in the water.

"You can't hide there."

If only he could press down into the well of his mother's thighs, escape the wild man with the wild hair that rose off his scalp like horns. He writhed in the shallow puddle of his mother's lap. The big man's hand reached deeper along the length of her thigh. His small fist struck it, the water splashing over his father's shirt. Mother's thigh moved beneath the fingers just as the breast had swelled behind his head. He hit the hand again and again. And the water splashed everywhere. The steam had vanished from the bathroom, leaving it cold and clear and empty. His mother kissed him again, laughing.

"Oh, you Hun! You Hun! You little Hun!"

Another memory came. He was six, a little older. His mother had made him an animal costume. She found an old fur stole in the attic, with the fox head still attached and a long furry tail. She peeled back the satin lining and hemmed it into earflaps. When she sewed on some shoelaces, he could tie the fox stole over his ears like a cap, the furred body trailing down behind.

What a little wild animal he looked, with nothing on but his fox cap and a dishrag for a loincloth! His black hair stuck out on all sides, and his mother gleefully patted his small behind, crying, "Run off now! Hide!"

Yes! Hide-and-seek! But where? The best part of it was how all the women, every one of them, came after him. At the start, his mother waited quietly in a corner of the living room, listening. And when she spied the tips of his fox ears moving behind the sofa, sounding the alarm:

"The sofa!"

First came big Henny, huffing and puffing and wheezing like a bellows — the fat old woman clung to every bit of furniture so she didn't slip on her bandy legs.

Then his sister, Dolphie. Dolphie, always so prim, but during the Fox Game going barefoot. Letting her hair down and fussing it into a mess, crouching on the floor like an animal herself. She came after him quick and hard, tearing over the hall rug, which slid on the polished floor.

They were *hunting* him. A thrill stabbed like fear and joy. They'd see! They'd see! He leaped over the couch like a real fox and plunged under the dining room table, hiding among its crossbars and legs. He tried to scamper out again, but his mother barred the way. Then Henny, down on all fours, thrust her head under the table, yowling fiercely. She snatched at him, but her heavy arms were too big and clumsy. "Aiii!" Dolphie shrieked. She seized his ankle, and they fought under the table. He kicked and broke free.

"On the stairs!" his mother called.

A flash of fox fur and a swish of tail, but when the women reached the banister, the stairs were empty. They clambered up, panting hard, the scent of him thick; they had his spoor.

His parents' room was quiet and shaded, the sun slanting in through the blinds, falling on the bright-red coverlet of the bed. He heard his own breathing and then the women's feet in the hall. A place to hide! Where to hide?

Under the bed? No, too tight.

The bathroom? No escape.

The closet door beckoned him. A trap with no exit, but there was a faint chance they'd miss him among the hanging clothes — and then he might break free. The women entered the room stealthily, spreading out. . . .

"He's here," Dolphie said in a hush. Her hair spread across her face like a web; her red-rimmed eyes roamed from the dresser to the chair, from the bathroom to the bed. His mother gazed warily up at the ceiling as though she would find him by searching her mind. She closed her eyes and concentrated. "Yes, he's very near."

"I can smell him," Henny whispered. She crept steadily toward the closet with a wicked smile on her face. Dolphie followed, her red lips drawn back, showing rows of pointy teeth. The women's skirts rustled about the door crack. His mother's legs paused outside the door. "Shhhhhhhh . . . ," his mother warned.

Far back in the musty closet, he wrapped himself in coats and dresses. If only he could crawl into a pocket and hide there like a mouse. His bowels yearned, and he wanted to go potty all at once. What a delicious full feeling, knowing how good it was, and how much better when he finally let go.

He wasn't a mouse — no pocket to hide! He'd break free now. Escape! He snarled like an angry fox, bursting from the closet. The women stumbled backward, tumbling over themselves. He was free! Free! Bounding across the room —

"Got him!" his father shouted, bolting from the bathroom. Half the man's beard was shaved away, soap clinging to one side of his naked face. The naked skin, white like a fish; a pink scratch and blood where the razor cut too close. His father swept him in the air with hands so strong he thought they'd crush his potty-go right out of him. A terrified squeak flew to the ceiling, and his father grinned, the shaved side of his face looking vicious and abrupt.

Deep inside, the delicious fullness squirmed, and he felt it moving on himself, as if those iron hands had squeezed it out. The man put him down shakily. While the women, faces bloated with anger, shouted: "No! No! No!"

His mother prodded him into the bathroom, but not in anger.

When he sat on the potty, he saw his father had backed off into a corner of the room, glowering silently. "This is ridiculous," he rumbled. "You act like a bunch of savages."

"We didn't ask you to butt in," Henny snapped back.

Then all the women came to the bathroom door, peering in as he sat on the potty seat. His mother felt his ribs, her touch gentler. . . . The soiled loincloth lay discarded on the bathroom floor. But his fox cap still clung to his head, the long red fox tail curled around his waist as he sat on the potty. He didn't feel like going anymore. When he looked at his loincloth, he saw most of his potty-go there.

His mother stared at his father in the most peculiar way. He had the strangest thought: that she hated the man. . . .

"I don't like it," his mother said. "Shave the rest and grow it all back."

The reedy nurse wiped the soap from a straight razor. The white goat's beard from half his face lay in a thousand cut hairs down the front of his hospital gown. Some lay on the floor, the shorn hairs blending into the white tile invisibly. The old man knew they were shaving his face because they suspected a tumor in the cheek. My God, he felt it throbbing there himself: the warm bath and the shaving had brought sensation everywhere. If the X-rays confirmed what he already felt, they would bring him into surgery early in the afternoon without wasting time. He must remember to call home.

"We're ready," the nurse said.

He caught the nurse's hand that held the razor. She didn't struggle in his grip but relaxed her arm as if to say, There's nothing I can do for you. Showing him how helpless he had really become. How impotent. Like an old gent walking around with his pants unzipped: open cage, dead bird. A terminal case, so why fuss?

"Please, Nurse." He let go of her arm. "My father looked awful with half a beard. I can't look much better. Will you shave the other side?"

Her fingers touched his shaven cheek; a tender gesture. She had cut it close, leaving the parched old skin waxy smooth. When she turned his face in her strong hand, a thrill went through him, like a far-off train whistle in the dead of night. He liked the feel of it. Her fingers on his jaw, her firm grip saying, You're not gone yet; I'll do what you wish. . . . He looked down the length of her, seeing how the starched skirt brought out the curve of her hips. He wished he could reach over and surround her bottom with his forearm. "You're a handsome man," she said out of nowhere. It sounded like something she'd told herself the first moment she caught him tottering in the hall: Ah, now *there's* a handsome man! He felt himself stirring, warm and bloody and alive. He began to laugh. The first time in a year! Where the hell was his wife! The reedy nurse looked at him, a little worried. "Are you all right?"

He smiled up at her; he liked her hard-bitten face. She'd make some man a good woman before too long. She drew close enough for him to see the pockmarks from a bad case of acne years gone by. His arm wanted to go around her bottom. He let it go.

"Stay still," she hissed with a naughty grin. "You're very bad."

They put him under the X-ray projector, a huge metal locust of a machine, his shaved face going into shadow. The white-smocked technicians murmured at him to be still. . . . This was the end, then. The gnawing pain in his jaw had returned, as if some monstrous blacksmith with knotted hands was trying to hammer off the side of his head. Anything had to be better than this. He was flaccid again, his cold groin far away, like a valley covered in mist.

He had been taken in by strangers. Men in white coats, with lean, sallow faces, machinists of the corpus. Like some elaborate death ritual of ancient Egypt, preparing pharaoh's body for its journey over the river of death. But instead of building a tomb and gathering the relics of his worldly reign, instead of painting the tomb walls with the deeds of his life and a picture of his soul, instead of waiting till he was dead before they cut out his organs, preserving them in jars — instead of all that, the white strangers wrapped his living body in a cold sheet and sent him under a dark machine.

Later, there would be the inspection, the prodding and the poking — when they took out bits of him, pieces of his bone and shreds of his flesh, which they threw in a pail at their feet: flecks to be picked apart by more sallow strangers, to determine if those shreds were good or evil.

Better to be a king cut down in middle age. So it felt now. For he wished to take the slim nurse's bottom in his forearm once more. Or even find his wife. Take her away from whatever and do it to *her*. But this ugly machine hovered over him like a huge carrion fowl sucking at his guts. And him too feeble to push it away. Better to be cut down in middle age . . .

One of the technicians asked him not to mumble. Why shouldn't he mumble? He had a right. He was a king who had lived too long: survived his wars, seen his men fall one by one, survived his assassins and the princely ambitions of his sons — survived them all. Alone in the end and waiting, when his body came to claim him. The last assassin. A cunning, silent watcher, standing ever by your chamber door.

Now he knew for certain: better, much better, to be caught alone while hunting in the bright forest daylight. Better to be caught by ruthless brigands far away from his soldiers and the finery of the court, to be tracked down and hunted like an animal. For even as your steed leaped over a fallen tree and a spear stove in your back, in your mind — in your heart! — you knew you might escape. In fleeing there was hope.

In the desperate struggle there was hope. Dying with a bit of life in your blood. How much better so . . .

When there was hope.

64

BOOK II

THE PATIENT'S SYMPTOMS

Chapter *1*

A Meeting of Minds

Was he dead? Professor Praeger was supposed to be removing a tumor in his cheek. He remembered that much. No, a little more. A glimpse of the black X-ray machine as they slid his body out from under it. Then an even briefer glimpse of the reedy nurse's flat stomach as she took his pulse. Perhaps not even her. Then a long pause as he lay on the gurney in a bright room somewhere.

Presently a voice said to him, "We're going to put you to sleep now," and he looked distractedly at the needle sliding into his arm. Then he floated over the operating table, looking down at the gowned assistants. He lay in white. A tube snaked into his nose and another dripped plasma into his thigh. What a grand ordeal they made of it! There were a few terribly vivid seconds when he saw Professor Praeger's narrow, delicate hands holding a scalpel and going in for the first cut. The dainty hands made a deliberate stroke, and the skin separated cooperatively as blood welled from the cheek. The flow came freely, while a nurse tried to keep pace with it, dabbing around the incision with one sponge after another, then dropping the soaked sponges in a waste pail under the operating table.

"Keep it clear," Praeger snapped. "If you can't keep it clear, we'll send you home and get someone who can."

He thought this remark terribly unfair — after all, everyone knows facial cuts bleed more than others. The assistant used more and more sponges, while Professor Praeger's spidery fingers probed deeper into his face. After a short while, the professor paused contentedly to gaze into the incision. At last he said, "*There* . . . you see?"

The narrow fingers held back the peeled skin, and all the assistants crowded round the table to look. Within the cavity of moist flesh and flowing blood sat a knot of bluish gristle, the tumor.

"You see?" Praeger sounded almost gratified with the chance to elaborate. "It goes back and back; there's no end to it. The carcinoma has spread to the bone below the right eye. If we probed further we'd find the brain pan affected. Local inflammation of the cranial membrane. Higher fluid pressure within the cranial cavity. That is why the symptoms are something like spinal meningitis. Pain in the limbs, searing headaches, acute sensitivity to light. But unlike a viral infection his symptoms ebb and flow, when the body manages to absorb some of the excess fluid draining from the skull." Then a long sigh. "I'd say the Subject has about a week to go . . . Let you be witness, ladies and gentlemen, to the long-term effects of a good cigar."

The light in the operating room flickered as though the hospital were experiencing a power failure. He no longer cared about the body on the table. Then came a brief foggy period where he sat in the garden of his new English home in a lawn chair under the leaves of the almond tree. Lün sat in the garden doorway of his office, with her hindquarters up on a step and her front paws planted stoically in front like a stone lion. Why did dogs sit like that? With their bottoms an inch or so higher than their fronts? She looked comfortable and ridiculous at the same time. From out of the faint French doors people came into the garden and spoke to him. . . . He tried to answer. Friendly faces. He knew them, but the effort to recall their names had grown simply too great. He smiled and waved feebly as each new face swam into view. Some took his hand, some kissed him on the cheek. Then everyone went away and the sun streamed through the leaves of the almond tree.

His wife came out and sat beside him in a lawn chair. They held hands. . . . He tried to tell her about wanting to make love to her in the last few weeks, but he had lost the words. She pressed his hand in her own as if she understood, but how could she? They had not made love in such a long time. Out of the blue he noticed the same thrush sitting in a branch of the almond tree almost directly overhead. The tree was in bloom even down to the tiniest branches, covered in pink blossoms.

The thrush turned its head this way and that, inspecting him with black, glossy eyes. Then the bird flitted from the branch and swooped off toward the house.

He lost sight of it for a moment in the streams of sunlight dappling the ground. Then his eyes caught up. The thrush had landed next to the chow on the garden doorstep. But Lün paid no heed, neither barking nor pouncing. . . . And there they sat, inches apart, as in that odd Hicks painting *The Peaceable Kingdom*, where the wild animals of the jungle reposed calmly side by side. The dog looked down at the bird and the bird looked up at the dog, as if they knew each other's thoughts. Then they both stared straight at him.

He wanted to call someone, to come and see such an odd thing. But now he couldn't even whisper. He groped for his wife's warm hand, to show her, but the lawn chair lay empty. He looked back at the doorstep: the chow and the thrush still sat there. What intelligent faces they had. How lucky they were. The sun came down through the pink blossoms of the almond tree, and he decided to go meet it. He could fly. Right through the soft pink petals and into the sun if he wished. He was free.

So had he found heaven? Or was this just the glow of his own mind continuing on for infinite moments, like the heated coal after the flame had gone out? Trains of thought feeding on the currents of a trillion living brains . . . where all the minds that had long known his person now suddenly thought of him at once? He fell along a shaft of sunlight, through a wire-mesh cellar window, and into the dark bowels of a city building. The shaft of sunlight fell on an old desk in a narrow corridor of metal shelving; row upon row, canyons of file boxes rising to the ceiling. How amusing: at last he had found the Almighty's Hall of Records! But that meant he would presently be held accountable — a rather disagreeable prospect, considering the volume and content of his lifetime's work.

A young man sat at the desk with a folder of London *Times* newspaper clippings open before him and several dozen scattered around. What a relief to discover that the most prominent thought on the lad's mind was a pretty twenty-year-old clerk up in Editorial named Nancy, who wore very tight sweaters.

True, God might employ such young men, but probably not in his holy Hall of Records. More likely the Almighty's clerks were skinny Quaker schoolmarms or Eton-educated male librarians with socialist vegetarian tendencies — not frothy bucks smitten by visions of tight sweaters. Between burning glimpses of Nancy, the *Times* feature writer was furiously estimating how quickly he could absorb all the periodicals before him and knock out a draft of an obituary about a dead duck whose works he had never read.

Easy, Spence, you're a quick study. A draft in an hour, two at the most . . .

A wicked thought: if only the obituary's first line could be planted in Spence's open and slightly desperate mind. The line should read: "Sigmund Freud, the world's greatest living [blank], is dead." Not a bad opener.

Let that quick study struggle over the blank. But Spence showed no signs of having taken the bait. The young man looked suspiciously over his shoulder, as if he felt someone breathing down his neck. Then he shot a disconcerted glance along the stacks.

"Who's there?" he called nervously.

Silence yawned on the linoleum floor; the empty corridor between the stacks marched off into the distance. Then a girlish giggle escaped from a tight sweater somewhere in infinity.

The shaft of sunlight drew him back along its path. Up and up into the sky and clouds, to where the spores lived upon thin air. The great earth below existed like a huge, curved, pregnant woman. The translucent sky, the deep blue of the oceans, and along the coast of southern India the lighter blue aquamarine of coral reefs and shoals. Great bands of clouds drove across the brown-and-green continents, covering and uncovering the ripe surface of the planet like that same swollen pregnant Venus covering and uncovering her belly with a veil.

Indochina passed slowly, and then the great lap-water of the Pacific, with the dark speckles of the Mariana Islands, a green crescent in the pale blue. A huge monsoon had risen, a coiling swirl of cloud hiding the ocean beneath. A creeping unease came with the gray-purple clouds, but it wasn't the storm itself — for the monsoon seemed safely remote, a mere hypnotic pattern. No, something *about* the storm, something wrong . . . Then he understood. The clouds in the monsoon's dark galaxy had stilled on the surface of the ocean, like a photograph laid upon the sea.

Now came the conviction that his soul's dying spark no longer moved across the face of the earth but hovered — flickering in a fixed spot in the heavens as the earth below ground to a halt. How long could the spark of the soul float above the world as the earth stood still? While the chaos and turmoil below froze in time, midstep, midbreath, between the beat of a heart and the blink of an eye? Ages seemed to pass without an answer, nothing moving, the planet holding its breath. . . .

Then with a silent groan the engine of the world began once more her immense rotation — a ponderous surge — now rolling backward, east to west. The gray-purplish monsoon evaporated into itself, vanishing into white nameless clouds that quickly melted away. Watching it had a profoundly irritating effect, like trying to read handwriting in a mirror.

So were all the people down below doing likewise? Writing backward, putting verbs before their nouns, or spouting nonsense like "Market to went piggy little this?" Were all the crops returning into the ground and disappearing? The rain falling upward and all the drains in the Northern Hemisphere sucking water down the wrong way — or were they sucking water down at all? Could water flow upward into a faucet? Did gravity work? Was the Eiffel Tower lifting off its moorings? Or was it being *unbuilt*, demolished by its own ironworkers, rivet by rivet and girder by girder? Moving back in time presented so many problems.

And yet he sensed that far, far below, the timepieces of the world were keeping perfect time: every wristwatch, every clock tower, every clock on every mantelpiece steadily winding backward, lap after lap, tock-ticking back through the years.

Did that mean people were growing young again?

Or was this all a singular absurdity only his soul spark saw, a private fancy lasting his eighty-three years, unraveling in the moments of his own brief span like a spool of thread and then running out forever?

He wanted a closer look.

The rugged coast of California grew hard and clear. Each time the land rippled, a great pressure surged upon him, like a voice about to speak into his mind but holding back with all its strength. As the searing white expanse of the Nevada desert rolled below, the pressure became a suffocating blanket. Night came. And then day and then night . . . He lost count of the sun and moon; they passed and flashed and came again.

His soul spark floated in the rarefied atmosphere, a thistle upon the winds — where seeds kept aloft for years were swept along, eventually to fall and root in strange forests or lie fallow for eternity on the dry sands of nameless shores. Up here the cirrus clouds drifted like thin gauze across the sky. And then the earth rolled slowly to a stop; the going back had ceased. The thistle of himself fell like a stone.

The cirrus clouds streamed by, and the planet rushed up with a smile.

Tiny blue veins grew into rivers. Green fields blossomed. Blue lakes spread from puddles into ponds, mountains erupted from the soft wrinkles of the hills. The thistle flashed over the Black Sea: water sparkling, with ships rocking upon its waves. The land of the Crimea rose and vanished. The wind whipped across the small Sea of Azov, turning it into a panic of whitecaps. The thistle plummeted into the dark blotch of a city by a river. Ships and barges plowed their way up the channel. Smoke rose from the city's chimneys. A hundred rooftops came at him. Alleyways, and people scurrying to and from their many tasks. The thistle fell right toward a slanting gray roof near the dockside wharves. The grimy slate came closer, close enough to see the soot everywhere. So the last spark of his soul was merely a thistle, plunging through the stratosphere to crash upon a roof. Destined to lie dormant then, until the end. Too bad, too bad . . .

The hard sooty shingles came up in a rush. He wished he could blink, but he quietly passed through the stone instead.

The plummeting stopped with one great suffocating thump. For a long time the fall left him black. But this smothering concussion was a calming pause, for his passing had been endured and the natural order of things restored: after the enduring, the blindness. . . . How many years had gone by? Three or four or a hundred?

If he listened closely, would he be able to detect his living self somewhere on the European continent? He tried, and faintly — yes faintly — even in the blindness, far off he heard a patient murmuring familiar words. He knew the year now: if the thistle had plummeted upon Vienna, falling into 19 Berggasse, he would have found himself a mere five or so years younger and listening to a patient consumed with a nervous tic and boils. Dimly he could taste the cigar that burned between the listening man's fingers. How easy to attach himself once again to his old self and travel about with the charming fellow, like a fly on his shoulder.

But he had already listened to that patient's problems, for better or worse, and already ground out the cigar that burned between those fingers. It held little appeal. Besides, what could the dry thistle of a soul spark do? Consult in the treatment of the patient? More than likely he would give the same advice and concur.

In the consulting room of 19 Berggasse, his old self squirmed in the chair with a touch of indigestion. A bubble of lunch gas was moving through the listening man's lower quarters. Presently his old self would have to break wind.

So that's how your old ghost speaks to you! It haunts you quietly from a great distance, sending you a curse: a phantom of flatulence to punish you for your gastronomic misdeeds!

No death? No dying, then? No end? Just hollow repetition, like the ticking seconds within the workings of a clock with no hands to mark the passing time? Oh, God, he wished the Lord would come and take him. . . .

The enduring was passing on. Frau Direktor's blindness slowly coming to an end, her strangling asthma drawn off for the moment. So it wasn't so easy to die after all. What a mad dream! Flying about the world and poor old Herr Professor sick . . . A deep hush lay upon the Rostov clinic. Her weary eyes rested on the wooden bedpost by her head. And there on the post sat a tiny fluff of thistle, waving feathery arms.

How very odd: just like in the dream . . .

She stared at the thistle on the worn post for a minute or an hour without the slightest inclination to move her gaze elsewhere. Sometimes the thistle became a little fly, staring back with weary eyes; then her own eyes would blink, and no more fly! Only a wavy bit of fluff upon the bedpost. *So I'm really not dead . . . but spared for today.* . . . But the wooden bedpost filled the world, and the sounds outside her door hardly mattered.

What a wonderful old bedpost it was, cracked down the center, with a worn knob at the top. And a bit of fluff. Or was it a fly?

She woke again in the darkened sickroom. Bare wooden lath showed through the cracked plaster on the ceiling. The electric lamp with a blue paper shade on her bedstand burned with a dim light. And the asthma had returned, like an unpleasant friend. The bed creaked. The floor cold. She found her slippers. Standing was a problem. Clutching the bedpost helped. Her breath steamed into the chill of the room. The stuffing had fallen from a broken windowpane, letting in the winter air. She crammed the stuffing back.

Voices echoed in the lower reaches of the house, the sounds of people talking like disconnected motes. And the asthma, which had been hovering like a black angel, closed its wings. She was slipping off again. Back to the mad dreams.

A tiny fly lit on the bedpost, its buzzing innocuous and far away. How puzzling: a fly in winter. A winter fly . . .

Talk to me! it said. Talk!

Ah, the Herr Kinderweise fly, come all the way from Vienna to keep her company. What was there to talk about? Nightmares and bad dreams? And then it became clear. All this time the falling sparks of their minds had been hovering around each other. Touching and retouching while they gazed at the great rolling earth, all throughout each other's long enduring. Each one had felt the other's presence, familiar and reassuring like a silent companion. Yes, even as she choked alone in her bed — and yes, even while he lay dying, years and years apart. Long ago their pasts had mingled, so they could relive, must relive, one last time, he and she.

Forever.

Frau Direktor would endure her passing just as Herr Professor a few years later: passing in and out of their last precious days like jumbled puzzle pieces, one upon the other, joining spark to spark in their infinite final moments. Herr Kinderfly and Frau Asthma would travel together for a time. A meeting of minds, their resurrection . . .

So you are here.
Yes, I am here.
I must tell you something, Herr Professor.
Tell me.

Yes, tell him. Before the asthma took her away. Before the huddled lump died in the bed, gripping the cracked bedpost of her future. Before the others took her children out of the country, safe and far away. . . . But not right now. Not this second. No, rest a moment. Rest and drift along a memory. Visit her old friend and grope her way into his hidden, secret places. Back to the stone madhouse where she was truly born. Back to the whitewashed solitary room where she floated like a bubble in the air. Where she finally met jung Herr Doktor Young. No! Not right! What he said was: "Hello, I'm young Herr Doktor Jung." Crucial difference. You should always get a person's name right. But young Herr Doktor Jung never knew her proper name. So she kept him waiting at the throne room door. Waiting for a thousand years while young Herr Doktor Jung peeked at her through the viewing slit. Didn't he know the viewing slit was really a rectum? The madhouse had devoured him and was now expelling him into her private room. Funny, he didn't seem particularly worried that his head had become a turd. . . . Perhaps in a clean and efficient Swiss institution —

Enough! Time enough for that!

Yes, time enough for the rest, to see everything that needed seeing — her sickness, her cure, his betrayal — to know everything worth knowing.

Chapter 2

The Sphinx

They found him alone in the tower room. He had built his house
when his mother died, stone by stone, until it rose to a tower where
he could sit. Oh, the workmen had done the actual masonry, but he
had directed the building. The circular ground floor had windows at
all points of the compass; a dug-out stone hearth in the center, with
a smoke hole; and bunks fitted into the curved walls. No electric. No
gas. And, connected by a narrow stair, a comfortable crow's nest that
rose up higher than the rest — an aerie where he could riddle with
the stars like an ancient sorcerer of old.

He had built the place because he liked to dream and had filled it
with papers and books and paintings on the walls. They found their
old colleague alone, spinning riddles for his own amusement. Dozens
of volumes were strewn about his desk and on the floor by his chair.
Broken pencils lay where he had discarded them after snapping their
points in a fury of writing. A Montblanc fountain pen left on a lined
pad, put down in the middle of a word and not picked up again for
months. The half-written word was "Götterdämmerung," that is, Twilight of the Gods. But the train of thought on the half-scrawled pad
was long since lost.

There were books on alchemy written by wise men of the tenth
century and books on Lenin the Antichrist written by cranks in the
twentieth century. There were issues of *Life* and *National Geographic* and
an issue of *Time* with Hitler on the cover as Man of the Year. There
was the latest issue of *Vogue en français*, cracked open to a feature in
which a feathery scribbler fluttered on about Philippe de Somebody's
"horned-breast-cup velvet backless ball gown, which produced an ag-
gressive *femme fatale très moderne*." And he had torn an article from an
American cooking magazine on the making of ancient Mediterranean

warriors' wine, entitled "The Drunkards of Troy." But peeking out
from under this recipe was yesterday's obituary from the *London Times*:

FREUD, 83, FATHER OF PSYCHOANALYSIS
by J. K. Spence
London. Sigmund Freud, the father of Psychoanalytic
Therapy, also the originator of the Oedipus Complex
theory of human behavior and perhaps the world's
greatest living —

Herr Doktor had stopped reading right there and let the obituary become slowly engulfed under other papers he was considering. He
called the process "layering" and thought it a legitimate method of
letting his subconscious decide what to bring to the surface. Or bury,
for that matter. Freud's obituary had reminded him of a passage in a
long-lost book. He suspected it tucked under a stack of tomes devoted to 600 B.C. black Attic vase painting.

No, no, no! Not a book; an *article* on the myth of Oedipus by that
half-cuckoo historian Graves. Near his feet lay a few books by the
same fellow, crammed with torn slips of paper marking sections that
intrigued him. He found what he was looking for. Several typewrit-
ten pages, now crumpled. A scholar friend had sent him the text of
a lecture the historian had planned to give. But the event had been
canceled and the text never published. A fragment of Graves's strange
lecture ran thus:

THE RIDDLE OF THE SPHINX
"What, being of one voice, has sometimes two feet,
sometimes three, sometimes four, and is weakest
when it has the most?" Those who could not solve the
riddle were throttled on the spot by the Sphinx.

He stopped reading, suddenly remembering that the very name
Sphinx *meant* "Throttler." But without trying to recall how he knew
this fact, he went back to the passage:

The riddle of the Sphinx was deduced from sacred
icons showing the winged Moon Goddess of Thebes:
her composite body — half lion, half serpent — was

77

a calendar symbolizing the Theban Year. A lion for
the waxing spring–summer sowing time and a serpent
for the autumn–winter harvest. The Queen of
Thebes, a living woman, was the Sphinx's Moon
Priestess, the Goddess on earth to whom all offered
their devotion and to whom a sacrificial Sun King was
married for the term of a year.

Brief was the Solar King's reign: for at the close of
his season another King was chosen to take his place.
And after a violent struggle, the usurper cast his master down. So a heap of skulls grew at the Sphinx's feet.
Yet the infamous riddle has been invented to explain
these rotting bones of fallen kings, *invented* from an
icon picture: an Infant, a Warrior, and an Old Man —
all worshiping the Goddess.

He stopped reading again. Invented by whom? To explain a supposed
sacred icon picture — what icon picture? On a plate, a vase, a cup, a
tomb? Mr. Graves never said where the picture might be found. The
thought of a massive search bored him. It meant going through the
whole picture catalog of the British Museum and possibly half the
Greek National Museum as well. Should he write Graves a letter and
ask him point-blank? Where was that rascal hiding? Majorca someplace . . .

That was the thing about Freud he always admired. The old Faker
never failed to give his sources. And any idiot could look them up if
he wished. But not the clever Mr. Graves; no, Mr. Graves had seen it
somewhere and you damned well better take his word for it.

The passage went on:

The icon picture shows not three individuals but the
same man — paying his respects to the Goddess from
cradle to grave. In other icons the Moon Priestess is
shown in the three stages of life: young, fertile, and
withering. Thus the great birth and death cycle mim-
ics the passing seasons of the year: the flowering of the
land and its fall to barren winter. Under the matriarchal
system the new King was often a prisoner of war or a
shipwrecked sailor — the usurper now called a "son" of

the royal family. Thus when the Queen Priestess helped him seize his bloody throne, this stranger had indeed murdered his "father" to marry his "mother."

Oedipus' guessing of the Sphinx's riddle still echoes the worship of the seasons. Man! is the answer. First going on four legs as a child, then on two as a youth, and in the end hobbling with a staff. Hearing the unraveling of her cultic riddle, the Sphinx Moon Goddess threw herself off a cliff in despair.

Was Oedipus a 1300 B.C. invader who suppressed the ancient Moon Cult, seeking to end the yearly ritual king-slaying in Thebes? Did the Moon Priestess commit suicide rather than alter the ancient ways? Was the myth of King Oedipus told from the invader's point of view? An invader branding the old ways incestuous and barbaric?

If we consider the Freudian theory of the Oedipus Complex as an *instinct* common to all men — we must now see that such a theory was suggested by the *perverted* telling of the myth. And while Plutarch records (*On Isis and Osiris* 32) that the hippopotamus "murdered his sire and forced his dam," Freud would never have suggested that every man has a Hippopotamus Complex!

He loved that last bit. What a clever retort to the old Faker, shattering his all-inclusive theory of sexuality. Ah, Mr. Graves, hiding on your Spanish isle, making provocative remarks. While singing songs of the dead ones — Plutarch, Apollodorus, Asius — making his own translations of all the lurid tales of rape and cannibalism and the bloody incest of the gods. Look anywhere on the Mediterranean: moon goddess cults flourished on every coast and in the woody depths of every mountain grove. Where June weddings saw a young man marry a Lady of the Fields, where the villagers knocked off a useless old man and planted him in the ground to seed the crops, or sent his smoke up to heaven in a cloud to lure the vital summer rains. . . .

The human-god ritual of birth and death stretched back into the past like a well-trodden path, dwindling to the barest foot track, ending at last around a fire in the wilderness, where men in skins stared up at the moon and carved round, fat stones in worship of the dark. Small, round, eyeless things with heavy breasts and a ripe pregnant belly. Archaeologists found them everywhere neolithic man made his campsites, in and around the lands of the Mother Sea — found them in the tens of thousands. Venus stones they called them . . . though Aphrodite and Roman Venus were but her great-great-granddaughters. Long before the King of the Jews, a little pregnant wench was God.

Who was this stone mother? Did a race of men worship their women? Or women worship her alone? Did she have a name? A thousand names? Or a secret name, never to be spoken?

Perhaps they only called her *She*.

He rose from his desk and began pacing anxiously about. He felt trapped in this little room. Graves's ideas on psychology were much too pat, too clever. And when it came to his German — "the Oedipus Complex . . . an *instinct* common to all men" — obviously the fellow had read Freud only in translation. The old Faker never used the word "instinct" when it came to describing a process of the human mind. Instinct was too knee-jerk, too goose-step. Freud saw human affairs as affairs of the heart, impulsive, compelling, contradictory. A sick man might be driven or seduced into some strange relation with his mother, but common sense told you it wasn't instinctual, like dogs sniffing each other's rear ends. No, a mother-tongue reader knew the old Faker used the word "drive" when referring to our human foibles and compulsions — in German, a different word altogether.

And what about the aforementioned problem of sources? How much simpler if Mr. Graves had decided to include a picture of the Sphinx icon. Was he really the gentleman scholar after all? Or would a man who misconstrued the word "instinct" be "driven" to invent an icon to fit a theory? Not the first time in the history of the Sphinx that a conqueror staged the propaganda to suit his purposes. After all, hadn't the emperor Napoleon suffered defeat after defeat in Egypt, while sending back victorious dispatches to Paris? His callous artillerymen used the Great Sphinx for gunnery practice and finally dragged home a huge obelisk to commemorate his triumph! The obelisk stood to this day in the Place de la Concorde. And the Sphinx smiled across the Nile with her nose blown off. Even the mighty Bonaparte had failed to wrest the secret from her.

80

Only one solution remained: write Mr. Graves. If the scholar put him off, then perhaps the codger had been caught doing a little inventing. Ah, the perversity of man's suspicions against a stranger when a little thing like a penny postcard of an ancient icon was left to the imagination.

Perversity.

Had not Mr. Graves used the word himself? The Oedipus Myth perverted by an invader for his own ends . . . Odd choice of words.

And which was more perverted anyway, a brigand invading Thebes to kill the Moon Priestess — or sleeping with your mother? It would depend on whom you asked: the Queen of Thebes or your mother. And what about Plutarch's poor hippopotamus, who murdered his sire and forced his dam? Herr Hippo obviously suffered from the deeply repressed wishes of a latent Oedipal complex. But whether they arose from a secret hostility toward his father coupled with a perverse lust for his mother, or simply because Herr Hippo needed more wallowing room on the mudbank, no one would ever know.

Perversion.

Not an innocent word at all. Who, indeed, had more opportunities to turn things to his own uses — a confused hippopotamus or a classical scholar translating long-dead languages, which only a handful of men really knew well? Perhaps the whole thing boiled down to one's reputation — the preservation or perversion of it! For what was "reputation" anyway but a *life path* open for the world to see?

Was this, then, the riddle of the Sphinx?

What creature, being of one voice: when was it the weakest? The child or the lonely, feeble old man who walked with a cane? No, neither. It was the creature of your public face, the creature of your reputation. . . . What people saw of your path in life, how it bottled you and throttled you and crushed you in the end. How many men had felt the errors of their life path killing them, strangling them — and longed to see the Sphinx's smile fade? She knew, she always knew. . . . She knew the errors you had made.

Jung picked up his fountain pen for the first time in three months and went back to the lined writing pad with the half-written word "Götterdämmerung" on it. He read once more the aging words:

Great leaders, such as Napoleon, are both Man and God; they are Mangod. Inspiring devotion, worship, sacrifice — the divine privilege of sacred beings. But Mangods also inspire savagery, war, and chaos — prerogatives of Men. And when such beings pass from their thrones, when the mantle of heaven is lifted from their shoulders, so too their works slowly pass into dust. Their deeds fade, or are forgotten. Even the tales about them shift and change, casting strong men as weaklings — and cowards as strong. . . . While the stone prizes of war remain like the Egyptian obelisk in the Place de Concorde. For the fallen Mangod leaves monuments in the cities of his followers and hateful memories in the Trojan fields of his slaves. Their godly reign, a twilight extending for long years, an endless sunset of affection from the grandchildren of his Palace Guard, beneath a bitter pall of spite from the widowed daughters of the vanquished, a Götter — a Götterdämmerung. The slow-falling dusk of their godness.

The pen hovered in his hand. "For the fallen Mangod leaves monuments in the cities of his followers and hateful memories in the fields of his slaves. . . ." He loved that last phrase. The carved neolithic stones of pregnant women were such monuments, surviving artifacts of a Götterdämmerung — but what of the memories that went with them? The memories were gone. The mouth-to-ear chain of storytelling long broken, garbled, confused. A charred jawbone in the dead ashes of time. With no one left to remember the stone woman's tales. How had she died? The same way the Sphinx died. When a Mangod unraveled her riddle. Long ago some Mangod had divined the secrets of the stones, only to replace them with mute silence. If her original secrets had remained unfound, she would have continued as a god. When had men decided to cast their stony mothers down to hell? How could women have let them do it? Ah, but women were always letting men get away with things. . . . With half a smile on his face, that he might finally write something worthwhile, he set pen to paper:

> But even though the monument of one Mangod
> may outlast his memory and his deeds, yet there may
> be a second life for them, a coming sunrise after the
> endless night. . . .

He hesitated, putting down his pen. An annoying itch prickled his skin. Two flies raced about the room, one on the back of the other in copulation. He looked about for a flyswatter. Where had he left it? The prickling humming came again. His skin crawled. Where was the damn flyswatter?

He found it under a stack of dusty books on Stonehenge, untouched since last summer. His eyes flitted about the walls. Come, come my young friends, show yourselves. . . . Ja, he knew them. The first bold flies of spring, eager little fornicators with nothing on the brain but an urgent glow that said, Hurry up and fuck and populate the lakeside with a plague of swarming children. He fancied he could read their minds. They had simple minds, with simple thoughts. Like: ME FLY/YOU NOT FLY and FOOD/NOT FOOD.

But now, as it was their season to reproduce, all thoughts were superseded by the one great thought: HE FLY TO SHE FLY.

And so they flew, one glued to the other, oblivious to everything else. There! On the windowsill! He crept toward them, hardly daring to breathe. He raised the flyswatter. . . . The two fat bluebottles shuttled sideways as if to make themselves more comfortable, the top fly rubbing his front legs together. He batted them both into the stone without the slightest feeling of remorse. More stunned than crushed, they sprang off and lay dead, hooked together like Romeo and Juliet.

Hah! He flicked them over the window ledge and sat down at his desk again. His mind felt completely refreshed. He stared eagerly at the paper with the word "Götterdämmerung" on it. The word meant nothing to him now. He had lost his train of thought.

As if to torment him, the silvery whine came again. *More* flies? He slashed the swatter back and forth, peering frantically about the room. His ear itched as if a fly were licking the salt off his skin. He snapped the swatter, spastically hitting the side of his face. His head sang. Something flicked by his desk, but when he turned to stare directly, all he saw was the corner of a book with the sun on it. He lost his temper.

"Where are you? I'll slap you! I'll smack you! I'll crucify you on a needle and watch you die! Come out, you buggers! Come out!"

He paced in circles, batting the swatter through the air. After a few seconds he sank to the chair, exhausted. A line of dribble ran down his chin. He wiped it off with the back of his hand. A dull silence fell on the room. He shaded his eyes against the glare coming from the window. His hand twitched. Now look at him! With a rattan fly-swatter stuck in his fist, striking it smartly against his thigh like a swagger stick. The flyswatter stung his leg, but he couldn't stop. As though a stranger were swatting him and he had to let him do it — wanting just to keep on hitting and hitting. He closed his eyes against the glare. A page turned in his mind. . . .

A story he liked to tell himself. He was an infant again . . . mysteriously outcast from his real family. In the cold gray dawn they took him from the house in swaddling. Who carried him? He did not know. A servant perhaps, on orders. Who gave those orders? Someone who wanted him taken off, carried off to die.

The servant bore him for miles, high into the mountain meadows where the air ran thin and cold. Then at last they stopped. The servant set him on the grass and went away. He was alone.

The sun climbed to the zenith and down once more to the empty blue that borders on purple. He quivered and shook and cried, and the sound of his tiny voice vanished into the light of the early stars. And then suddenly he stopped crying: a deeper, evil dread came over him. The meadow was hushed.

He heard a growling, a snuffling, and a long howl that echoed against the craggy peaks. At the edge of the meadow a wolf came up on the horizon. And then another. He tried to crawl, to hide, to bury himself in the grass, but he was too small, too cold, too weak. . . . The first wolf looked up and cried at the stars. Then all the others sang with him, howling their hunting song, a song of torn flesh, cracked bones, and tongues in warm blood. . . . Leaving nothing behind but a stain on the grass when the sun came over the mountains in the morning.

Suddenly the wolves fell silent. What were they waiting for? One by one, each wolf slunk below the lip of the meadow and vanished.

The faint sound of tinkling bells came to greet him. The gawky shapes of goats with bells tied around their necks trotted up the dark swath of grass. He heard the friendly bark of a dog and then another. . . . They were marching the goats: telling them to "Get along there, Graybeard!" "Stop dawdling, Missy!" "Keep in line, Curly!" And the goats bleated back, saying: "Oh, stop pushing." "You needn't snap!" "Watch it, Fleabait, or I'll punch your snout!"

How he understood the language of animals he did not know. But it seemed so sensible how the goats and the dogs got along. The dogs barking orders and the goats complaining as though they'd been ill-used.

Two dogs sprang across the last stretch of grass. Stopping short a few feet away to smell him very seriously. Both their minds thought at once: *Not a wolfcub.* Their lolling tongues lapped him around the ears and neck, their noses colder than the air. And then they both laughed as dogs laugh, with smiling jaws, and began to dance. Sending up a chorus of barks, crying: "Mancub! Mancub!"

Quick feet swished across the grass, and he was lifted into another pair of arms. Strong, clean-smelling arms. A shepherdess had found him.

He was safe.

His fat face pressed into her sweet-smelling flesh. The cold flowed out of him like steam. Her fingers touched him in a place that made him warm and swollen; spreading coils through his body. . . . Her sweet-smelling flesh hung above his face; he was putting his lips to it, greedily sucking the life from it, and the life flowed down his throat. He was swollen and erect, pointing at the face hovering above the flesh he sucked. An olive-skinned face. Her eyes deep like pieces of amber, dark like the dilated silky brown nipple he sucked in urgent gasps. There was a mole on her lip, and his pudgy hand left off clutching her breast, fingers reaching up to touch the mole. Her dark lips were smiling at him and he smiled back, letting her breast fall from his mouth. She was his. His alone. Mother. Lover. Goddess. She was the Sphinx.

Chapter 3

The Stag King

At last his thigh became so painful he stopped striking it. Two more flies had appeared on the windowsill to torment him. The swatter fell from his hand. While he stared dumbly at his empty fingers, the two flies, glued in love, darted from the sill and dropped smartly into his palm. He could have closed his fingers on them if he wanted, pulled their wings off if he wanted. . . . Part of him loathed the mating flies, part of him had no urge to crush them. Old man Jung felt as if he had finally plucked at the spool of a personal truth. And if he drew it to him, like Ariadne's thread from the labyrinth, he would draw from oblivion not the slayer of the bull, but the bull monster instead. No child could do that.

The infant knew only the dark life of the nipple, wanting it utterly and irrevocably. The warm nipple in his mouth to suck. The amber eyes. The smile. But in time even the dark nipple began to fade, a lost fragrance from her yielding self. So dim and vague a memory, he wondered if it had been real at all. . . .

Then at last he became a grown-up boy of four. The lost nipple had changed into a full person, and he knew so many things about her. That she was his Nanny Sasha, a farm maid from up-country, Piz Sardona in the Glarner Alpen. That she was twenty and unmarried. That his mother kept her in the house long after she stopped giving him her breast, because "He was so easy with Sasha. And no matter what anyone said, Nanny really was a good girl."

Who said? He didn't know.

She had tucked him into bed for the night, but he had gotten out to look for her. And now he wanted her to tuck him in again. He walked the long, gloomy hall past the kitchen. The white porcelain sink

86

shone ghostly pale, like the flesh of a fish. He listened for the Scuttlers, who always came out of the dark. The Scuttlers, who crouched along the walls or under the dining room chairs, like black water bugs in a coal cellar. Ready to swarm out of the shadows with their thin snatching pincers . . .

The dining room was empty too; a sliver of moonlight reflected on the surface of the oily walnut table. Then he suddenly came to his parents' study. A panel of blue pleated drapes stretched along one wall of the book-lined sitting room. Behind the curtains stood a pair of glass-paned French doors. And behind those doors, his parents' bed. A quivering came over him, till it felt like a strong hand grasping him between the legs. Where was she?

"Here!" she whispered, clasping him over the mouth. He wriggled in delight at the closeness of her body. A naughty current passed between them — of being where they weren't supposed to be. "Shhhhhhh," she warned. And with both hands, she pushed him into the cloaking folds of the curtains. Slowly she drew him closer to the panes, forcing him to look. Her hand caressed his shoulder, and he pressed it back. A warm glow flooded the bedroom, a single candle burning on the nightstand. His parents were entangled on the bed, locked together. The man was struggling with his mother. His face hidden, but not hers. Her eyes gazed blankly at the ceiling. As she lay passively, his father grunted. "Here . . . No, wait. Yes!"

Nanny Sasha had called his mother "noble looking" once, but all the spirit seemed to have fled her features: staring up from the pillow with her light hair thrown back, her face flattened, mouth open slackly. His father's struggle pressed down harder. "Help . . . ," he begged. Then weakly, ". . . why don't you help . . . ?"

His mother shrugged her shoulders as if that might do it, and the struggle began once more. Then Nanny Sasha tugged him back through the blue curtains. The last thing he saw through the glass was his mother, turning her head. Moodless eyes staring at the burning candle. Yet not with flame or light, but blackly. Dark marbles of hate.

Back in his bedroom, Nanny Sasha's cheek grazed his as she tucked him in. Questions. Questions. Did mother hurt? Was it father's fault? Or *his*? But instead he asked, "Do you love me?"

The mole on her lip touched his forehead when she kissed him. "That's why Sasha's here . . ."

He stared at the four walls of his room for a long time after she was gone. A parade of painted animals marched along the top border. A duck in a waistcoat with a gold watch fob, a spotted cow in a pink tutu, a rooster in boxing gloves and trunks, a fat white pig in a butcher's apron, holding a cleaver in his knuckles . . . A band of three gray mice played flutes, and a not-so-fierce Doberman in a policeman's uniform offered a bunch of flowers to a coy lady poodle with ribbons in her hair. All the animals looked so natural in their human clothes, he wondered why ducks never wore waistcoats when he saw them in the farmer's pond. And then he fell asleep.

When he looked along his body, his hands seemed miles away. Out the bedroom window he saw the moon against the sky. Beyond the house he felt the deep cold of winter, the tree branches naked and swaying in the wind. A shape passed across the face of the moon. Not a cloud but like the groping fingers of a hand, passing before a pale face. Then he saw the shape more clearly.

They were antlers.

A stag stood outside his window; the animal's antlers silently searched the face of the moon like the fingers of a blind man. He heard the beast's scraping hooves on the frozen ground. He wanted to cry out for Nanny Sasha, but no sound came no matter how hard he twisted his mouth to shout.

The cool night breeze flowed over the bed, and he heard a distant thundering. The Stag! Running right at the house, right at the open window. Too big, too big! Break the whole wall. Crush and trample him!

The thunder ceased, and the Stag leaped over the bed on a breath of cold air. A graceful, silent, languorous leap. So slow and heavenly he had plenty of time to watch, to see its sleek belly arch over, mottled brown and white. What terrible fluid strength. Legs that could run for miles. Leap over anything. Crush anyone. The Stag landed on the floor without a sound.

He followed it into the hallway, down the black stairs, the hooves of the beast striking quietly before him. A white tail darted around the corner. Sickeningly, he heard the Scuttlers hurrying up behind him. He glanced back into the darkness. Yes, they were chuckling and laughing, pouring thickly into the hall like a crowd of black beetles to snatch him and catch him and pick him apart. He stumbled into his parents' sitting room, a great dread crawling up his legs. A certain knowledge of what he would see. At his heels, thousands of Scuttlers swarmed all over themselves to get at him. And then he saw:

The Stag and his Mother. She had her thighs wrapped around the animal's belly, her face pressed to his neck. She clung to him, holding herself off the ground. And the beast was struggling into her, just as his father tried before. Only this time the woman urged him on, hands reaching to touch the curved horns. Teasing them, toying with their sharpness. She was going to turn her face from the animal and look in his direction. Eyes begging him to come and help Mama, begging him to mount the Stag as the beast galloped into her. Riding her stud as he rode her. To help them. Urge them. Whip them along!

He fled down the hall, barging over the Scuttlers, trampling their insect heads, breaking their shells, squishing the liquid guts out of their backsides. He yanked at his bedroom door. He pounded it. It wouldn't open! He couldn't —

Wake!

His eyes snapped open in bed. The sheets were real. The window part open. No moon. He heard the rustle of leaves in the trees; he felt the warm breeze of a summer night. The painted border at the top of his walls stared down as ever. He slipped quietly out of bed and peeked into the hall. No Scuttlers.

Candlelight burned within Nanny Sasha's room, casting a red outline around her shut door. He heard murmurs and rustlings. And the familiarity of it dawned on him as though he'd heard it in his sleep. He kept telling himself to leave now: don't touch the doorknob, don't turn it, don't —

The door opened by itself . . .

Two bodies twined on the bed. She was urging him on as his mother had the beast, her hands reaching above the headboard for a plaque that hung on the wall. A hunter's trophy. Stag horns . . .

She grappled for the horns as the man struggled between her legs. Her fist clenched one antler. Nanny Sasha moaned, or was she sobbing? She broke the deer horn from the plaque. The man lunged into her, and she drew the sharp points across his back. Lines of sweat and red welts. The candle flame jumped as she cried out. The horn clattered to the floor.

Then suddenly her cry ceased and she was sighing. The bed rocked still. A silence . . . The man was his father.

He went back to his room and was sick in the chamber pot. Weak dawn crept in at the window. He walked grim-faced to his parents' bedroom just as daylight threw blue shadows across the study.

He tugged back the curtains. Light dashed across his father's face. The face looked slack and pale, his beard rough. His eyes opened; he put a finger to his lips. "Shhhhhhh . . ." A glimmer of a smile on his face. "Go back to bed."

And then his father rolled over, throwing an arm over his sleeping mother. The man's back shone white and unmarred. No scratches. No welts. He turned from the French doors with a black smoke in his gut. Back to Nanny Sasha's room. And once again the door was shut against him. She still slept in bed, wrapped in her sheets. Just one breast exposed; the dark, distended nipple beckoned him. He wanted to run to the bed and touch it. When he looked to the wall, his heart stopped.

The antlers on the hunter's trophy were intact, unbroken. Both horns fixed to the varnished wooden shield. They pointed at him like accusing fingers, saying, It never happened, it was in your mind, you made it up . . .

She stared at him. Pouting a little, eyes roving over him from head to toe. He fought to stare her down, but she unwound the sheets from her limbs, slowly asking in a husky voice:

"Did you have a bad dream?"

No! He shook his head, not trusting his mouth to speak. She lifted the corner of the sheet. Her tan legs stretched in long supple lines for him. It seemed cool under there, inviting, dark and safe. "Come," she called. "Come to Nanny Sasha. Come . . ."

He wanted to cry. And maybe even wet himself. He came.

The old man in the tower slid from the chair and leaned against the stone wall, the two flies still cupped in the palm of his hand. They were doing a mating dance, showing each other their private parts. And even though their private parts were too minuscule to make much of an impression — still, they were showing off for him too. Should he be flattered? No . . . Animals copulated anyplace — in a cave, on a tree, in the palm of your hand. Lice bred in the seams of your clothes or in your hair. Mating like that meant nothing. Only the other kind of mating meant something. The human, warm-blooded, brain-wrenching kind.

Nanny Sasha had shown off her private parts for him. And he had returned her giving, pressing his little body toward all her secret places, loving them, worshiping them. How many times had he exposed himself to her? In the bath, on the potty, getting undressed. And how often she to him? Letting him in the water closet as she sat on the seat. Letting him stay with her as she searched for her clothes. She was a country girl, used to seeing things thrive or die. And he — her rooster chick, her piglet, her little nothing . . . She showed herself to him shamelessly. Guiltlessly. Endlessly.

The man in the tower stared into the upturned palm of his hand. He felt a tear roll down his cheek. He had gone shamelessly with Nanny Sasha, in his *heart* he had. And his father too. His own father. Had the two of them mended the broken antler in the small hours of the night? Mended it to make him doubt his eyes? His father lusted after her; he knew it in his bones. The desperate, insane wanting . . . His mother must have known. Any woman would.

In a horrible flash he saw his mother in a rage: he had overheard his parents having an argument early on a Sunday morning. His mother clad in her pink satin robe, his father frozen in a chair, sitting in the book-lined study. His face remote, incomprehensible as big words in a book. As though nothing Mother said made the slightest difference.

"Deny it!" Mother was shouting. "In my own house. Deny it to my face!"

But what *it* was was not clear. As though *it* were some kind of vermin Father had brought in on his shoes. He hoped not beetles or cockroaches or anything related to the Scuttlers. His father mumbled something in reply.

"Do you think I'm blind?" Mother snapped back. "Or stupid?"

His father shrugged as if admitting what she said, that she was blind. Stupid. He glanced away and mumbled again. His mother's voice rose in outrage.

"I should have expected it!" Shrieking. "Expected it!"

Father's voice came distinctly, stern as old wood. "In my opinion, you gave permission long ago."

Mother stared the man to hell, her face red and swollen, her eyes yellow. "Permission . . ." The words choked out of her, a strangled sort of sputter. She went quite pale. An invisible line had been crossed between them. Something unforgivable had been said. Or suddenly admitted.

His mother went into the bedroom and closed the French doors. Then from inside the bedroom came the sound of glass breaking. Immediately the French doors swung open so hard they shattered, broken shards falling to the carpet. Mother was crawling out of the bedroom on her hands and knees, sobbing as she came. "This is what I'd do to you! This is what I'd do to you!" She had the long white bolster that always lay on their bed. With a broken piece of mirror glass she ripped at it. Streaks of blood had smeared across the creamy bolster. "This is you! This in you!"

Hanks of stuffing came out as she stabbed with the jagged glass. A rosy sweat floated over the pale skin of her arms. From where he crouched in the hall the woman seemed to be coming painfully toward him, straight at him, stabbing as she came. And every time she sobbed, "This is you! This in you!" her eyes seemed to be staring into his own.

The man strode stiffly out of the study, staring straight ahead. His mother remained on the carpeted floor with her blood-streaked arms around the shredded bolster, and her face sank into the satin, sobbing, "This in you . . . you . . . you . . ."

The man sitting in his tower mumbled, "You — you — you." He meant all of them: his mother, his father, Nanny Sasha. They had all transgressed. His head felt terribly swollen, like two great fists grinding his brains together. What profane arrogance to waste your life on the mere appearance of a thing. A career. Religion. An empty marriage. Only your own family mattered. Your tribe protecting you in the wilderness. How miserably his own tribe had failed him. They sent Nanny Sasha away, of course. One day there, the next day gone. And he never saw her again. Passing into the realm of warm and swollen dreams . . .

He leaned against the stone wall. Where were those blasted flies? He felt one stuck in his ear. Now buzzing, keening furiously to be set free. He wanted to jam his finger in, gouge it out, but his hand wouldn't budge. For a brief moment he understood the language of flies. A tempting siren of unbearable sweetness. How dare anyone talk about him inside his own head! How dare a couple of mealy-mouthed insects hold a personal conversation inside his own cerebellum! He became dizzy; he closed his eyes and shook his head, begging them to cease, but they didn't listen. He'd shut them up the minute he could stop drooling all over his chin. Amazing how much drool came out of a person's mouth when he let it hang indecently open. Puddles and puddles. Someone should really wipe this idiot's face.

He tried to groan out loud. But all that came was the thread of spittle that ran down his throat. Doktor Jung should really know by now how to handle a difficult patient like himself. After forty years of practice, high time to learn, ja? First, the patient should commit himself into the care of a reliable institution. That would be the Burghölzli of Zurich. Get a nice corner room overlooking the garden. And then Herr Doktor Jung might come and see him. Ah, but see here now, sir — Herr Junior Physician Jung resigned his post at the Burghölzli thirty-odd years ago. And the methods they used in 1905, ach! Disgraceful! Of course, the patient would have to take into account Herr Junior Physician's relative inexperience. Perhaps they might consult Herr Professor Freud. Somewhat of an expert in cases of this kind. But would the great man consult on such short notice?

Of course he would! Freud loved him! They would consult as they always had. When had you last slaughtered your father? Herr Freud would ask. Hah! His father was years and years dead. Too late to track the old man down. But had he not killed another man, another father? That was what Herr Freud really meant to ask. Oh yes, he had. Another man. Another father. In a crazy girl's dream. Oh yes, he had.

Chapter 4

The Institution

He had come out of his seizure (a fit of neuro-spasmodic paralysis, should he call it?) and managed to wipe the spittle from his shirt. Somehow he had tumbled down the tower stairs without breaking his neck. Once in the round hearth room, he had collapsed on a bunk to sleep a deep, dreamless sleep. How long? The fire that burned in the central hearth had died to embers. Perhaps the same day, then. A sultry dusk lingered at the windows.

As he lay on the bunk the slats beneath the rag-stuffed mattress made his bones feel brittle and achy. His paralyzed hands tingled, the circulation returning in hot needles of blood. Thank God the interminable itching in his head was gone. Those flies would certainly have driven him mad in the end. . . . He *had* killed his father once. Not the one in Nanny Sasha's bed, as would have been proper, as it should have been. But he'd found another, a lord and master. And cut his throat not once but a thousand times, to the roaring applause and wild cheers of the mob. They gave him garlands for the killing, garlands and devotion and love. They all wanted the old Faker dead.

As the seizure passed, he dimly remembered grabbing at an old framed photograph that sat on his desk. At the time, he had half a mind to burn the picture — that was why he came downstairs! — but he had collapsed on the bunk too soon for that, saying to himself, "I'll just rest here a minute first . . ." He still clutched it in his numb hand. He wondered how he had managed to break the frame and get the photograph out of the glass. He pried his fingers loose and let go.

The faded picture showed the imposing edifice of the Burghölzli Mental Hospital. On the back, a credit: Hans Hunisch, Photograph, 10 Hellestrasse, Zurich, February 15, 1906. He stared again at the

94

cracked photo; the name Hubert Prisson & Co. leaped to mind. The building's architects and also builders of elaborate, elegant mansions along Fifth Avenue in New York City. What a ridiculous, absurd piece of useless information! How could he ever —

Ah, he recalled now: veined marble pillars flanking the doors of the main lobby — he had passed them a dozen times a day, for years on end. . . . A bronze plaque embedded in one pillar proclaimed a paean to the architects:

Hubert Prisson & Co.
New York — London — Paris — Rome
"Addresses of Distinction"

Distinction was perhaps too light a word for what Messrs. Prisson & Co. built. They favored wrought-iron gates in the Gothic style, with spiked lamp cages on the gateposts. The Burghölzli had huge windows on the ground floor that opened like doors, the fittings of gold plate. The lintels over every window were red sandstone against blue granite. Then row upon row of half columns designating the various rooms and suites, five stories up like a layer cake. Round turrets at the building's corners, with circular rooms on each floor; the turrets of a different color than the rest, a black stone like the bastion of the Bastille. Then along the top of the layer cake, gables with triangular Flemish windows, the design stolen from the château of Chenonceaux on the Loire, with the palest blue slate roofing, the copper trim gone green. And finally, above the four spired turrets, smart brass flagpoles.

By the time he arrived there the building had aged fifty years; cold rains and sun and Zurich dirt had cracked the exterior stone. Inside, the marble wainscoting had yellowed with the grime of bodies and cigarette smoke. In some places, the orderlies' gurneys had scraped the walls, leaving marks.

A lush, well-planned garden flowered behind the building, but all this photo showed was window after window: staff offices, examination rooms, lecture rooms, communal wards . . . His own office had been in the back, in one of those cylindrical turrets overlooking the garden —

No! No! No! This photo had been taken *from* the garden. His office had been in *that* corner turret, the fifth window up. There! Partly open, the way he always kept it, summer or winter, even on the worst days.

Was that him? A dark blur leaning back in his chair, elbow resting on the sill? A smudge in the photo?

How little photographs truly showed of a place. The fresh garden fragrance of the leaves and grass after the rain. The steamy food smell from the kitchen. The ozone cloud in the hallway outside the Galvanic Room. The fetid, musty odors in the lower reaches of the basement. No talking, no calls for help, no ringing bells. How could a mere picture show how they went about the business of treatment? Show triumph or failure. Or the common rhythm of life . . . ?

What damn few choices they had back then. They held unruly patients under warm water to soothe them. They wrapped lethargic ones in cold, wet sheets to stimulate their systems. Hydrotherapy they called it: your choice of hot or cold.

There was also the electroshock apparatus: a long wrought-iron table with overhanging cables attached to an electrical generator. A wide range of volts could be applied to different parts of the human body. It worked in some cases of nervous paralysis or memory lapse. And it always worked in those cases suspected of shamming.

Lastly, they had a limited kind of surgery. Excess cranial fluid might be released from within the skull to relieve pressure, or fluid drained from the spinal column with a tap. And on rare occasions a violent case was brought under control by removal of several grams of brain tissue.

But what photo could show any of that? An iron table was just a table, a shower room just a place to wash your hair. No photo could show the forlorn cries falling on the stony ears of nurses and orderlies who had been around too many crazy people for much too long. Nor show the shallow look of bored cruelty on doctors' faces as their patients' imploring cries went unanswered; or the dull hum of staff conversations while a filthy young woman banged her head against her room door, laughing to herself minute after minute. . . .

This was a mental hospital, a *madhouse*. And no photo could ever truly capture the dayroom. A glass-enclosed solarium that gave onto the garden. Where they put the Incurables. For so they were. Forty or more . . . all curious cases, the odd and the notable. Some were war veterans with shrapnel in their brains, whose tiny government pensions had been turned over to the Burghölzli for their indefinite care. A rich widow who had willed her entire estate to the Pan-Germanic Society of Maidens for Moral Decency now spent her days under the delusion that she ran a bordello, with the dayroomers her stable. Most of the Incurables were not paying patients of the hospital but rather kept as specimens — living diagnostic examples. And when one ceased to function, that is, died, the Burghölzli hurriedly replaced it with another suitable specimen.

The dayroom obsessed him, drawing him to it day after day. He used to find a spot to sit, and there he gazed through the glass inner doors as though into a pit of roiling chaos. Beyond the glass the noise was deafening: twenty voices babbled at once; one voice stronger than the rest rose in tone-deaf verses, singing the same lines over and over:

> We stuck it in!
> We twirled it round!
> Yes, she took it all,
> Right on the ground!

This ditty from an Incurable who fashioned snatches of black cloth and white paper to make himself a minister's collar. A narrow, horse-faced man of about fifty-five, with protruding purplish lips and graying hair that he sometimes pulled out in tufts. He had been a school superintendent — who suddenly one day failed to appear for work. But soon he warmed a bench in the public park and there, nine parts drunk, sang his lewd verses. From that day forward no one had gotten any more from Herr Superintendent than that ditty he chose to repeat. Because of his previous position, the local magistrate had to get involved in the man's commitment to the Burghölzli. To the delight of the whole court — spectators, clerks, and sergeant at arms — the magistrate maintained a straight face when each question asked was answered by:

"We stuck it in!" or "She took it all!"

In the end an exasperated magistrate finally inquired, "Pardon me, Herr Superintendent, but do you realize where you are going?" To the howls of the court, Herr Superintendent urinated nervously down his leg, replying meekly, "Yes. Right on the ground. . . ."

Delusions ran rampant in the dayroom: a young peasant lass had

97

convinced herself she was a little boy from China. She tied a head-band around her head so tightly her eyes went slanty, and she always spoke accordingly in "Chinese." There was a dignified dowager who had become Queen Victoria and went regally around the dayroom, inspecting her territories and protectorates. Occasionally she would mount punitive actions against the Pathans in the Kandahar — "Those devil blackies!" — and would have to be restrained.

The Barber of Seville, a small, sallow Spaniard, offered to shave anyone who would sit still for him, yet he wanted to shave nothing but their genitals.

Only by great vigilance did the staff manage to keep a razor from falling into his hands. Despite this, he cleverly fashioned a piece of cardboard into a "razor," which he stropped on his belt, and he often shaved one particular man; a fellow so withdrawn he never noticed anyway. . . .

The hospital also cared for the Sisters of Mercy, a pair of pinheads who stared happily out into the garden all day long. Both, pale, hair-less creatures with narrow pixie skulls and fairly sunny dispositions. Obviously content with each other, they never tormented any of the others. And though called sisters, they weren't biologically related. The male (he had a penis but no testicles) came from a convent hos-pital and was perfectly harmless. The female had been sold by a cir-cus when her huckster died of drink. This sister was sexually active, and in everyone's mind her strange appetites were linked to her mas-ter's excess. She required an eye on her at all times when she went into "heat." Still, the two sisters were drawn to each other out of some mutual sympathy. . . . While watching them chatter back and forth with no apparent content to their speech, Herr Doktor slowly came to see them as the menagerie's two most human attractions. Unhap-pily they proved him prophetically correct: when one of the sisters died of a bad cold, the other wasted away shortly thereafter. Died of grief, people said.

And finally the repugnant cases . . . A man called the Bricklayer, as he had really been one once. He defecated on himself with such reg-ularity the staff had long ago ceased trying to tidy him up more than twice a day. Periodically, orderlies assigned to the dayroom could be heard calling out sadly, "Ach, another brick!"

There was an aging hormone case, a giantess, whose pituitary

98

gland had gone rampant, making her grow seven feet tall. She licked her fingers and toes as if she were a house cat, and so she had always been known as Le Chat. During years of attempting to clean her "paws" she had twisted her limbs like a yogi contortionist. A select few of the staff knew her identity: the illicit offspring of a renowned Hungarian count and his twelve-year-old sister. The institution was amply compensated for the care of the count's "niece." Rumor had it the pitiful child's "aunt" committed suicide at the time of her birth, abandoning into a cruel world yet another poor orphan.

But perhaps the most engagingly disagreeable case was Herr Tom Thumb, an unctuous, talkative dwarf about twenty years old — delivered to the institution by the same local magistrate after a brief court appearance. Herr Tom Thumb was lucid and congenial, always ready to regale a willing listener with the true stories of his early youth. "People spit on you when you're made like me. You can't even walk down the street in peace. Once I went to Zermatt to take the mountain air, and right there on the street a workman stepped out of a *Braubaus* with his stein in his fat fist and spat on me. Spat on me! Pah! Just like that!"

Yet while Herr Tom Thumb talked, he masturbated almost continually: on his clothes, on his listener, against the windowpanes of the solarium. . . . The staff had quite given up trying to stop his chronic ten-minute bouts. And like most things repeated ad nauseam, the sight of Tom Thumb, little pecker in his pudgy fist, aroused no more reaction from the orderlies than a dropped cigar butt in the gutter. More amusing by far was Herr Doktor Jung engaging the dwarf in conversation. Herr Doktor sitting calmly on a bench by the glass windows while Herr Tom Thumb held forth from the top of a packing crate marked THIS END UP.

"I can't imagine why I do this," complained the dwarf. "Do you know why, Herr Doktor? Well, I don't either. But I have to. I do it when I get up, I do it when I wash, before I dress, after I dress, I do it when I eat — I think I even do it in my sleep. You wouldn't believe how sore I get."

"Then why don't you leave off for an hour or two, Herr Thumb?"

"Leave off!" cried the dwarf in scandalized terror. "I *can't* leave off. That's what I'm *telling* you."

"Well, my friend, it's no use wearing the thing out, is it? You must see that you run the risk of infection — when who knows what might happen? A surgical operation could leave you with less than you have already — how would you like that?"

The young dwarf paled, swallowing his fear. "Never! I'd kill myself first." Then, paling even a shade whiter, he demanded with quiet resolve, "Don't you believe me?"

The little man was so earnest, only a cruel person would have laughed. "Yes, I believe you," Herr Doktor assured him. "But let me see if I can get you some salve."

The dwarf looked to heaven, clasping his hands to his breast. "Sweet succor in my hour of need!" Suddenly he leaned over the edge of the crate, whispering secretly, "See if you can make it petroleum jelly."

"All right, then. But I'll have to prescribe it officially, you know."

"Is that a problem?" the dwarf asked, looking really worried.

"In the case of a baby with diaper rash, no . . . But in your case, Herr Thumb, I have to avoid making it look as though I approve of your conduct. This means submitting a procedural note defending the request for your prescription. First, there's the incurable degenerative nature of your affliction."

"Yes, there's that," the dwarf agreed readily.

"Then there's the hope of postponing the inevitable and drastic consequences from your . . . from your . . ."

"From the willful misuse of my bodily parts," the dwarf tried hopefully. "The magistrate said that, not me."

"And quite to the point, my friend. Admittedly this prescription only hastens the overall worsening of your condition, so I shall stress the alternative: that the situation ignored can only lead to more radical deterioration, irritation, inflammation, infection . . ."

"And *surgery*," the dwarf murmured, appalled. "Help me," he pleaded.

"I will do what I can, Herr Thumb. There's no point in letting you whittle yourself away."

The dwarf ceased handling himself for a moment and hurriedly crossed his breast in the Christian manner. "Bless you," he said piously. Then peered suspiciously around the room. The nearest orderly was lounging against the wall not paying the slightest attention. Herr Tom Thumb leaned dangerously over the edge of the crate and asked conspiratorially:

"Why the devil do you come here?"

"Why, to be with you," Herr Doktor said immediately. "And to help, of course . . . Would you rather I sat in the cafeteria with my colleagues over limp strudel, doing those droll impersonations of Le Chat, for instance?"

Herr Tom Thumb knocked his heels against the crate and began handling himself again. "Filthy practice," he agreed. "I've never seen the humor in callous jests at other people's expense."

A newly admitted patient was always called the New Victim.

"Your New Victim needed restraint this afternoon."

Or: "Victim in 504 needed a bath and purging."

This time it was Nurse Bosch who passed by him as he sat in his regular chair, watching the Incurables in the dayroom. The Bricklayer had just laid himself another lodestone and was proudly showing it off to anyone who would admire it. Herr Doktor heard Nurse Bosch's skirts swish as she approached.

The head nurse was an irrepressibly sunny woman with a broad Slavic face and one of those eternally optimistic dispositions. About forty-five, a large woman whose stoutness had no flab, she kept her hair in a starched cap. The first time young Herr Doktor saw her, he thought, *Ah, at last I have met the Happy Pig.* But all he said out loud was: "Pleased to make your acquaintance, Nurse Bosch."

Now she passed him without breaking stride and said offhandedly, "Your New Victim has arrived, young man."

When he turned to have a word with her, Nurse Bosch was nowhere in sight and he had to go about finding his New Victim himself.

On his way to the registrar's office, he glanced out the window into the garden. September was in its dusty middle days, the air still hot, and the branches on the trees hung parched, ready to shed their green. That morning he had noticed a few fallen leaves on the sidewalks and in the dry rain gutters, omens that the heart-quickening days of autumn were not far off. He passed an electric fan whirring noisily in the hall, stirring the dead air to no purpose.

The registrar knew the whereabouts of the New Victim's parents. They had been waiting in Herr Doktor's office for a quarter of an hour. He bounded up the stairs two by two. His mouth felt dry and awkward; he hated meeting people for the first time. The soft sucking sounds of a man drawing on his pipe came out of his silent office, then the stiff rustle of a woman adjusting her dress as she sat. The parents were not talking to each other. Herr Doktor went in and apologized for keeping them waiting. The registrar's admission form told only that the family owned a printing house for the preparation of legal briefs in the Russian city of Rostov-on-Don. They lived somewhere in the German quarter. The husband's age was fifty-two. A cursory glance yielded the impression that the parents were nice, respectable, and bourgeois.

"Rostov is a long way off," Herr Doktor remarked, waving his hand in the general direction of the east.

"That's very true," the husband agreed. And then the three of them lapsed into the consuming silence once more. The man went on smoking his pipe in an amiable, inoffensive manner, as though he had plainly said all that needed saying. Yet mixed in with the unmistakable smell of expensive tobacco was the calm, assured way he left his matches in the ashtray on Herr Doktor's desk — as though it were his ashtray, his office, his desk.

The registrar's form told even less about the wife. She had omitted filling in her age. She had the rich, satisfied air of an aristocrat, perhaps because of her fine clothes and the ease with which she wore them: the fur stole about her shoulders, the long black feather in her hat, the diamond sparkles in the veil she never raised, the touch of perfume. . . . Yet beneath the veil Herr Doktor saw the face of a hawk. She was at least her husband's age, maybe older. And the first to break the silence, asking Herr Doktor questions in the matter-of-fact tone of a woman accustomed to getting down to business. "Forgive me, young man, but aren't you a little youthful to be a physician?"

"No forgiveness necessary, Frau Schanderein," he replied. "I'm barely thirty. I've been a doctor for three years. If I look too young, I suppose it's my mother's fault."

The woman smiled thinly under the veil. And then more questions. How long at the hospital? she asked him. Three years, he told her. And who were his immediate superiors? Senior Physician Nekken and Direktor Bleuler, he told her.

"And why didn't one of these men decide to take on our case?" she demanded.

So that was it! They felt snubbed for not being handled by the Burghölzli's Herr Direktor personally! Insulted for being delegated down the chain of command to a junior physician. Weren't they important enough? Weren't they entitled to a Herr Direktor — or a senior physician at the very least?

Oh, lord; he wanted to laugh. Should he tell them Herr Direktor Bleuler had already looked in briefly on their child, that what he saw gave him little hope, and so he passed the case along? Should Herr Doktor tell them that if they found their way to his office, most of the other senior physicians (Nekken included) had also rejected taking them on? And what would the parents think if they actually met the lofty Bleuler? Herr Direktor was an addleheaded, forgetful, morose old wheezer. Not particularly brilliant: perfect, in fact, for the bureaucratic administrative post he commanded.

His colleagues called him "distinguished" and "eminent." Harmless, meaningless words for a man whose sole achievement had been to hang on forever without the blemish of a scandal. He had sad, puffy eyes, and his gaze wandered about when you spoke to him, glancing down at his black laced boots, or over the top of your head as if you weren't there. But most revealing was his beard. He had the habit of continually stroking his thick badger's beard while he engaged people. A matted furrow ran down each side of his jaw; and he had even worn some of the hair away. Irreverent staffers raised gales of laughter in the cafeteria mimicking the old codger, pulling on their own faces and mumbling, "Ahem, ahem, gentlemen . . . To be a doctor, the first thing you must learn is . . . ah . . . to find your patient's room. And secure, if possible, ahem, a *correct* billing address."

In point of fact, the Direktor had more than enough reason to be morose — for the Burghölzli Hospital almost never cured anyone's madness. And Direktor Bleuler was often heard to say, "Ahem, gentlemen . . . we are not in the business of results. Results are for hotel chefs and . . . ah . . . hairdressers. We are in the business of diagnosis. So I urge you, the first thing you must learn is how to find your patient's room and, ahem, if possible secure . . ."

No, Herr Doktor knew, the eminent Herr Direktor had already had his look-see, stroked his beard, and sighed sadly. The senior physicians had had *their* look, smirked coldly, and passed the case on without a second's remorse.

Let some junior physician take it on if he wanted. Who knew, he might be saved an embarrassing failure if the bills were paid on time.

So perhaps the parents suspected as much, as clever, self-important people often do. The wife's interrogation went on, her voice provoking him at every turn.

"How many patients have you handled personally, Doktor Jung?"

"How would you diagnose our child?"

"You mean you haven't examined the patient yet?"

Frau Schanderein used the word "patient" as if she assumed all the doctors and staff called them that, instead of by their real names or cruel nicknames: Crazy Hans, Le Chat, Herr Tom Thumb . . . So he told them that seeing the family first was not that unusual, and that yes, he had glanced into the child's room, which was only one floor below. Now he asked them to tell him about their family history. And this demand raised a rumble of consternation. The husband blew out a great cloud of smoke as if the question were excessively personal, while his wife spoke up sharply:

"Oh, come now, Doktor, we're not the sick ones here, the child is. Perhaps if you can get her to talk, she'll tell you herself. As for our part — we were a normal family. Until the recent attack, the child was like any other. An attack of nervous *hysteria*. That is the right word, isn't it, Herr Doktor Jung?" The woman's hat and veil turned dramatically toward her husband, as though demanding he confirm every word she said. Cocking her head as if to say, Well, go on, you tell him.

But Herr Schanderein had let his pipe go out and held it impotently in his hand, staring idly into the bowl of ash. So the wife took up again. "We came to Zurich to see our child enrolled in medical school. The first attack occurred in the back of a carriage, near the railway station."

Rostov station or Zurich station? Herr Doktor wondered. But he asked instead:

"Does the girl have any special interests?"

And the wife answered, "No; just the usual."

"Nothing at all? Does she draw, or collect butterflies, or play a musical instrument?"

The husband was shaking his head no. He let the pipe fall on the rug, spilling charred tobacco. "Erik!" the wife snapped. The moment passed into uneasiness as the husband collected his pipe.

"Are you saying your daughter has no keepsakes, no personal things, no other interests aside from . . . ah . . . entering medical college here?" The father had become sadly crestfallen, as if the questions were intended to hurt him personally. The mother stiffened behind the feathered hat and veil, becoming priggish and tight-lipped.

"Moreover, it seems the patient is not exactly a child, being nineteen years of age."

Again, no comment.

Finally Herr Doktor leaned back in his chair and let out a long-drawn-out sigh. At last he said, "I don't believe either of you is being candid with me."

The husband seemed to shrink inside himself. The wife swelled with indignation, bristling all over.

"Don't be absurd, young man. I demand to see the Direktor, so he can be informed as to the extreme tone of this interview, the insolence of your *personal* questions." Herr Doktor remained calm and silent, letting her go on. But she deflated as he failed to meet her on the rampart of her anger, trailing off with, "If you think you can just get anything you want from us . . ."

After a few more quiet moments, he said, "In cases where a person is withdrawn, I am always curious to discover the conditions leading up to the attack. I apologize if such curiosity seems inquisitive to the point of rudeness. As to your seeing Herr Direktor Bleuler — by all means, let me make an appointment for you with his secretary. Perhaps I am at fault for not explaining everything fully. But I was under the impression you understood Direktor Bleuler is already familiar with your case, as are several of the other senior physicians. And that it was decided I should look into it further." Herr Doktor paused for a moment.

The husband was working himself up to say something. "No, no one told us anything," he said doubtfully, as though long suspecting a hidden truth.

"Of course," Herr Doktor went on, as gently as he could, "if I am not suitable for you, or you don't think the Burghölzli can help, we can sometimes recommend private physicians in town, or specialists in other cities."

A grim eventuality was dawning on the parents. An understanding, as they now saw the possibility of having their child back on their hands. In her present distressed condition, this prospect was dreadfully unnerving. With a sharp turn of the head, the wife shot a look at her husband that said, He'll do as well as anyone. Go on, tell the bastard what he wants to know.

Clearly irritated, she fiddled with the brim of her hat and, as she did so, twitched aside the veil. For a brief second, the black lace fluttered from her face. And in that moment Herr Doktor saw a strikingly beautiful woman, once upon a time young, but now glittery and brittle like the crystal prisms of a broken chandelier. . . . Hard, mascaraed eyes, sharp mouth, piercing nose. Not really a woman any longer but the statue of a woman, ruthless and cunning, imposing her stony will at every opportunity and hardened with discontent at every turn. When the veil dropped back once more, it fell like a shade, shutting her off from the world. Herr Doktor knew he would get no more from her this day.

The husband put his pipe away, since it had proved only an encumbrance; and by shoving the brown briar into his coat pocket, he seemed to concede all at once the uselessness of fighting anymore. He started haltingly, as though pained to admit:

"She never was really normal. What I mean is, she can talk — when she wants to. She can read — on and off, that is. Some years were bad."

"Bad?" Herr Doktor asked.

"Some years were bad. Where she fell behind. But she seemed to catch up. I suppose we spoiled her, the way people do with their children —"

"*You* spoiled her," the wife cut in. She seemed to think this a crucial point of some kind. Like a disadvantage.

A flash of anger came into the husband's eyes, and then died without a trace. "What I mean," he went on, "what I mean is, maybe we weren't strict enough, but I always thought she caught an infection." An *infection.* He seemed to put a lot of stress on that word, as if it explained everything. "You know, like the grippe. Only in the brain. Getting in her skull and making her sick. She was so young when she had her first attack. Maybe five years old. She didn't eat for a week. I was sure she had caught something. But then every couple of years she'd have another attack —"

He halted suddenly. He had a handsome, fair-weather face, which seemed just right for easy smiles and breezy summer days, but now it was clouded and crumbling. He hid it in his hands. . . . The wife looked away in disgust, stiffening noticeably, humiliated by his weeping. She cast a sidelong glance at him, with a cruel twist of her chin. "Stop it, Erik! Erik, pull yourself together!"

She said it with almost a ventriloquist's voice, her lips barely moving, as though the young doctor across the desk wouldn't notice a papery hiss. He was reminded of a silly woman at a dinner party trying to kick her drunk husband under the tablecloth to shut him up. And since everyone pretended not to have seen her, she felt perfectly safe.

Now the wife spoke up sharply, as though to distract him from her husband's disgraceful behavior. "Herr Doktor!" she chirped. "Herr Doktor, if you discover an infection, will you be able to cure it?"

He could see that in her heart she wanted to believe her husband. That their daughter had an infection like malaria, that reappeared throughout a person's lifetime. With an infection there was some hope at least — this Herr Doktor might concoct some potion to cure the child. But he couldn't simply ignore the husband's behavior, even if that's what the Schanderein woman clearly wanted. So he addressed the man, face still buried in his hands.

"Herr Schanderein, how long do you and Frau Schanderein plan to stay in Zurich?"

Herr Schanderein's fair-weather face came up a deep shade of pink. His eyes were wet, and he wiped them before speaking. "How long do you think we should stay?"

"I need a chance to observe your daughter — examine her if possible. Then we should have another conversation. Shall we say a week?"

"And then you'll know for certain whether it is an infection or not?" This from the mother, in an imperial tone.

"Am I the first doctor you have consulted in all these years, Frau Schanderein? I seriously doubt this. So let me be frank. There is slim hope that I will discover in a mere week what has eluded so many of my predecessors for so long."

Frau Schanderein became chilly, pulling herself up properly in her chair and demanding once more, "Now tell me, how old are you, Herr Doktor?"

"Thirty," he repeated evenly. "And you asked me that before." That made Herr Schanderein smile, but his wife ignored it. Was she unaware of repeating herself? Or was this some sort of ploy to dominate him? She hammered out a steady stream of questions:

"So you say the hospital specializes in nervous disorders? Does that mean disorders of the brain?"

He said it meant that. And other parts of the body.

"But curing a disorder of the brain is rare," she objected. "Isn't it true no one can even agree on what disorders of the brain really are?"

He said it was true: no one agreed.

"But then you imply disorders like my child's have been cured. What were they? Who cured them?"

By way of an answer, he reached into a bookshelf by his elbow and took down several thin pamphlets and a larger book. He told the Schandereins the persons in those pamphlets suffered disorders of the brain; he told them some had been treated with success. He told them they could read the pamphlets if they wanted. Herr Schanderein tentatively picked one. He paged limply through it, seeing without comprehending. He read the title softly to himself as though not sure what it meant: *"Studien über Hysterie . . ."* He lingered over the authors' names, as if partly recollecting them. "Breuer and Freud." Then he picked up the larger book. "Freud by himself now, I see. *Die Traumdeutung* . . . but this one's about dreams," he said, confused.

Frau Schanderein sniffed at the pamphlets. "There are plenty of Gypsies in Rostov who'll listen to your nightmares. Are you trying to tell me my daughter has the same disorders as are in those little papers?"

He told her no, that every person was different; cases might be similar and yet not alike.

Frau Schanderein physically exulted in the prospect of catching him in a contradiction, ruffling with pleasure where she sat. "Oh, so these are not the same disorders. Something similar, perhaps." She seemed to swell in triumph. "So in fact my daughter's affliction is not in those little papers at all."

She picked up the dream book, demanding with some contempt, "And what about this one?" She flipped through the opening pages to see where it was published. Then she closed the book, putting it back on the desk, plainly having seen enough to satisfy her curiosity. "We could have gone to Vienna as easily as Zurich," she said disdainfully. "It's a good deal closer, besides."

"But I thought, Frau Schanderein," Herr Doktor reminded her innocently, "you came here to enroll your daughter in Zurich University Medical College."

The woman went silent for a moment, staring at him flat-eyed as if what he said had not penetrated. At last she changed the subject entirely, saying with satisfaction, "Then you're admitting you don't know very much about the disorders of the brain. Or much about a cure."

"Admittedly, Frau Schanderein," he said, "we face a very troubling state of affairs."

There was little more to be said; the interview clearly coming to an end. Frau Schanderein thanked him politely for his time, rose to shake his hand, and led her husband from his chair. Herr Doktor got up to show them out, bowing at his office door. Herr Schanderein took his hand. "We'll be in touch in a couple of days to see how you're coming along," he said hopefully. The man gently pressed Herr Doktor's hand like a silent apology, as if to say, I'm sorry, terribly sorry for this whole episode.

When they had gone, Herr Doktor sagged behind his desk. What an impossible woman! Mystifyingly obnoxious; and worst of all, she had managed to ruin his shirt: the perspiration under his arms had turned sticky, body-sour. Why attack everything? Him, his science, the hospital . . . ? As if she had to wreck the foundations of his whole world before she'd allow him the privilege of examining their daughter. No, far preferable for Frau Schanderein to prove the whole works useless before anyone laid even a shred of doubt upon her parenting. After all, didn't everyone know nervous hysteria was all but incurable? Rendering questions about their family life totally irrelevant?

And as for any diagnosis . . .

Disorder of the brain or elusive infection? Surrender the girl or whisk her off to Vienna? Doctors or Gypsies? Who cared? So long as in the final analysis the good Frau Schanderein wasn't found guilty of any wrongdoing.

The pamphlets and the book he had offered sat ignored on the desk. He hefted the heavy one back to the shelf. Then changed his mind, deciding to leave it be. Gathering dust in reproach if the parents ever returned.

Chapter 5

The New Victim

This was the case that launched a saga of notes. And though in time he wrote hundreds of pages, at the beginning, at least, most were like this:

Sept. 15: Visited Patient. Was not allowed in room.

Hardly an indication of what really occurred. In fact, he had not been able to "examine" the patient at all — except from the corridor. Small glass viewing slits in the room doors allowed anyone standing in the hall to peer inside. Almost everyone working at the hospital had gotten into the habit of taking sidelong glances into the rooms as they strode by: a patient would never know whether he or she was being watched or not. When Herr Doktor caught any of the staff peeking in that way, he always barked at them to look in properly or not at all.

As for Herr Junior Physician's own looking in, after a week he had still not managed to gain entry to the New Victim's room for more than a few seconds at a time. At first, of course, he had stood outside the patient's door and peered through the viewing slit. He saw a whitewashed room with a wrought-iron relic of a bed jammed in one corner by the window. Over the bed hung a Catholic icon of the Virgin Mary. Even though it was September and quite warm, the window was shut. He noticed several indolent flies dreamily bumping their heads against the glass in a fruitless effort to escape into the wild before winter came. As a general rule, the hospital left the private rooms unlocked, though supervised, and supplied each with both a bedpan and a chamber pot: the first in case the patient didn't wish to rise from bed, the other in the event a second use was required. Herr Doktor thought highly of this arrangement, as though the staff were demonstrating their readiness for any occasion.

The Schanderein girl sat on the bed. She had wrapped sheets and blankets so tightly around her body she looked like a mummified corpse, one of those neolithic bodies you saw in Ice Age grave holes, sitting head to knees, hands clasped around their withered legs. How did she breathe? As little as possible, he decided. And then that day he opened the door.

The Schanderein patient shrieked, the shriek so piercing that patients in nearby rooms sent up a wail themselves. The sound of the shriek lanced through his brain, flashing like a blinding light behind his eyes. At once a fierce headache gripped him. He fled the room and, before he knew what he was doing, slammed the door against the sound. The shrieking went on for several moments, rising and falling, and then ceased abruptly.

His first thought was: *If I can't get into her room, what the hell am I going to tell the parents?* What an impotent thought.

He glanced furtively up and down the hall to see if anyone was watching.

But no one cared enough yet. Soon there would be a time when his standing in the hall brought Nurse Bosch and smug young orderlies strolling insolently down the corridor, not even bothering to hide their sneering smiles at his pointless vigil. But the taunts came later.

The first day with the girl felt like an eternity. The quality of her shriek totally unnerved him. Not just the noise, not just the intensity . . .

What then?

As if the mummy on the bed were being stabbed with a hot wire. You felt the outrage in the shriek. Despair. Violation.

And so, barred from the room, he had plenty of time to study his new patient through the glass viewing slit in the door. He contemplated the folds in her swathings and watched for signs of movement. Meals were brought, spurring a shriek, and left hastily just inside the room. The pawed-over meal plates were taken away as quickly. But it was not clear whether the meals were eaten.

One night in the first week he happened to pass the patient's door.

The light from the hall shone into the dark room through the glass viewing slit. The bed lay empty, the mummy gone. Then he heard the soft slurping and feverish gobbling. He spied the mummied form crouching on the floor, grabbing food off the plate. The gobbling ceased. A shriek came. Had the girl sensed him standing in the hall? *Felt* him listening in?

"Excuse me!" he said hurriedly at the viewing slit. "I won't sneak up on you again." The shriek had wakened others on the floor. A grumpy orderly padded from room to room in the confusion, checking to see that everyone was all right.

"Wake them up, why don't you!" snapped the orderly as he made the rounds. "There, there, Mitzi — go back to sleep. Hush, Tante — it's only a noise. . . ." And one by one his charges quieted down.

"The only sound sleeper on the floor is you," Herr Doktor retorted irritably as the orderly clattered down the stairs.

Once Herr Doktor tried standing in the patient's room no matter how loud she screamed. Awful mistake. The noise from the girl's throat, even muffled through her mummy wrappings, rose octave upon octave, higher than the shriek of a jungle bird, higher than he ever imagined a human voice could go. He stood it twenty seconds or so, until his hands started sweating and his head caught fire with the sound. He fled the room.

Now his actions had become quite celebrated, and he often found an audience waiting for him when he arrived for his daily visit. On the miserable day of his trying to wait out the girl's screams, he found Nurse Bosch smiling mildly at him from the end of the hall. He had half a mind to walk to the end of the corridor and slap the smug piggy smile from her fat piggy face. The fact was he *had* to flee the room, for as the girl's shrieks rose and rose, he had an image of the blood vessels in her brain pumping more and more until one of them ruptured and burst.

As for Nurse Bosch, she too seemed to think the prospects for this New Victim were far horizons of wasted effort, with the patient leaving her private room when the money ran out, finally reaching the horrid dayroom — to be watched sadly from afar by an older and much wiser Herr Doktor.

*　　*　　*

Sept. 22: Visited Patient. Was not allowed in room.

Entries for the rest of September would say little more.

What could he have lost by giving up and saying, She is incurable — there is nothing to be done? Incurable. Nothing to be done . . . The words echoed like a Hindu mantra in his head as he sat with the Schandereins for the last time in his office. They had allowed that the Burghölzli was as good a place as any to leave their daughter. They would send sufficient money for her upkeep. Herr Schanderein seemed particularly adamant that she be kept in a private room and was willing to pay any price to assure this.

"Can the hospital arrange for her steamer trunk to be fetched from the hotel? It's very large. You'll need a couple of men."

Frau Schanderein seemed almost indecently satisfied with Herr Doktor's failure to come within a yard of her daughter, a failure that plainly confirmed a conviction she had nurtured for some time: since no one was able to do anything for the girl, there was obviously nothing to be done. As the interview began, Herr Doktor found himself staring unconscionably at Frau Schanderein's figure as she sat proudly before him. A fine woman, she took pains to show it off. Her dress was made of china-blue silk, an evening shade like the light of the sky just as the sun goes down, and woven into the silk were the masks of Comedy and Tragedy, at tilted angles to one another. The embroidered motif was a tiny one, each mask no larger than your thumbnail, so you had to look closely. It struck Herr Doktor that the masks were placed on her breasts exactly where her nipples would be. The thought of the laughing and crying faces at her breasts was arousing and horrifying at the same time. The woman was haughty and menacing; she repulsed him, but her breasts did not. Somehow she had separated them off from the rest of her. He imagined her luxuriously peeling down the front of the china-blue gown as they all sat there. Showing off her splendid self and offering up the rest of her, making him fall for them, press his face into their yielding warmth . . .

How could he *think* of such a thing? This was the parent, the guardian, perhaps the very maker of that shrieking thing on the bed in 401. He tried to shut out the invisible spell she cast around herself, to tear his mind away from the all-consuming scent of her womanness. He felt it wafting about the room. Was her husband immune? Or had she long ago ceased to arouse the man? In their first encounter Frau Schanderein had been provoking and clever, trying to trip him up. But now that Herr Doktor had fallen, having failed to examine their daughter, she could afford to turn the coy side of her face to him, the smile of victory. After all, Herr Doktor had proved to be no threat. Why not seduce the young man, preen a bit, fluff his feathers . . . ?

God, what was he thinking? As the fog lifted from his head, he noticed her indulgently touching the edges of the pamphlets left for them the week before. She ran her finger across the dream book, leaving a streak in the dust.

"They really ought to send a girl to tidy up," she remarked casually. Almost like saying, Dust them off and put them away, my good man — they shan't be any use to us.

As for the fare-thee-well Herr Schanderein, Herr Doktor saw no trace of the remorseful weeping man of their last meeting. Now assured of his daughter's comfort in a "room of her own," he was at peace, all his responsibilities properly discharged. He sat cavalierly; a thin trail of smoke rose beside his head. His dark hair swept back, gleaming; his lip curled about the pipestem clamped between his teeth. A handsome man . . . In fact, the two of them made a smart, striking couple. He, something of a pirate — and she, an Empress de la Valse: regally sensual and remote. A beautiful, unattainable woman whom you saw across a ballroom floor in a rival's arms.

Yet Herr Doktor found their business wearing him down. After all, why in hell should he squander his energy just to prove the naysayers and doomsayers right all along? But even as he stared at Herr Highwayman lounging contentedly in his veil of smoke and Frau Empress with her untouchable bosom thrust out, all the weariness turned to cold, hard anger. . . . What right did they have to be insolent? What lurked behind the social posture? That was their daughter down there in 401. A shrieking invalid on a bed.

Their own *daughter!*

If only Herr Doktor could find the place in their brains where the simple answers lay. But their minds were closed to him. He saw in their faces the Empress and the Rogue relishing their freedom, tasting the clean air outside the sickroom, away from the endlessly repellent task of caring for their daughter. Was this one of the reasons they had come so far? he wondered. To abandon the girl in a strange land from which there was no return? Yes, he was jealous of them; jealous of their freedom — for leaving him behind with that mad thing in room 401.

Should he refuse the girl and make them take her back?

Who in the hospital would care? Not a soul.

Diagnose her. Pronounce her incurable and hand her back to the parents. They deserved getting their Shrieker back. Deserved the long suffering life of tending to an invalid. The endless mess, the cleaning up, the ceaseless watching and never sleeping. The slow wasting away. For a sweet moment he relished the thought, turning it over in his mind. There'd be other cases coming along, better cases. . . .

Then he saw the girl on the bed in her room once more. A wrapped thing in blankets, not moving, hardly breathing. Barely alive . . . Give her back? To the makers and breakers of that screaming wretch in 401? Send her back to *them*? What a heinous, detestable act. A wicked utterance blossomed on his tongue; he picked up the dream book and dusted it off, saying calmly to Frau Schanderein:

"Since examining your daughter has proven so difficult, as you yourself anticipated, madam, I think we must take the possibility of an organic infection all the more seriously. Therefore I must examine you both, in order to determine whether an infection is at the root of your daughter's troubles. And whether the Burghölzli should be involved in her case at all."

He said this mouthful in the blandest manner possible; by the end of it, Frau Schanderein was trembling from neck to bosom, her mouth working as if to spit bile from her lips . . . But her throat made only cracked sounds. Her husband's face had gone strangely pale. He suddenly looked right at her, stricken, imploring her to speak. Do something . . . Say anything.

"Examine us!" the woman cried. "But we're not the sick ones. She is!"

"That may be," Herr Doktor went on calmly, ignoring their discomfort. "But nevertheless I will have to arrange for full physical examinations so we can look for any signs of hereditary or congenital defects that might contribute to your daughter's condition. Defects that you yourselves might not even be aware of. Signs of past exposure to venereal disease. Syphilis. And the possibility of gonorrhea. Which in your case, madam, will require a pelvic examination."

The parents' outrage gave way to a long moment of stupefied numbness. "Venereal disease . . . ," the woman said in a bare whisper as if she'd never spoken the words before.

Whatever possessed him to pursue this line? he wondered bitterly. Oh yes — the way the parents looked. So smug and satisfied, so secure in themselves. He wanted to scrape a bit of that away. Well, at least some of it had gone now. The man and the woman were glancing furtively at each other, fearing something of their own transparency.

Herr Doktor took two lined writing pads from his desk drawer and two sharpened pencils from a laboratory beaker by his elbow, put one pencil on each pad, which he slid across the desk.

"These notepads are for you. Please write down your full medical histories, listing any diseases, chronic ailments, or bouts of sickness you may have had. Also, Frau Schanderein, please note the date of your last internal pelvic examination, if any. And you, Herr Schanderein, the date of your last prostate examination, if any. And lastly, please list the series of your daughter's attacks and the dates they occurred. If you can remember what activities precipitated them — family outings, school life, activities, whatever — that might be helpful. I'll leave you alone now. The lavatory is down the hall to the right. I'll send Nurse Bosch by in a little while if you'd like something from the cafeteria. If you need me, I'll be outside your daughter's room. Or the floor orderly will know where I am."

The two of them stared dumbly at the pads, paralyzed. He paused at the door with an afterthought, addressing the husband:

"I am of the deep suspicion, sir, that Frau Schanderein and yourself have ceased to live as man and wife. And that it has been some time since your last relations. Did you cease relations before your child's first attack? Or was it later, as the dismal prospect of caring for your daughter *indefinitely* began to weigh on your marriage? Please note any contributing factors this state of affairs may have had on your daughter's condition."

Herr Doktor was glad to be able to finish this last bit without any objections. The parents had not turned to look at him as he paused by the door, but now Herr Schanderein bowed his head slightly. A gesture of supplication, of pleading, of imploring Herr Doktor not to leave him alone with himself or his wife.

Frau Schanderein appeared outside the girl's room ten minutes later, saying simply, "We'd like to talk to you, Herr Doktor."

Back in his office, the yellow pads lay empty. He saw the Schan-

116

dereins were terrified of writing, of putting their hands to the blank empty sheets as their own banality welled up to meet them. But they were willing to talk now, tell him anything — anything but write. Their story came out in broken bits, falling before him like the dislocated pieces dumped from a puzzle box. Lies, truths, half-truths, half-lies, foolishnesses, incoherencies — he let them run on. It was good to hear them speak. He made some notes: the specialists they had consulted, the number of attacks, snatches of family medical history, all the little innocent things he had wanted in the first place.

Nothing really helped, but in giving of themselves this tiny bit, they were giving him their daughter. He felt it, like a silent agreement being struck: the girl was changing hands. Just their saying, "This is who we are," was a token of faith, like an offering. Please, Herr Doktor . . . please take care of her. And he was satisfied they meant it.

By the end, the Schandereins were actually leaning toward each other in their chairs, adding to one another's stories as they spoke. And when they had finished, Herr Doktor Jung poured them each a glass of sherry from a green decanter he kept on the bookshelf. The man tossed it back in one gulp; Frau Schanderein took it down deeply in two. Herr Doktor saw them out of his office with the sugary sweetness still on the tip of his tongue. He put the yellow pads away, the sharp pencils back in their beaker. He dusted off the two pamphlets and the dream book, putting those away as well. He never saw the Schandereins again.

Later in the day, a gang of orderlies fetched the girl's steamer trunk from the parents' hotel; they lugged it, sweating and grunting, up to the fourth floor. The big trunk sat in the hall beside her door, where it remained untouched and unopened for a very long time.

Frau Schanderein also sent along a bouquet of flowers, addressed to "The Good Herr Doktor Jung," with a card that read: *Thank you for your continued effort.* He was tempted to throw the flowers out his office window, but something stopped him. So he tucked the card between the pages of his early case notes and gave the flowers to Nurse Bosch instead. Who in turn gave them to Tom Thumb, the dwarf, with his first prescription of petroleum jelly. To the small fellow's undying gratitude, Herr Doktor's request had been approved — provisionally.

Chapter 6

The Siege Engine

Every day he went to the patient's room. Every day the patient shrieked. And every day he leaped out again. The ritual went on, unchanging, as summer waned. In the early days of October, the garden below the girl's window turned to fire and flame. When the wind blew on a bright day, bread-loaf clouds raced across a Spanish sky, and the red-gold light from the faces of the tingling aspen leaves flew up into the patient's window, dancing about the whitewashed walls of her room.

The hospital staff went about its normal routine: patients were admitted or discharged, meals were cooked and served, the dirty dishes carted off, bedpans filled and emptied, cases diagnosed, reports written, filed, then forgotten. And whenever a certain Herr Doktor tried to enter his patient's room, a murderous shriek rang out and the young fool leaped back into the hall as if stung by a wasp.

Days passed. And weeks . . . Then one morning when Herr Doktor came for his visit he noticed the patient had opened the window. A dun-colored sparrow perched on the sill. The bird pecked at a crumb and then looked brightly around the room. It chirped once, twice, thrice! The girl, wrapped in swathings from head to toe, now sat facing the bird as it bobbed for crumbs at the open window. The hair on his legs stood up; a creeping invisible hand going down his spine and between his buttocks:

She hadn't shrieked the bird away!

He turned from the viewing slit and removed his glasses. Someone passed in the hall, speaking to him, but he didn't hear and nodded his head, hoping the person would go away. A bird on the windowsill . . . a harmless little sparrow . . . Was it only *people* the girl didn't like?

An oily sweat broke out on his forehead, and he mopped it off with his handkerchief; he must look into the room again. He hastily cleaned his glasses with the same rag, smearing them worse than before. He looked into the room. Ja, a sparrow on the sill. The patient still facing it. Fact: the girl was discriminating. Actively choosing her company: *I'll have this, not that.*

And her company was a bird.

Yet all else remained as before. The thing on the bed like an immovable, shrouded idol. A statue of a person, hung with a drape. Just like a real statue, waiting . . . waiting for someone to pull the drapery off and reveal her stone form to the world.

No! No! No!

How easy to get it all wrong. The patient wasn't waiting like a wallflower at a dance. The patient was saying: *No one — Absolutely no one —* can come inside unless I say so.

All these weeks and days of September gone . . . What an obvious statement! He wanted to hit his head against the wall. Her silence was not withdrawal! The dead mummy was not hiding but aggressively exercising her authority over the immediate space of her hell. The air around her body, what people saw of her person, her bed, her room — the girl's silence a stifled shriek of . . . *defiance.*

And now her parents' words came back at him. "She was always trouble. Always putting her nose where it didn't belong, sneaking up on us when we were in bed."

"How old was she then?"

"Three or four," Herr Schanderein said.

"And what did you do?"

"Nothing," Frau Schanderein said.

"You ignored it?"

"Of course not," the woman said, annoyed. "We simply locked the door. Locked her out."

"But didn't she stand outside the door and cry?"

"Children cry all the time," the woman said. "Who remembers?"

"And so you left her there in the hallway. Alone."

"Yes," said Frau Schanderein, with a hint of a smile. "A child has to learn."

Herr Schanderein glanced at his wife sourly, savoring a private reproach. "She liked to get the little bugger mad," he said.

Frau Schanderein didn't contradict but thrust her dignified bosom at him. "And why not? When you were always ready to be Herr Küssen-Küssen."

Herr Kiss-Kiss she called him, in soft-mouthed contempt, as if her husband kissed all manner of unclean things — rotten fruit, soiled rags, sewer grates. But now it struck Herr Doktor as he stood outside the daughter's door how the whole business had come full circle. Once little Fräulein Schanderein had been kept out when she wanted to get in. Now she made *him* the little bugger waiting in the hall.

It had taken two orderlies to carry the girl bodily into 401. Was this a girl on the verge of entering medical school? In America, maybe, but certainly not in Europe. Here you had to walk and talk and present yourself. No shriekers. No mutes. No huddled mummies alone in their rooms.

Yet she allowed a sparrow . . . The bird had succeeded where the man had failed. What distinguished a sparrow from a man? Fool . . . of course! The sparrow was an animal. Not able to ask politely, "Fräulein, may I come in, please?" Only people asked permission when they wanted to enter. And the girl knew it. Any child knew it — if she'd walked unbidden into her parents' bedroom. Or been locked out, stranded before a bolted door, begging for attention yet studiously ignored. Any child would know enough to ask, "May I come in?" But no, no, not the birdbrained junior physician, not the highly educated, self-important Herr Doktor, who doesn't even know enough to knock-knock-knock!

Oh, God, three weeks of barging into the room. Days and hours of barreling in and getting shrieked out — squandered! More time wasted standing stupidly in the hall each day, watching the wrapped mummy on the bed. All leading up to thirty seconds of watching a dun-colored sparrow peck at some crumbs. He shuddered with embarrassment, at his own stupidity. He wiped a sweaty palm across his forehead and back over his scalp. Then spoke through the door:

"Forgive me, Fräulein, for being so needlessly rude these past weeks."

An orderly mopping the floor at the end of the hall leaned on his mop to listen. Herr Doktor breathed deeply and plowed ahead.

"I realize now, Fräulein, that I must apologize for rudely entering your room without permission. I apologize. Please forgive me. And all of us who have thoughtlessly thrown ourselves at you."

For three weeks then, orderlies and nurses had also barged in several times a day, to bring the girl's meals, to remove the dirty dishes, and to replace a bedpan or chamber pot, as necessary. "Fräulein," he said squarely to the glass viewing slit. "Henceforth, I promise these daily intrusions will end."

He glanced at the orderly leaning idly on his mop.

"Don't you have anything better to do?"

Without a word the man went back to mopping the floor in a desultory, spiritless way. He could tell the orderly's ears were perked for any more juicy bits to repeat later. So now, there would be new opinions formed when a certain junior physician denied the hospital staff access to the room of the New Victim in 401. Unfavorable opinions. Imagine the gall — barring nurses and orderlies from a private room!

Christ, how stupid! Was she even listening? And why say "I'm sorry" when he probably couldn't do anything about the comings and goings of the daily routine? There must be a way to bring the girl food without intruding. Cut a slot in the door? No, too much like a prison. And what of clean sheets? A hospital was nothing if not a place where clean sheets came whenever they're wanted. Forget about clean sheets for now. Eating and eliminating were the main problems at hand.

And then he saw how it was to be done.

"I'll bring the meals myself," he said to the viewing slit.

So far he had not looked into the room. He imagined any minute a shriek erupting from within to cut him off, shatter the momentary calm, crush the tiny crumb of understanding he had gleaned about the girl. . . . At last he dared a glance through the glass viewing slit. The sparrow now gone. The mummy on the bed had curled itself up like a dog. For the first time he saw part of the patient's body: grimy white socks on her feet, the socks matted and twisted so the heel came about in the wrong place. Could a sock get that dirty in only three weeks? Or had the same pair been on the girl's feet since the middle of summer in Rostov? He wondered what else he might find under the mummy's wrappings. The girl's underclothes, hanging in looping gray shreds beneath. Bedsores. Scabies. Fleas . . .

He imagined a face with a hideous harelip, with two front teeth showing through a slash of pink gums. What else had the Schandereins failed to tell him? How long since the girl had stopped washing herself? How long had they given up trying to tend to her?

Why hadn't he asked the parents the questions he needed the answers to? Because they tried to make him feel inferior? So he cleverly insulted them and sent them on their way. They must have felt deserving of his punishment, swallowing it like a dose of medicine and making good their escape. A headache crept up the back of his neck, crawling around his ear.

"Fräulein, I will return later tonight with your meal."

To the mystification of the kitchen staff and the floor orderlies, Herr Doktor made out a list of new instructions. So twice a day a scullery maid brought the girl's meals to his office; and in the quiet of the afternoon, or even late at night, he brought the patient her food himself. In an odd way, it brought him close to Fräulein S . . . as though by touching her plate, he touched the girl herself.

Herr Doktor sat at the end of the hall, with room 401 far down the row of private doors. The chair under him was an uncomfortably severe Puritan meetinghouse chair, meant to keep the sitter awake and alert for long periods of time. The usual occupant was a muddle-headed orderly named Zeik, a soft dumpling of a fellow who always managed to outwit the chair. First, he curled his hip around this way, then he twisted his torso the other way, settling his bulk, and presto! he fell instantly asleep with his head thrown back, his Adam's apple jutting out as he snored.

But tonight Herr Doktor had relieved Zeik from floor duty and, try as he might, had not found the secret position that would relieve the pulsing aches in his lower back. How had that idiot Zeik done it?

Earlier in the evening he had gone to Fräulein Schanderein's door and announced, "Fräulein Schanderein, I have brought your meal. I shall leave it outside your door. I have sent the floor orderly away for the night and will take his place at the end of the hall."

He set the covered plate from the kitchen near the door crack, where, if she reached outside, she could easily slide her meal within. Then he watched the hot plate of food, with the steam rising from the little hole in its tin cover, slowly cool, the steam vanishing. . . . He had given up looking at the plate. Perhaps she didn't understand anything at all. If she didn't know there was a "door," how could she open it? If she didn't know about "plates," how could she eat from one?

But all that was some time ago.

A mess of papers lay on Herr Doktor's lap. Notes-of-Procedure destined for the desk of Herr Direktor Bleuler: pointless justifications of his eccentric treatments for the girl. He had long since ceased trying to finish the reports.

"You will never enter the Victim's room, Herr Jung." He had heard no sound of footsteps approaching. Herr Senior Physician Nekken. At last Direktor Bleuler's favorite diagnostician had come around to "consult." Nekken. What an unpleasant name. Spelled slightly differently, with a *c*, Necken, and you had the word for tease — a kidder, a joker, Loki the Trickster. . . . Had that been the original spelling? Just pondering it made Herr Doktor warm behind the ears. Controlling his face around Senior Physician Nekken was the single most important goal. Controlling his face so as not to show fear. Nekken always wore a long, swallowtail coat, reminding Herr Doktor of a tall praying mantis. He had thin, tapered fingers like forceps and a narrow embalmer's face: a face filled with gray and tepid thoughts, like peeling back layers of epidermis with his clean fingernails to stare lovingly into a cold dead brain.

The man's hooked nose and stiff red hair always made Herr Doktor want to say, "This is a Jew's face." Though it wasn't true. Nor could Herr Doktor account for this nasty bit of hatred. Branding Nekken a Jew called up pictures from those fairy books of long-nosed Rumpelstiltskin as he pranced by the fire, gloating over the firstborn he'd snatch from the pretty maiden trapped in the high tower once he spun the king's straw into gold . . . misformed, ugly thoughts of poisoned wells, ravished virgins, loathing, greed, and cruelty. Cursing Nekken a Jew made him the lowest form of life, lower than a louse.

For Herr Doktor felt Nekken *was* the lowest form of life: a brilliant diagnostician always ready to pronounce a given patient's state incurable. Nekken's favorite therapies were the radical ones that showed immediate results. Hydrotherapy — where he calmly directed his favorite goons to sling an old grandmother under cold jets of water — no wonder the chronic melancholia over the recent death of her husband suddenly vanished. Or in the case of a lusty young ironworker whose arm trembled after a finger was crushed in a forge: strap him to the electroshock table and apply a good galvanic dose to the entire side of his body. Miracle! The lad bounded out of the Burghölzli like a jackrabbit, with his bill paid and a letter from Herr Senior Physician certifying the young smelter fit for service at the mill. But give Nekken a talkative dwarf who continually handled himself or the stoically quiet Bricklayer, and the easy pronouncement "incurable" fell from his thin lips with a sad look for the idiot who wasted his time with such patients.

And now Herr Senior Physician Nekken stood over the chair with that nauseating look of sympathy for the hopelessly deluded. "It's a pity you have to go through the business of those reports."

"A pity," Herr Doktor replied, keeping his eyes on the plate sitting far down the hall. "Would you care to finish them for me? The recommended treatment is simple: leave her alone and see what happens."

Nekken smiled indulgently. "Alas, I don't concur. In fact, I wouldn't have taken on the case at all."

"The parents obviously didn't want her any longer. And besides, they can afford to pay."

"Ah, the profit of it all . . . How long do you intend to relieve Nurse Bosch and Orderly Zeik of their duties?" Nekken inquired politely.

"I don't know."

"How long do you intend to sit here tonight?"

"I don't know."

"What are you going to do when the Victim doesn't open the door and get her meal?"

"Probably eat it myself for breakfast and then return the dirty plate to the kitchen."

A dry, mirthless chuckle. "What's for breakfast, then?"

Herr Doktor twisted around in the uncomfortable chair. With a wan smile he answered, "Honestly, Herr Nekken, I didn't look under the cover. But I suspect pot roast."

He stared once more at the plate sitting on the hall floor outside 401. He did not try to shuffle his incomplete reports, nor look too busy for further conversation. He had parried Nekken's jabs without cracking. It was enough. . . . And though he knew the gaunt Herr Senior Physician looked far down his nose at all below his station, Herr Doktor felt some pity for the tall man at his side. No one to talk to. No friends. Wandering about the Burghölzli for lack of anything better to do. The tall man stood quietly against the wall for several more moments, perhaps joining Herr Doktor Jung in the contemplation of the cold food plate at 401. . . .

"Well, my headstrong friend, I wish you a productive vigil."

"Thank you, Herr Nekken."

The senior physician clicked his heels and bowed sharply. Herr Doktor nodded his head in reply. Nekken made to leave, but paused on the stairwell. "Oh, by the way — I'm afraid the Executive Committee reconsidered the dwarf's jelly. We'll be cutting it off at the end of the week. You can, of course, appeal."

Herr Thumb meant nothing to the man; this was just pure spite. The exercise of arbitrary power. Herr Doktor stifled the urge to spit.

"Cutting it off at the end of the week?" he said lightly. "And then you'll be cutting it off for good. Why don't we preserve the dwarf's member in spirits and return it to him?" He went on blithely. "Or maybe stuff the dingus so he can handle it as the need arises."

Nekken stared at him wide-eyed. Then suddenly showed his teeth. "Cutting it off for good!" He clicked his heels and bowed again, then clattered down the stairs, laughing as he went. "Cutting it off at the end of the week — then cutting it off for good! Ha-ha-ha! By all means, return it stuffed! Ha-ha-ha!"

The clattering laughter faded. Herr Doktor wondered what kind of report Nekken would make to Direktor Bleuler about his pointless vigil. A benign one, probably, something like: Herr Junior Physician Jung is proceeding cautiously and with a good deal of candor toward the girl in 401. It is too early to say whether it is the proper course. Naturally, if it is *not* the proper way, some organic trouble will soon materialize and 401 will have to be rediagnosed. I'll want two orderlies, Nurse Bosch, and restraints in order to make the examination myself. . . .

Ja, that's what Herr Nekken would say, giving his junior colleague enough rope to hang himself. And after the elapsed time of wasteful coddling, the news would worm around the hospital that Herr Doktor Jung had ignored an organic condition for X number of weeks. Willfully ignored or misdiagnosed . . . which was worse? He stared at the pile of papers on his lap; they were blurry and indistinct, one shifting into another. . . .

The sheaf of papers fell off his knees onto the floor. He woke with a start. What a wonderfully comfortable chair, he thought. Soft as a feather bed. Then he realized his lower back was numb. Maybe the plate would be missing from its place beside the door! A wild, heart-leaping hope that persisted for several seconds, even though the girl's meal plate sat so obviously still untouched.

125

He went to it and lifted the cover. Pot roast. Green beans. Boiled potatoes. He took the plate back to the puritan chair, eating the beans and meat, leaving the potatoes. Then he returned the plate to its place by her door — the potatoes for her, if only she would take them. Through the big bay window at the end of the hall he saw the night coming to an end. A single bird chirped outside. Perhaps the sparrow who pecked at her windowsill the other day . . . ? That was his last thought until he woke again to the bustle of the day shift at 7 A.M. Nurse Bosch leaned over him, saying, "Why don't you go home, Herr Doktor, and change your shirt."

This seemed the stupidest remark he had ever heard, but he simply got up, gathered his papers, and said, "Danke, Nurse Bosch."

Before he left the corridor he retrieved the patient's untouched plate and announced through the glass viewing slit: "Fräulein, I'm taking your plate away, but I will return again with something from the kitchen for you to eat. If you wish your chamber pot emptied, I would be happy to take it with me now. . . ."

He was dead tired, an aching, shallow-sleep, have-to-urinate, have-to-stretch-out-flat tired. Mouth dry and tongue puffy, grains of grit in his eyes. He wondered how many days he could keep this up. How many days could she go without eating?

He said to himself, Three days — three days before he surrendered and went back to the way it was before: a stone-faced orderly yanking open her door, dumping her food plate, and snatching out the chamber pot. But could they really go back to "before"? Three days seemed an awfully long time to go without eating.

Surely some hospital snoop was already ticking off the number of meals the patient refused. How long before someone hollered, Your patient is starving! Is that why he ate the crazy girl's meals — to cover the fact she hadn't eaten them herself?

Give it up! He didn't want to think about it. He had to pee. He wanted a drink of water. And ja! he wanted a clean shirt. He stood outside 401 for a few more minutes, willing himself not to move, not to budge. Waiting. Waiting for what? A slop pot . . . He turned away.

If someone snickered at him when he returned the girl's plate to the kitchen, he didn't remember. . . . He stole a couple of hours' sleep at home on the couch and made it back to the hospital by eleven for rounds with Direktor Bleuler and company. The next night sitting in the hall went almost exactly as the first. The two differences being that he finished his papers and Nekken never appeared. A third difference: he discovered the comfortable position in the chair. You twisted your torso one way, your hips the other, and threw your head back, settling into the weight of your body. So! Orderly Zeik wasn't so stupid after all — he must really remember him at Christmas.

In the morning when Nurse Bosch came to wake him, he went to the patient's door and repeated what he said the day before.

Now, on the third night when he came to the cafeteria to collect the plate for 401, his speech at the patient's door had become a standing joke. As he passed the orderlies' table, one of them said, "Fräulein!" in a low voice, and the rest of them collapsed into hiccuping laughter.

Early in the evening Nurse Bosch came around with one of his prescription slips in her hand: Herr Tom Thumb's last dose of salve. She had prepared the prescription herself — a tablespoon of clear petroleum jelly sitting in a fluted paper cup. She included a flat wooden spoon, which they often used as tongue depressors. What possible use could Herr Thumb find for the spoon? he wondered. Clearly Nurse Bosch didn't approve of his prescription in the slightest; the fluted paper cup dangled from her fingertips as if she held a dirty, contaminated thing.

"Here is the dwarf's final application, Herr Doktor," she said coolly. "I thought you'd want to know."

He took the prescription slip from her; on it someone had overwritten: *Canceled*. An illegible signature. Nekken's signature. In a bold script he overwrote Nekken's order with the word *Appealed* and his own signature, then gave the slip back to Nurse Bosch.

"I've appealed to the Executive. In the months it'll take them to reach a final decision the prescription still stands. If anyone objects to using hospital stores for this therapy, you'll find a small quantity of petroleum jelly in my office, which we will make as a present to Herr Thumb. One tablespoon daily."

Nurse Bosch's face flushed; her chest swelled as though to protest. She struggled against herself for a moment. Then blurted:

"May I speak plainly, sir?"

Here it came. . . .

"Yes, of course, Nurse."

127

Emboldened, she thrust her soft chin out and plowed on: "You're wrong, sir. It won't do the little fellow any good. They might as well cut it off like a harem guard's and be done with it!"

"I see," Herr Doktor said quietly. "But what if it does do him some good?"

"I don't see how it can do anything but make him worse. It'll come off sooner or later, mark my words. And what if the jelly got out of his hands? What if one of the Sisters swallowed some and got sick? What would you say then?"

He looked dumbfounded. The *Sisters?* Two nights of sleeping curled up like a hunchback with his neck broken, two nights of waking up cotton-mouthed in a rumpled shirt, two nights of eating cold food at four in the morning. And now this — the pinhead sisters spooning petroleum jelly into their gummy mouths. Did this stupid woman really think little Herr Thumb would ever let the precious stuff out of his sight? He heard himself barking:

"Oh, just give the dwarf his goddamned grease, will you, Nurse? If one of the idiot sisters swallows some, she'll have the first normal bowel movement of her life!"

For a long moment Nurse Bosch said nothing. Her happy pig face had fallen to frowns. She folded the prescription slip, tucking it into the pocket over her breast.

"Very well, Herr Doktor."

She left him sitting in the hallway. They did not speak again for over a week.

He gave himself a limit of three days. But when no one on the staff seemed to care whether the patient starved to death or not, he let it go another day. And then another. Room 401 had a small sink in one corner, and once late at night he heard the tap going — so she was drinking at least.

The fifth day came. Again, he had fallen asleep around midnight and awoke at four. But he had Sunday off. Ah, to be home with Emma. A bath. A bed. A clean shirt . . .

The plate was gone.

Gone!

He wanted to shout, Look! Look, everyone! She's feeding herself. Feeding herself! He dashed off, trying to find someone, a witness, anyone. He found Orderly Zeik sound asleep outside the Incurable

Men's ward. Wonderful Zeik, snoozing away on a high backless three-legged stool, supported on no sides whatsoever. Amazing!

But he didn't pause long to admire Zeik's knack for comfort; he nearly tugged the orderly off the stool. The poor man first thought he was being punished for sleeping on duty. He fell plaintively to his knees and began to grovel for his job, mumbling, "Please, Herr Doktor, don't get rid of Zeik. Zeik won't fall asleep again. I promise to be good. Promise to stay awake . . ." And so on.

But after some sharp words, Zeik tucked in his shirt and groggily followed Herr Doktor back to the fourth floor. He had heard about the junior physician's new "therapy"; he wasn't stupid like everyone thought. The two of them stood in the stairwell a moment. Herr Doktor smoothed back the bristles of his crew cut, polished his glasses, and put them on again. At last he led the orderly into the hall.

The plate was in its usual place by the door.

"Oh, yes, I see," Zeik said, not seeing at all.

Herr Doktor almost rushed down the hall to throw the plate back into room 401. The orderly looked dumbly at him, pouting a little for being yanked off his stool. Herr Doktor didn't trust himself to speak without screaming. But he did manage to utter quietly, "Wait here a minute, please."

With every bone in his body screeching at him to bolt down the hall, he took his deliberate time and calmly walked to the plate before her door. Was it all a hallucination? Him, wanting to see the plate gone? Simply *overlooking* it when he woke? In his heart burned a little flame of hope. Maybe he wasn't wrong. Maybe . . .

He stooped and picked the cover off the plate. Then stifled a sob. But he knew he must show absolutely nothing — to anyone — or everything might collapse. There on the plate lay the scattered remains of a meal. It had been thoroughly wolfed down, with only little shreds of this or that left behind. He couldn't even tell what the meal had been. He swallowed several times before he spoke. . . .

"Zeik?"

"Yes, Herr Doktor."

"You are my witness. On the thirteenth of October, 1905, Fräulein Schanderein consumed her first meal in five and half days, between the hours of one and four in the morning."

"Yes, Herr Doktor."

From the tone of Zeik's voice, he knew the orderly was missing the significance of this. He may not have been aware that the victim had been refusing food. Or had taken the incredibly bold step of drawing the plate inside her room, eating it, and then putting it out for collection.

Zeik started for the stairwell in a hurry, obviously thinking him a little cracked. "Oh, and Zeik —"

The orderly ground to a halt.

"Sorry for waking you."

Zeik brightened, magnanimously. "Think nothing of it, Herr Doktor. Feel free, anytime."

For the first time in five days, Herr Doktor curled up in the puritan chair and really slept. Still sound asleep when the day shift arrived, but no one dared to wake him. Orderlies and nurses tiptoed around his spot. At last Nurse Bosch decided to do something about it. But since she was not on speaking terms with Herr Junior Physician, she found Zeik to do the job, sending him up to the fourth floor with the words: "Maybe we should get a double bed for the both of you."

Zeik chewed this over as he thumped upstairs. Could there be a conspiracy somewhere, its sole object the undoing of Orderly Zeik? Doctors and nurses in it together . . . ?

After much tugging and calling of his name, Herr Doktor finally came awake, smiling into Zeik's face as if it were the loveliest face in the world. Then he shot a worried glance down the hall. Ja, the plate sat just where he left it. . . . Herr Doktor rose from the chair, dragging the orderly by the wrist: just to be sure, just to be safe. They uncovered the lid from the plate. The meal had been eaten. Devoured. He peered closely into the orderly's soft apple eyes, asking:

"Well, I didn't eat it. Did you, Orderly Zeik?"

"Certainly not, Herr Doktor!" said the orderly in protest. "As I distinctly recall, you found me asleep!"

Zeik caught his breath, shocked at his own frankness.

Herr Doktor ignored the lapse. "Well, that settles it then. The girl ate it." He drew himself up proudly in front of her door and exclaimed, "Fräulein! I hope you enjoyed your dinner last night. I must admit I was getting worried. I shall return this evening as usual, but if you wish me to collect your chamber pot right now, I would be happy to do so."

He waited ten minutes. As no chamber pot emerged, he took the empty plate back to the kitchen. On the way past the orderlies' table, one of them turned to another and whispered something inaudible. The table rattled with laughter. The sound following him across the cafeteria all the way to the used-plate slot. . . . He had an image of himself hurling the empty plate back at them. But then he looked at the bare china in his hands. Carefully, he placed the girl's ravaged plate as the precious thing it was, upon a heap of soiled dishes.

For many days the ritual of fetching the victim's meals remained the same. Herr Doktor Jung set up permanent residency at the end of the fourth-floor hallway. How he managed his married life no one knew, but clearly he did manage it, for he always appeared in fresh clothes when he did rounds with Direktor Bleuler and company later in the morning.

"Nekken tells me young Fräulein has begun eating again. A good sign, no? When do you think you'll be able to examine her?" This as Direktor Bleuler tugged wearily at his beard, gazing at him from under heavy eyelids, a weary gaze that said, Come, come, don't waste our time with a lot of poppycock now.

"If God knows, he hasn't told me, Herr Direktor. And if he knows, he hasn't told her either. I wish he'd tell one of us."

Direktor Bleuler ran a thumb and forefinger into the crease of his beard. A dour smile. "Well, don't look at me, young fellow — the Almighty hasn't been to my office all week."

But suddenly the ritual did change. He noticed it immediately and was at a loss to account for it. Where once no plates went into the room while the girl refused to eat — now plate after plate vanished into 401 and none came out.

A casebook entry from that week:

> Fifth day since the change. Fräulein S has collected at least a dozen plates already. And while I can clearly see her chamber pot from the viewing slit, it appears virtually empty. I checked the garden below her window on the off chance she dropped her stools into the bushes. No luck. My guess is that a person eating sparingly would have perhaps one elimination every three

or four days. Maybe once in five. But if she kept them in her room, we'd be smelling them in the hallway by now. The patient must be forcing her feces down the drain in the sink. I suppose this is possible to do a little at a time using your fingers. I have not had the heart to try it myself — [Entry broken off.]

Entry a day later:

I tried *it*. With my own, naturally, and at home. Emma was not as put out about it as she might have been, though a considerable amount of explanation proved necessary. The explanations proved beneficial, however, for they completely took my mind off the revolting nature of the task and I found the whole business of messing about with the stuff had a calming effect, like modeling clay. One stops noticing the smell, especially as the water rinses it off your fingers. Cold water is essential, as warm water only cooks it.

The ritual remained the same for about another week and then changed again. During this period Herr Doktor had actually indulged in the luxury of going home to bed. Then, on the night of the change, Zeik, who was on duty, sent a message to his home at 3 A.M. The message ran: "Fräulein is giving back her plates. What should I do with them?" Herr Doktor was too confused to stumble back upstairs to bed again. So Fräulein gave them back — what the hell *should* he do with them?

He appeared on the fourth-floor hallway an hour later in a savage state of mind. "Did they come out one at a time, or did she push them out all at once? *Describe* how they came out the door, Zeik."

Zeik wrung his meaty paws, avoiding his eyes, then looked down the hall. He licked his lips as he stared at the plates outside 401 for some time.

"Well, Herr Doktor . . . ," he faltered. "Well, Herr Doktor . . ." Zeik seemed to want to make this his whole statement.

"You were asleep, then, were you, Zeik?"

"Yes and no, Herr Doktor," he said, fidgeting. Then, pleadingly, "You won't tell Nurse Bosch, sir? Will you, sir?"

"Out with it!"

Zeik began to fret, shifting from foot to foot. Then, "Herr Doktor, I know this may sound strange, but I might have dreamt it after all. I was dozing pretty lightly, sir, you know, with my eyes half open. I mean, sir, I *am* supposed to keep watch on things, even if I do steal a wink now and then. So I'd swear I saw her put the plates out first, sir, one by one. And then she put out the" — he began to search for the right word — "the presents. And then she put her presents out afterward, one on each plate."

He almost laughed out loud.

"Why do you call them presents, Zeik?"

"Well, they're wrapped, sir. Like presents, you know."

They were: just like gifts. From the score of plates Fräulein had collected in the last weeks, she had pushed thirteen outside the door of 401. Precisely the number of days from the moment the girl had begun to keep the things inside. And on each plate Fräulein S had made a deposit of feces, individually wrapped in a strip of bedsheet! He now saw the reason the room and hall had not smelled in all this time: Fräulein had avoided the meat and vegetables, eating only the potatoes. What she eliminated was not particularly full of waste products: toxins, acids, alkalines, half-digested fats — all the elements that produce a smell. But what made the gifts horrible was *how* they were wrapped.

Fräulein S had gone to some trouble molding her business: she gave each of the feces the shape of a little papoose, an infant, wider where the head would be and narrowing toward the toes. Wrapping each one as though in swaddling clothes, leaving an opening for the face. Even the swaddlings were wound to scale, with a tiny strip about the neck to bring out the slope of the shoulders. But oddest of all, she had contrived to make a bonnet or cowl over the face, cleverly pushing the fecal matter back with her finger. The result: an empty-hooded darkness. Thirteen wrapped phantoms. No wonder Zeik wished it were a dream. The orderly had plenty of time to contemplate their strangeness while waiting for Herr Doktor. Little infants made of feces, each wrapped in a cotton bedsheet, with a cowl making a shadowy void where the face should be.

"I guess she got them all ready beforehand, then put them out pretty quick," Zeik said. "Why do you think she'd give you dolls?"

Ah, clever question . . . But first, how *did* she make them? Had she done it under the mummy covers, in the stifling dark, by touch and feel? Timing her bowel movements until the very moment they were needed? Molding them in a strip of sheet, then wrapping the exact length of swaddling around that . . . All in secret in the thirteen days it took to make them?

Personal artifacts.

What else could you call them?

He was reminded of preserved bogmen found in English peat bogs, the brown leathery remains of druid sacrifice, the blank eyes staring up through a thousand years of mud. Thirteen meals and thirteen dead bodies, the product of her own insides. Food, dead babies, and her own feces.

Why assume they were dead?

No reason to.

And why thirteen? That seemed to ring a faint bell. He tried to recall if the parents said anything about the number thirteen. . . . Yes! He remembered now, a strange stroke of fortune. A few slips of paper had arrived at his desk from Accounting downstairs. The Schanderein bills. Bills they left without paying, which had been forwarded by their hotel to the hospital for collection. They ran to a hundred francs or so — a few nights on the town. Two expensive meals at the Storken Restaurant and a "liquor bill" from a well-known establishment, Der Geschmeichelte Kater — The Flattered Cat, a brothel. The establishment was located at number 13 Drosselmeierstrasse. But the girl couldn't know that. Just a coincidence. Yet the number 13 brought the parents to mind once more. How odd, really — Herr Schanderein had paid his daughter's bill three months in advance, but then this: the dun knocking on the door for a handful of coins. . . .

Forget them, then. Forget them. His struggle was not with the parents' erratic behavior but with the girl. With the girl's struggle.

So what of her creations? The hooded faceless shit babies. *Kotkindgeister.* The Ghost Children of Excrement. Her creations were faceless fecal infants in their swaddling clothes, made of the stuff of her own body. But whoever said they were dead? Her creations might represent anything: a childhood playmate who went away, a character from a story, a make-believe sibling — even something she had seen in a museum. Ask the smug Herr Doktor Nekken, and he would tell you the creations were the product of a demented mind, that they didn't represent anything.

The haunting thing about them wasn't the effort she lavished on their making, or the scaled precision of their shape — but the macabre effect of the cowl. How cleverly it revealed a shadowy void where the face should be. She could just as easily have chosen to fill it in, with a wad of paper or a button. . . . Why omit the face?

Some personal taboo?

He didn't pretend to know.

It reminded him of savages: How they hid a thing too sacred to be seen. How they forbade the speaking of a holy name. How their gods were often eyeless, mouthless, a smoothed-over blank cipher. For if you knew a god's face, then you owned him with your eyes. If you spoke his name, you possessed his soul. Greater the unseen power: as when the Hebrews forbade the making of a graven image. Not locked under a temple roof that might be set afire, or residing in the body of a statue, prey to thieves and vandals. But Unseen. Unconquerable. Forbidden even the writing of His name. For Yahweh meant nothing — comprising only the letters on either side of the ones that *made up* his name. The name of God invoked, a gap left in the alphabet where His Letters were removed. His was the void. His the hidden coils of sacred purpose. The untouchable likeness of soul: *I am that I am.* . . .

Herr Doktor stared silently at the faceless papoose babies on the plates. In a way, it all fit with the patient. She herself, wrapped and mummified — and so the images were wrapped. She herself, hiding her face — and so the Ghost Children had no face. Had she made a minuscule treasure of herself? How long had she been at the hospital? About seven weeks . . . God, how much longer it seemed — months and years almost. What was the girl trying to say? I am an infant. I am faceless. I am shit.

You're running in circles.

At his side, Orderly Zeik remarked sheepishly, "I think they're very well done," as if afraid he might be overheard having an opinion. Orderlies didn't have opinions.

"They *are* well done."

"Pity we have to throw them out."

135

He hadn't thought of this. They were made of feces; everyone would expect them to be disposed of. In his guts he knew this was wrong. The girl wouldn't want them thrown away.

"Zeik, get me a shoe box, some packing paper, and some string."

The orderly went, looking profoundly doubtful. But even if Herr Doktor didn't know what the Ghost Children meant, he did know what was proper and fitting to do. The orderly himself had been closer to the truth: they *were* well-made gifts. Not meant to be discarded. That she had only the contents of her room and herself to work with — remarkable! The Ghost Children were not to be thrown out.

At last Orderly Zeik returned with shoe box, packing paper, and string. Quite sure now, Herr Doktor planned to keep the things after all. . . . Not to disappoint him, the junior physician wrapped each one in a fold of packing paper and put it in the shoe box. Then the cover went on and the string was tied tightly around. Last of all, Herr Doktor labeled the box boldly with a pen:

Fräulein Schanderein
Rm. 401
Gift to Herr Doktor C. G. Jung
<u>Personal</u>

Afterward, he stood facing the patient's door, box in hand. Orderly Zeik, next to him, held the stack of plates like a waiter.

"Fräulein Schanderein," Herr Doktor called out. "I want to thank you for these . . ." For a second his mind went completely blank. These what? What should he call them? Just these, that's all.

"I can see you went to a lot of trouble to make *these*, and I want you to know I think them very fine. I've put them in a box for safekeeping and thought perhaps you might want to see how well they've been wrapped. If you don't object, I'll open the door and show you."

He waited several moments for a shriek of protest. Then hesitantly, gently laid his palm on the doorknob. The first time in a month . . . His hand was sweating. He twisted the knob and heard the latch slide free. He paused there, breathing long and deeply, waiting to see if Fräulein S would scream. The door eased open a crack, just wide enough for him to fit the shoe box through. He thrust his arm quietly into the patient's room without even trying to peek in the crack.

The box felt awkward and leaden, and soon his arm began to ache.

"There's a label on the box, which says they're a gift from you to me. If that's not right, I'll change it." He thought he heard the girl breathe. Her breath coming fast — but perhaps that was only himself. His arm grew weak. "I've also labeled it Personal, so no one will open this. I hope that's agreeable to you. . . ."

Again, nothing. It didn't matter — his arm was *in* the room. At last he withdrew the box and closed the door. He was shaking and half laughing to himself.

"Not a peep!" Zeik exclaimed, now totally in awe of Herr Doktor. Then, with a hint of suspicion, "She might have been sleeping, you know."

The words went through him like a dagger. "Ach, don't ruin it for me." The girl wasn't sleeping, he'd heard her quick breathing, hadn't he? He'd spoken loud enough to wake her, hadn't he? *Hadn't he?*

Tomorrow he would try to enter her room.

He would *try.*

Herr Doktor and Orderly Zeik marched down into the depths of the hospital, making directly for the meat locker behind the kitchen pantry, Zeik carrying the stack of plates thirteen high and Herr Doktor holding his precious shoe box with both hands. In unspoken agreement they didn't even stop to drop off the dirty dishes in the slop sink. But the meat locker was locked against them.

Herr Doktor went almost frantic. "You have a key, don't you?"

Now came Zeik's turn to show his supreme mastery of the ways of the place. His eyes clouded over with a bureaucratic glaze of obfuscation. Quietly muttering to himself, he put down the plates and jangled a ring of a dozen keys between his fingers. "Ah, Herr Doktor, you know the rules, ja?" He picked through the keys one by one. "The rules say only Herr Meister Küchenchef Prunk has the key to the meat locker. You know the staff are all thieves! Yes, believe me — they'd sell their mother for a slice of ham at two in the morning. Truly a shame no one can be trusted these days, ja?"

"Well, do you have the key or don't you?"

The meat locker door stood open. Herr Doktor nodded to the orderly and entered, going back to the coldest part of the refrigerator. There, on a high shelf, behind a stack of frozen meat patties, he placed the shoe box. He would give instructions in the morning for the box never to be touched. For a moment he stared up at the shelf, feeling the coldness of the wood-lined ice room sink into his limbs. His breath came as smoke. He heard the ice blocks near the door dripping drop after drop through the open cedar slats at his feet. He read the label he had written:

Gift to Herr Doktor C. G. Jung
Personal

How many months would her gifts sit on the shelf before he understood what they meant?

Behind him, in the less frigid reaches of the refrigerator, Orderly Zeik was happily paring slices of lamb from an immense joint. Zeik offered him a slice, but he shook his head. Herr Doktor wanted the last detail of this strange procedure perfect. He picked up the heavy stack of plates and went to dump them in the slop sink. They made a cheerful clatter, as if saying, So there!

"In my opinion," Zeik said with his mouth full, "Herr Meister Küchenchef Prunk makes a better side of ham. But I am forgetting the other important rule around here: Everything must be cooked precisely the same." Zeik finished his slice of the joint and pulled out his keys to secure the locker again. "But the first rule is really more important," he said as he locked the refrigerator and put the keys away. "Since no one in this hospital can be trusted around the supplies." And they both laughed.

He went home exhausted and took four hours' sleep. Toward the end of the night he had a ridiculous dream, in which he and Zeik were eating together in the cafeteria while Herr Meister Küchenchef Prunk served them portions of the patient's Ghost Children. The carving knife cut smoothly through one of the little wrapped infants, like slicing a salami. Already Zeik and he had eaten several of the relics, and they were delicious. But suddenly he wondered what the head tasted like: after all, it was void and empty. And how had Meister Küchenchef Prunk managed to cut a slice off this void? Zeik must have eaten that slice, he decided. Well, Zeik was empty-headed enough that eating a slice off the void wouldn't trouble him very much.

He should really lodge a protest, make Küchenchef Prunk understand that this was a gift, that they ought not to be eating it. Now

138

the master chef managed to cut a very tender morsel from the hooded, shadowy void of the cowled head and offered it to him. . . .

He woke up, saying, "No, thank you, I've really had plenty."

Behind the closed bathroom door he heard the shower running; his bedclothes felt damp and rumpled. He wanted to go back to sleep, but he knew he wouldn't. Too late now for easy sleep. As he dressed, he became more and more annoyed, irritably mumbling to himself, "No, I don't want to interpret it," as if to someone in the room.

He pictured the dusty dream book he had once offered the Schandereins as they sat in his office. It was nothing but an offering to himself: afraid that if he took on the girl, he'd need it before long. The success of the early-morning breakthrough meant nothing now. He had his arm inside the girl's room, but he no longer cared. All the pent-up misery of the past weeks churned in his stomach: the thought of the ten reports he had already written, the smirking orderlies, the happy pig Nurse Bosch, the smug condolences of Herr Senior Physician Nekken, the wordless, reproachful looks from Herr Direktor Bleuler every time he overslept and missed morning rounds. So! He had stuck his arm into the crazy girl's room without her tearing it off! Who noticed?

Who cared? Nobody! Nobody!

A printed page from the dream book stood out clearly in his mind. Chapter II, "Analysis of a Specimen Dream." So . . . nobody cared . . .

Except the man who had recorded that specimen dream in his book. That man would appreciate the significance of the early-morning breakthrough. He'd understand why Herr Doktor saved the ghost dolls in a cardboard box. And the meaning of his Eating Dream. And why he had to take the time to write it down.

Ach, but what a dismal dream. If he wrote it down now, he'd miss morning rounds again, with new "rumors" springing up: Did you hear, Wolfi? Herr Doktor caught an infection from the Victim in 401 by standing outside her door all night. Sleeping sickness. He's home in bed. . . .

Herr Doktor tried getting dressed. He tried tying his tie in the mirror but gave up on the fourth attempt, his face ashen, and slumped into an armchair. To think, an Eating Dream devouring him skin and bone. Yes, he'd probably miss rounds with Bleuler and company this morning. Already he had found a notepad and a pen.

*   *   *

139

He and Zeik were eating together.

For weeks he had been seeing to stupid tasks: cleaning chamber pots, running and fetching, bowing and scraping. So if Zeik and he were eating together, his dream had distilled reality down to the thought "You are what you eat." He was eating with an orderly. He was eating like an orderly. He was an orderly.

They were eating the Ghost Children.

Children. Plural. Wasn't it only one ghost child that truly concerned him? And how many problems neatly solved if Fräulein herself were nothing but a ghost? If dead and gone, she no longer suffered from nervous hysteria. And he no longer obliged to cure her. If dead, the girl would be free at last of her cruelest affliction — the painful condition of life.

He wondered what the head tasted like: after all, it was void and empty.

If only he could steal a taste from inside the girl's head. Know what she knew. Feel what she felt. If only . . .

How had Meister Küchenchef Prunk managed to cut a slice off the void?

How indeed! And who was the master chef anyway? The eminent Hofrats and pompous Herr Dozents of the university? The fine surgeons who lost every other patient on the table? The knowledgeable specialists, prescribing the same potion for every complaint? The bumbling Herr Direktor Bleuler? The goose-stepping Senior Physician Nekken?

He wanted to laugh and cry.

Because of course he knew one. There was always one. Not invited to the right soirees. Resigned from all the influential committees. Professionally ignored. Outcast.

Herr Master Chef *Freud* was the only man he knew to have cut a slice off the void. Discovering the Two Great Secrets: that hysterics concealed a method to their madness. And that dreams spoke in tongues the adept could master. Two secrets great enough to bring the world of men to their knees. Yet no one believed him. People said he paid his rent on the borrowed money of wealthy friends. By entertaining lonely middle-aged ladies with "therapies" for their innumerable and mysterious "female complaints."

Am I jealous? Is this envy?

140

Ah . . . the familiar burning at the back of the neck. The bitter longing. So how had Master Chef Freud done it? With his own dreams. Done it on the scraps flung at him from other men's tables. Done it with the dregs of his colleagues' referrals. With patients nobody else wanted.

A wild, sickly hope ran through Herr Doktor, like a lame man hobbling hurriedly down a crooked street. What the world ignored from one, another might reveal. Surely sooner or later the world must listen. Why not to him . . . ? Such ideas were mankind's property, not one man's alone. Why shouldn't he be the prophet, shouting the Word from out of the wilderness where Herr Freud had wandered lost all these years . . . ?

If fame came, and recognition, mightn't they share what there was to share? Herr Doktor's stomach burned.

What crazy thoughts were these?

To rob another man of his discovery. He felt exultant and horrid at the same time. Sitting alone in Zurich, sharing these secrets with a man who didn't even know he existed. Yet coveting them. God, he was despicable.

Zeik must have eaten a slice (off the void) . . . he was empty-headed enough so it wouldn't bother him.

Eating slices off the void didn't bother Zeik; just another way of saying Herr Orderly kept an open mind. Zeik — who called the Schanderein girl's creations "gifts." And Zeik again — who spontaneously felt pity at throwing the infant images away. Zeik — the intuitive one, the sympathetic one, saving Herr Junior Physician from a serious error. Putting Herr Doktor doubly in debt. Not only to the ignored man in Vienna but also to a floor orderly for showing him the proper way. So which one really had the empty head?

Suddenly he wanted to protest, make Küchenchef Prunk understand that this was a gift.

Who wouldn't want to lodge a protest with the proper authorities! The gift of insight given Master Chef Freud. The gift of mind reading given fluff-brained Orderly Zeik. The girl's gifts of her own personal artifacts. His eyes were watering, squeezing out hot, embarrassed tears. He had almost thrown out her gifts! What a blunder to have cast them away.

141

Had he no gifts? None of his own?

The notepad hung loosely in his hand, his pen fallen to the floor. All gifts were sacred, wrapped in packing paper, put in a box marked "Personal." Why hadn't he seen that the moment Fräulein put all those plates outside her door? She gave of herself and expected him to know her offering as sacred. My God, how *close* he had come to failing her!

Now Herr Meister Küchenchef Prunk had managed to cut a very tender slice off the hooded shadowy void of the cowled head and offered it to him.

Master Chef Freud cutting a slice off the void, drawing reason from chaos, spinning straw into gold. And soon it would be Herr Jung, offering up the cowled head of Fräulein Schanderein to one Herr Professor in Vienna. Finally defeated by the girl, until at last he surrendered and begged the older man for help. And in so doing, offering up his own head for examination. Oh, what a lovely tender slice might be taken from it! A tender slice carved from his own head and shown naked to the world. The last dread sacrifice . . . And now you must wake, Herr Junior Physician. Unless of course you wish to continue this cross-examination of your flawed character a little while longer?

"No, thank you. I've had plenty."

He sat in the bedroom, depressed and deflated. At some point he had mindlessly doodled an ugly sketch. The face of a screaming woman with a wild, open mouth, tangled hair, and bloody eyes. A Medusa face. He added some finishing touches — the malevolent line of her jowl, cruel crow's-feet about the eyes, a lick of the tongue, a glimmer of spittle. Whose nasty face was this? The girl's face, howling beneath the mummy covers?

No: the face of an unscrupulous plagiarist. The face of a worm, jealous of an orderly. The face of a nincompoop, ready to throw out a patient's precious gifts.

"Does she want me to wait outside the room forever?" he asked out loud. How much longer? Days, weeks — forever? He would make himself a statue waiting in the corridor of the hospital. Strong. Resolute. Quiet as stone. For sooner or later the door would slowly open. Even after eons, while the hospital rotted away to dust about the statue's feet, even if the door itself disintegrated. In the end she would

142

see him standing there, waiting for permission to enter. Waiting till she let him in.

What was there to tell the man in Vienna? That the girl shrieked? Hid her face? Made strange dolls out of her feces? No: now was the time to wait. Wait for the door to open.

Wait till he got inside her room.

Once again he stood outside 401.

"May I come in, Fräulein Schanderein?" he asked through the door.

At the end of the hall a new orderly sat in Zeik's accustomed place, Orderly Bolzen, a thick fellow with the neck of an ape and a heavy ridge of bone across his brow. Like Zeik, Orderly Bolzen seemed to have found the chair's secret, as if somehow all orderlies knew how to slouch for long periods of time in uncomfortable hard-backed chairs.

"May I come in, Fräulein?" Herr Doktor asked again. He recalled that in the past, her only answer to his questions was a steady silence.

In her silence he saw the nod of consent, as in, May I leave your meal beside the door? In her silence, her answer: Yes, you may.

"May I come in now, Fräulein?"

He opened the door and put his foot in the room.

The shriek went up for the first time in weeks, echoing all along the hall — her shriek answered by other patients in other rooms. Herr Doktor leaped back into the corridor and shut the door. Orderly Bolzen leered at him from the chair. The girl's shriek slowly dwindled inside 401. Then all along the floor the answering calls fell off. Finally the hall became quiet again, except for one patient weeping softly down at the end.

"Orderly, wipe that smile off your face," Herr Doktor said sternly, "or I'll have you assigned back to the dayroom." Bolzen dropped the leering grin.

Herr Doktor put his hand on the girl's door again.

"Forgive me, Fräulein. I suppose I should have asked first, 'May I open the door?'"

Again, only silence from the room.

He took a deep, shaky breath, then turned the doorknob. It creaked horrendously as the lock unlatched. A long silent yawn. He exhaled with a shudder that sounded like, Thank H-h-heaven. . . .

Fraction by fraction the door eased open. He gazed steadily down at his black shoes, not daring to look in. Afraid to break the silent spell by a callous glance, by any careless gesture. His head bowed in respect, hands by his sides, nothing more. He stayed that way for many minutes. . . . At last, when his heart slowed and his breath steadied, he spoke softly into the room. "May I look in?" he asked.

Nothing. He waited. Still nothing.

He raised his head. The mummy sat on the bed; the air in the room, stale and overused. The door stood open.

Chapter 7

Inside the Room

As the first weeks of November swept by, the leaves in the garden below the patient's window froze and shook themselves free. Scrambling over the garden wall, they scampered down windy streets. And as the garden's leaves blew off to other courtyards, foreign leaves from the wild countryside flew in to settle on the hospital grounds. Very little changed in 401.

Now the meals were brought at normal times. Often Herr Doktor did the bringing, and Zeik helped too, on time stolen from other duties. Orderly Zeik was the only other member of the staff allowed to set the girl's plates by the door and make the announcement that food had arrived. Thrice weekly the patient left her chamber pot right inside the door, indicating her desire for an empty one. Herr Doktor and Zeik took to carrying chamber pots with them when they brought her meals, not knowing which day she might yield up a filled one. Only in the middle of the night did Fräulein push her empty meal plates out into the hall and quickly shut the door. And so far the new night orderly, Bolzen, had not managed to catch her at it. He too liked to sleep at night — but denied it all around.

Herr Doktor assumed she washed herself in the sink, for the place would have smelled much worse if she hadn't. Yet as for the bedsheets, her wrappings, those hadn't been changed since she arrived: two months slept in, never washed.

Every day Herr Doktor went to room 401 and asked permission to enter. Every day came the mute silence and the ten-second pause while he gave the patient time to change her mind. And every day he opened the door, putting her meal on the floor, asking, "May I come in?" But always — a shriek in answer. He might look, but not enter. No crossing the threshold. He stood at the door.

"Maybe tomorrow then," he always said. "Perhaps tomorrow."

He lost count of the days and stopped looking at the calendar. November passed into December. He stopped reading the newspaper. Or answering his mail. He abandoned his casebook and moved through his duties as though in a daze. The rounds with Bleuler and company seemed endless; he made sensible responses to questions he hadn't really heard. He lost Herr Tom Thumb's petroleum jelly appeal — and didn't care. He was assigned two New Victims by Senior Physician Nekken: young women with nervous paralysis of the legs. He cured one when she admitted her uncle had been sexually abusing her. The other miraculously shuffled along after galvanic treatments to the hips. A treatment she herself insisted upon. Herr Doktor suspected a tumor at the base of her spine, but his diagnosis was rejected. Both women left in high spirits. Nekken congratulated him on his success; he didn't even remember their names. He had forgotten there was anything but the black-and-white-checkered marble floor leading from the stairwell to the door of 401. Forgotten who he was, except for the twenty seconds when he stood at her door, asking, "May I come in?"

And then it came. The nothing silence of consent. His neck stiffened, bracing for the shriek. He flinched anyway, almost saying out of habit, "Maybe tomorrow, then."

But the silence drifted from the room, while he heard the faint noises of the hospital all around him — two nurses calling each other in the garden, the whir of hard rubber wheels as an orderly pushed a cart down the hall, the incoherent whine of another patient, complaining. Had he given Fräulein Schanderein enough time to change her mind? Who knew? He went through the door and stood there, head bowed. Leaving the door open.

Silence.

"May I close the door now?"

Again silence; he counted to ten, pausing once to ask, "May I?" And when he reached the full ten, he closed the door behind him. God, he didn't even know today's date! No later than the second week of December. His eye strayed to a naked tree bending outside the girl's window. A few faded maple leaves clung on, refusing to let go. The sun slanted across the mummy's shoulder. Shredded rags of white clouds fled into a blue sky. He was alone with her.

Alone.

An immense blackness settled on him like chimney soot; a weight too, like a wet overcoat. . . . He listened for her breathing. She sat on the bed, knees to chest, exactly as he had seen her that first time. Seeing her so unchanged made him limp and watery, daunted by the power of her will to remain of stone. Only he himself had changed over the passing months. The blood seemed sucked from his limbs; he felt his legs going out from under him.

"May I sit down?"

Nearby stood a hard-backed chair, brother to the one at the end of the hall. As he slumped down, the figure on the bed began to gasp:

"Ah —! Ahh —!" building to a crescendo, in half a moment to a full-blown shriek.

"Never mind." He leaped to his feet, shoving the chair to the wall. Then paused awkwardly, his hands hanging foolishly at his sides. He let the seconds tick by . . . afraid he'd wreck it now if he said the wrong thing.

At last he said, "May I introduce myself? I'm Doktor Jung. I'm your doctor." The blockish idiocy of the remark . . . she might not even know she was in a sanatorium.

"Your parents brought you to the Burghölzli Mental Hospital. You've been in this room for about three months. In the beginning ing I meant to ask if you were comfortable, but, well —" He shrugged, admitting, "I still haven't examined you." He was speaking too hurriedly, his voice a note too high. He tried to speak slower. "If you're not comfortable, I'll see you get whatever you need. If I'm not acceptable, perhaps you'd like to choose another physician. . . ."

If the mute thing on the bed understood a word, it made no sign. He forced himself to speak evenly and clearly.

"I apologize for not realizing sooner you wanted the room to yourself. I hope I come to understand things better as we go along."

He had run out of ideas.

"Would it be all right if I came to see you tomorrow?"

*   *   *

Every day he returned. The routine repeated. First the announcement in the hallway: "Fräulein Schanderein, I have brought your meal. May I open the door?"

Then, standing in the open portal, "May I come in?" Then, once inside, "May I close the door?" And finally, "May I sit?" To each question came the mute answer, during which he counted to ten, bracing for the coming shriek, his nerves on razor's edge. And then, when the silence of consent lay before him, he always replied, "Thank you," into the hush.

On the third day after his gaining entry, she allowed him to sit in the uncomfortable chair. Within several days, the various "May I"s had been condensed into only two: May I come in? and May I sit? On the eighth day, he glanced through the viewing slit in her door to see her standing by the window. At first he feared some new change had occurred in the night that would prevent him from entering — and only with the greatest strain did he ask, "May I?"

But no screech came and in twenty seconds he sat before her in the uncomfortable chair that dug into his ribs with wooden fingers.

Fräulein Schanderein stood in the corner, cloaked head to toe in two blankets clutched together. Outside her window the branches of the maple tree shivered in the wind. An ice storm the night before had lacquered one side of the tree trunk so it glistened with ice. The midday light turned the tree's frozen sheath to silver, with blue sky reflected along the bark. No more leaves clung to the tapered branches, just bare translucent fingers. Was she looking at the beauty of this too?

He glanced at the bed. The sheets, free at last of her body, were yellowed and grayed with constant use. He saw the place where she had torn the strips of swaddling to make the gifts. Almost a perfect square hole in the center of the top sheet. Most amazing. She'd done it without scissors or shredding the sheet completely. He must try it at home sometime. But why give up the sheets now?

He almost laughed. Of course, of course!

"Ja, Fräulein — it's about time, no?"

He got up and said, "May I take them off the bed?" The briefest pause. "Very well, I'm going to take them off the bed." He stripped the mattress, wrapping her sheets into a damp ball.

"And may I go to the door, ja?"

He opened the door.

"Bolzen! Come here, please."

Apelike, Bolzen lumbered to the door. He tried to peek around Herr Doktor into the room.

"Bolzen, I didn't ask you to stare into Fräulein's room."

Bolzen latched his eyes to Herr Doktor's tie, then took the yellow sheets as they were thrust into his paws.

"Please have these washed and ironed and returned within the hour. I'll wait for them here."

"Very well, Herr Doktor."

Bolzen disappeared. The girl and he were alone once more. She had not strayed from the window. And now he realized he had sat without asking permission. The sun had shifted, making the ice on the bark gray and opaque. A peculiarly splayed branch reminded him of something. It looked so familiar, the way the taloned fingers curved and hooked. For some reason he imagined Orderly Bolzen doing the washing and ironing. Bolzen in a white apron and washerwoman's dress, Bolzen sweating over a hot iron . . . And then he recalled the dancing animals that ran around the border of his childhood room. My God, he hadn't thought of them in years. Wasn't there a dancing bear in a pink tutu? Bolzen the bear. Wasn't there a monkey too? What was the monkey supposed to be? Oh yes, he remembered now: the monkey was a doctor in a white coat with a stethoscope.

What did those taloned branches remind him of? It had something to do with his childhood room. Or a dream . . .

Bolzen knocked on the door. He had returned with the sheets. The hour had passed. He took the sheets from the orderly; they smelled fresh and starched. He began to spread them over the bed, first the bottom sheet, then the top —

The hairs on his neck rose. Something wrong. Wrong with the sheets. He felt the mummy stir and gasp, "Ah —! Ahh —!" building to a howl.

Wrong sheets! No hole in the top!

Bolzen had given him a fresh pair, not the same pair. These weren't *her* sheets. The gasps came faster now. "Ah —! Ahh —! Ahhh —!" Soon a shriek.

"I'll get them! I'll get them!" he stammered. "Wait! Just wait a moment!" Frantically he tore the fresh sheets off the bed and plunged headlong into the hall. Orderly Bolzen was reading a magazine in the chair. He looked up, surprised to see Herr Doktor barreling down on him with the sheets balled in his fists. "Where are the sheets?! These aren't her sheets! Give me her sheets!" Bolzen sat in the chair, too startled to argue.

Herr Doktor plucked the magazine from his hand and flung it aside. He shook the balled sheets under the orderly's nose. "What were you doing for an hour? Sleeping? Drinking? These are new sheets from the linen room. Not the ones from her bed!"

Bolzen tried to say, "Yes, yes, they are —" But Herr Doktor hammered him down. "Where's the hole? There's no hole!" Bolzen cowered. He didn't know — God, he didn't know.

"So we're going to find her sheets," Herr Doktor ordered. "Wherever they are. In the laundry room. In the wash bags. The tubs. The baskets. Right now!"

Bolzen found himself dragged off the chair by his coat lapels and plunging down the stairs. Madly trying to remember! What the hell did he do with those damn sheets from 401? Did he even bring them to the laundry, or did he throw them away somewhere? What had he done after that bolt of schnapps from his bottle in the boiler room?

They turned the laundry upside down — tearing through the baskets of sheets and towels, fishing through the sopping tubs, dumping out the stuffed wash bags. They scrounged the lower depths of the hospital like rats, until Bolzen finally remembered where he had tossed them. Mashed in a corner, near the black, oily door to the boiler.

Herr Doktor marched the orderly and the sheets back to the laundry. All other work came to a halt. The sheets with the odd square hole were bleached and washed and ironed dry. Orderly Bolzen looked uselessly on.

In thirty minutes they were back outside room 401. Inside the room you could hear the faint gasping, "ah — ah — ah —" as the girl waited for their return. She kept gasping as Herr Doktor made the bed. He put the sheet with the hole on top and smoothed out the wrinkles.

"I'm leaving now," he said.

The mummy's faint gasps faded away. For a moment they stood together in silence. Outside the window, the sun had shifted again, turning the ice-clad tree shiny black. The branches were like antlers.

Ah yes, *antlers* . . . In his father's house. Antlers on a plaque over Nanny Sasha's bed.

Before Herr Doktor left for the evening, he went once more to the girl's room and stared through the viewing slit. She had the sheets off the mattress and twined about herself. She draped the one with the hole over her shoulders like a poncho, while wrapping her head in the folds of the other, making the whole getup some kind of eyeless burnoose. But in a trick of the light or her clever winding, Herr Doktor saw a black hooded cowl where her face ought to be, a shadowy void instead of wound sheets.

When he got home that night, Herr Doktor had a glass of whiskey from a bottle his wife, Emma, kept in the parlor for guests. He never drank much, so the stuff slid into him like a liquid club and he slept the whole night through in a black sleep.

The "incident" with the sheets took up more than thirty minutes of his time. The head of the Orderly Section protested. The old washerwomen in the laundry room protested. There were even protests from other physicians when they found their private patients in an agitated state later that day. And to top it off, Junior Physician Jung had lost his temper at a valued member of the staff. Shame on him.

His Note-of-Procedure regarding it all promised to be a small book in length. The whole point of which boiled down to why young Herr Doktor thought this highly uncooperative girl (who had yet to utter a single word in four months) was more partial to one set of bedsheets over another.

Somewhere in his justification he disclosed the nature of Fräulein's gifts in the hospital's meat cooler. The result? Yet another protest from the kitchen staff. Why did the girl's excrement have to be kept, and kept in the kitchen? Another report. Through it all Herr Doktor tried to demonstrate the establishment of a limited, slim line of communication with the creature. And some members of the executive staff even disputed this, saying that most of Herr Junior Physician's claims of dialogue were mere stuttered salvos fired at a mute imbecile. Or worse, that Herr Doktor was only talking to himself. And yet . . . here he was saved.

Since in all fairness the patient's original condition *had* changed since her entry to the hospital, and in view of Herr Junior Physician's outstanding record so far at the Burghölzli . . .

Direktor Bleuler kept all the reports and various protests on his desk in a single pile tied with a blue ribbon. And there the pile languished in an impenetrable lump.

Another note had dropped on the top of the pile. This one from the hospital librarian, reporting that Herr Doktor was checking out an inordinate number of medical texts. Should anyone call for them, the texts were most likely in his possession. In fact, he had already informed her not to expect one book returned and had paid full price for it — Kohl's *Biology*, a standard text for first-year medical students.

How curious . . . what could Jung possibly want with a first-year medical text? the Direktor wondered.

Herr Doktor had brought Fräulein Schanderein Volume I of Kohl's *Biology* and left it by her meal plate on the floor. How dismaying then, the next day to see its cover torn off and pages missing. But he had the feeling her act of destruction established her possession over the thing. As she had with her room, her body, the food she ate, her excrement. And now the book he gave her. For if a book was damaged, clearly it could no longer be returned and must remain.

He brought her other books: Leaman's *Anatomy*, Grunfeld's *Neurology*, Elsen's *Psychology* (a very thin text), but she never touched them. They stood in a stack by the door.

Then one day as he made to leave he heard the sound of a heavy book falling to the floor. She had pushed a thick volume out from under the covers. The anatomy text. Here again the book had been handled, the pages folded or crushed, the spine cracked.

Reading . . . ?

"You know, Fräulein, I'd be happy to get you any *sort* of book." But the girl said nothing, made no sign. He thought of a trained chimpanzee given a fork and spoon by its master. The chimp eats with the spoon for a while, then sticks it up his nose. The audience howls. Was she like that, dumbly pawing the pages of the books he brought her?

December had been unusually mild. A dusting of fallen snow had all but melted. With the window closed, the air in room 401 began to get fetid. Perhaps Fräulein S had ceased to wash from the sink; he smelled the tang of her perspiration. One day in the middle of

152

December, he went to remove her chamber pot, as usual. But now the mummy on the bed began to shake and tremble, gasping, "Ah —! Ahh —! Ahhh —!" So he hastily put the pot back in its place on the floor. It was about a quarter full, with a mixture of stool and urine.

The gasps came again when he tried to remove her meal plate. And so he left the partly eaten meal on the floor. The onset of a new stage? That night he wrote in his case notes:

> Is she hoarding in preparation for some new gifts or artifacts? I think the patient's diet is too varied now for any creations. If she means a message here, I am deaf to it. If a signal, blind to it. I wait on her pleasure. . . .

Chapter 8

A Parade of Chamber Pots

When he looked at the last sentence of his case notes, he wondered if there was not something to it after all. Yet what was he waiting on? Should he write the man in Vienna? With a dull ache in his throat and a leaden hand, he began to draft his letter to Herr Freud . . . but after only a few lines abandoned it, a scrawl of unfinished phrases. The curtains in his hospital office were drawn tight against the cold. Soft creakings came against the glass, soft patters. He drew back the curtains and saw the moon shine briefly through torn clouds. The silvery light caught the snowflakes as they leaped upon the glass panes before their ghostly vanishing. . . . The mahogany wainscoting of his walls and the dark beams on the ceiling shone redly. He sat in an armchair of dark-green leather, as if in a quiet grove of trees, while the snow whirled without.

What kind of tale to tell? A child's toilet-training tale. *Wunderbar* . . .

He opened the window a crack. A few flakes danced into the room, holding their form for a moment before melting on the sill. So it was to be a snowy Christmas. And ja, he wanted to get her something, but what? Good question. What do you get a girl who has nothing? Some people in the hospital said openly Fräulein had made no headway whatsoever. That everything Herr Doktor claimed was an illusion. He folded his arms over the desk and rested his head. A snowflake blew into the room and coldly kissed the back of his neck.

*   *   *

After two more days her single chamber pot nearly brimmed over. Several dishes were strewn over the floor, overlapping each other. God, the smell! You got whiffs of it in the hall. And when inside the room, you breathed in shallow puffs. After twenty minutes it became unbearable. And then the flies! Three or four little black devils. In December! Amazing!

He hoped these were the adventurous few lured up from the warm, dark reaches of the basement, where they lived all year round, and not some winter breed, spawned from maggots in the meat. They were puny, drowsy things, buzzing lazily over the patient's refuse. One always crept across the top of his shoe. Whenever he flicked his foot it flew off, then darted back. How he hated them!

"May I get you another chamber pot?" he finally asked, having at last the sense to think of it.

Now came the long open-ended pause he had almost grown used to, the silence saying, Leave it here and get me another one. So after a few more moments he rose, going to the door and calling out:

"Bolzen, *Achtung!* Please fetch another chamber pot. Thank you."

A little while later, Bolzen came back with a clean chamber pot made of polished brass, with a broad lip curving inward so someone could squat comfortably. When Bolzen knocked, Herr Doktor announced, "I am going to open the door now. Bolzen has brought a fresh chamber pot." As the door swung open, the smell struck the big orderly physically, a spasm of revulsion wrinkling his face. He thrust the chamber pot into the room blindly and stomped down the hall without waiting to be dismissed.

The smell was that bad, then. . . . Perhaps he had grown used to it. Better expect another protest soon and be ready with another report. He thought he caught a flicker of movement on the bed. He felt minutely examined, peered over, as if the patient was staring with one eye through a clever fold in the sheet. But when he looked directly at her, he saw nothing but the sightless burnoose.

He wanted to believe she looked at him on the sly, that she noticed him. How he tried to make everything right for her, how he tried to anticipate her every need and whim. What needs? What whims? The girl never said. He was guessing.

All at once the putrescence of the room overwhelmed him, as

155

though a hundred drowsy flies were settling on his bare skin. He had heard people got used to flies crawling over them — but refused to believe it. He stood, weak and pale all over.

"May I come tomorrow?" he asked.

The next day was worse. . . .

A new nurse, one Fräulein Simson, came on duty. She had been with the Burghölzli a week, having recently come from one of the public wards in the city. On the public wards she had learned mostly how to ignore patients calling her names and making lewd suggestions. Tired of it at last, she had hoped to find a more refined position under the eminent Herr Direktor Bleuler. And so far young Nurse Simson had been lucky, tending mostly to the cooperative paying patients on the fourth floor. Easy patients, whose wealthy families preferred them not to languish at home, the kindly sad ones . . . And so Nurse Simson felt sorry for the "poor dears" having to sit alone every day in a tiny room in a big stone hospital.

And since fetching meals and making beds had been her business up till now, she extended that business to the poor Schanderein girl in 401, despite the standing orders given by the extremely odd Herr Doktor Jung. So Nurse Simson went herself to fetch poor Fräulein's meal, adding an extra covered dish to the stack of plates destined for the fourth floor. Back upstairs, she unloaded the dumbwaiter, piling the plates on a cart, and started her rounds with room 401, at the end of the hall.

Calmly, then, she fetched the meal for 401. Calmly she opened the door and entered. Calmly she tried to ignore the overpowering smell. Calmly she tried to ignore the patient's gasps, which shortly turned to howling shrieks. Calmly she tried to set the place to rights, attempting to carry out a few dishes, make off with a brimming chamber pot. Calmly she even tried to make the bed. But in the screaming room, it appeared Nurse Simson had gone berserk. Completely rattled, like a mannikin imitating the movements of a real person. A puppet, jerked about — stooping and stopping, fetching and putting down — never finishing a task she set out to do.

In the end she managed one thing only, to collect a few of the dirty dishes. And she almost made off with them, but for the full plate of food thrown at her head as she opened the door. Nurse Simson saw a flicker of the patient's arm out of the corner of her eye — and then

156

the plate exploded against the wall, covering her with splinters of glass and flecks of hot stew. She dropped the dishes and fled.

They called Herr Doktor to the nurses' lounge, a dingy room on the third floor. Nurse Simson was being comforted by Nurse Bosch. Nurse Bosch seemed to revel in this role, for she had taken young Fräulein Simson right into her arms and pressed her face to her bosom, stroking the back of the sobbing girl's head. She reminded Herr Doktor of a dowager cat mothering a bedraggled kitten. Nurse Bosch shot him a glance that said, See! See what you've done!

He noticed a dark-colored stain running down young Simson's white starched uniform — feces or food? The skin of Nurse Simson's neck was mottled bright red. When she tore her face away from the great mothering cleavage, she gulped air between sobs and spat, "She's the devil! The devil's in that room. The devil!" in a shrill, pointy voice — and then went back to sobbing between Nurse Bosch's breasts.

Herr Doktor felt another protest coming. . . . As things turned out, Nurse Simson left the Burghölzli the very same day. But he still had to answer the business in writing.

"And why didn't anyone stop her?" Herr Doktor demanded.

Nurse Bosch and Orderly Bolzen stood in the hall outside 401. Echoes of the turmoil fled into the stairwell, escaping from the fourth floor. The patients along the corridor were still moaning and wailing, laughing and singing, calling for their doctors or arguing with long-dead relatives. And underneath the din came the rising and falling "Ah —! Ahh —! Ahhh —!" of the sobbing young woman in 401. How many days till the girl returned to the way he had her before that idiot Nurse Simson barged into her room? How would they ruin it all next time?

Neither Bosch nor Bolzen replied. Herr Doktor tried to reason with them. "It's about treating the girl decently. Respecting all the little things we take for granted. That no one will disturb us on the toilet. That we can sit and eat at peace. You think her habits revolting? If you didn't, our good Doktor Nekken would slap you in room 402, next door. But that doesn't give anybody the right to barge into hers. . . . We can't help the girl and fight each other at the same time. Tell me, when will she realize we meant her no harm today?" He halted. Orderly Bolzen stared dumbly at the floor. Nurse Bosch's eyes had snuffed out like candles, the lines of her face darkening with resentment. He suddenly saw what she disliked about him. His fair good looks. His take-it-or-leave-it manner. The fact that he bossed her around. But most of all how he called her attitude into question. As though she didn't know the first thing about crazy people. This was going about it wrong.

He tried another approach.

"A physician's standing order regarding his patient was broken today," he said. "Surely, Nurse Bosch, you know no one is allowed in Fräulein's room?" A short, irresolute silence elapsed as Nurse Bosch considered this. "Do you think we might have Orderly Zeik back on this floor during daytime hours?" Herr Doktor suggested mildly.

The dim lights in Bolzen's eyes flared to life like grimy lamps. . . . Asking Zeik back — what an unforgivable insult! Bringing Bolzen's own record and seniority into question. Somehow it had gotten around that Junior Orderly Zeik had rendered special "services" to Herr Doktor — i.e., gaining entry to the kitchen meat locker. Zeik was now spending six months on waste disposal in the bowels of the building. The Orderly Section sending out a message to all concerned: junior nobodies were in no position to do anyone favors.

Nurse Bosch gazed into Herr Doktor's cool gray eyes. She must make him an answer: a standing order had been broken, a patient disturbed, and a Burghölzli physician's treatment temporarily halted due to the inattention of the staff. A price must be exacted. God . . . Bolzen was going to hate her for all eternity.

Slowly Nurse Bosch said: "Well, we'll see what we can do about your request, Herr Doktor. In the end Orderly Bolzen and Orderly Zeik may have to swap shifts. It can't be arranged all in a minute."

"I understand," Herr Doktor replied.

Done. Bolzen would leave the floor.

By the end of the day, the spot on the wall where Fräulein Schanderein threw the plate at Nurse Simson had dried, a long streak of decayed food smeared from shoulder height almost to the floor. In the coming days the streak would remind Herr Doktor of dried blood.

Once again, five days passed since Fräulein S began refusing to yield up her meal plates and chamber pots. If the mummy wanted to keep them, fine, she could have them. Half a dozen plates lay scattered in their congealed grease about the floor. . . . He had even stepped on one by mistake and nearly broken his ankle. But the mummy showed nothing, and he had difficulty during his visits not to stare continually at the chamber pots slowly filling up.

A few more days passed, and each day he inspected the condition of the receptacles on the floor of her room. Then going to the door and announcing, "Orderly Zeik! Another chamber pot, please!" Or whatever was needed. He no longer asked for permission to rise and go to the door — he just went ahead and did it. Perhaps a small omen of change.

On the eighth day, Nurse Bosch appeared personally with a clean chamber pot.

"Something wrong, Nurse Bosch?"

"Nothing, Herr Doktor. Zeik was having some trouble finding fresh ones. Our supply is not unlimited, but I knew where a few extras were kept."

The gesture touched him, and he bowed to her. "Danke, Nurse Bosch."

She handed him the polished brass chamber pot with a simple "Bitte." Nothing showed in her face, though the sickly smell of the room flowed like a heavy fog in the hallway, almost liquid . . . Nurse Bosch nodded her head once in parting, then turned smartly on her heels as if to say, I am up to this — this and anything else. She might just as easily have appeared empty-handed, with excuses instead of a chamber pot: So sorry, Herr Doktor, we've run out. But she made it her business to find him one, gone out of her way. He had the feeling that if he asked Nurse Bosch into the room to sit with him that moment, she would have come. Even known enough to ask Fräulein for permission to enter. And known enough to wait for the silent answer. Something had changed between them.

She moved.

The mummy on the bed moved. Right in front of him. Ja, he was sure of it. Fräulein S was moving. . . .

He froze to the chair, gripping the seat with both hands, as if someone had stuck an icy thumb up his behind. Even when she wanted her wrappings washed, he always found her standing in the corner by the window, with the blanket tucked around her, like a mannikin in a store waiting to be put in place.

159

But now her limbs were moving, rippling the sheets. She unwound like a snake. . . . First her foot came out. It reached over the bed to gently touch the floor. A grimy, dirt-streaked foot. The toenails almost black, long and curved, tremendously thick. Months had passed since anyone bothered to clip them — long before Fräulein's entry into the Burghölzli. Her rough toes crept along the floor, wavering like insect antennae. The stubby faces of blind worms, sniffing ahead, searching. The big toe of the foot touched the smooth surface of a chamber pot. Sniffed along one side, then crept around the other . . . Her dirty toes found a point close to the middle and shoved the half-full pot a few inches in the direction of his chair.

The contents sloshed a little, threatening to spill. The foot disappeared into the folds of the covers. The mummy moved no more. Herr Doktor stared at the chamber pot. The toes said, Take it. Take it away. He picked the thing up; maggots waved in the sloppy stuff. Before leaving he paused in the door and said:

"Thank you, Fräulein."

The next day she pushed another pot toward him with her toe; and the day after that, another. Offering up the putrid contents of her room.

The dirty meal plates too . . . Nurse Bosch came to the door without his having to call, solemnly bearing off whatever he gave her. On the sixth day of Fräulein's change, Herr Doktor asked the girl:

"May I introduce Nurse Bosch and Orderly Zeik? They have helped us in this matter. Carrying chamber pots, washing sheets, and so forth. They are waiting outside."

The long pause, the answer of silence.

When the door opened, Nurse Bosch tucked up her white skirt a fraction, crossing one leg behind the other in a smart little curtsy. She probably hadn't curtsied since she was ten.

"A pleasure to meet you, Fräulein. I hope I have been of some service."

Then Orderly Zeik bowed gravely, clicking his heels. "Enchanted," he said.

The mummy on the bed of course made no sign. Within four more days, Nurse Bosch and Orderly Zeik were allowed in the room for various purposes: to bring fresh chamber pots, to take away dirty dishes, to strip the bed, wash her sheets, and return them. The floor

160

was scrubbed and the room aired. But when Orderly Zeik made to wash the crusty streak from the wall, the mummy gasped, "Ah —! Ahh —!" and Zeik left off. The crusty streak would stay.

In the week between Christmas and New Year's, Herr Doktor bought her a present. A dozen sprigs of hothouse freesia, which he placed in a vase on her dresser. Some a royal shade of purple and others butter-cream yellow. They must have come from a very lusty hothouse, for they filled the room with a sugary-sweet smell like apricot jam. When Herr Doktor had seen them in the flowershop, he thought at once of Fräulein Schanderein. Their color glowed so violently and their smell was so mouth-watering — it must have taken the rankest dung to fertilize such a sweet, sugary flower. Their price stunned him, but he bought the buds anyway.

January came, and a brief week of January thaw, when the bleak winter sky warmed, the ice melted, and the earth breathed. People thought of spring and took off their heavy overcoats. Old wives said this was when the winter killed you: you ran outside without a coat, caught a cold, and died. But who lived his whole life listening to old wives? Herr Doktor's coat came off, and he ran around like everybody else.

Nurse Bosch and Orderly Zeik were now regulars in room 401 and performed their duties with little effort and hardly a thought. They barely noticed Fräulein Schanderein, the girl being merely a mummy who sat on the bed. Insignificant and of no concern.

Herr Doktor caught a cold that lasted three weeks and almost killed him. At the start of his Old Wives' Revenge, he ignored his own advice — "Stay home, you're getting sick" — and went to work anyway. What a wicked, vicious old wife of a cold which either stuffed his head and wouldn't let him breathe or sent mucus running out his nose so that he used a dozen handkerchiefs a day. The skin around his nostrils turned red and sore, his eyes puffy. And as the cold grew worse, he felt as if people shied away from him in the corridors, while a year's worth of poison oozed from his system.

The girl's Christmas freesias had dried to sad tatters. Gone their lively scent, or was it his sense of smell? The distance between himself and Fräulein S seemed to increase by the layers of cotton wool encasing his head. When he left 401 after his usual twenty minutes,

161

Nurse Bosch waited for him at the end of the hall with a chamber pot in her hand. She showed him its contents, swirling a puddle of urine around. His ears were clogged; her voice seemed far away.

"No bowel movement," she said evenly.

The empty chamber pot didn't bother him as much as the scratchiness in his throat, which no amount of honey tea seemed to help. "Well, do you go every day?"

"I," said Nurse Bosch with some authority, "am *not* the patient."

"So log it on her chart."

Nurse Bosch frowned, clearly dissatisfied with his lack of reaction, but visions of the cafeteria and more honey tea danced in his head. He cleared his throat, croaking, "What do we know about her? Nothing! First she won't let anyone in her room — then it's all right. Next she won't have her meal plates inside — now it's okay. Then she won't let anyone remove her things — but now we take them out!"

His voice was as harsh as a magpie's. "What can I tell you, Nurse Bosch? You know as much as I do. So last night she forgets to have a bowel movement. What should we do? Call out the fire brigade? If she doesn't go in a week, I'll start to worry."

Through all this Nurse Bosch stared at him imperially from the head of the stairs, chamber pot in her hand. "I shall log as you instruct," she said stoically. "I hope you feel better tomorrow, Herr Doktor."

The next day he felt worse. At home, Emma said to him, "Here, drink some orange juice for your head and eat some prunes with cream. How many days since you went to the —"

"You too!" he snapped. "You're getting to sound like Nurse Bosch." His wife hadn't the faintest idea what he was referring to.

"I see," she said.

At the hospital, he met Nurse Bosch coming out of the room with the chamber pot.

She showed him its contents. "Nothing."

The cold had gone to his throat and he could hardly whisper, "Two days, then. Sometimes my wife and I don't go for a week."

He shocked Nurse Bosch with that one. Proper folk never talked about themselves or their wives. The nurse bore off the pan, saying, "Consider prunes. . . ."

And the next day he met Nurse Bosch again, exactly as before. Now he couldn't even talk; his head felt stuffed with moldy bricks.

"Where does she keep it?" the nurse asked him. A daring remark for the old sow, but he hadn't the wit or whistle to reply. Late that afternoon, he checked the patient's sink for signs she sent her bowel movements out that way. And then went outside in something of a blizzard to check the ground below her window, as he had done some months before. Of course, he found nothing. He thought he would die that night when he got home. He felt light-headed. He knew he had something of a fever but didn't want to take his temperature. He sat in bed and drank honey tea, whose waxy taste was starting to nauseate him. In the morning he had just a bad cold again.

On that day Nurse Bosch deftly swirled the chamber pot and remarked without expression, "This is not healthy."

"Could you bring tea to my office?" he asked in a bare whisper.

Three more days passed. It had been a week — the magical "week" he had so blithely joked about. At home, Emma sat at breakfast eating prunes and cream as if to mock him. He glowered at her when she offered him some. "I'm doing just fine," he wheezed.

The girl ate too, if you could believe that. The food on her plates disappeared every day. My God, she must be tight as a drum. . . . That night he dreamt that when he blew his nose he had the most magnificently formed and satisfying bowel movement out his nostril. He had woken at 6 A.M. laughing and promptly passed out again in the act of wiping a crust of mucus from his lip.

At the nurses' station in the hospital, Nurse Bosch was also feeling slightly sick. Herr Senior Physician Nekken had chosen this day to come around. And for ten minutes he gazed torpidly at Fräulein's chart from under his pale-lidded eyes. Nurse Bosch pretended to work on some forms, but as the mantis figure of Nekken remained staring at the chart, she gave up the pretense of paperwork and tried not to fidget. A troop of first-year interns passed the window of the nurses' station joking among themselves, but their mirth fell as they crossed Nekken's cold shadow in the hall. Even Orderly Zeik stopped short when he saw the elongated body of Nekken standing like a funeral monument. Zeik retreated, deciding to come back later.

Only Orderly Bolzen seemed attracted by Herr Senior Physician's lingering silhouette. The sloping shoulders of the apish orderly appeared in the window of the nurses' station and stayed there as if waiting for orders. All the hairs on Nurse Bosch's neck began to stand

163

straight up. Nekken spoke at last, never taking his eyes off the chart:

"Where is Herr Doktor Jung?"

"He hasn't come in yet, Herr Doktor Nekken."

Nekken kept looking at the chart, his voice silky and scaly at the same time. "Are you familiar with the patient's condition?"

"I am familiar with it."

"So you are aware that it has been eight days since the patient has had a bowel movement."

"I am aware of it," Nurse Bosch said quietly, not sure she could trust her voice again.

"And you checked the patient's chamber pot today?"

This time Nurse Bosch really did whisper. "I checked it."

"And you found her condition the same?"

Nurse Bosch tried to say, Yes, the same — but no sound came. She tried to tear her eyes away from the tall man staring complacently at Fräulein Schanderein's chart. The scaly soft voice came again. "You were going to *wait* for Herr Jung before bringing this to the attention of your superiors?"

"Herr Jung always checks her chart first thing," Nurse Bosch managed.

"Does Herr Jung often come in so late?"

"Herr Doktor Jung is suffering from a bad cold, Herr Nekken. . . ." Her voice fell as Nekken's head creaked around on its stalk of a neck, staring at her through those pale, cavernous eyes.

"Aren't you going to do *anything?*" the scaly voice asked.

Nurse Bosch's throat closed again. She felt a touch of sweat on her forehead and the hot tears spring to her eyes. She blinked them away and wiped her moist face. . . . She went limp, the struggle over.

"Very well, Herr Doktor Nekken."

Nekken barely glanced in the big orderly's direction. He dropped the chart on the desk with a soft slap.

"Help her, Bolzen," he said as he glided away.

In the deep sleep from 6 A.M. onward, Herr Doktor had a dream: The hordes of Asia Minor were invading Switzerland. He could see the great dust cloud from their baggage trains rising from the horizon. There must be millions and millions of those brown-skinned devils ready to sweep over the mountains and crush his little country. He was afraid, terribly afraid that he wouldn't be there in time to repel the coming invasion. Well, he thought gaily, if they've come for chocolate, they'll have to dig it out of the ground like everybody else!

And then he woke up. Damn, late for the hospital again. He stumbled about his bedroom, searching for his clothes. Yesterday's crumpled shirt would have to do. As he tried to tie his tie in the mirror, he couldn't focus on the knot. He got Emma to help him, but he wasn't able to focus on her face either.

"I don't think you should go," she said.

He wanted desperately to get back into bed; his bones ached, each one separately. He slogged from the house anyway. A gray rain lashed down outside, a cold, biting rain that chilled him each time a droplet flew in his face at the tram stop. But it cleared his head and got his blood moving. When he tramped down the long marble entrance hallway, he felt almost human.

He came upon the empty nurses' station — no Nurse Bosch in sight. And Orderly Zeik wasn't in the uncomfortable chair at the end of the fourth-floor hall. Panic and pain jumped on his spine. "Ah —! Ahh —! Ahhh —!" came from the room. The door ajar. He ran, his wet shoes skidding on the marble. He tripped and fell, sprawling. His hand must have been in his jacket pocket; the pocket had torn to a flap. He staggered up and flew in at the door of 401. The shock of what he saw staggered him.

Nurse Bosch and Orderly Bolzen struggled over the patient. Fräulein Schanderein was clawing and fighting, yet managing to keep the sheets wrapped about her head. Bolzen had ripped them from around her buttocks and floundered over her flailing legs. The girl's buttocks were exposed, round and plump and very white, shaking with tremendous violence. Very *white?* He saw a sallow grayness to her skin — of course, she never washed. Nurse Bosch was trying to administer an enema with quaking hands, but each time she went to penetrate the patient's behind with the spike-nosed india-rubber bulb, the mummy wriggled so violently soapy water squirted everywhere: across Nurse Bosch's bosom, into Bolzen's face. The orderly got some in his eyes and bellowed in fury, drawing back his hand to strike the naked legs beneath him —

"Get out. Both of you."

Nurse Bosch dropped the enema bulb, and Bolzen looked up, blinking stupidly, wiping soapy water from his face.

"Get out!"

165

The mummy on the bed, going "Ah —! Ahh —! Ahhh —!", broke free of Bolzen's weight and clawed the sheets around her body, vanishing from sight.

Outside in the corridor, he told them to *wait* in such a way they would have waited all day. Then he returned to the room, banging the door. For a moment he felt the solitude of being alone with the patient, alone in her room. She was still going "Ahhh —!" in pulsing gasps. He didn't know what to do: tear out his hair, gnash his teeth. He wanted to stop his ears to the steady, maddening momentum of her gasps, or shut her mouth — anything. A sheen of wetness glided across his nose and lips. He didn't care. He had failed. Months would pass before she returned to where they were just before the attack. Months!

The enema bulb rolled by his foot. Soapy water leaked from the nozzle. He stamped on it, and stamped again. The ugly thing split like an overripe pear. And in the rattling pause between the girl's gasps, each time she gulped for air, he said, "I'm sorry. I'm sorry. So *sorry* . . ."

Back in the hall, Bolzen had shuffled to the wall, cowed. "I don't ever want to see you on this floor again," Herr Doktor told him. The orderly nodded humbly, his eyes locked to the tops of his shoes.

To Nurse Bosch he said, "Tell me this, and tell me the truth. Why did you do this? Why . . . ?"

The nurse opened her mouth to speak, her eyelids spread wide open, exposing the whites all around the iris. Her mouth kept opening and closing in time with the patient's gasps coming faintly through the door. He wondered if Nurse Bosch was even aware of what she was doing. Finally her mouth formed a word — not even a word — a sound, like a child choking on a bone. The sound a cracked whisper: "Nek —"

Her soft face crumbled in running tears and sniffles. Pathetically, she clutched Herr Doktor's sleeve and then began to pet his hand. He let her pet it for a while, until her sniffles finally ceased.

Then off in a rage to find Nekken. He pictured the senior physician begging for his life, squirming on his knees. Herr Doktor walked faster. That's what he wanted — Nekken down, down on his knees.

Herr Doktor reached the stairs. He felt dizzy, and a waxy film drifted before his eyes. He must go calmly, so as not to break his neck.

166

Nekken would wait for him, wait beside that grand bronze statue sitting on his desk . . . Bologna's Mercury, perfect for the bastard. A slim lad leaping off into Renaissance flight, forefinger raised to the sky, his staff of Caduceus crooked in his arm as though taken aloft on a last-minute whim . . . Herr Doktor's feet slipped out from under him, but he caught the stair rail, clinging precariously for a moment. He lowered himself to a step, pausing to catch his breath. Why did Mercury point to heaven? he wondered. He really should know a simple thing like that.

Oh, ja, ja, ja . . .

That pointing finger was the finger of augury, of foretelling the future and hidden signs. Weep! O marble Romans, wagging your fingers in the air. For behold His Majesty Nekken! The Infallible. The Seer, probing a mad girl's rectum with an enema nozzle of Divine Sight.

But beware, O Nekken. Beware the ides of Jung!

Herr Doktor dragged himself to his feet. Down he went, a fog opening up before his eyes and closing in hazily behind. On the second floor he clasped a doorpost, panting through his teeth. His legs felt wet and raw inside his trousers, rasping his thighs at every step. From the rain, or had he wet himself? But what about that winged-footed nancy-boy's staff, Nekken? The Hippocratic staff of Caduceus, Karyx the Herald!

He Who Brings Tidings.

Do you know these tidings, *Signor Il Magnifico?*

Do you?

His legs were shaking. Shaking like snakes. Yes, there were snakes entwined about the herald's staff. Mother Earth's serpents, her children of the moon. Offspring born of nothingness. He-snake and she-snake coupling about the herald's staff, bringing order out of chaos — and All-Life from the great world Egg.

Those were the herald's tidings, Nekken! That a truce had been declared between man and woman, so that love be made in the thighs of the Earth. For She had decreed —

That the world shall be born!

Steady. Don't slip again, don't lose your balance. Herr Doktor took a baby step away from the doorpost. He touched the wall for guidance and support. A face swam lazily out of the mist, staring at him as he slid along the wall. The voice familiar, ja, a friendly person. He mumbled, "Yes, I'm fine, thank you. I've an appointment with Doktor Nekken. We must consult . . ." He tried to rub the mist from his eyes. There — Orderly Zeik, asking him if he was all right. Ah, good old Zeik, good old fellow! To show he was all right, he left the safety of the wall and walked stiffly down the middle of the corridor. Zeik must think him drunk. He really must try and get a grip on himself.

Herr Doktor stopped for a moment, resting his head against the cool marble of the wall. The smooth coolness cleared his head. Soon he would reach Nekken's office and come face-to-face with the man. He felt light and transparent, but all the crazy thinking had wiped his mind clean. He knew what to say, what to do. Ready for Nekken, ready to see him sitting beside his pretty-boy Mercury. His catamite god leaping off on an urgent errand, a forced purge for the girl in 401.

Herr Doktor touched his lips to make sure he'd left off mumbling.

He had reached the office door.

Nekken sat poised behind his desk in a chair of the Empire style: carved lions'-head armrests and lions' paws at the feet. The upholstery was malachite-green satin, the backrest crowned with a gilded crest, the imperial Napoleonic N, which now stood for the physician himself.

The only thing moving in the room was Nekken's white, languid hand, flowing leisurely across the creamy slip of paper. The hand seemed to move by itself, straight from the elbow: a department store mannikin writing a letter. The mannikin did not look up.

A few papers — one of his own innumerable reports on Fräulein — lay beneath Mercury's winged feet, the nonchalant sign that Herr Jung had long been one of the great man's daily concerns, displayed intentionally to dismay and to intimidate. His own papers trapped under the god's feet, as if to say:

You're underfoot, Herr Jung. You might get squashed.

Off to one side hung a small oil painting. A finely executed Tiepolo, a detail from some larger work. It showed the pudgy, twisting body of a cherub, Cupid himself. The painting hung on the same level as Herr Nekken's narrow, cadaverous face: a pudgy yearling with baby angel wings, laughing across the sundown blues and pinks of a Venetian sky. Tiepolo's Cupid with a pink rosy bottom, a fresh, moist bottom that begged to be lovingly spanked.

At last Herr Senior Physician Nekken deigned to recognize his colleague's presence. Slowly the long, pale face looked up from his writing paper. He smiled cautiously, as if quietly delighted to see Herr Doktor coming into his office.

"Why, Herr Jung! At work already? We didn't know when to expect you."

But the smile flickered as Herr Doktor leaned heavily over the green-blottered desk. His hands instantly darkened the blotter with sweat. He spoke quietly and clearly, as though to a slow learner:

"How would you like it if I ordered Bolzen to sit on your legs while Nurse Bosch ripped down your pants and gave you an enema?"

He felt the sweat run down his arms. At last Nekken replied, "Your patient was nine days overdue —"

"My patient" — Herr Doktor's voice sank — "is my patient." A drop of sweat fell from his chin and splashed on the blotter. His voice sank lower. "And she will evacuate. Without being tortured. Eventually. On her own."

He caught a whiff of his own perspiration. Sickly. Violent. And across from him, Nekken's controlled, calm face, smoothly shaved to the point of waxiness. The skin so taut and flawless, Herr Doktor wanted to slap it.

"You are losing control, my friend," Nekken said in a sympathetic whisper. "You see progress where there is only mindless parroting. In the past months you have turned this staff and this place inside out with the ceaseless demands of a petty tyrant. And you have neglected whatever other duties you may have had. What happened to that young man I sent you last week, the one with the fluttering eyelid?"

"I sent him away. He wasn't sick. He was nervous. A vacation. A few days drunk, a few nights with a girl — that's what he needed."

Nekken leaned back in the chair, folding his hands. "You sent away a paying patient. Tell me, what are we paying you for, Herr Jung?"

He had no answer for that. Herr Doktor saw more droplets fall from his chin. Oddly, he didn't feel hot. . . . He found an answer:

"I have been employed these many months establishing a rapport with Fräulein Schanderein. A paying patient. You destroyed that this morning."

"Then it wasn't much of a rapport, was it?" Nekken said, his fingers touching in a church roof.

"It was the best we could do."

"The best? Really? Then you define a rapport as no talking, no eating, and wiping up excrement all day long . . . ?"

Herr Doktor noticed that Nekken had a very prominent Adam's apple, almost grotesque in the way it protruded from his throat. He wondered what it would feel like to crush the ugly lump between his thumb and forefinger. Would Nekken scream the way the girl screamed? The way he wanted him to scream right now? The way Herr Doktor himself wanted to scream? How amazing when his voice came out stern and severe, commanding:

"Leave my patient . . . *alone.*"

Nekken gazed at him over his praying hands, saying nothing. Then he seemed to relax, chuckling and folding his fingers together: "All right, all right, my dear Jung. I'll leave her alone." He rose from the Empire chair, coming around the side of the desk. Gently he took the junior physician by the elbow, leading him to a full-length gilded mirror against one wall.

"But tell me, what should we do about you, Herr Doktor?" the man demanded gravely. "What should we do about you?"

The morning flew back at him in a rush: the waking, the panicked dressing, flying through the rain, sprawling in the hall, sneezing all over himself. . . . The mirror showed it all. His tie had come out of his collar; the torn pocket of his jacket flapping. And God, his face.

His hair plastered sideways; his spectacles bent and crooked. His nose ran wetly into his mustache. Face ghastly pale, lips redder than normal life. A pathetic vampire . . .

Herr Senior Physician stood next to him in his crisp swallowtail coat. Impeccable. Daunting. "Yes, what *shall* we do with you, my friend?"

Herr Doktor started to laugh. He found a rain-damp handkerchief in his breast pocket and began to wipe his face. "I don't know, Herr Nekken. I really don't know." He blew his nose. "Perhaps we should check me in as a paying patient, file a report with Direktor Bleuler, and work up a diagnosis."

He pried his bent glasses back into shape, more or less. With them perched on his nose, he looked merely dim-witted. Straightening his

170

tie helped. So did tucking in his shirt. He combed his hair. Better. He left the mirror and made his way around the end of the desk. He lingered for a moment over the statuette of Mercury, gently touching the god's muscular bottom. "Sweet lad . . . Very engaging."

He looked to Nekken for a reply, but the man stood silently by the mirror. Now two Nekkens watched him: the real one and his reflection. Ach! Two Nekkens! One was enough. . . . Herr Doktor went to the Tiepolo portrait of the pudgy cherub. He shook out his wet handkerchief like a sheet.

"That's just how I caught my cold," he remarked to the little laughing Cupid. "By running around outside at all hours with nothing on." Then aside to Nekken, "You should cover him up, or he'll catch his death." The older man seemed to be wondering whether Herr Doktor had lost his mind or was merely playing a poor joke. How delicious to see the senior physician irked by a touch of doubt.

"You don't want this child getting sick, do you?"

Without waiting for an answer, he delicately held his damp handkerchief from both corners and smoothed it carefully over the pudgy bottom of Tiepolo's laughing infant. The wet rag clung to the canvas. Now the imp peeked over the sheet in glee, no longer indecently exposed.

"That's better, my little fatty," Herr Doktor said. "Just like a patient I know, in 401." He bowed sharply to his colleague, clicking his heels. "Shall we file a report of our conversation," he asked, "or will a gentlemen's agreement be sufficient?"

Nekken did not return his bow. He had gone to the Tiepolo cherub. Taking a compact manicure case of shiny black leather from his coat pocket, he extracted a pair of silver tweezers and began trying to pick the damp nappy off the painting without using his fingers. The man's thin face had grown ashen with silent anger.

"A gentlemen's agreement, then, Herr Senior Physician?"

Nekken's hands shook, the tweezers unable to pinch the dirty rag from the rosy buttocks of his beloved oil painting. "Just get out."

171

BOOK III

THE DREAM

Chapter 1

Speech with the Queen

He was quite sick for the next few days. Chill, fever, vomiting. Zeik waited for him to emerge from Nekken's office, led him to a free room across the hall from Fräulein's 401. He clung to Zeik, climbing up the stairs, letting the orderly undress him and put him to bed. He felt too wretched to care how it looked. . . . But bedridden or not, his patient still retained her stool, and going home to recuperate wouldn't help.

It must be said of Nurse Bosch that in the days following the enema attack, she did as much as she could for their cause, bringing Herr Doktor constant doses of beef bouillon at all times of the day or night, which gave him the strength to crawl across the hall, to sit for an hour or so in room 401.

A grim afternoon followed the attack. In a lull between waves of chill and fever, he stood outside Fräulein's door, listening to her gasp, "Ah —! Ahh —!" until he was nearly faint. When at last he found the courage to enter the room, she kept on as if he weren't there. Sitting with her until a mounting bout of diarrhea forced him to leave. All through the night he heard the muffled beat of her gasps through his own door. Then at some point in the blackest hours he awoke to silence. She had left off. . . . And he passed into sleep again.

The next day Fräulein let him into the room but began gasping hoarsely the moment he asked permission to sit. So he stood with her, sweaty with chill as the pulse of her howling throbbed in his head. . . . He'd heard of sailors cast adrift in small boats not defecating for weeks. But only because they had little food and what they did eat was absorbed almost wholly into their bodies. They were prone to attacks of tenesmus, the futile effort to defecate. Painful, like dry-heave vomiting. The body going through all the motions with none of the results . . . But this girl wasn't even going through the motions.

Back in the quiet of his private room he fell asleep in the chair, his head dropping to his chest for a moment. Eyes fluttering, he dreamt one word:

Dokpox.

He awoke with a start.

Dokpox. Ja . . . The parents had brought the girl to Zurich to enroll in medical school. But at the last moment she had become sick with an attack of nervous hysteria. "That is the right word for it, isn't it, Herr Doktor Jung? Nervous hysteria?" The mother's bosom heaved for him. The beautiful, ornate china-blue silk of her dress, dotted with the masks of Comedy and Tragedy. Her daughter had come to Zurich to become a Doktor — so once they thought she could master the art. But the poor creature had fallen sick instead. First medical school, then sick: *Dokpox.*

Well, if the mountain won't come to Mohammed — Mohammed would go to the mountain. He decided to lecture her.

He found Leaman's *Anatomy* pushed under her bed.

"I presume you've had a look at this," he began. "There's a first-year lecture that goes with it. Old Groaten at the university used to give it. He's dead now."

He paused for a second. Did she even hear? Ah, it didn't matter. He hadn't thought of old Groaten for years. If only he gave the lecture half as well as that dry old goat. The anatomy book opened in his hands; when he stared at it, the print glided in and out of focus. He must really get back to bed soon.

Outside her window he saw the rain of the last few days had stopped. The sun shone in great shafts that struck down from the clouds, which were torn and ragged, with slashes of blue showing through. He fancied he heard birds chirping and even saw the flickering of a bright leaf peeking in at the window. Oh, he must be really sick to be seeing springtime leaves in the dead of winter.

"I'm sorry, Fräulein," he said brittlely, "but I'm not feeling well. We'll start the lecture properly tomorrow."

He didn't remember lumbering up from his chair, or going across the hall. Or falling into bed.

*   *   *

While he lay in the room across the hall from 401, people came and went before his eyes. He tried to speak to them, but they ignored him. He found it difficult to forgive them. He pondered this for a while. People were so naturally rude. Then he perceived that they were actually trying to help him. First off, his old underwear was gone and he lay naked in bed, the sheets cool and crisp. Then he heard voices, worried but gentle. At last the faces came. Nurse Bosch's round piggy face hovering over him, her small eyes glistened. She was swabbing his forehead.

But even as she drew the cool washcloth across his burning head, her face changed — and now Emma dipped the washcloth into a basin of water. *Emma* wiping the sweat from his forehead and wringing the drops away. Emma. Owl-eyed, sharp-beaked Emma the maid. (The maid! Never tell her that.) No, Emma his wife — that's what he meant to think. How had she ever come to marry him? Did he actually ask her once? Or had they just silently agreed on it? He thought of her body, which sometimes hung above him as they lay in bed. A soft, fleshy rail that squirmed this way and that until he grabbed it by the thighs and speared it, spread it open, and searched its quivering insides. He must be laughing, for Emma looked at him strangely, as if he were mad. Feebly he tried to take her hand and draw it down below to show her how big and warm he felt. He wanted to make her understand. But she freed her hand from his, placing it back on the sheet, saying, "Rest now, darling. . . . Rest now." If only he could show her the huge beastie under the covers. Why didn't she let him? Was she afraid? He just wanted to *show* her.

Then she went away. Or did he close his eyes for a moment? He still felt a bit of washcloth trailing across his face, its annoying frayed ends tickling his skin. No, not the washcloth — the mummy's hand. Frayed bits of the mummy's swathings draped from the girl's arms as she gently touched his face. Would Fräulein Schanderein uncover herself for him now? He peered intently at her: the eyeless, sightless burnoose encased her head. The mummy stopped patting his forehead, and the sweat ran freely into his eyes. If he looked at it again, would he see the girl's swathings — or the empty-hooded cowl of nothingness? The black void of the shit doll staring down at him? He prayed as the sweat ran down his neck: Please don't be an empty head, please don't be a cowled head.

The wrapped mummy mumbled at him.

177

"What? I can't hear. . . ."

The mummy spoke. "We have some mail for you, Herr Doktor."

No, not the mummy — Nurse Bosch. She had brought him a letter.

"How long have I been out?"

"All night."

"Was Emma here?"

"She's here now. . . ." Nurse Bosch quietly withdrew.

He saw a soft armchair had been brought into the room. Emma's body folded into it, sunk in a deep, limp sleep. She had brought clothes for him: his slippers, his checked bathrobe. He felt remarkably better, like someone recovering from a hangover when it lifts its gray weight at last. Nurse Bosch had left the letter on the bed. His eyes focused slowly on the print. Addressed to the girl. From the father. Ach! The last thing in the world he could deal with now. He flicked it across the room, and it landed on his folded bathrobe.

Emma did not stir. She had curled up with Leaman's *Anatomy* and still clutched it. . . . Had Fräulein evacuated during the night? Had she eaten? He had promised to lecture her today. He tested his joints, feeling his limbs, twisting his neck around. Everything ached. He could manage a little.

His mouth felt dry and parched. A pitcher of water stood on a table by Emma's chair. He picked it up and put it to his lips. The water ran down his chin. His genitals felt cool and hidden. "Genitals" seemed the right word. So inoffensive. So harmless . . .

Emma shifted in the chair; her narrow bottom pressed toward him, showing its curve through her woolen skirt. For a second he saw himself locking the door. Saw himself rip open his robe. Yank aside her skirt.

Rape her.

Covering her mouth so no one would hear.

But . . . the doors didn't lock inside. And then there was the viewing slit. He sighed and put the pitcher down.

Before he left the room, he slipped the book from Emma's grasp. Her fingers clutched the air for a moment, then went still again.

"Herr Doktor!" Orderly Zeik started from his seat in the puritan chair.

"Feeling much better, Zeik, thank you."

Nurse Bosch stormed down the hall to face him. "Herr Doktor, we have strict orders about you too! Now back in you go —"

He stowed the book under his arm and took both of Nurse Bosch's hands in his own, feeling her cool, dry skin. "Thank you for yesterday. Thank you for taking care of me."

She drew her hands away shyly, rubbing them . . . telling him what he wanted to know.

"No evacuation last night. And she ate about half her meal."

The nurse glanced at her wristwatch. "It's about noon now. Time for lunch. Shall I fetch hers?"

Nurse Bosch brought the meal while he sat in her room. When he held the steaming dish in his lap he imagined Fräulein's swollen belly, ready to split, intestines distended, too packed to breathe. If only he could pass his hand along her stomach to feel inside. Had either Nurse Bosch or Bolzen noticed the state of her belly when they tried to force an enema on her?

What if there was blockage?

What if the girl had swallowed something and stopped her bowels? Giving her an enema might have revealed that — or even freed the blocking object. In which case, the enema, forced or otherwise, *would* have been the correct procedure. His halting its implementation might cause a rupture. . . . She could hemorrhage, the contents of her bowel spilling into her lower body cavity. In a few days she'd be dead of fever or infection.

He tried to recall if he'd ever heard of a case of a person physically retaining bowel movements. Holding on to them . . . What an insane force of will! But to what end? What purpose did it serve? Pain an end in itself? Eating and eating and holding and holding until she became a carcass packed solid with food and feces . . . Pah! Ridiculous.

The smell of the steaming plate wafted into his face: knockwurst and sauerkraut. Now the folds in her mummy wrappings were moving. Was she really going to eat?

Ja, the hands beneath her wrappings rippled back and forth. A grunt came from the sightless burnoose, a wet gurgling. He placed her plate on the bed. A claw snatched a handful of kraut and knockwurst and vanished under the covers. The mummy made the sounds of chewing and slavering. God, still *hungry* . . . He willed himself to sit calmly and watch the lean fingers going from plate to swathings.

179

Very soon the food disappeared. Why had she let him back into her presence so quickly? He had imagined months of knocking at her door, begging, "May I come in? May I this, may I that?" But in his blunted, fevered state he had completely forgotten to knock when he came to her room — just barged right in! And now of all times — why was she eating in front of him? He prayed she'd move her bowels, right where she hunched, anywhere — just so she wouldn't rupture, die, and end it all too soon. . . .

Before he got to see her face alive.

"I've promised you the first-year university lecture. And so you shall have it." He cleared his throat, opened Leaman's *Anatomy* to the frontispiece and then to the table of contents. "The study of anatomy is the study of the body structure — that is, the body's structural relationships: skeleton to organs, organs to nervous and pulmonary systems, and those systems to the musculature. None of these systems is independent; all of them are connected and integrated. In this lecture I shall deal with the precise nature of the human skeleton, the nomenclature of its parts and their functions; from there, the muscle fibers working from the extremities toward the trunk; and the contents of the body cavity itself. Then the head, its bones and muscles, the organs of the eyes, throat, and ears, and finally the nervous system. My last lecture will end with the brain."

He caught his breath. He had not fully thrown off the grippe. His brow was damp. "Even naming all the body's parts is a considerable task, and those proficient in its naming have been held in high esteem for many thousands of years."

He went on with his lecture for another half hour, devoting himself to the skeleton and musculature of the foot, starting with the phalanges, the little toes, working through the various cuneiforms, metatarsals, and cuboids. He found he was incredibly rusty and needed constantly to refer to Leaman's text for the Latin names. At the end of this stint his body felt chilled and slightly loose in the bowels.

The mummy had devoured her plate of knockwurst.

Emma stayed the night with him in his room across the hall, curled up as before, like a lanky cat in a soft armchair. He could not know that for most of the night she lay awake and watchful, simply staring at the dull glare from the hall lights shining through the smoky glass of the viewing slit in their door. The lights from outside made the viewing slit an oblong full moon in the black sky of the darkened room. At last she fell off, long after the sick one muttered himself to sleep.

In the morning he went back to 401 in his bathrobe and slippers. This was the eleventh or twelfth day of her retention, and he lectured her on the skeleton and musculature from the tarsus, the heel, to the patella, the knee joint. When he first entered her room he thought he heard her whimper. In gladness or fear? Did she actually *want* to void herself now? Or was she afraid?

That evening, the unwashed claw snatched another plate of food. He had to interrupt his second lecture of the day, on the fibula and tibia, to rush off to the hall lavatory and let his guts run out. It seemed he could keep nothing in. Whatever he ate turned to water. In the dead of night he voided himself again, begging the girl silently to go, damn you! go! While Emma stared at him, saying nothing as she lay awake . . .

On the morning of the thirteenth day of Fräulein Schanderein's retention, his lecture had at last reached the pelvic area, including the first spinal disks, the sacrum, the coccyx, and the contents of the pelvic cavity. He wondered whether to go directly to the lower bowel or begin with the bladder and urinary tract.

He stood at the window, staring down at the winter garden. Frost covered the gravel pathways, the ground ice glittering in the morning sun like glass dust. Holly leaves clung stubbornly to the shrubs by the path. The other trees were bare and dark, brittle sentinels on a winter day. He decided on the bowels. . . .

"The intestines of the bowels are the tubular portions of the alimentary canal. They extend from the stomach to the anus, leading from and forming an arch about the convolutions of the small intestines." In the brightness of the morning light he saw his own reflection in the glass, his face a ghastly thing, hollow cheeked, pinched. He saw a flicker of movement in the glass. The mummy had crept toward the edge of the bed, as though about to rise. He tried to go on, to keep his voice on an even keel.

"Food mass is carried along within the intestines by contractions of the muscular walls. The small intestine, a tube of approximately twenty-three feet in length, is where bile, pancreatic juice, and the acidic secretions of the glands within the small intestine's lining complete the digestion of proteins, fats, and carbohydrates. The digested nutrients pass through the tubular lining and into the blood and lymph systems. . . ."

The ghostly reflection of Fräulein Schanderein in the window moved again. The mummy, swathings and all, vanished from the corner of his eye.

He heard the hollow grating ring of the brass chamber pot being pulled across the floor. If someone knocked now, he would kill him, beat his brains to a pulp in a rage. If someone knocked now . . .

"What remains of the food mass are various undigestible compounds, which finally pass into the large intestine, up the ascending colon, across the arch of the transverse colon and down the descending colon to the rectum — and at last to the anal canal."

A deep grunt came from the floor. Another deep grunt and a gasp for air. Then a long pause ending in a pleasant sigh of relief. . . . The girl began to breathe in deep drafts. He forgot the lecture and smiled down into the garden below. A satisfied silence filled the room. It might be cold outside, but inside, the heat whistled up the metal radiator, and his toes were warm and dry in his bedroom slippers.

The patient went back to the bed. And he to his chair, his own dearly beloved room 401 chair. All the time sitting in that chair, all the effort and patience and doubt . . . No, nothing in vain. He glanced at the chamber pot. Fräulein's stool lay there — a meager five pellets the size of deer droppings. Somehow he had desperately wanted to see more, a pound or two at least. But logically he knew this impossible; the body could not hold a pound or two for thirteen days. The stool's compactness revealed that her body had used up the greater portion of her waste product. The clawed meals and half rations went part of the way to account for this, but not all. In order to consume that much of the indigestible bulk, the patient's metabolism must be operating at a furious rate. She digested food and burned calories like a hard laborer working in the deathly cold. Yet all she had done was sit in bed. This — obviously — was not rest in the normal sense. He saw the truth in the saying: "Sitting still is harder than jumping about."

Great hands clamped about his gut. He wiped away some tears that had sprung to his eyes. . . .

"Thank you, Fräulein, for attending my lecture."

He picked up the chamber pot and went out into the hall. Zeik

182

jumped to his feet, followed closely by Nurse Bosch. They halted at attention a pace away.

"We have now resolved the issue of elimination," he said.

He presented Orderly Zeik with the chamber pot, and the orderly accepted it as if it held the holy relics of an ancient order.

"Nurse Bosch," he commanded, "the contents of this chamber pot shall be noted as belonging to the occupant of room 401."

"Yes, Herr Doktor."

"Furthermore, the contents of this chamber pot shall be labeled immediately as such."

"As you wish, Herr Doktor."

"Moreover, a specimen of the contents of this chamber pot, one sample from each of the five deposits, shall be presented to Senior Physician Nekken for dissection and analysis. It is my personal request that he handle the dissection himself and oversee all the details of its execution. The specimen of the patient's stools shall be examined for trace elements and compound residue persisting from the patient's meals during the last thirteen-day period. I shall help Herr Nekken work up a full report, stating all the findings and any suitable comments thereon, complete with laboratory analysis and forensic results. Copies to myself, Direktor Bleuler, the entire intern staff, the patient herself, and appropriate members of the hospital support personnel . . ." He paused to catch his breath. "Will you please be so kind as to draw up a memo to this effect for me at once."

Nurse Bosch preened with hidden delight. "It shall be done as you instruct, Herr Doktor."

A great wave of relief seemed to have swept over the three of them, a feeling of conspiracy and triumph. As though the doctor, nurse, and orderly were the girl's secret helpers, having begged her to go all this time, wishing they could go *for* her. After the days of waiting, no fuss, no dissection, no amount of paperwork was too great regarding the girl's meager pellets.

"At the very least," Herr Doktor said slyly, "no one will accuse us of supplying the specimens ourselves."

Nurse Bosch and Zeik both bowed. "No, Herr Doktor."

The five small specimens were taken away.

Herr Doktor ordered tea in his room for himself and Emma. But he saw her comfortable chair empty, save for the impression of her body.

183

She left only a note behind: *Glad you're feeling better. Dinner at six. E.*

Not even love and kisses: no, not her way — beautiful, cold Emma. Either the master of her face or spent and sated beneath his body. He tried to remember if he had heard her laugh recently. Yes, not long ago when he spilled egg down his front and almost walked out of the house with it congealed on his shirt.

Now, where the devil had she stuck his clothes? He poked his nose into the small closet, but all he found was his overcoat. Pinned to the lapel another note from Emma, this one reading: *Remember, don't be late!*

So! She had taken his clothes and meant him to go home by tram in his bathrobe, slippers, and overcoat. Ja, the price to pay for disrupting their home life, for two nights sitting up in a hospital chair and five months of him talking to himself about a patient no one had ever seen. He must stop at Yenkel the florist (whose wife was her best friend) and buy Emma some flowers. Maybe stop in at the butcher's dressed in his pajamas, or the greengrocer's, and pick up a tidbit or two. Just put it on my bill, please. . . .

He plucked the note off his coat lapel and stuffed it in his robe pocket. His finger touched stiff paper.

The letter from Herr Schanderein. Forgotten in his pocket. No: ignored — put aside. Truthfully, the letter frightened him. Perhaps someone else in the hospital, Nekken or even Direktor Bleuler, had written to the parents. About his notable excesses. About his weird attempts at therapy. And this a response, fallen into his hands by mistake. His skin crawled, that he and the girl could be undermined so easily. Everything must be set to rights at once.

He went straight back across the hall without taking his tea. This time he knocked, and the answering silence came. He opened the door. He asked for permission to enter. She gave the wordless permission.

"I forgot something," he stammered truthfully. He showed her the unopened letter out of his robe pocket. "This came from your father two days ago. I'm dreadfully sorry I didn't give it to you at once, but I was afraid you might not move your bowels. Perhaps I was more frightened that people were talking behind our backs. Maybe writing your parents about us. This was weak of me. Nothing people say should matter. I should have known this in my heart. Forgive me. Shall I read the letter to you, or just leave it?"

He thought he saw a trembling through the length of the mummy's wrappings, a shifting of the folds — yes, he definitely did.

"I'll leave it," he said at last, putting the envelope on the edge of the bed. "If you want to share it with me, just leave it out where I'll find it."

He turned to go, his hand on the doorknob. A soft mumbling came from the bed. A murmured, stuttered sentence, spoken so faintly it might have been a person speaking in the room next door . . .

"Did you say something?" he whispered.

Again the soft mumbling came, with a few distinct words as though escaping out of a deep well. "I'm the muh-muh-muh. With a quonk-quonk end."

He shut his eyes and leaned his head against the door. "I'm sorry," he said. "I couldn't catch everything you said." The wood of the door felt cool against his cheek. "Is this about the letter from your father?"

A long silence followed, in which he thought he heard the mummy trembling; then he realized you couldn't hear a person tremble. But you could. The sound of her swathings rubbed together, and the bedsprings groaned as she squirmed. . . . The groaning stopped. No sound at all. She had given up, changed her mind. The moment lost.

He put his hand on the door with a sigh —

Then came the caw of a harsh voice:

"Tell him I'm the Queen of Sparta!" said the wrapped head. "Tell him I'm the Queen of Sparta with a hot rear end!"

Chapter 2

The Twiddle

"What?" he asked stupidly.

The trees beyond the window in the garden creaked sadly; the midday sun covered by a tuft of cloud. The wrapped head spoke hoarsely again, the voice rising and falling in cracked octaves from her months of silence.

"Tell my father I'm the Queen of Sparta with a hot rear end."

"If I write him saying that, will he understand?"

A pang of instant regret. Stupid question. He was there for *her*, not the father.

The voice rattled like gravel falling into a pit: "You make him understand. Make him."

"But *I* don't understand."

"Yes. You do. You understand."

They were having a conversation. Him talking, her talking back. Saying things to each other — who cared if it made any sense or not? And each time her voice fell off, how terrifying she might never speak again.

"I'll try to make him understand," he said. "As much as I can. As much as *I* understand. . . ." For a vivid second he hated her for making him wait so long. What a twisted bit of shit she'd been. Now he had to go home through Zurich's streets in a bathrobe and slippers. Did she know he spent nights across the hall? Tying himself in knots for her?

She rattled on. "You make him. Make him. That the Queen rules the earth and the sky at night. And the men from the mountains and the woods. Kill each other for her lovely hand. Lie with her in her temple under the light of the moon."

He looked about for his damn writing pad. What was she saying?

186

Moon goddess and the men who slew each other . . . Who fought for her bed . . . How strange — as though he'd suddenly turned down a familiar street at dusk in an unknown part of town. The streetlamps being lit and the lights coming on behind curtained windows. Had he been there before? Only to wake in bed?

He called this lick of déjà vu by a private name. It was Lamplighter's Street. A dreamer's street. Existing only in his mind.

The folds in the mummy's sheets began moving in ways he had never seen before. First her hands appeared, slithering from under the covers. Long and thin — not emaciated, but quite elegant . . . Her skin coarse and gray, as though shriveled in a dungeon. He saw a bedsore at the back of her elbow, the skin flaking off whitely from the red knot of a boil. Her hands moved hesitantly across her knees as though lost. . . .

He wanted to rush to the door, make sure no one interrupted! All he had to do was tell her, Wait! Let me make sure no one comes. But she was on the verge of unwinding the swathings from around her head. Already her hands fluttered, picking gently at the burnoose, faintly touching the first tucked folds.

She was going to show him her face.

Her self.

She had risen from the bed and turned toward the window. Her thin hands clutched hold of the burnoose: slowly they peeled back the lower layer of sheet. The cloth unwound, a strip from her forehead, another strip. More strips, uncurling like a bandage, falling about her neck. Just a cowl remained, casting a black shadow. Her hands went to the edge of the hood to peel it back.

Someone knocked on the door. He writhed. Fräulein Schanderein froze, her hands to her head. Perhaps the person would leave.

Another knock.

"Stay here," he managed to croak at her. "I'll send them away."

The intruder knocked for a third time. A little gasping pip escaped from her, and she began to wind the strips of burnoose around again. He turned on the door's viewing slit with a gathering weight in his brain, a pressure that would explode his head, splattering the room. The moronic face of Orderly Bolzen peered furtively at him through the glass.

187

"Stand away from the door, Bolzen," he ordered. The orderly moved obligingly to one side, wringing his hands and blinking stupidly. He had not forgotten his banishment.

"Well, what is it?"

"I have a message from Senior Physician Nekken." Bolzen came to a full stop, waiting.

"Ja, what is the message?"

Orderly Bolzen clasped his hands in front of his pants as though repeating lessons from school. "Herr Senior Physician Nekken offers you his heartiest congratulations on the events of this morning. And" — here, the ape-man struggled to remember — "and regarding your personal request, he is at your disposal." Obviously Bolzen hadn't the foggiest idea what he was saying. "Is that all right, Herr Doktor?"

"Fine, Bolzen. Thank you. Offer Herr Nekken my sincere gratitude for his good wishes and cooperation."

Orderly Bolzen bowed deeply and left, mumbling to himself, ". . . my sincerest gratitude for his operation. No, my sincerest . . ."

Numskull!

Neanderthal!

Knuckle-scraper!

Herr Doktor wanted to heave a brick down the hall at Bolzen's retreating head. The mummy had gone back to the bed, the burnoose wrapped, her pale, elegant arms gone. Everything as before. He wondered what would happen if he smacked his own head against the wall, again and again until little spots of blood appeared, and then a few more and then a few more.

"May I come tomorrow?" he asked. The answer came. The heartless pause of long reproach.

"There's always tomorrow," he said.

But no more today.

He went back to the room across the way and drank a cup of tepid tea.

Why hadn't he just told the big cretin to go away?

Leave us alone, Bolzen. That's all he had to have said.

He knew the answer. Fear. Because when the girl shed her wrappings, she was no longer his safe, bedridden patient. If she walked and talked, if she spoke and showed him her face — so much more would be required of him. More than the simple knock on the door, the May I come in? The May I leave now? . . . The daily May I? and then home to bed himself.

Forget about home. Forget about bed. He really ought to send Emma a note saying he wasn't coming. He really ought to do this, but he felt Mistress Sleep's soft fingers touching his brow. . . . Go on, she said, write Emma. And so as his eyes drooped he composed a wonderfully sensible letter to Emma, explaining everything. Especially how important his staying across the hall was right now. And toward the end of the letter, he imagined Emma's strong, thin thighs as they warmed him in bed. He ended his note: "P.S. Darling, I'll ravish you tomorrow." And then he slept.

Twenty minutes into the next morning's lecture, the hand began moving under the covers again. This time he had prepared. Early in the morning Zeik fixed up a sign, Do Not Disturb, which hung outside the door. Herr Doktor also tacked a rectangular piece of paper across the viewing slit, making them as insulated as possible.

He watched Fräulein Schanderein slip off the bed and face out the window. As he lectured, she unwrapped the strips of sheet from her head at the same slow pace, but now it seemed to take ages just to reach the same stage as yesterday. His tongue grew thicker and thicker. If anyone — *anyone* — ignored his sign . . .

A deep shadow fell beneath the lip of her cowled hood. The shadow's reflection stood out blackly in the window. Her thin white fingers pulled the cowl back. He glimpsed the pink curve of her ear and a lank mouse nest of hair. Indeed, it seemed a horrible tangled mess, limp and unwashed, hanging in greasy tendrils. Thick mats fell clean out of her scalp as she uncovered her head. He saw white skin through the patchy wisps — the ravages of half meals. Red and black scabs speckled her pate, surrounded by a freckling of dry flakes. . . . A long, stringy lock hung across her face. She seemed to lurk behind it, as behind a half-drawn veil. He must see about coaxing her into a bath — but how?

The window reflected her ghostly face. She was wilted and ravenous, cheeks sunken, the muscles around her mouth sallow and drawn. Her eyes gazed dully into the middle distance of the garden. He wondered that the blazing light of the blue sky didn't sting her eyes. Perhaps an innate dullness shielded her even from the sun. She played

189

with a twist of hair that hung across her face. Twirling it now one way, now the other. Then curling the last little end around her mouth.

She had been pretty once. But what a waste now. What a waste . . . Then by slow degrees he saw yet another face: as if by looking at the girl he had stepped through an unseen door and found himself on Lamplighter's Street once more. No, not a face. A smell . . . the secret scent of *her*. Richer than all the perfumes ever sold with names like Night's Close, Autumn Moon, Amber Chase. The scent of . . . Nanny Sasha.

He closed his eyes. Nanny's dark scent wreathed him like a cloud. And he smelled the sweet-scented nipple that hung above his face, a rich dilated nipple, swollen and tender and ready for him. He put his lips to it, swelling in his mouth, giving everything of itself. . . .

The crazy girl had turned her face toward him. He gripped the chair's arms, terribly afraid some force would drag him to the nape of her unwashed neck, inhaling deep and hard . . . afraid that Fräulein *too* would smell like the cherished suckling of long ago.

Get a grip on yourself. Nanny Sasha was then. This was now. The girl and his treatment. Here and now . . . Only yesterday she had spoken: "Tell my father I'm the Queen of Sparta with a hot rear end." And today she showed Herr Doktor her face. She had even left the letter on the corner of the bed. For him to read? He took it up now. What a pitiful excuse for a letter. A bland apology for not writing more frequently, with a scant word of hope for her speedy recovery tagged on the end. Written in a single pallid hand, signed: Love, Father & Mother.

Tell him she's the Queen of Sparta with a hot rear end? Where the devil had she gotten that? All he knew was the urgency of her command. Tell him! Make him!

She stood at the window, twirling a strand of hair around her pinkie.

"Shall we send your father a message? A message from the Queen? I'd write whatever you say. We can try to make him understand —"

She stopped twining her hair around the spindle of her finger. Then began sawing her thigh with the heel of her hand. Rhythmically sawing back and forth without a second's pause. A compulsive insane movement. A pointless, repetitive sawing that made her seem an idiot. Twiddling. He had seen enough of it from the Incurables in the dayroom.

190

Suddenly she repeated childishly over and over:

"You'll never make him understand. You'll never do it. Never do it. Never make him understand. Never do it! Never —" Sawing her thigh to beat the band, hopelessly twiddling.

Now ordering him in a high, shrewish voice, "Lecture me! Lecture me!" He picked up Leaman's *Anatomy* from under the chair. Her twiddle went on. And though he lectured her for an hour, she was still going strong when he finally closed the book. Still twiddling alone in her room when he left the Burghölzli at the end of the day.

Chapter 3

The Letter

The winter deep of February surrounded him in a frozen silent hush. Broken only by the crackle of ice underfoot as he walked home from the tram stop. A few flakes of snow drifted down from a clear night sky. No moon; the stars glittered cruelly. He dawdled before his door, reluctant to enter. The thought of warmed-over dinner, of talking to anyone or sleeping, choked him. He thought of the hospital. . . .

Did the girl twiddle in the dark and in her sleep? He crawled into bed beside the warm body of Emma. She barely stirred.

When Fräulein's twiddle didn't cease after a few days, and when their conversation failed to proceed much further than "Queen of Sparta, you'll never do it, lecture me!" Herr Doktor gave up — he gave up exhausted, incapable of any fresh reaction to her. Idiotic rantings weren't communication, just complicated riddles, nasty taunts. He had opened box after box, only to find yet another box, this one with a mouth. While his own life slipped away. He liked her better mute.

Unknown to the girl, her most immediate problem was not her twiddle or the nonsense spewing from her wrapped head, but the fact that her room bill was unpaid. Her father had let it slip two months, with several hundred francs due on hospital room and board. Herr Doktor settled it himself, along with an additional two months.

So when Fräulein's spastic twiddle kept on, he finally began the letter to Herr Professor S. Freud of 19 Berggasse, Vienna, Austria. Avoided for so long in the vain hope of gaining ground with the girl, which he could tout and brag about. Now the letter he wrote struggled before him — torn up, or started again with a line lifted

192

from another version. He lost count of the days. . . . But as the letter evolved, so did his picture of the Schanderein girl's situation. A short conversation with Herr Tom Thumb accidentally sharpened his insight.

"Well! Well! Well! How wonderful to see you at last, Herr Doktor. Ah, but don't fret — I can see what you're going to ask me. Yes, yes, just the same. But I must say, Nurse Bosch has been quite liberal with the petroleum jelly. It fell off for a time — the dosage, I mean — and that caused some anxiety. . . . But over all a great comfort. I've got a little pot of it, you see. Get it filled when necessary. . . . But enough of me! What of you? We've heard all sorts of things down here" — he cast a dark glance about the room — "that is, those of us who listen. . . ."

"What kind of things?"

Tom Thumb began to chuckle, his fat body quivering with delight. "That you got the little bitch to eat and shit and talk and show you her face. Wunderbar! What next, Herr Hofrat?" Then, conspiratorially, "But they also say you're paying for her room. Tsk-tsk-tsk, paying for your patients. What a shame . . ."

The remark rolled around in his head like a bean rattling around in a gourd. That he got her to talk and shit and show him her face. He had done something after all. And so had she. Even if he did dole out money for her keep, in his gut he knew she paid deeply too. The letter began to write itself:

> She is a highly intelligent nineteen-year-old: bound for the University Medical School at the time of her last attack; now in a pronounced demented state. (Routine physical examination impossible; details of recent case history enclosed.) All her acts can be likened to the tyrannical control she exercised over the immediate space of her room. Though mute for months, she made one command clear: So with my room, so with me.
>
> The eternity gaining entry to her presence. The offering of the cowled sculptures. The attempted violation of her person. I see a common thread. First — she

had the power to reject me. Next — I the power to reject her. And in the last — both of us defending against the outrage of her person.

To her command: So with my room, so with me, we added: So with Us.

Even as he wrote these lines the girl's situation changed; one morning he entered her room to find its familiar disorder completely gone, as if recently cleaned by the maids. Had he entered the wrong room? But no, there stood the books he brought her, in a neat row along her dresser. And the dresser itself dusted, the wood gleaming darkly. Automatically he looked to the wall by the door where the girl threw the plate of food during the meteoric passing of Nurse Simson. The brown stain no more . . . a shocking pale streak in its place, cleaner than the surrounding wall. Her shallow sink basin gleamed too.

She had made the bed, the covers turned down in proper girls' school fashion. The pillow fluffed — but no girl. She had crawled underneath, wound in a sheet of her mummy wrappings, which bore the dirty marks of all her cleaning. He peered cautiously under the bed. Her hand still sawed her thigh in that furtive spastic twiddle. She had brought along the neurology text, free hand clutching it in her dark little cave.

Within ten days she began to parrot some of the ordinary things he said. So different from the harsh bitter caw when she croaked, "Tell him I'm the Queen!"

"May I come in?" he would ask her. And she would mumble, "may i come in."

Then he'd ask, "How are you?" And she'd answer, "how are you." Speaking softly as if recalling the echoes of words long forgotten . . . Unnerving at first. Voices in room 401 — rising and falling while the thrum of the hospital rumbled beyond their door.

She has begun talking. Ejaculating words. Expelling her insides. Is it any wonder bodily excretions of all kinds fascinate her? Though you might say I tolerate her behavior, the truth is I willingly participate. And since I am not particularly revolted by her behavior, why should I pretend for the sake of social convention?

194

During his lectures she often went in his presence, half shielding herself with a scrap of blanket as she squatted. She even dabbed him with flecks of food and bits of dung. Often, at the close of his visits, bodily matter and the remains of dinner clung to him, to the chair, the room. . . . Yet each morning, when he appeared in fresh attire ready for her daily assault, he found her place clean as well, dirt vanished as though a host of fairy elves had helped her through the task at night.

But there *were* limits. She once managed a bowel movement so quietly he failed to notice. Hovering over his chair for a moment, as if to sit where he usually sat. And his heart leaped. Ah! she wants to sit where I do . . .

But she returned to the bed. He had the vague notion of sitting luxuriously, showing her the great comfort of the chair. See, Fräulein, see how wonderful it is to sit here. . . . So he sat — only to slide in the warm dampness. A surge of giddy revulsion raced through him. She twiddled on the bed, her wrappings loosened, her free hand twirling a lock of hair, pulling it around the curve of her mouth. A strange coy gesture.

"I am really awed, Fräulein," he said, aghast.

And she repeated, flat and hollow, "i am really awed fräulein."

Was she heaping dirt on me in the ordinary sense of the word? Or was this feces play an offer of her finest parts? These first few weeks of February seemed so much cruder than the time of her wailing, gasping, and filling chamber pots. Cruder than the time of the fecal dolls. Indeed, those early days seem a golden time. Now, due to the state of my clothes, I leave the hospital by the back way. And often spend an hour searching for a carriage, since the drivers are reluctant to pick up a gentleman in such condition, and going on the tram is unthinkable.

As Fräulein ate more food her sickly pallor receded, though she remained thin in the flesh. She began to gorge herself. Orderly Zeik often ran to the kitchen to fetch her another portion. One day in the middle of February she languidly uncovered her arm. A dried red smear flashed at him. Burnt lightning on the bare whiteness of her skin. At first Herr Doktor panicked, thinking she had wounded herself somehow.

But in a moment better sense took hold, with a dull shock. . . . Under the covers her thighs were spread open, her twiddle hand going in between them. It came out smeared red. With a toss of her head the burnoose fell away; she had smeared some on her face. Now she smeared more, around her mouth and eyes.

The regular meals, her recent gorging, had all taken effect. Now fatter, she had gained enough weight to start her menstrual blood flowing. Her first period since coming to the hospital: he made a note of it in her case file.

> So with my room, so with me. Shall we now add:
> So with my blood?

On the second day of her period she included him. Her red-tipped fingers went to his face. She used quite a bit, going back between her legs again and again; her fingers going around his eyes and over his eyebrows. Then last of all his mouth. At the very end she pushed her wet finger inside and ran it across his teeth.

He let her do it. First under a wave of disgust, then with a growing sense of amazement. He went to the mirror over the dresser for a look. A bloody-faced wild man stared out at him, a splattered savage with dripping teeth from where he plunged his fevered face into the pulsing stricken body of his kill. Here at last, the real face of the Stag King, needing only the twigs in his hair and a knife in his hand.

What was she doing to him? Her hand came again for a last touch, and he flinched. What final outrage? Rings of blood around his nostrils, where he inhaled his enemy's last dying breath? But the hand stopped short of his face. She gripped his bow tie. She tugged at it, untying the knot. Leaving it limp around his throat.

And then he heard the oddest thing. She laughed, flat and shrill, "Heh-heh . . ." A pause. "Heh-heh . . ." Slightly evil. Wholly mirthless. But finally a human expression on her dull face. Pleasure in cruelty. His own hand fluttered to his limp bow, and he smiled weakly back at her.

The laughter ceased. Her face blank again. He caught a flicker of movement in the corner of his eye. The rectangle of stiff construction paper had slipped from the viewing slit.

Direktor Bleuler's watery blue eyes gazed through the thick glass. Herr Doktor stared into the white-bearded face. No shock. No revulsion. Yet somehow sensing, as though reading the old man's mind, Direktor Bleuler felt deeply ashamed for his young colleague. Disgraced that some sacred laws of intimacy had been transgressed, rules of conduct between doctor and patient, man and woman . . . But wholly fascinated, terribly drawn by the audacity, the subtle skill. How many years had the old man wished for an impossible patient to unravel bit by bit? Longing to do what his junior was doing in this very hospital? A lifetime.

And so they struck a silent bargain, the terms of which both men understood without speaking. That the younger man would never embarrass the elder by calling him a failure. And that the older man would say nothing of what went on inside the room. Nor stand in his way. Bleuler to keep his cloak of dignity, and Jung his naked patient. The white-bearded face nodded tightly once and vanished from the viewing slit.

Alone with her again, the smell of menstrual blood wrapped him like a damp towel. Terribly familiar, waking the souls of his primitive ancestors in the cells of his veins. Deeply personal, private. Making him Fräulein's *possession*. The heavy scent so like the warm air space under the bedsheets where he used to crawl to be near Nanny Sasha, the smell of her smooth, strong legs . . .

How had men come to revile a woman's monthly time? Come to name it unclean? Ja, it smelled damp, muddy. But healthy and living. Alive and seductive . . . The smell of fullness and fertility and the fearful power of life. How many barren centuries had passed into dust since man craved the damp life-odor of his woman's monthly time? Craved and feared it as he craved and feared the passing of life's power. Eons of progress and civilization, of coats and boots and forks and spoons and clean linen on the table. Of which wineglass to use. And which hand to wipe your ass.

No wonder she laughed so cruelly. What pitiable foppery. All the frivolous tatters of mankind's finery conspired to hide a person from the knowing sight of others: everything from clothes that distorted your shape to polite society's pretty white lies that hid your meaning. Every woman a whore, every man a secret enemy. How many times had he said, "So good to see you, Herr Bump," when he really thought, *Drop dead, you old fart?*

And with all the niceties the very pulse of life had faded — gone into the long, ancient Before Time, when the blood of life streaked the face of the world. When it meant something to hunt down an enemy in the dark, hunt him alone and catch him alone, and then tear your teeth into his raw flesh. Feeling his life pour into your heart as you tore his lungs out, his death scream shivering into the wild lands.

What would Emma think if she saw him now?

Or Nanny Sasha?

She, who broke the antler plaque to scratch raw welts down his father's back. Ja, she'd laugh the bitter, mirthless laugh too.

"You're laughing at me," he said.

"You're laughing," he persisted.

"Laff," she repeated stupidly, showing her teeth. Blood on them too, as if the girl had eaten from the same carcass. He smiled, showing her his bloodied teeth as well. "Laugh," he said.

Her lips drew back in answer. "Laff," she repeated. Now, distinctly, "Laugh." He wanted the next word, the one that would add to what they had.

"Laugh," he tried again. But she had wilted, going dull again. With a sigh, he rose from his chair. "Well, perhaps tomorrow."

"Always," she said.

He paused at the door. Her face withdrawn into the cowl, a spray of tangled hair covering her eyes.

"Tomorrow," he tried again.

"Always," she whispered.

A reply! Hoping he would always come tomorrow? Or saying that she'd always be there waiting? He didn't care. His words were with her words. Hers with his. Tomorrow and always. At last. At last . . .

> Our first word-association encounters did not follow the exact pattern you set out in your book (title? must find it). But I swear before Eternity that no feeling, no act, no success or failure, will ever compare to

the triumph of that first time. My God, we'd done it.
To talk and talk back!

To swear before Eternity: no feeling, no act, no success or failure —
compared to that first time. To Swear. Before Eternity.
A thing no mortal could *ever* know.
Oh, happy fool.

Progress seemed everywhere. On a sudden impulse he decided to introduce her to the idea of a bath.
"Bath?"
"Laff," she answered.
"Bath," he repeated.
After a moment: "Baff."
How simple if her private room had been built with a bath. Most of the fourth-floor patients were marched out weekly in a troop. First women, then men an hour later. Down to the shower room where all hell broke loose: soap flew and water splashed over the towels. Measly towels, barely wide enough to wipe a person dry. Afterward, damper versions of the fourth-floor patients were marched back to their rooms, in various states of dress and cleanliness. Just dumb luck none of them cracked their skulls.
As for the girl, the idea of her white, skin-and-bones body standing naked in the immensity of the shower room, with its twelve-foot ceilings and jets of water, screaming again, while a nurse and an orderly stood grimly by, making scrupulously sure they hosed every nook and cranny . . .
No, there had to be a more private, tender way.

Zeik solved the problem. One day he passed the sixth-floor laboratory, with its long black laminated tables, rows of gas jets and boiling beakers; there he spied a coiled length of rubber tubing about ten yards long. The tubing gave birth to an idea. Down he went into the hospital's forgotten reaches, plunging deeper, scavenging in every corner until he found what he was looking for. In the slimy blackness of a storage bin dating back decades lay a fifty-year-old copper bathing tub, long abandoned, filled with oily rags, dead paint cans, and indescribable filth.

Zeik cleaned the worst of it, bringing the tub upstairs in a more presentable state for the kitchen staff to scrub and polish. After he checked it for leaks, they placed the copper sitz bath in a corner of the girl's cramped room. Rubber tubing ran from the hot-water spout of the sink. But the thing had no drain. Originally it must have been tipped over onto a stone floor, the water running out the gutters of a bathhouse. So he improvised, bringing along a two-kilo tomato can to scoop out the dirty water.

"Bath," Herr Doktor said.

"Baff," the girl repeated doubtfully. The presence of the big tub agitated her. She hid from it, twiddling furiously. But she didn't shriek; and let it stay. Her first bathtimes were hesitant, touching the water with a trembling finger like a cat's paw, the other hand fluttering across her thigh. Eventually the girl came clean in stages; soon dangling her hand in the copper tub, then swirling the warmth about and letting the bathwater run through her fingers. After a few days the wrist and forearm of one arm were clean to the elbow, a dark ring on the white skin like a ship's waterline.

And then later, all of herself. Getting into the hot water wearing the sad remnants of her chemise and bloomers, she stripped off her sodden rags and slid them into a heap in the corner. She dried herself on huge towels that Herr Doktor bought specially from a Turkish bath. A half dozen of them, kept freshly laundered and neatly stacked on her dresser. Herr Doktor took away her gray rags and left her a white hospital gown, which disappeared under her sheets and swathings. Following her bathtimes, he scooped out the dirty bathwater; later Nurse Bosch or Zeik took care of the chore. As the weeks passed she soon took baths herself and drained the tub herself, but not without several episodes of flooding — generally in the middle of the night.

Their talking went on.

Not the normal "How are you? I am fine," but a slow exchange of single words. Seemingly random. One word bringing on the next, their sounds a code. One day they had a "conversation." She lay at his feet as he sat cross-legged in the chair. She tugged and fretted with his shoelaces, playing with the bow and the knot. A bright sky of mid-February burned into the room, the sun silvery and the tree branches rattling like a tangle of skeleton bones.

200

"Blue sky," he said, as you would say, Nice day, isn't it?

She paused in twirling his laces. Then one single word:

"Lawning," she said. He was stumped a second or two before he knew what she meant. Longing.

Blue sky.

Longing.

"Family," he said, as in, You don't say?

"Hospital," she replied at once.

"Blood," he said right back.

"M-m-m's gash," Fräulein sputtered. She tied his shoelaces in a hopeless, unpickable knot. Her vulgar word snatched the breath from his throat. When he felt he could talk, he tried:

"Doktor Jung. That is, myself." He switched legs, giving her the other shoelace to tie in knots.

"Nothing," she said, pulling at the lace.

Nothing? It hurt that his name meant nothing. Ja, she could hate her mother all she wanted, but now he courted her good opinion. Surely he was more than just a nothing? What of his influence? His presence? His devotion?

"This chair," he said, tapping it with a pencil.

"You," she said immediately. "You."

Ah . . . pleased for a brief moment. Then he resolved to say the one black word that always brought their conversation to an end. Just to show her he knew its power.

"Father."

Not "your father." Just the black word. Alone like a dark pebble on a white sandy beach. She'd stop playing with his laces. And start to twiddle, sawing her thigh. He hated saying the word, to halt their talking in the middle. The room went so quiet you could hear a person walking on the cold gravel path down below in the garden.

"Father," he insisted.

This last time shook her loose. She convulsed on the floor and sprang to her knees. She ripped the notebook from his hand, flinging it away. Crouching before him like a rabid monkey, the tangled hair swept off her head. A wild vicious thing. Eyes glittering as though she might grab him, tear off a finger with her teeth.

"Queen of Sparta!" she snarled. The hatred surging out of her. Body rippling with the need to spring. "Queen of Sparta!"

As she crouched at him, the sweat ran in streaks inside his shirt.

Waiting her out, waiting until she finally ebbed with a sigh of contempt. Giving up on him and crawling back under the covers. The burnoose going over her head.

Who was the Queen? I remember her saying: She who rules the earth and the sky at night. She who rules the stone crags above and the men below. Killing for the pleasure of her hand . . . The chosen one, lying in her temple under the moon.

How many times did I provoke her with the word "Father," sitting paralyzed while she boiled before my eyes? Did she crouch so I would crouch? Seething to frighten me, cow me, humble me down . . . ?

"Father," he'd say. And she crouched as before, like a Sphinx on the bed. While he — entranced — sat frozen, her timid prey. His will crumbling. Weak all over. She wanted him thus. The chair slid away, and he knelt before her, cowed so that she might see. Humbled by her surging wrath. Rage at his not giving her what she wanted. Bow to me. Go low. And slowly she rose up before him like a tower of smoke, graceful and deadly. To stand above him like the beginning and end of the world . . . So began the first act in an elaborate play, an intricate fantasy, a ritual that they performed over and over. For the simplest beginning had been the hardest part to learn:

All Must Kneel Before The Queen.

Chapter 4

The Ritual

They had to play out the Ritual several times for him to fully grasp all its parts. A long time it seemed: the winter days of February lingering before March. But since the parts never varied, when their meaning became clear the two of them acted out the Ritual quite deftly. She forced him to learn a number of facts in order to play out the fantasy, and if he failed to pick them up (say, acting the role of the old, decrepit King) she was quick to anger. She crouched on the bed, that furious look in her eyes, watching in pleasure as he squirmed in fear.

Fräulein called herself the Queen of Sparta. And for the time being, Herr Doktor put off many of the obvious questions as to the meaning of her "Sparta" and her "Queen," and how she hit upon the fantasy, with the knowledge it required of history and ancient peoples.

Could she have known the far older name, Arcadia? The backward mountains of the Peloponnese: where slaying and sex and death had been acted out since men lifted their muddy eyes to the icy sky. Acted out long before the empires of the Mediterranean mother sea, long before they built Palace Mykonos on the high rocks. The ritual rose out of the dark time, when heroic Mycenae was but a dank stronghold, overlooking a rain-sodden crossroads. Out of a time when a handful of hungry brigands gazed down like vultures for easy plunder on the winter plain. Happy enough to steal an old goat or a new cloak — if either could be had without too much of a fight . . .

Strange ritual indeed. More than simply a fragment of her madness — for clearly the Ritual once existed. And he knew in a vague but powerful way that her play came out of the depths of time: a thousand years before Helen's betrayal of Menelaus, before warlike

203

Agamemnon's sea raids off the coast of the Troad. So when the girl used the word Sparta, he took it as a signpost on a road, directing his gaze toward a small part of this immense world she wished him to see.

But for the time being, whether Fräulein invented the Ritual or had read about it somewhere made little difference to Herr Doktor. He sensed hidden meanings pulsing through, for the action felt dreadfully familiar. It stirred the marrow of his bones, rumors from dim ancient spans, the glimmer of another man sleeping within him all his life. Suddenly waking beside the charcoals of a campsite fire — that oldest home of man — and sensing all around a circle of cold faces gathered in the dark.

And so the Ritual was played — a familiar dance, knowing in his heart the next turn of it as they went along. The circle of faces drew close enough to see, streaked with dirt, twigs and leaves woven in their hair: a tribe surrounding him as he stood by that first fire. Tongues of flame, sparks, and smoke curled into the night. While the clan of faces chanted slowly, "You — you! . . . You — you!" pausing long heartbeats between each murmurous blow and the next. "You — you! . . . You — you!"

"Queen," she snarled. The Ritual had begun.

He knelt on the floor before her, head bowed to the ground like a Moslem, not daring to look up. She stood above, remote and terrible, a queen blessing him with her mere presence — at once his mistress and owner of his soul. Moments passed . . . during which his knees began to ache and a numbness crawled down his shins. A change came over him; the cramps grew, withering his flesh. No longer young and supple, his skin shrunk and wrinkled. Old age descending on him like a cloak of troubles.

"Up," she commanded. "To your knees."

At last she allowed him to rise. His back straightened stiffly. His hands trembled at his sides; his forehead numb from where he rested it on the floor. And he beheld her. Immovable and stony, not deigning to drop her eyes or lower herself to look upon him.

"The wreath," she said. "Wear the wreath."

Her hands moved, twining in and out. She wove an invisible wreath of leaves and green twigs into a curved braid. He smelled the fresh tang of the woven wreath and the clear sap at its broken ends. The plant scent mocked him; he shrank from it, touching his crown in loathing as she placed it on his brow. From out of the darkness he thought he heard the bark of a dog. A wind from the night licked his neck, and all the hairs rose like marching ants along his spine.

He always tried to remember the hospital room, with the life of the building buzzing around them like a great beehive. Every so often he glanced out the window at the cold, bright winter sky, to reassure himself that, ja, this was Switzerland and the clever, smart city of Zurich — but it seemed to him he looked through faded glass, a smoky daguerreotype sucked of all its color. The real vision came up the marrow of his bones: nighttime on a craggy hill, the circle of dirty faces, the young woman beckoning him to rise with taunting eyes.

"The wine." She meant for him to drink. They brought a stone cup, leaking bloody drops. Palsied hands took it, spilling down his front, great red drops splattering his throat as he tried to drink, choking on it. Laughter cackled from the ring.

She took the cup from his hands, swilling the rest in a long, even swallow, carelessly dropping the cup to the ground. He wavered like a frail reed. The chant spiteful and slow: "You — you! . . . You — you!"

Inside the hospital room she had begun to dance around Herr Doktor. A coy, graceful dance, unchanged from its first step, a dance of wooing and courtship, of families and friends. Peasant people danced it in country villages from Arles to Odessa. An old dance, the same in Crete as in Albania, the same everywhere, anywhere people sat and drank, sat and laughed and drank some more.

The girl stepped slowly round him in a tight circle, first in one direction, then the other. A teasing one-step — pressing her fists in at the hips, bringing out the curve of her waist. She dipped once and took a step.

Then stopped.

Dipped again and took a step.

Then stopped.

Now, again, the slow dip-and-step, leaving the old man by the fire, weaving her way toward the ring of faces standing in the dark . . . At the circle's edge she paused. The faces parted, and a stranger passed through their midst.

She knelt before him, offering the cracked stone cup with out-stretched hands, as if the cup were his alone. He took it and looked about the circle, daring anyone to say different. The cup vanished into the shadow of his face, a trickle of wine running down his throat like sweat.

The old man's heart pounded in his ears: they let the stranger take his cup. His wine to a stranger's lips. How dare he touch the old King's cup!

The old man knew its every crack and curve. The father-son cup, made from the rock of the Moon Spring, where the crag water plunged into the thighs of the valley. A fist of stone broken from the rushing waterfall. Carved in the Before Time by the Forgotten Ones who spoke no words. But who, then as now, bowed to Her. The Silver White Face, whose body they saw in the snowy peaks, shining brightly on a moonlit night.

With long age and many owners, the cup had cracked. You drank and the blood-red drops dripped from the flaw, running in the creases of your palm. She filled it for the stranger.

He drank once more.

And let the woman lick the drops that ran down his arm.

She rose and danced for him again. Teasing. Dipping once and stepping lightly. Circling round and coming back. The weakness had gone from the old man's limbs — a lust for the Dancing One. How dare she dance for him like that? A spark flew from the fire, and the old man saw himself young again. In the flow of his fine strength, how he caught the woman in the woods and dragged her down. Clamping his hand over her mouth, holding it there to let her bite it. Wanting her to bite it as he *did her* sprawled on the ground, laboring in and out as she writhed and cursed and called for her father and her brother and mother and sisters and tried to crawl off as he mounted her in the cool dirt, clawing the soft moss and wet fallen leaves . . .

The old man looked at his withered fingers in the fire's flickering light. The cold was back upon him, purpling the teeth marks of that mating long ago. She had forever scarred the thick flesh below his

206

thumb. How small and crude the cup had looked in the woman's hands. The stone all black. And along one side the carved faded image of Her Above, graven in the Sleep Time — a crescent moon, with thirteen chiseled lines. Her thirteen births, her thirteen deaths, her rising and setting tale of each year's passing. He took Eldest Daughter of the Claymaker to wife, and she drank his blood that day, the blood of his manhood's veins. Then drank wine from the cracked stone cup. Long time he lived with her. And made her mother of the Dancing One, who, a lifetime later, teased him in the darkness, while the faces chanted:

"You — you! . . . You — you!"

Alone and womanless, he shivered by the fire that threw no heat to his old cricket bones. The faces drew off like ghosts . . . the Dancing One stood still. Only the stranger's eyes remained, red coals in the blackness. The father-son cup had fallen to the ground between them. Young man daring old to pick it up.

The bright Swiss sky lit the hospital room. Heat piped up the silver-painted radiator, and a thread of steam hissed out the valve. By the bed, Herr Doktor still trembled in the guise of the old man. At this point the dark grove of trees faded from his mind, and he found himself drawn back to the stuffy room. The dry reality of the hard wood floor on which he knelt, the soft contours of his clothes, the thrum of the hospital beyond, and finally the gawky scarecrow of a girl towering at the end of the room.

Now he rose and changed persona. Shedding his palsied old age, revealing the strong sturdiness of his limbs, becoming the other, his rival — the shadow man. But no longer faceless. The stranger's face his own. Himself standing in the grove, straight and tall, a hunter of the night.

Fräulein Schanderein came to him now, dipping once and stepping lightly. She chanted flatly:

> We gave the wreath
> We drank the wine
> We saw the darkness fall.
> The Old Moon wanes
> The clouds fly off
> Tonight the New Moon calls. . . .

Her voice growing cold and pitiless, each word sweet pain upon her tongue:

Tear off the wreath
And spill the wine
In manly terror hide.
The eyes of stars see
The new moon hunt
Tonight the Old Moon dies. . . .

She came to a full stop and looked scornfully toward the corner of the bed, where she saw the old wreck, too terrified to pick up the cup. Hissing:

"He thinks he can hide."

Then, peering intently into Herr Doktor's face, searching for any sign of doubt: "But he can't, can he?"

"No."

"Then what shall we do to him?" she demanded. The fullness of her voice leaped eagerly. She knew the answer.

"Yes, what *shall* we do with him?" he asked quietly.

"I want to see his blood." Her breath came in rapid jerks. "I want to see you bring him low and take his skin off in strips while he's still alive and calling my name. I want to hear him beg me. Beg me. Beg!" Spittle flew from her lips. "I want to tear his thing off with my hands, yank it off and shake it in his face!" She was pawing Herr Doktor, breathing in gusts, erupting:

"Look! Look! The old man picked up the cup. He's running. Trying to hide! After him! After him!"

Herr Doktor leaped to the chase, first into the corner by the bed where last the old man knelt.

"No! No!" she shouted. "Behind the tree!"

Herr Doktor looked sharply from side to side.

"That one!" Shrieking at her wit's end. "Are you blind? That one!"

He sprang across the room, barking his shin on the copper bathtub. He didn't care: the bloody hunting heat coursed through him. He landed like a cat in the corner by the door. Too late.

The room went silent. She stood stock-still: her eyes flickered toward the bed. The signal. The time had come for quiet — the noiseless stalking. Slowly, slowly, Herr Doktor crept toward the bed.

Inches and half inches. The seconds crawled like sweat. Minutes passed. . . . He had drawn close, gliding like smoke. His legs quivered from the strain. At last he stopped.

Inside, all his strength gathered, a winding rope of fury and lust, tied like a heavy calmness around the fist of his heart.

"He's near . . . ," she whispered. A fleck of spit glistened at the corner of her mouth. She licked it away with a wet pink tongue.

"Ja," he breathed. "Here . . ."

He crouched low for the final spring, staring intently at the bed. He groped at his side, drew out a make-believe dagger, and ran his thumb along the invisible blade. "Do it!" she urged him. "He's right there. In the thicket. I can smell his fear."

He closed his eyes, forgetting everything. The room, the hospital, the girl breathing urgently beside him . . . The old King was very close. Wanting to die. To die running, before he'd yield his neck for the kill.

"Now!" she cried.

He jumped on the bed, clanging it to the wall. A shout went up from a patient across the hall, but who cared? The killing heat rolled to a boil. Fräulein strangled her pillow; he stabbed it with the dagger.

"Again! Again!" she shrieked.

He plunged in the bloody knife. She clawed the pillow, tearing the linen case. The seam opened, spilling an ooze of goose down — the life ripped from its guts. Then, finally, they tired, their blows coming to an end. Her hands unclutched bit by bit. Herr Doktor threw away his invisible dagger. They sweated, panting in long, hard gasps of murder. As the killing heat passed like smoke, the two of them lay exhausted, side by side on the bed. He waited for his heart to stop pounding in his chest. She stared intelligently into his face. No signs of a twiddle. No dementia. Haughty. Self-knowing. And she always recovered before him.

She leaned luxuriously against the wall, reclining. With one hand she languorously stroked the beaten pillow as if it were a purring cat. Indeed, she started to purr herself; her lips glistened in a naughty smile. So much more in control than he . . . She stopped petting the pillow cat, and both hands came to her rib cage. She caressed her ribs, then brought her hands under her breasts, cupping them for a moment and letting them fall. An easy, natural gesture, shamelessly satisfying. And as she stared at him, a dreamy smile came across her face, her eyes drowsy and drugged. Petting the pillow-cat.

"Come to the Queen," she said like honey. "Come, she wants you. . . . You can have her now. Come and take her."

He said nothing. Drained and spent. Part of him crushed, ashamed, but that passed too. Poor, poor dead pillow, he always thought. And then he wanted to laugh. Poor pillow! A petted pillow-cat. Lucky thing.

His heart slowed as he regained his composure, tucking his shirt-tails back into his pants. The great intelligence he saw in her eyes was dying out.

"Come to the Queen," she murmured in a silly drawl. Losing interest.

"Why?" he asked.

"Because . . ." Her eyes dead. "Because," she said again, but this as a final answer. Just because.

His skin prickled. They were being watched. The thick piece of construction paper for the viewing slit lay on the floor. In the hunting and the struggle and the wild murder, it must have come loose as it had before. Senior Physician Nekken's narrow Satan face floated behind the glass — watchful and expressionless and numbingly calm. The face disappeared. Then Orderly Bolzen's eyes flitted past as he stole a forbidden peep through the viewing slit.

Herr Doktor replaced the blue sheet of paper. He looked back at the girl on the bed. All the fiery candle flame of intelligence — extinguished to nothing. The burnoose had wrapped itself around her head, covering even her eyes. A sheet hid her body. Underneath the tent of her wrappings he saw the rhythmic sawing of her twiddle. The Ritual was over.

He must finish the letter soon.

210

Chapter 5

Consultation with a Fantasy

Fritzi the postman knew his daily visit to 19 Berggasse was of the utmost importance to Herr Professor. So after delivering the mail to the butcher's shrewish wife, whose shop fronted the street — "Vhat! Only dese stupid bills again! I've paid dem ten times already!" — Fritzi the postman passed through the carriageway into the courtyard where Herr Freud waited anxiously at his door. The man came out in good weather and bad, in rain or freezing cold, greeting him with a simple "Guten tag, Fritzi. And what have we here?"

The postman had a theory about the letters he carried, a sort of parlor game. That you could tell what the letter said just by looking at the envelope, the style of the address, the manner of the handwriting . . .

Take today's packet for Herr Professor: not your ordinary mail — catalogs, magazines, fees from patients with no return address, and so forth. Nor what other professionals routinely received: fancy envelopes with black or gold or silver lettering, which Herr Professor of 19 Berggasse never got. But now this: a creamy gray envelope, smooth, flat, and *heavy*. Beautiful Swiss stamps showed a noble William Tell with crossbow, and another the Swiss Guards of the kind they sent to the pope in Rome. The return address printed in raised British Lion red:

> Krankenhaus Burghölzli
> Zurich
> Schweiz

And printed by hand in the upper left corner: C.G.J. RM 501. The sender's initials. His office number. A man known at his place of work.

211

Fritzi had always meant to tell Herr Professor about his theories, but instead he always made a joke about it. Pretending to be a mind reader, holding the letter to his forehead and gazing blankly into the Great Beyond, uttering the essence of its contents.

So he played the mentalist as he handed over all the mail but this creamy gray envelope. He pressed it to his forehead with a sly glance at the sky. The postman's fingers gently rubbed the edges of the packet as though receiving its inner vibrations. "I feel confusion here. I sense chaos —"

"That's because you can't decide what's in the wrapper, Fritzi."

"No, no, not so . . . The chaos, the confusion — this is the *subject* of the communication. And I feel the plea here. Someone is desperate."

"The human condition is desperate."

"Your vibrations are very bad, Herr Professor. Very disruptive. I can feel the sight slipping from me . . . but ah! I sense here an opportunity. Yes, that's it, an opportunity."

Fritzi handed over the envelope. Herr Professor took it rather doubtfully. "My vibrations are always bad, Fritzi. But we shall see."

Yet when Herr Professor felt the weight of the thing, yes, he knew the oddness of the package. He paused for a moment at the bottom of the stairwell. If only there were noises coming from the waiting room above, the murmur of many voices . . . Impossible, of course. His waiting room always lay empty. He arranged it that way, letting each patient out by another door so no two would ever meet. But as he gazed up the carpeted stairs he imagined the clamor of a dozen voices. The smoke from their cigarettes and pipes, the scraping of chairs, the creaking of the floor as they paced to and fro. Ladies in black with their hats, gentlemen standing with their umbrellas: a veritable throng begging for a few minutes of his time. Oh, it could have been that way — so easily, so easily. If only his practice had been podiatry, internal medicine, dermatology — even proctology!

But not good-for-nothing psychology. An obscure field where no two patients might even sit in the same room together. How impossible to make money this way, to raise a family. How futile.

He stared blankly at the gray envelope from Switzerland. He knew the Burghölzli, of course. Who didn't? Direktor Bleuler ran one of the great ones. . . . He should have liked a position there. They paid well,

212

and earlier in his career old Bleuler had smiled upon him, might even have given him a job. But no more — too late to go begging at the door of a strange institution in another country. So what did the Burghölzli want with him?

The rest of the mail fluttered to his feet. He tore open the gray envelope and saw there . . . much too much to read on the staircase. But he knew how to get to the point without reading every damn word. His shoulders sagged. A case history from outside his little circle of Vienna.

A consultation.

The one thing he never let himself hope for. Not from an émigré this time, no, not from a Jew or an angst-ridden hausfrau disenchanted with life in general and her husband in particular — but a genuine request from a sturdy pillar of Swiss society. A blessed physician from the golden halls of the exalted Burghölzli Sanatorium, seat of all power, font of all knowledge. How eminently just. Exactly the type of referral his Gentile colleagues fawned over; because when they paid, they paid so well. And when they didn't, they still enhanced one's reputation, drawing other consultations in their wake.

Then a twinge of disappointment. Not the director himself writing. Jung — who was that? He skipped frantically to the end of the letter. Junior physician. Another twinge. *Junior* . . .

But after a moment he squared his shoulders and strode up to the consultation room. Hah! Congratulations, Fritzi! It had happened at last. Junior, senior, director — who cared? He had slapped them in the face and they had woken up. It had become embarrassingly self-evident: the Institutional Method was a failure. They were desperate for help. Praying on their knees.

He laughed as he strode through the empty waiting room. The lonely umbrella stand, a clean ashtray, a couple of vacant chairs . . . He chuckled again as he threw the torn gray envelope onto the end table in the consultation room. A cramp seized his chest. The pressure sharpened for a moment, making him wince. He felt weak and shaky and groped for his chair. Don't die now. Before you even get a chance to write young Herr Whosis! Be a man, already.

Be a mensch!

Is this what it meant to be a mensch? Waiting half a lifetime for bankrupt methods to die so that bright young junior doctors would someday seek him out? While strange pains preyed upon your aging body?

He let the womb of his consultation room embrace him and massaged the red crab that sat upon his heart. Too many pictures on the walls, too many books crammed on the shelves. Over the couch hung a French artist's rendition of the colossal Egyptian god-kings guarding the temple of Abu-Simbel. The carved stone kings watched him mutely. This stricken man and those who came to lie upon his embroidered couch, their last human worshipers.

He gripped the armrests of his chair: carved sea serpents with scaly spines, bulbous eyes, and lolling tongues. Years of stroking, gripping, and mysterious chest pains had worn away some of the wood. "Help," he whispered. "Help me. . . ." He reached for Pan from his watchful tribe of gargoyles. The lecherous fellow grinned at him. More staggish than goatish. With sharp deer hooves and the stubs of antlers poking from behind his ears. The Romans actually had a staggish Pan, he now recalled. They called him Faunus. How easy to see him leaping off along the trampled deer runs to gambol with the herds. Foraging their berries, browsing their moss and leaves. Standing in the cold rain at night, drinking from the same streams, bedding down in the same matted grass . . .

And then, at the rutting time, bellowing with the long-antlered bucks, fighting them off and even taking a harem of hinds for himself. This little Faunus gave him the feeling that he would have found a doe's rear end just as attractive as a farm girl's creamy behind. Taking one or the other, as chance allowed. Herr Professor had paid a hundred and fifty guilders for him in an overpriced shop. Ach! The crab of pain scuttled sideways in his chest. The indulgence! A week's fees!

But what a proud little bastard. Herr Professor could almost hear him whispering naughty suggestions: forget about your morning patients, say you're indisposed . . . just sit back and read young Whosis's case. Tell Donna the maid to send everyone away. What's wrong with you? Afraid someone will find out? Close the office for a day. Just for today. Go ahead. . . .

He did nothing. He shifted in his chair, stroking the armrest. The crab scuttled quietly behind his lungs and mysteriously faded. A long morning's work lay before him like a dreary road. If only one of his patients would send word, cancel because of a head cold or a bout of rheumatism.

Wishful thinking.

No, only Herr Schuyt, his next patient, held claim to his attention. Not this scrap of paper from a stranger. And Herr Schuyt wouldn't vanish just to suit his mood. He heard Donna's footsteps in the hall. She poked her head in at the door. "Herr Schuyt is here, Herr Professor." A reluctant shudder went through him. The Hat Fetish. The Drone. Pan appraised him coolly, with the hint of a sneer. Go on, cancel the hat man — or are you afraid your precious envelope will lead to nothing? Herr Professor frowned at the statue.

From her place at the door, Donna the maid politely cleared her throat. His eyes glided to the table by his elbow. He found himself staring longingly at the gray envelope.

"Herr Professor . . . ?" Donna tried again.

He hefted Pan into his lap and let him grin. "You win." Then to Donna the maid: "Tell Herr Schuyt we must cancel. Beg a thousand pardons. As you can see, I'm not feeling myself today."

In an hour or two of delicious stolen time he read it through and through. Even going back in some places to read it again. How had Herr Junior Physician addressed him? Erwürdigster Herr Professor Doktor Freud? Or Sehr geerter — straight and to the point?

Erwürdigster. *Most venerable* Professor. A supplicant. Even under all the dignified language you could feel the imploring, down-on-bended-knee supplication. Oh yes, they politely called it "consultation" — by all means try to call it something nice.

Not since he ended the friendship with Fliess had anyone implored him. With good old Wilhelm they had inaugurated the exclusive Vienna-Berlin Society of Mutual Masturbation. Membership requirement: total obscurity. Honorary founders: the rhinologist Fliess of Berlin and Herr Doktor Sex Quack of Vienna.

He had been waiting for his imperial appointment to professorship back then. And he might have gone on waiting forever if he hadn't luckily cured a woman with connections to the ministry. After interminable years and mysterious delays, she pressed his case down avenues of her own: the appointment came through in a month. Now hearing the title Professor always gave him a tinge of pleasure followed by a lick of hate.

God, how he and Fliess had stroked each other up and down, like a couple of lonely cats wrapping themselves around any available table leg for comfort. What a bleak, desolate time: when the Nose Doktor of Berlin had been the very first to hear every cracked theory, every half-baked notion. And Fliess responding with even wilder fantasies of his own. Theories about an immutable twenty-eight-day rhythm cycle in every condition or affliction — whether you were male or female or a dog or a duck. Ideas about how the human body's whole nervous structure was somehow guided through the nose — oh, God! While Herr Doktor Sex Quack — so insecure — tested every bit of gibberish. Forcing him to read all the available literature on cycles: immutable, pathological, seasonal — *and* nasal. Months during which his own work floated aimlessly in a sea of doubt. It embarrassed him now just to think of it.

Then once in a blue moon one of his holier-than-thou esteemed colleagues deigned to send him some scrap of human flesh for a second opinion. Invariably he found nothing to work on; and so inevitably returned the human scrap to its point of origin with many thanks. Herr Professor had long ago given up on second opinions. And now this, the elegant Burghölzli envelope. A ray of hope, that maybe this time it would all be different . . .

For the gray envelope meant only one thing.

That Herr Doktor Whosis had consulted every jackass in his own hospital, sought out every second opinion, third, and fourth — and still came away empty-handed. So he might as well give the Vienna Sex Quack Method a try. Well, well, well! Young man Jung. I like you already!

He scanned the pages for that nutty thing the girl had croaked. Ah, yes! "Queen of Sparta with a hot rear end." Hah! And then what had she purred after they murdered the pillow? "Come to the Queen . . . She wants you. . . . You can have her now. Come and take her." First you kill a pillow, and then she begs you to take her on the floor. What's stopping you, Herr Whosis? Propriety? Let me tell you the story of the foxes.

The she-fox fleeing. And the he-fox chasing her. The scent of her body dragging him madly onward. He saw them dashing through a birch wood, in and out of snowy hillocks and white trunks, flashes of red fur across the snow. Their breath shooting steam, but still they kept on, panting, gasping, never resting — and still they ran. Their pawprints fleeing back behind them, over hill and dale across the cold white ground.

Why did he chase her? And why did she run?

The red-tailed he-fox had to be the perfect beast. To snarl off all the other males who wanted her. Then chase her down himself, right to ground. And then — and only then — have enough guts left over to take her in the snow.

But why did she run? So only the best one got her. Her match in strength, in drive, in will. And cunning. For even in the end she might squirm out from under him, biting and scratching, denying IT to the last.

"Find a little mouse for me," she'd taunt, "and then I might consider." So, tired, hungry, still aroused, he'd trot off looking for a mouse. Spend two days starving to catch one peeping out of the snow. Denying himself the pleasure of gobbling it there and then. Keeping it clamped between his teeth, still alive. Trotting back over the miles to where she waited for him — to set it at her feet.

For you. I caught it for you.

And for the little foxes to come.

While she, going hungry, and waiting in the birch saplings while her mate hunted for a mouse, wondering whether he would ever return to do the thing he was born to do. The deep animal satisfaction of being caught at last. And in the end, when he had brought the mouse and she had eaten a dainty bite of it, she would smile a gleaming, foxy smile at him. Turning her hindquarters for him at last, lifting her soft red tail, inviting him into the cloud of her hot scent once more. And him, to smile a foxy smile back. Frisk his tail. And take her in the snow.

That was sex!

Call it what you wanted: it didn't change a thing. Say, Oh, we're human, we're different, we're above all that — you were wrong. The cunning primitive mind lurked in the overheated genitals. The he-fox chasing her up steep hills while he took shortcuts, forcing her to wade across the stream while he stepped over the stones, driving her through the brush while he dodged the roughs, cunningly saving his strength for the end. The mad drive to defeat her. The lust to mate. To seize her. The rage to kill anyone who stood in his way, between him and the scent coming from the crack between her legs — and

217

the glorious moment when he plunged in his hot thing, her yelp of protest vanishing into the trees!

Herr Professor broke off his reverie.

The various truths concerning men, women, and foxes were not the issue here, but Herr Doktor Whosis and his Fräulein. Come to the Queen. Come and take her. You can have her now. . . . How direct and to the point. How like a crazy person to say something frank and candid when you least expected. So unlike all the "normal" people he knew in everyday life, who always talked in euphemisms, in secret code. In his dream book, in the passage dealing with Flowery Language, he had analyzed a dream filled with hidden sexual ideas, in which one of his patients was climbing down from a great height carrying a BIG BRANCH in her hand, thickly studded with RED FLOWERS that looked like OPEN CAMELLIAS. . . . To someone familiar with his method of interpreting dreams and their concealed thoughts, the sexual imagery was obvious. The camellia was a showy, hot-colored, open-petaled flower. Though perhaps a lily or a gladiola might have represented this woman's vagina better by virtue of having a deeper crevice, but then there would not have been even the shred of a disguise. And a good disguise on a thought let you bring it out into the open. With this girl's odd fantasy, however, there seemed little or none. No, that couldn't be right. There's *always* a disguise. Some secret hidden behind the clever tale. Fräulein S told this particular story in order to hide an even stranger one. . . .

Years ago, when his publisher sent the five-hundred-odd copies of the dream book to the secondhand stalls, Herr Professor looked over the shoulder of his life and realized he had lived simply to discover the Method. Like a castaway coming upon a lost island in the ocean. And by combing the washed pebbles along a deserted beach, he had found the long-sought-for philosopher's stone, hidden among the worthless wrack and crushed shells. Holding up the long-sought-for rock, what had he seen? Hidden passions? Secret dreams? The glowing caverns of the heart?

Only chaos, lust, and terror. His own inadequacy staring him in the face at every turn. How many times a day did he say one thing when he really meant the opposite? How many times had he smiled when he really wanted to cry? And laughed when he wanted to murder? All in the name of getting along, making do, getting by . . .

Was forgetting someone's name really so innocent? Arriving late or early really so accidental? Wasn't there meaning in every little act? A convenient correctness in our errors, as when you missed a streetcar but suddenly recalled the burning gaslight in your empty office? A hidden achievement in your faults — avoiding a stop at the delicatessen but finding yourself at the jeweler's on your wedding anniversary.

How to explain to Herr Junior Physician of the Burghölzli that in the beginning, the very beginning, he spent his days dissecting layers of dead brain tissue in a bleak, cold laboratory, staring at the lifeless cells through a greasy microscope, inhaling the funeral-parlor smells of alcohol and formaldehyde. Before a Method existed at all.

And then the awkward, clumsy years of those first sessions, when early patients stumbled over some minutia or couldn't recall a simple fact from the day before. Driving him half insane with eagerness to know, to discover what or why or how — leaping from his chair to place his hands on their head and press their temples. Yes, actually *squeeze* their skull, pleading, imploring them to:

"Think! Think! You can remember. Just try. Try!"

Years it took to abandon the dissection of dead brain tissue, cold baths, hypnotizing, shouting, and squeezing heads in his hands. Years to discover the simple innocuous question:

"What does that remind you of?"

And then let the talk ramble out until all the evasions and lies, all the wishes and fears, had been exposed. Revealing a person's hidden rooms, seeing all the gross injustices of childhood papered over with pleasant recollections. Smiling strangers. Gruesome parents. A promised gift. A failed grade in school, a second helping of dessert, a good-night kiss, just one more chance . . .

Subconscious. Unconscious. Censorship. Distortion.

Stilted words like that only got in the way.

He crawled case by case. And circumstance by circumstance.

What *method* was there in any of that?

As for the "analytic" part, it lay in paying attention to what people said and recalling what they overlooked the day before. A misrepre-

sentation. A little fib. And by examining these "oversights," penetrating the disguise to reveal a truer thought. A finer perception.
Deeper sympathy. Cowardice. Or hate.

Then how did you cure people afflicted with hysteria? Nobody
knew. Anything else was a lie. But none of that mattered anymore.
Only the young man's question. The wise man's answer.

He had gone in to lunch; a plate of steamed noodles and goulash
sat before him at the kitchen table. The paprika scent in the meaty
gravy rose into his face, but he sensed another smell inside his head,
more delicious than the plate of goulash, sweeter than the orange tea
he drank. The scent of victory.

Because he knew how to cure this sick girl for young Whosis.

Indeed, he did.

The pungent steam from his plate curled into the nothingness of air.
The kitchen seemed far away. He hoped that if he went for a brief
trip, no one would notice his absence. Just go on with their meal without him. He glanced back and saw them still engrossed in their food.

Ah, all was well, then. . . .

Around him the dark wound like an eyeless shroud. Church bells
tolled the midnight hour, and he heard the distant whistle of a train
moaning to silence on the outskirts of town. Herr Professor found
himself standing in the street. A curved cobblestone carriageway led
to a tall, iron-spiked gate. Lights burned behind the blue glass of the
lanterns. The iron gates swung silently open, and he passed inside.
Before him the fortress of the Burghölzli towered, floor upon floor,
window upon window. He remarked the absolute murkiness of the
night itself: no moon, no stars . . . impenetrable.

By chance he glanced at his own hands. They gave off a lumines-
cence, a faint radiance, as when you cupped a candle flame. But this
glow came from within himself, without any outside source. *He* was the
candle. *He* the flame. Glowing into the dark of the lifeless hospital.

Then he went inside. The clean marble halls glided by. He drifted
past doctors and interns sitting in their offices, reading or writing,
never bothering to look up or wonder at the puff of air at his passing. . . . Then the hallways slid away, and he stood in a huge glass-
enclosed room swarming with crazy people talking and howling,
whispering and laughing. Ah . . . the solarium where they kept the

Incurables. A horse-faced chap wearing a homemade reverend's collar stood by himself, braying, "We stuck it in! We twirled it round! She took it all! Right on the ground!" While off in one corner a mad barber shaved a catatonic man's genitals with a cardboard razor. Curled on the floor, a huge woman licked her fingers and toes like a cat, pausing every so often to mew. Two pinheads with silly Chinese eyes swam into his vision, their heads bobbing on rubber necks. Herr Professor felt himself slowly sinking. A gleeful dwarf darted out of a musty corner, masturbating furiously —

He saw the pulsing glow of his inner light dying. The dwarf babbled at him. "So you think you can cure her, eh, my good man? We'd like to see that. Indeed, we would. But can you cure this, eh? How about this?" The little shrimp was flicking his tiny slug right in Herr Professor's face. "Let's see you cure it right now!"

"No! No!" he cried. "I can't help any of you! It's the others I want. The *curable* Incurables!"

Fräulein and Herr Junior Whosis! Find them and never mind the mentals. No man could save them. They were too far gone. Just like himself. Why, look now! Look at him crawl on the floor.

Walking like a dog.

Ja, just like the children's red corgi, Hansel, back home. Crawling between everyone's legs. If they're crazy, he barked, I'm crazy. If they are, me too! He scratched himself behind his ear, sniffing the ground for somewhere good to pee. Now barking. He gripped somebody's leg between his paws, just like Hansel back home. Oh, what a fine, attractive leg! He gripped it more firmly and began humping it with great ardor and affection. Just as the children made Hansi do when guests were in the house. Oh, what a beautiful leg!

After a few minutes of fruitless humping, the great overpowering affection for the leg began to wilt. His humping ebbed. A bottomless remorse took him. Please don't let this fine leg belong to Herr Junior Physician Jung. But as he looked warily along the leg, he knew he'd prayed in vain. Just as bad as he imagined. Worse, in fact. For the leg he'd been humping with so much love belonged to none other than Herr Direktor *Bleuler!*

What a terrible first impression.

At last, a little shamefacedly, he discovered his hands and feet and brushed himself off with as dignified an air as possible. What could he say? He tried to think of some gracious remark to show Herr Direktor that being a dog was really all in a day's work. . . . But nothing suitable came to mind. Except:

"Herr Direktor, I presume."

And then:

"Would you be so kind as to introduce me to Herr Junior Physician Jung?"

Direktor Bleuler tugged doubtfully on his thick beard for some time, as though deciding whether to answer. Perhaps they wouldn't let him see Herr Junior Physician after all! Perhaps they'd misdirect him, or pretend the fellow had left the hospital. He almost dashed off, calling, Jung! Doktor Jung! When Direktor Bleuler cleared his throat and said in a bleating voice:

"Ah yes, Judas, we've been expecting you. Why don't you look for your new friend over there." Bleuler waved a vague hand in no particular direction.

He saw the shadow of a man and woman in silhouette, heads bent together in private conversation. All at once he felt the pulse of life return to his limbs. He held his hands out and they glowed with a golden light. He thrust his warm fingers into the gloom, touching the huddled figures' wrists. Watching his own warmth flow into them . . .

"Come," he beckoned. "Let me lead you out."

They followed his touch, fluttering after him. He drew them through the crowded solarium, weaving among the tangle of madness. Even as he tried to save them, droves of Incurables gathered about to block their escape. Yet each time he shone his outstretched palm to the mob of deformed faces, some shielded their eyes and shrank away; while others, as if transformed by magic, shed their madness, becoming whole again. The cured ones following in a line, their thread growing longer . . .

Once safely beyond the dayroom, in the hospital garden, the shadowy cloak fell from young Jung and the girl like rags. Their faces were lit by the dawn sun coming over the garden trees. Herr Junior Physician bowed gravely to him. And then Fräulein Schanderein dipped her knees in a curtsy. Oh, so demure, such a lady, so obviously touched by her cure — but too thankful and smitten for words.

222

A few paces off, the entire staff of the Burghölzli stood in ascending rows as though gathered for a formal photograph. Worshiping him, enthralled, in awe of such a sacred being. And now Herr Direktor Bleuler walked across the gravel path to greet the Blessed One.

To offer his supreme respect.

To make the most wonderful gesture.

Bleuler turned to face the assembled staff and raised his arms like the conductor of a great orchestra. The chirping of the garden birds ceased one by one — so too the rustling leaves in the trees, until the very air stilled. Then, as the man's hands dropped slowly to his sides, the staff of the Burghölzli knelt silently to the ground, prostrating themselves for the Blessed One, like the shepherds at the manger. Kneeling to him, one and all.

And to Mankind's Second Dawn!

"Your Method is a gift to us all . . . ," Bleuler whispered gravely. "How can we ever repay you, my dear Freud?"

And for a happy, breathless moment, his mind went totally blank. The thralls had finally bowed to him.

What was there to repay?

The plate of goulash had been devoured and pushed aside. A hunk of bread lay beside drops of the fragrant reddish sauce. The life of the kitchen bubbled around him. Across the table, Donna the maid dipped her spoon into a small bowl of stew. She smiled briefly and then turned her attention back to the bowl. Near the sink, one of the boys scrubbed the goulash pot with great mounds of suds that seemed to crawl into his hair, while the other boy was clanging two rinsed pot lids like cymbals. Through the racket, Herr Professor's daughter had been trying to ask him a question. "Are they going to marry?" she asked him. When he did not answer immediately, she insisted, "Well, is he going to marry her? Yes — or no?"

"Is he what?" Herr Professor yelled over the din. "Who?"

"Those papers!" she retorted, completely exasperated. He had brought the gray envelope to the table. The pages were spread about and splattered with goulash drops. He had been eating as he went over Herr Whosis's crazy case again. "You've been ruffling them and shuffling them and mumbling, Young man and a girl . . . young man and a girl. And so I asked: is he going to marry her?"

"No, I don't think so," he said over the noise. "He's probably married already. To somebody else."

"Married to somebody else!" His daughter rocked back in her chair, completely scandalized, then crossly blurted out, "Well, he'd better stop fooling around, then, and make up his mind."

Herr Professor gaped at her, speechless.

Chapter 6

Emma

She was his wife, wasn't she? With her own title. Everyone called you Herr Doktor Frau. Just an empty title, no? The "wife" tacked on as an afterthought, making her *his* Frau. The forgotten fluff at the end of his name, with everyone assuming the man did the thinking for the both of them. But what *was* she supposed to think? Didn't you ever wonder?

The way he spoke to her changed in the passing months as the new patient took over more and more of his time. Nothing drastic. A tip-toe of slow degrees . . . And then it hit Emma all at once, in one of those sickening revelations that made her feel physically ill. The revelation came after a dream.

She dreamt of the Burghölzli Hospital in the time of his terrible head cold, during which she stayed by his bedside across the hall from room 401. What were they waiting for? Then she remembered drearily: the girl had retained her stools, and they were waiting for her to go again. Where was Carl? He should have been in bed, delirious with fever, sweating and twisting.

As she left the room a horrible loathing came over her . . . as though what waited in the hallway beyond was something supremely repulsive. A lump in her stomach worked its way into her throat, a gag to keep her from screaming.

She went out into the fourth-floor hall, but instead of standing on cold marble she waded ankle-deep in a river of slow-moving feces, like a river of lava. So! His patient had gone at last, she thought. Won't he be pleased! Yet she made no effort to pull her feet from the

225

flowing mire. Instead her eyes riveted on the door of 401. The patient's door.

The lump in her throat stifled her to silence. She tried sticking her fingers down her gullet to pry it free, but she couldn't get a grip on the slippery thing. The patient's body had trapped her husband in the room. It had grown huge, reminding Emma of that illustration in Lewis Carroll's *Alice in Wonderland:* poor Alice grown immense inside the rabbit's house, with her head pressed to the ceiling, her elbow jammed out the window and her foot stuffed up the chimney. Only, the patient had grown far, far bigger. Fräulein Schanderein had swollen to fill the whole boxlike room. Grown so huge she crammed every corner of the box, bulging out the open doorway, the layers of flesh and skin packed like meat. Emma had the impression of a gigantic cooked ham, squashed into a tiny tin: solid flesh with a sheen of jellied aspic dripping off.

"That's her," Emma said in her dream.

And then she saw her husband.

Carl had tried to crawl from the girl's room before her body engulfed him. His outstretched arm protruded beneath the packed layers of flesh. He had scored the marble floor with his fingernails, trying to pry himself free.

Emma woke up in a silent groan. Their house cat, Geschrei, sat amicably on the empty pillow next to her head. She stared incuriously at Emma with that infuriating aloofness so common to well-fed house cats. Without warning Emma struck her, sending the cat off Carl's pillow in a streak of orange fur. Geschrei halted at a safe distance, pinning Emma with a look of indignant reproach. And now, as the dream faded, Emma clearly heard the changes in the way he spoke to her.

When he said, "I'm off to the hospital. See you later." When he said, "Let me concentrate. I'm writing a letter." When he said, "No, I'm not hungry. Take it away." When he said, "God, I'm starved! Why isn't there ever any food in this house?"

It all meant the same thing: Never mind. I can't think about you right now. *Dammit, just leave me alone!*

Emma remembered how it used to be.

At first they shared the Schanderein business. Talking in bed at night, discussing the events of the day as man and wife. The early nights of September lingered with summer's heat, while their skin on the sheets seemed blessedly cool.

The nights ran together as they pondered the meaning of Fräulein Schanderein's shrieks and the question of how to examine her without resorting to force. Emma felt a secret thrill at the thought of him making the girl strip and show herself for examination. Then, subtly, Emma put her own self in the girl's place, fantasizing her submission in bed. Seeing him as the devil when he roughly pulled the covers off, and when she thrashed about to get away, imagining his hooves leaving streaks across the sheets, hearing his long, scaly tail whipping back and forth through the air in the darkness of the room. How forbiddenly delicious to have the devil in your room at night and feel his strong body press you down in bed. It made her want to faint and snarl foul language, mouthing words she did not even know she knew. . . .

But the girl had not touched her deeply yet. Merely a thing of the hospital, suitable for fantasy — and far away.

So as the bright October days shortened to cooler nights, she waited with him in her mind as he languished at the door of 401. And the wait became interminable and dreary.

Their talks in bed stopped when he began spending nights on the fourth-floor hall, watching for the girl to take a plate of food into her room or send a chamber pot out. Once, Emma came in from shopping and was appalled to find him trying to force feces down the bathroom sink. He looked up from his task, grinning idiotically, and launched into an explanation about how "this was the way the patient did it, you see, in order to keep her room free of excrement."

Later in the week he sat at the dinner table while his food went cold, drawing a picture of the gift Fräulein Schanderein made for him: a repulsive, faceless little doll. "You see, she made them out of strips of her bedsheet and her stools, which she somehow made in small regular amounts —" He broke off, admitting sheepishly, "I was all wrong about her trying to force it down the sink. She wasn't doing that at all. She saved them up. One a day for thirteen days. Making them for me!"

What could Emma say? All that day she had shopped for the meal herself, and cooked it herself, and sent the servants away early. Now the food lay on his plate, hunks of spongy meat and tired vegetables, growing cold. Her own plate barely touched.

"Yes, I see," she said.

November came, blowing cold each day and colder at night. The bed was cold and she lay alone. He came in at odd hours, muttering to himself in snatches she couldn't catch. If he spoke to her at all, he did so in asides, his face brightening for a moment when he told her, "I opened the door today and stared inside."

Then, on another day, "I got inside the room." And on the next, "She allowed me to sit." Then finally, with a grim smile, "Three months to the day, exactly. I introduced myself."

Nothing else existed in his life. Emma stopped asking questions; waiting silently for him to speak, yet all the time wanting it to change, to go back to the way things were before. Far easier to hold her tongue than to put the hard questions now. Questions like "Do you still love me?" And "When will you come home?" November was the silent month.

Then one day he did come home. On a day when the ice glinted blackly on the windowpanes in the December dusk, barging in livid, shouting, "The idiot lost her goddamn sheets! The very *raw material* of her gifts. What did the moron think? She didn't want them back?"

He shut himself up in the kitchen, letting the teakettle whistle. She heard china shattering in the sink, heard cursing. He broke two cups making tea. She told the maid she could leave early.

He left the kitchen a wreck and went to the parlor sideboard, where he took a bottle of whiskey from a cupboard, the only liquor in the house. Emma watched him pour three slugs one after another, then push the shot glass away after the last. Finally gripping the bottle, head bowed as though praying to the whiskey god before putting him back in his dark hole. From then on he shut her out completely.

When he began composing the letter to Herr Vienna Professor in earnest, Emma crept into the study to read his notes. Consumed with curiosity and loathing — swearing never to look again but knowing all the while she would. For now she saw through the viewing slit into the patient's room, seeing what he saw. How Fräulein kept full chamber pots around her bed for comfort. How she sent him out in frantic searches for more vessels in which to store her excrement. Offering up her chamber pots and used meal plates. How her husband finally saw the girl's unwashed foot as it pushed a slop pot toward him.

He said one thing to her during this time, right at the end of December, murderously happy. "Hah! She threw a plate at a nurse named Simson. Almost killed her. Pity!"

In early January he began to get more cooperation from the staff; and for a little while at least, he came home regularly and in a better state of mind. She caught a light cold, which she passed on to him. He fought it for ten days, yet going each day to the hospital, and the cold grew worse. He looked more and more drawn, as if some hidden physical bond with the patient robbed the very life from his blood. She brought him sugared tea with oranges squeezed in it as he lay hacking in bed. . . . He said thank you. And she said you're welcome.

The next day he overslept, woke up in a panic, and fumbled about the bedroom, trying to disentangle clean clothes from soiled ones. "I don't think you should go," she told him. She could have stopped him if she wanted, just by holding his hand and drawing him back to bed. But she let him go, tying his necktie to speed him on his way. Part of her hoped he would get really, really sick, and leave the Schanderein girl to someone else.

Emma's vile Whisperer suggested that. Her secret Whisperer who said things like: *Try to understand and not be too critical.* But he whispered it in such a mealymouthed way, she knew he really meant: *Let the fool hang himself. Then he'll come back with his tail between his legs.*

Who was this secret Whisperer anyway, always poking his long, blue-carbuncled nose into everything she thought? A figment of her mind, of course. A vile incubus who took pleasure in feeding off all the sensible and mature words she used to hold her life together, only to spew them out again as cheap, smelly virtues, the nice words she used to fool herself into seeing everything as normal. She knew his face. Bulbous eyes, swollen from crying in the dark and feeling sorry for himself. Running nose, from the cat hair that collected in the bottom of the closet where he lived. Spidery fingers, perfect for picking at all her open sores.

And forever cajoling her, whining from his dark corner, interjecting some nasty piece of counsel. Every time she thought she knew her mind, he just made matters worse. One day insisting, *Try to understand — after all, he's your husband.*

Yet the very next day whimpering fearfully, *Say something, do something. Save yourself before it's too late.*

Yet when her Whisperer went back to his smelly hole and she saw her husband trembling with fever, putting on his clothes, determined to make it to the hospital . . . her heart did leap out to him, knowing how alone he was. Knowing how much courage it took to drag himself forward as the whole sea tide of things battered like a gale to flatten him down. While her Whisperer sneered, *Help him Emma — after all, he's your husband.* Licking his chapped lips, making it sound so dirty.

Only he could put those quotation marks around the word "husband." . . . And it had been a long time since Emma found it possible to remove them.

Ja, her "husband" . . .

Running off half dead to save his little Fräulein.

Then came Orderly Zeik straight from the Burghölzli. Herr Doktor had fallen sick, and they were keeping him in a room across from the patient. An open war had been going on over the body of the girl in 401. That very morning Herr Doktor had arrived in the nick of time to prevent a major catastrophe. And all the while her vile Whisperer chided, *After all, he's your "husband."*

Yet the days she nursed him in the hospital brought them closer than they had been for months. Emma found a reason for being. He needed her and she could serve. There was a wholesome center in that, a warm place where the Whisperer never shoved his nose. She sensed that even as her husband lay sick, part of him wanted to "make love" to her. Sensed it like a smell rising from the sickbed. But as for "making love" . . . quote marks had been placed around those words too. That night her eyes fluttered open to see him creeping close to her, almost close enough to take the quote marks away from making love. She felt him wanting it then. And she wanted him to want it. And take her in the chair . . .

Nursing him was a little like making love. She wiped the perspiration from his forehead while his eyes glistened up at her. And every day she waited while he went to Fräulein's room to try to cure the girl for a few minutes, returning shaking and weak. How sensually ironic that during the time Fräulein S defiantly clamped onto her bowels, Herr Doktor noisily expended himself in his own chamber pot. While Emma babied him and wiped his bottom. Making them more intimate than they had been in months. And yet horrible too, touching him that way in the hospital and not at home, in private.

On the night the fever broke, she knew she would not be needed the next day. Indeed, he had already gone to the girl's room when she awoke in the morning, stiff and cramped in the chair. How galling! She had worn herself to a fray keeping a death watch over him three nights running. *Don't even leave him a note*, her Whisperer suggested. She wrote one anyway: Dinner at six, Darling — or some such nonsense. *What a good little doormat . . .*

And only when Emma walked in at the front door did she realize she had taken her husband's dirty clothes from the hospital room to press them, twisting his jacket and pants into knots as she mumbled furiously to herself all the way home.

Suddenly she laughed. Served him right. And she tried to stifle her smiles and smirks that evening when he stepped out of the carriage in front of their house with his bathrobe tucked around him, bare calves and feet in slippers. He came right into where she sat in the parlor, hooking his thumbs into his bathrobe belt, and announced with quiet pride, "Fräulein Schanderein spoke today."

Thence straight to bed.

The next day his head cold seemed to be waning fast. "I'm going to see her face," he told her.

Emma stared out their bedroom window into the broad dome of a brittle blue February sky. The sun warmed a triangular patch of their bed . . . the winter passing. God, I hope she dies today, Emma thought. Before he can finish the letter, before the man in Vienna writes back.

Now, as Emma watched the triangular patch of sun creep higher and higher on the bedspread each morning, Fräulein Schanderein seemed less and less like a flesh-and-blood person. More like a living vegetable lying in a hospital bed, which clung to its miserable existence by sending out fungus-like tentacles, sucking the putrefied essence out of everything it touched. The girl had long since ceased being ill, ceased being fascinatingly crazy. Now every time Emma thought of her husband with that girl, she called the girl a name —the Cunt. He was with the Cunt. He's seeing the Cunt. He's just come from the Cunt. And nothing she could ever do erased this ugly word from her mind. An unspeakable word — the mealymouthed Whisperer was too afraid to say it. And then one day Emma discovered she could not even keep the cunning word locked up in her head. But that it cunningly managed to escape.

This is how it happened. Emma's final university paper was due for her baccalaureate in archaeology — to be finished in five weeks' time — and she had barely begun to collect the materials! In desperation she had turned the kitchen into a study of sorts, working long hours there when no other chair or room in the house seemed to suit. After a few days of cloistering herself among the smoky bricks and pots and pans, she began to think she might actually deliver the paper on time. . . .

How snug and comfy the kitchen was: rows of china plates smiled down from their shelves, and teacups gossiped with their saucers. A net of onions hanging from a dark roof beam amiably consoled a smoked ham nearby on the tasty fate of being eaten. A place of her own, where she ruminated to her heart's content while a cheery fire hissed, a bubbling pot of water whistled for tea, and Geschrei purred sweetly in the chimney corner.

She made the kitchen table her desk. And beside a pile of half-peeled turnips for a stew she stacked old volumes. Various tomes on the European Grave Builders, with long-winded titles such as *Prehistoric Times as Illustrated by Ancient Remains and the Manners and Customs of Modern Savages;* and dubious pronouncements bordering on the pompous, like *The Geological Evidences of the Antiquity of Man.* And still further leaps of the imagination, such as an obscure medical paper titled "The Marking of Lunar Time Through Synchronized Menses in Tribal Females of the Tahitian Islands." Also strewn in sheaves across the table were some pen-and-ink drawings by the Frenchman Abbé Henri Breuil, who sketched bones and artifacts he uncovered while digging holes in the Aurignac caves at Les Eyzies in the Vézère valley.

What made a person carve the soul-image of a bison onto a round flat stone? Why cherish a reindeer antler etched with the figures of spearmen on the hunt? She had traveled through Les Eyzies once — a gentle rolling valley with a sparkling river, tame and secure. The huntsmen chipping flints and stalking game were long, long gone. Only a quiet, cultivated valley, where peach trees laden with fruit swayed in the wind and where a plump gendarme in his smart blue uniform pedaled along the road, ringing his bicycle bell . . .

In the midst of her pondering, Helga, their housegirl, brought a note into the kitchen. Helga, a sweet, sheltered creature, didn't mean to disturb her, but an irritation welled up in Emma, as if some nasty substance embedded in the envelope itself had passed from her husband's hands to hers. Of course the note came from him; who else? Once thoughtful gestures, now they were fast becoming annoying interruptions. Each one the same. Dear Love, I'll be home late tonight, will you please see to something or other of no particular importance. So Emma just took the note silently from Helga, glanced at it, and tossed it aside — thinking to herself, *He can't come home because he's with the Cunt.* And blithely went on paging through the pages of Abbé Breuil.

The housegirl gaped at her from the kitchen door.

"What is it, Helga, dear?"

The pale maid pressed a dimpled fist into her moist red mouth and fled with a mousy squeak. Had the word really been said out loud? Into the air?

He can't come home because he's with the —

A damp sigh ebbed slowly down in Emma, a sigh that sounded like *die Fräulein.* . . . She hadn't even read her husband's note.

In the middle of the next morning she found his shirt from the day before slung limply from the wooden bedpost. Streaks of blood ran along the collar and down the shirtfront, slashes of bright red on the starched white cotton. And along one side, the warped smear of a finger. He must have killed the Cunt, Emma thought instantly. What'll we tell the police?

Later, as she tried to work, a great blackness descended on her . . . like a stone pressing upon her head. She turned from books to notes and back to books again. While Geschrei flicked her orange tail to beat the band. Before noon, Emma crept into his study again, tiptoeing around the edge of his desk, sitting stealthily in his chair. Her hands hovered over the layers of papers. Sifting through the heap, she searched for some clue to the blood.

I'll only stay for an hour, she promised herself. An hour ... But when the long shadows grew to dusk, Emma had still not solved the riddle of his bloody shirt, for he had yet to write that into his case notes. But she did learn other things. About Fräulein's twiddle, and about the girl's first speech. About their word association tests: and chuckled to herself over the abject nonsense of it. Blue sky. Longing. Family. Hospital. Was he really going to tell the man in Vienna any of that?

Then suddenly, in panic: how could she keep her husband from making a fool of himself? Was it already too late?

Her next day's search answered that. Yes, much too late.

She found the page describing the Ritual. So now Emma knew. Her husband let the girl smear feces on him. Even her menstrual blood. And they danced together alone in her room. Playing a game of murder. Her husband doing Fräulein's bidding, crawling to her, killing for her . . .

Emma hid her face in her hands. She wanted to scream. How had it ever come this far? *Yes, how?* asked the Whisperer in mock tenderness. *After all, he's your "husband."*

The weeks of waiting for an answer from the man in Vienna turned to weeks of pacing, of grumbling to himself, his voice rambling about the empty rooms of the house. . . . Then it came. The Reply. A thin standard mailer. Reluctantly she laid it aside on the gilded table under the long hall mirror, beside a crystal vase. She primped the yellow roses in the glass. There! find it yourself. And I hope he tells you to forget the whole thing. Give up. Send her back — wherever she came from.

Emma caught her face in the mirror. Lines of spite had appeared about her eyes. A stark, malicious face. Her chapped bottom lip had taken to growing a new layer of skin every other day. And her blouse misbuttoned — walking around half the morning with her collar askew. Looking like the school dunce, her shirt bottom hanging out and her shoes untied, the little girl all the other little girls laughed at. Emma raised her fist over the glass tabletop; she saw herself flinging the yellow roses to the floor, tearing up the letter, pretending it never came —

That night at dinner he sat through the meal, reading and rereading the Vienna man's answer: saying nothing, picking at his food, finally shoving it away. A spoon clattered to the floor; he ignored it. He pushed his empty coffee cup in her general direction. Without a word, she went to fill it.

When she brought the coffeepot, she put the cup back near his elbow — then accidentally poured the burning liquid across his sleeve. He jumped, glaring at her. "Goddammit to hell!" A few drops had touched the edge of the Vienna letter. The Reply! And his eyes went murderous, as if some sacred totem, scroll, or tablet had been defiled. Now a price must be exacted to purify the thing again.

She was crushed with remorse; and she furiously dabbed the coffee drops from the letter, nearly weeping. "I'm sorry. So sorry!"

But he did not notice her welling tears. The glare had vanished, and he mindlessly repeated, "It's all right. I'm all right. It's all right." After a moment forgetting all about her, sinking even more deeply into the Reply. Emma's tears dried in her eyes. She cleaned the table coldly and efficiently. When she had set the place to rights, his empty coffee cup reminded her it wanted filling. She brewed another batch in the kitchen. Back in the dining room, she finally poured him the long-awaited cup.

Spilling it *again*.

Soaking the letter this time.

For an awful moment he stared at her clumsiness in frowning disbelief, then said in a thoughtful way, "I know you went through all my notes. Do you think I'm stupid? Why don't you write your own paper and stop mucking about with mine? You're about due, aren't you?"

Emma set the coffeepot down with a clang and listened to him rant.

"They say at the hospital I'm in love with her. They say I like menstrual blood smeared on my face. They say I taught her how to do tricks with her shit. You think that's true? Then say it. Say it to my face!"

Emma said nothing. She silently tried to mop up the soaked letter; it had stuck to the table. She tried to peel off a page, only tearing it.

He grabbed her hand to stop its fussing. She snatched her hand away and clutched it to her breast. His words hammered into her.

"When she first came she was wrapped like a cadaver. Now we see her face! She smelled like a goat. Now she bathes! Every second she shrieked like a banshee. Now she talks! So you *talk*. What the hell is wrong with you? Come on, tell me. Let's have it!"

Suddenly a vision overcame Emma. A picture of herself tipping over his chair until he fell flat on his back with his legs up, still shouting, "Let's have it! Let's have it!" Hiking up her dress, ripping open her underwear, to straddle his face, to shut his jabbering mouth, while he thrashed helplessly and she grinned down in an angry sexy rage, grinding her hips into his face.

"You have it now?" she said down to his muffled head. How wonderful finally to have the last word, finally getting his loose tongue just where she wanted it, all pressed into her open ready —

Cunt! grunted the Whisperer from between her legs. Emma went red hot with shame. She squirmed off the vile thing's head, flying right up to the ceiling. But he came after her, zeroing in again, long nose to skewer her to the ceiling, to splay her just like a rag doll —

The dining room came back. The table empty. No Whisperer. No husband either. Carl had gone off to his study, leaving her alone with the orange house cat, purring watchfully in the empty chair.

Chapter 7

Mind Traveler

The hearth fire in the Bollingen Tower had crumbled to ashes; the night was burned away. The old man had not stirred from the bunk. After lying long hours on the thin, rag-stuffed mattress, his brittle back ached as the wooden slats dug quietly into him. Then, in the endless remembrance, he had ceased to care. Pain no longer mattered.

Gray morning light peeped in at the window. He swung his stiff, cold feet onto the stone floor. Mein Gott! His legs felt old, so weak and fleshless. . . . Sweat from his fingers had ruined the faded photo of the Burghölzli Hospital. How long had he worried the sad relic as he wandered those long-forgotten halls in his mind? Was it only last night he stumbled downstairs from the tower in a fit? Only yesterday he read the old Faker's obituary in the paper? Oh, his body ached. Too much ancient history. Living whole lifetimes in the past — a sixty-five-year-old man doing the work of a thirty-year-old. He wondered idly if Freud had kept that first letter about Fräulein Schanderein. What a sincere youthful bit of fluff!

And yet . . .

He rolled up his sleeve and looked at the scar: a small brown patch where Emma's spilled coffee had soaked through his shirt and burned him. Funny how a little burn hardly noticeable at the time had blistered and broken and left a dark mark. The scars you carried with you . . .

Should he start the fire again? See the bright tongues of flame warming his bony hands and smoky coals glowing darkly red . . . ? He tried to rise. But no. His thighs were glass strings. Another seizure, then. Hah! to die a day after the old Faker. While the other man's body was still warm almost. And the idiots would all write about the poignant coincidence of it, the two of them dying a day apart like that. Headlines like: TRAGIC SYNCHRONICITY! Giving the old Faker his last death rattle of revenge. Oh, they were all idiots: the smart writers, the smug critics, the clever editorialists — anyone who made their middling way in life by judging other people's talent for a living. Well, no third-rate hack aspiring to the editorial board was going to scrib his obit with some sanctimonious crap like "Enigmund Freud, the world's greatest living *blank*."

His breath came sluggishly in his chest. A lifeless hand rested on the sill as if it belonged to somebody else. More flies had returned. He tried to shoo them away, twitch his hand, flick them off. Simple.

The hand ignored him.

One of the flies creaked its head sideways and looked wisely at him, then rubbed its forelegs together as if immeasurably pleased with the state of things. Thousands of hairs bristled from its watchful black face like spikes from a black iron helmet. Its horned jaws worked: saliva gleamed wetly in its mouth. At last he understood . . . it had come for him.

When you died, a fly came and took you away. The beaked face tried to say something — but its fly's jaws were no good for words. He could barely make out what it was saying. . . . Come along, Herr Doktor. Follow me, please. This way now . . .

The little black fly leaped from his hand, whirring off on a wing of grim-reaper wind. So I'm going to die after all, he thought. How nice.

The shaft of sunlight went on forever, as he fell through its brightness; sparkling motes of sun-trapped dust whirled pleasantly around him like a universe of stars. Enduring . . . continuing on like a bright blindness that never died. He heard the great babble of humanity's common voice, like a thousand people laughing and crying, singing and shouting, all at the same time.

Of course! The gales of light were a *brain* . . . his *own* brain. The whole world in the arched cathedral of his thought! Oh, what a confusion of noises and tastes: a wailing siren heard at noon yesterday, a bitter gulp of seawater swallowed thirty years ago — all the memories of the mind existing side by side. The brain was eating a thousand meals and living a thousand days. Every moment, every tear. Even the skin had memories: cuts and bruises, scrapes and bumps, a lifetime of minor accidents all clamoring for attention. Then came the kisses and caresses, beginning with Mama's and Papa's — to a little cousin's in a dark closet, to a girl in school, to a fiancée, to a wife's — to where yours and hers became mixed together.

While never far away the emotions slumbered like restless mountains. Some towering, some crumbling, some at rest like dead stones. Years of terror and happiness, despair and joy, boredom and loneliness, triumph and defeat. Yet sitting high above it all, on a throne of its own design, Formal Learning gazed down upon the rabble. There was A-B-C and One-Plus-One and Pi r^2. A miserable page of physiology memorized intact and the touch of fingers on a cool scalpel as it sliced some cadaver's heart in sections. While the words of a teacher droned on forever: "Well, have you finished that dissection yet? Have you finished that dissection? Have you . . ."

And finally the little thoughts too, resting comfortably like old married couples on a bench in the park. Washing his wife as she sat in the bath, smelling her wet fragrant skin, feeling the simple pride in the act of running a washcloth along her arm . . . Then a lash of anger: he was shouting at someone recently — an orderly? Then a moment of peace as the body slipped off to sleep.

But even in his sleep there were memories and dreams: Herr Doktor dressed as Brunhild in a circle of fire while Nanny Sasha galloped on horseback and armor to save him . . .

The brightness and the noise seemed to lessen; a dirty lightbulb filled his vision. An old, naked bulb — was he waking up? Not in the tower, surely. The tower had no electric.

An annoying feeling persisted, as it did in dreams, that no matter how hard you looked at a thing, the object stayed blurred, obscure. Whereas other things, on the perimeter, stood out sharp and clear. But never what you wished to see when you tried to pin it down. He saw only the pale, sickly glow of the yellow bulb, while the rest of the room kept slipping from his view.

Yet he sensed other rooms . . . the feelers of his thoughts wandering through half-open doors and down deserted hallways. He went past huge dust balls and dropped coins, past a sleeping cat, and around a corner. Then came a narrow flight of steps, leading down. Bleak twilight seeped from a round compass window, vistas of slate roofs and chimney pots leaking weak streams of smoke into a dying sky. A cold wind beat against the glass. Flecks of black ash flitted across, and then the lazy flakes of an afternoon snow swirled down, the big white flakes falling with the black flakes of ash. While off in the distance, the deep, lonely hoot of a boat whistle sounded.

He found himself within a town house. An institutional kitchen with large pots and pans hanging from metal ceiling racks, strainers and slotted spoons. Skillets clung to a wall near a huge black grill. Something burned on the range, smoking away. An old wolverine of a woman, puffing a filthy cigarette, snatched the pot off the flame, then darted back to the slop sink to redouble her attack on a battalion of dirty dishes. Her cigarette fell from her mouth, hissing into the gray, soapy water. A trembling film of grease closed over the sinking butt. She paused and rested her elbows on the sink, shaking her shaggy head, mumbling stubbornly, "This will never do, Madame! If you weep now, I shall get very angry. What would Frau Direktor say?" But she remained there with her head bent, motionless and silent, a ragpicker of defeat. . . .

The kitchen door banged open. A younger woman and a child bustled in on a gust of wind, clutching sacks of groceries. The bag in the little girl's arms spilled, sending its insides rolling across the kitchen. A sack of sugar split, and the child went straight for it, greedily licking the sweet grains off her damp palm.

"Marie! Marie!" the old woman despaired. Then, pleading: "Petra, don't just stand there!" The younger woman hadn't bothered to retrieve the spilled groceries. Her coat hung off her shoulder. She looked over the kitchen in a kind of numb disbelief, then dipped her hand into the lathered dishes, shuddering in disgust. "Is this all you've done? These are from breakfast. We've been away hours. You haven't started dinner yet. What's wrong with you? What's wrong with you!"

"I'm sorry," Madame whispered to the dirty dishwater. "I'm tired."

But Petra didn't hear her. She snatched the sugar tin off the shelf and began scooping up the mound of sugar with a spatula. "The vegetable seller knows something. He wouldn't sell to me. Just that hunchback Jew in the back of the market. Probably tomorrow the Jew won't sell to me either."

"What about the butcher?" Madame asked faintly. She had gone back to her mound of dishes with creaky effort.

"I had my pick of the garbage pails." As evidence, a brown-wrapped bundle leaked slow blood onto the floor. Petra scooped the last grains of sugar into the tin, while little Marie stared at nothing, idly tracing lines on the floor where the mounds of sugar used to be. Searching for a grain, licking her finger, then searching again. For a moment the child left off and quietly mumbled into the sleeve of her coat, as though piping an order down a ship's speaking tube.

"She's at it again," Petra said with a note of dread.

Now they could hear the child's soft voice as she spoke down the tube of her sleeve. "Engine room, report. Report . . ." Petra gathered Marie in her arms, stroking her. And the child let herself be taken, silently curling into the young woman's arms as the older one looked on. Spilled groceries lay on the floor. The pot on the stove grew cold. A sink of dirty dishes. No one spoke.

He slid away from the kitchen, gliding toward the front of the house. Here again he found the dimming yellow bulb casting a sickly light over everything. But now the annoying vagueness was gone. Behind a cluttered desk sat a middle-aged woman. She had taken off her reading glasses and polished them on the sleeve of a plum-colored sweater, which hung above her shoulders. She resettled her glasses and turned her heavy eyes toward the papers before her. What was it about this woman? The graying hair? The strong, weary face? Her glasses? A severe tortoiseshell type, industrial looking. A central-economy standard issue, millions of people given millions of the same. The tortoiseshell frame only brought out the heavy squareness of her face —

But the dress!

Ja . . . once upon a time such a dress: a daring off-the-shoulder black velvet gown. Cut low over the bosom, showing off the bust as though the woman's hands were cupping them up for you herself, feeling their weight and offering them for you to admire. The youthful bosom he remembered, so strong and so yielding — Fräulein Victim's bosom, yearning to be touched. But wait now! When he bought her the dress they didn't call her Fräulein Victim anymore, no . . . and the way of the dress itself, it had clung to the girl like the petals of a lily.

But the woman at the desk was all wrong. Flabby and sagging, while the dress had grown frayed and worn; the seams opening and a panel of coarse material sewn in to make room for a larger person. He noticed creases in the black velvet where the heavier woman had spread where she sat. He strayed to the wide expanse of bosom, pale and luminescent. How coppery Fräulein's skin had been, even in the depths of winter. Still, the woman wore the thing with dignity, as if this were the very last garment of value she possessed. The black velvet dress recalled tender memories, sweet social conquests, and past glories in its very fabric.

And ja! Here the same row of rhinestone buttons set in silver buttercups, four of them, down the left shoulder strap . . . How those rhinestones had glittered! Glittered and flashed in the crystal light from his own dining room chandelier above the great honeyed oak table in the Zurich town house. Her bosom, the glittering and flashing crystal light, the gleaming table: it set a man's teeth on edge, making you think about undoing those rhinestone buttons, unbuttoning them one by one to watch the black velvet peel off her white shoulder, to see the butter-cream skin beneath. Too precious, too sweet to touch . . . He had picked it out himself, paid more than he could afford. It glowed so darkly in the narrow shop window as the snow curled down through a cold February twilight. Enchanting him completely, the row of sparkling buttons, the darkly gleaming torso of the mannikin sheathed in black velvet . . . while the decorative accessories so casually displayed — the alligator purse, the kid gloves, the string of pearls — faded before the dark power of that lush, seductive dress. He saw it and knew it had been made for her alone. How many weeks did he lurk before the window of the shop, waiting for the courage to go inside? Pondering how long till the girl herself would be ready, sane enough for a fitting? At last, before his courage failed or the dress was snatched by other hands, he did the deed. The pretty shopgirl clucked in admiration as she wrapped it in crinkly pink tissue paper. "A fine lady's dress," she said with a trace of jealousy.

A fine lady. Hah! Months he had waited for her to stop smearing shit over everything and everybody and dancing about like a spastic at the drop of a hat. How long before he brought her out in public without her exploding into a fit of verbal nonsense? Ja, for this was a fine lady's dress, made for a fine lady. How many months passed before she could even do an impersonation of one? Whatever possessed him to buy the damn thing?

Because he thought he could cure a mad girl.

Cure her!

That was begging for trouble. Ja, ja, he should never have tried. Just stuck her in the dayroom, as Nekken and the rest wanted. Then crawling to the old Faker for advice! Ach! How low could you stoop . . .

The vision of this place and its people was slipping from his grasp. He felt the gales of wind in a bright light, gales of wind eating away the years.

He was going back again. . . .

Chapter 8

Shadows

Herr Doktor sat in his office on the fifth floor of the Burghölzli. The Vienna reply sat on the red leather surface of his desk. The dried coffee stain from Emma's jealous fit marred one side of the white paper. Like the long-forgotten streak of decayed food that had once defiled the wall in Fräulein's cell. How long ago that seemed. . . .

But Emma wasn't the crazy one. The girl was. And his wife had better adjust to that fact, because he wasn't going to stop now. Not for Emma.

Not for anyone.

Now that his playacting mayhem and his wild dances with the girl had become generally known, another spate of treachery had run through the halls like a virus of malice. A crude Star of David had appeared on Fräulein's door, scrawled in red lipstick. A sign meant to cow him, to daunt and intimidate . . . Naturally, they never caught the prankster. But what truly frightened him was how the powers of the place — Bleuler and Nekken — remained so conveniently neutral, obliging Herr Doktor, Zeik, or Nurse Bosch to wipe off the malicious star every time they found it. "Well, this is an asylum, you know," Nurse Bosch remarked sadly. "Everybody's crazy. . . ."

He turned to stare out his office window. The cold stung him. A clean blanket of March snow lay on the garden grounds in sloping drifts. The darting tracks of a hare cut across to a burrow in the bank near a vine-covered wall. How he wanted to drift out the window, find a safe burrow of his own, and sleep till spring. He leaned back tiredly in his chair. The Vienna reply seemed to hover over the desk, his lazy eyes seeing the letters blurred and hazy. . . . He set the paper down and let the haze gather over it as smoke from some Aladdin's lamp.

Like a genie, Fräulein emerged on the surface of his desk, wrapped in a filmy sheet — lying across his blotter like a love slave. Salome. A single eye reproached him from the folds of her turban.

"Can't I have a fantasy?" he asked.

But there came no answer. Instead she began to writhe like a serpent, her body undulating, showing him its seductive curves and voluptuous parts. He grew warm for her as she coiled on the red leather. . . . Her voice came for him, honeyed and melodious. A sweet voice gently urging him to take himself out of his trousers and show himself to her. Telling him she wanted to see him take it out, see him touch himself. And then to have him watch her too. Watch her while she touched all the dark and lovely places.

Her silky shadow spread over his face. It smelled like gardenias . . . jasmine and warm baths. . . . If he died now, it would really be all right. She parted herself, and he heard the words that ran down him like water . . . "What if the others see us?" she asked. "You and me and this?" Answering the question for him like the stroke of an omen: "Then they'll see us. And then they'll know."

Herr Doktor lifted his head off the stained reply. Had he fallen asleep? A passage from the Vienna letter lay faceup on his desk:

> What caused her trauma? The girl may have had years to build up a veritable house of cards around some dangerous misconception. While at the heart of her labyrinth she hides the sacred minotaur of an idea — Her Self — a monster of wrong thoughts, suspicions, and discord. Are you the one to lead that monster from its lair? What shadows of her past guard the dungeon ways you seek?

But oh, God, if Fräulein made up what she saw, or what she thought she saw, or what happened long ago, or what she simply *wanted* to happen . . . then there'd be no unraveling the madness. No end to the fantasies, insane creations, lies, and dreck. To cure her, impossible. Impossible!

A gust of wind sucked the window shut with a metal clang! He jumped up, shouting, "Ahhh!" Then, after a moment, sheepishly latched the window, rather glad no one had seen him leap from the chair like an electrocuted frog. He waited for his heart to settle down, with the nagging sensation something was wrong nearby. He looked under his desk, feeling foolish. Of course nothing but his own limbs, some dust, and a wastepaper basket. Still the anxiety gnawed at him. Like that crooked picture on the wall. Was it always tilted, or had it slipped recently?

A print, almost invisible in the gloom. *Actaeon and His Hounds.* Actaeon, the young prince who stumbled on Artemis bathing. Lest he brag of seeing the goddess naked, the huntress turned him into a stag and hunted him down with his own dogs. The print showed the creature, man above, stag below, with antlers growing from his head and a strip of fur that ran down his neck, blending into the broad, strong haunches of the animal. Four dogs clung to its flesh, tearing him apart. The engraver showed in lurid detail the snarling teeth and the ripped entrails of the stag-man. The print had been hanging on the wall when he first moved into the office. And he didn't know if he liked it or not. . . . Perhaps that's why he never took it down.

He glanced out the window. A moon had risen over the garden wall, casting white light across the snow. Did the moon rise early or late this time of year? He looked at his pocket watch, but to his dismay he saw it had stopped at seventeen minutes to seven. Seven this very night, or seven in the morning — who knew? Why didn't he wind it every day, the way normal men were supposed to do?

Then he saw what was wrong.

A shadow fell across the floor in the hall. The shadow of a person standing quietly outside his door. Someone playing tricks.

"Who's there?"

No one answered. The hair on his calves had risen. The malicious star artist, come to scrawl on his office door? Now, shrilly, "See here, who's there?"

The shadow vanished. He cursed himself for being such a coward and poked his head out into the hall. Empty. Then he saw the shadow coming from behind one of the columns that flanked the turn in the corridor. He knew the form, the silhouette of folds and wrappings. A draped figure. The true goddess who chased him through his days, laid sleep upon his eyes, and caused his watch to stop. At his feet he found a book. The neurology text, given Fräulein ages ago, left outside his door. Well, she had supposedly been on her way to medical

246

school, so why not give it to her? But until this very moment, Herr Doktor had not realized how much he hoped she had actually *read* the words. . . .

Why bring the volume? As if to say, Someday I'll be better, and when I'm better I'll study neurology and learn to be a Fräulein Doktor. . . .

"Neurology," he said to the shadow. "Well, why not? After all, someday you'll go back to your studies. It's an open field at least. Indeed, I should know. Why *not* neurology?"

The shadow from the column wavered as if trembling in a draft. No, she had never read it. Only pawed it, smeared it with bodily matter, tearing out pages. He really ought to stop playing around with his life and try another field before it was too late. Would another hospital take him? Perhaps if he mastered a degree in surgery. Keep this book, though, keep it as a reminder of how he kidded himself for so long, hoping that if only he tried hard enough, listened closely enough, empathized enough, *sacrificed* enough . . .

The shadow wavered like a ribbon of smoke, threatening to disappear. But instead her voice came back at him.

"You don't know anything," the shadow said.

As though he'd never know anything. Ever. As if he was immeasurably stupid. And would remain so. Forever.

Her footsteps pattered off. He had half a mind to chase her down, yank her roughly by the arm, and yell, "What do you want from me?" Push her against the cold marble wall, rip away her sheets and turban, while he pried her thighs apart and took her. Shouting, "Is this what you want? Is it? Is it?"

The vision collapsed with a sigh. He was too tired to follow her. He clumped back to his seat, dropping the book on his desk. The cover flew open to a dog-eared page. She had made a streak across the white paper. Ja, he knew the place. Knew it chapter and verse. Knew the very lines she'd been reading. And *now* he knew why she had come up to his office that night. Why she brought him the book. Why she said he knew nothing. She was right. He didn't know anything.

He bolted out of his office, running for the stairs. He had to see if his guess was right. He had all but forgotten her steamer trunk. Her damn trunk! Standing mutely outside her door for months, ignored like a dumb beast of burden. Once a week one of the maids wiped the dust off. Now he had to see if the trunk was still there. He almost tripped at the top of the stairs. Zeik stood like a soldier at attention, as if he'd been expecting Herr Doktor. The girl's steamer trunk had vanished from the hall. Had she dragged the monster through the doorway alone? No, impossible! The trunk was huge. He'd tried to lift it once. A gang of four orderlies had lugged it up. God! she must have really wanted the thing inside to drag it those few bitter feet into her room. She was right, of course. He hadn't known anything. At last he understood.

Chapter *9*

The Patient Exists

She was a bee in a huge beehive. She even knew what kind of bee — a worn-out worker drone, worked to death and hiding in her cell. She felt the living stone hive above her and below her and on every side. The many-celled Beehölzli . . . the Burghive. Swarming with other bees, busy bees going in and out of rooms and up and down stairs, humming all together.

But she had been broken and no longer worked. So they put her in a cell alone. And wrapped her like a budding larva and sealed the door with wax. Just before they sealed the cell, the nurse bees wrapped her in a healing gauze from the spit in their mouths. The gauze softened the armor of her exoskeleton, and while she slept the black and yellow markings of her thorax began to fade. . . . She became soft mush, now splitting in two, with wriggling legs that thrashed about, with bones inside and flesh and blood. Soon she was not a bee any longer.

How sad not being a bee . . . When she felt her warm limbs and not the hard insect armor, she wept and shrank down in the covers of the bed. The blankets were stiff from overuse, from rubbing her skin day in and day out and never washing. Down below she smelled herself, not sweet beeswax and honey, but sour and goaty. And even farther away, her feet were cold. . . .

In the dark room a shaft of white light fell through the viewing slit, like a shaft into an underground chamber. How she hated the electric light. It burned night and day from great opaque white glass globes that hung from the hall ceiling by iron rods, casting a steady, blinding glare. . . . She shut her eyes against its emptiness.

Her skin itched where she picked a scab on her elbow. She kept

249

picking and picking, sometimes not even letting it crust over before she went at it again. The picking of her elbow had become a private thing, her own, and she wasn't going to show the sore to anybody. Not even Herr Smarty Pants.

She also called him Herr Guten Morgen. And: Herr May I Come In? But his real name was Herr So Polite. Yet he certainly could be called Herr How Are You Fräulein. Or: Herr May I Sit Down Fräulein. He had a lot of names. Though his latest and most recent name was Herr Smarty Pants, because he tried to be so smart all the time.

Herr Smarty Pants even thought he'd gotten her to talk. Wrong! Wrong! He hadn't *gotten* her. She could have talked anytime. Anytime she wanted — even the first day if she wanted.

She laughed under the covers, dry, choking laughter, waking up the sick bee in the next room. Another worn-out worker drone lived there; she always heard him whimpering and trembling. Sometimes he rocked back and forth so his whole bed creaked. His constant babbling sounded to her like gurgling water over flat stones, so she named him the Gurgler.

"Shut up, you!" she hissed at the wall, then slapped it with the flat of her palm. "Shut up, Turd Mouth!"

Sometimes she called him that — Turd Mouth. If she ever went into his room, she would surely strangle him, choke him to death to stop his gurgling forever. Her hand thudded against the wall, and she hissed louder: "Shut up, or I'll come in and eat your tongue!"

She laughed her dry, gagging laugh, challenging the Gurgling Turd to make one more tiny sound. Then strained hard . . . holding her breath, listening with all her might. But the whimpers faded to silent fear. Now nothing. Not a sob. Not a whimper.

Good. Let the Gurgler whimper to himself for a while. At last she could ignore the shaft of light from the hall, falling like a blinding weight through the viewing slit. Ignore everything: her own bed, the little room, the great stone Burghive outside. . . . Just rise above it all and float, float like a soap bubble in the air wafting in the darkness of the room, never touching, never landing, drifting and never breaking . . .

She had things to think about.

Such as: how long had she been there? Thirteen years at least in this same bed. Under these same sheets, smelling this same air. That

250

would make her about six hundred years old when she first arrived.

No, six was very, very bad. Mustn't think six. Or eight or ten or any of it. Not thirteen either.

She'd been here a *week*, then. A long week, or maybe a month.

It was a secret.

A safe secret from the tall one, Nek-Nek, who stared at her blandly through the waxy viewing slit. When his face came into view, she closed her eyes and went away. And with her eyes closed she rose from the bed like a ghost, right through the door, through his body and down the hall. And when she opened her eyes again, she was elsewhere! Sometimes outside the window, hanging from a drainpipe like a spider. Sometimes in Herr Smarty Pants's office, watching him sleep at his desk. And very soon she was going to float into the Gurgler's room next door while he sniveled in bed, to strangle him with her own hands until his thrashing stopped and his gurgle was gone.

Nek-Nek's long, narrow face appeared in her viewing slit again and again. The deadskin face, she called it. And when it came she always closed her eyes. Floating away in the stale air of the room, drifting through him . . . Then waking up in some other part of the Burghölzli, in some quiet place beyond the bee cell — with her back to the cool marble wall and her chilled feet on the cold, shiny floor. There she might stand like a statue of herself, blending into the surroundings as people passed by, never noticing, never sensing her presence, merely glancing briefly at the noble statue of the Queen and passing on.

Sometimes when Nek-Nek came in the dead of night, he trapped the safe bubble on the bed. Then she shrouded herself from sight, peeking through the folds of her covers, watching him stare down through the waxy slit of the bee cell. The deadskin face always stared a long, long time, and she always hid until the face was gone.

Then there were the books. At first she did not remember what the blockish things were supposed to be. They looked so familiar, so touchable, and she felt she ought to know all about them. Their insides and outsides, and what they did. For a moment, a name came to the tip of her tongue. Yes, it was . . . it was . . . A great vagueness lay upon her, a warm, wet fog that covered her and took away her brain. . . . She knew there were scratches and marks on the thing. And for a long time (twenty years?) she stared at it, stared at it right on the floor, waiting for it to speak. She pushed the dead block around with her foot, trying to get it to show itself, but for the longest time it stayed dead.

Then Smarty Pants gave it away, coming into the cell and saying, "I've brought you another — "

Book?

Book . . . Not right at all. She tried it out several times to see how it sounded: book . . . book . . . book . . . until the feeling came over her of wanting to jump and shout and tear it apart. Then she closed her eyes and floated in the bubble through the winding tunnels of the Beehölzli. Up and down stairs, along the corridors and back into her cell again. When the bubble laid her gently down in bed, she opened her eyes and saw what made her vibrate so. It came into her mind as out of a clear blue sky, like Mother Mary in those stained-glass windows — the Book. Her Book. And she recalled the title . . .

The Exegesis of Aching Dottery

Her book from home, with green and blue marble swirls on the cover and gold paint along the edges of the pages. Even the binding was sewn with gold thread. Did Herr Smarty Pants have it sent?

The bubble came and took her away. She floated with her eyes closed. Ages and ages went by, during which the stars wheeled about and slowly went out blackly one by one at the rim of the universe. When at last the bubble let her down on the bed, she felt beaten and crushed. She knew the worst now. Herr Smarty Pants's book didn't come from home. It wasn't titled *The Exegesis of Aching Dottery*. Not at all. It was called . . . *Anatomy*.

But how long had it taken her to understand that?

Herr Smarty Pants talked and talked, droning on about the fibula and the tibia and the sternum and the coxae. . . . And all the while she had the deep feeling of tightness, a swollen stretching that was lovely and painful and expectant. An urgent thing was about to happen. She was becoming a big, round egg. Becoming all yellow yolk and clear albumen — and soon she was going to hatch.

But it was still not safe to be born. Not yet. Because she suddenly saw a wolf staring through the wax viewing slit. Snarling and slavering, saliva dripping from his fangs. Odd, she thought, what a striking resemblance he has to Herr Smarty Pants. Of course, Herr Pants had come to look in at her, dressed in a wolf's costume.

"Go away, please," she said. Or did she scream it? And then, as if to oblige her, the wolf closed his wet jaws and went away. But then Nek-Nek's face came instead.

And it never did what she wanted it to. Watching her touch the book. He knew she touched it even before Smarty Pants. Long before. Because he came in the dead of night, his silent presence creeping like a smell as she cautiously touched the pages of . . . *Anatomy*. And she knew if she peeked through the folds, his face would have changed again, into the armor-plated helmet of a soldier bee, with its huge, domed prism eyes and horned, clicking jaws. There, behind the milky wax of the viewing slit, the armored face stared silently, occasionally jabbing its spiked head from side to side, examining her with huge, sad eyes. And when the soldier bee came to watch her, she always went back to being a bee herself. . . .

Always listening for the roar of his wings beating the air in the hall — but there was never any sound. Only the soldier-bee face hovering silently. And she, deaf in a soundless world. She felt a pressure in the very air, so great her eardrums threatened to burst, pressure enough to crack her armor-plated thorax. Then little by little the fierce silence went away and Nek-Nek's deadskin face came back, sneering mildly at her with his heartless human smile.

She might have understood things better, except for the pretty floating bubble. Sometimes it saved her and sometimes it snatched her away. Sometimes it made her human and sometimes turned her into a bee. . . . Obeying rules of its own, rules she did not understand. Taking her off on endless journeys through the worm-crawls of the Burghive. Then setting her down on the bed once more, lonely and confused. If only she could remember how it had been at the very beginning . . .

The sound of laughter. Then angry shouts. The huge form of the

Burghive loomed above her, like a painted stage set, seeming to fly up on the hinges of an immense trapdoor. And she saw that in fact it *was* a beehive, with thousands of bees hovering about and darting in and out among the windows. They dragged her into the great Beehölzli, to be stung alive by soldier bees' barbed stingers, crushed by their armor plating, swarmed over and suffocated. She closed her eyes, slipping into the warm, safe bubble . . .

And slept for a thousand years.

Chapter 10

Labor Pains

Someone somewhere was always screaming. The immense stage front of the Burghive loomed above for a moment and then swallowed her. Huge hands, strong as metal clamps, hoisted her and dragged her along. She floated over the floor, her feet barely touching. A long marble staircase glided by and then a set of glass doors that opened onto a sunny solarium. She saw it as a bright fishbowl, a glittering aquarium with people-fish inside, pressing their wet faces to the glass doors with big unblinking eyes to see her passing. Then came miles of twisting corridors and being hoisted up dingy stairwells, one flight after another — and all the while, some abominable person was shrieking in her ear.

Last of all a door opened, and they threw her inside a room. No, not a room, but a sort of tube with five waxy sides, open at one end and then canting out in the shape of a pentagon. The walls smooth and translucent. A bee cell. Two man-sized worker bees hovered at the opening of the tube; they danced delicately about the angles and edges, secreting wax from their horned jaws, sealing up the entrance. The wax came from a pulsing gland inside their beaks, flowing out in thick, warm streams that instantly adhered to the cooled portions. Before the new layer hardened, one of the workers deftly molded it into a smooth wall. Already the two worker bees had secreted half the opening shut. In a few moments they finished, and she lay alone inside her cell. Her body felt puffy, white, and uniform: she had become a white larva waiting to be born. A little brainless egg without a center. She went to sleep.

She woke and glanced about her, wondering vaguely at the change that had come over the cell. Now it looked like a person's room, with a bed and dresser and a window facing outside. The door had a glass slit in it: a shaft of ugly white light slanting down. She closed her eyes and stopped her ears to make the person room go away. At last she felt her separate human legs begin to fuse together, and she knew she was turning into a bee-egg again. Soon her human legs jelled and she was safe once more . . . just clean liquid inside a translucent larva case. And the five-sided tube snug all around, the walls waxy smooth. It was much, much better being a clear little egg without a center.

But the clean, waxy tube always returned to being a people room, dingy and cramped. Suddenly the door would fly open, but instead of people coming in, a wolf would burst through. A wolf in a suit and tie, its thick neck bulging out of a pressed white shirt. And sometimes she saw a large bee in a tight white nurse's uniform, who squeezed in and hovered over her bed, taking up all the space and leaving her no room to breathe. How she loathed seeing the wolf and the nurse-bee.

If she had been a larva then, it would have been all right. But when the cell was a room, she was also a soft person. With the awful bees pushing and prodding, and scraping her with their sharp pincers. Then zip! the bee vanished, and the wolf in his suit and pants came back, growling at her in a wolfish voice she didn't understand.

How did the wolf fit into a man's suit of clothes?

Wasn't it terribly uncomfortable, cramped and hot?

While ever some awful person screamed his lungs out right in her face. While the pounding in her head throbbed like a kettledrum and her legs slowly fused together, losing their bones and flesh. Until she became an egg once more, the walls of her room turning to pleasant wax. Clean and empty inside.

Safe.

Time came and went like this. A long time, during which she was either a sleeping egg, clear all the way through — or watching the bees come into her room, then hiding from the wolf while the cretin went on shrieking. Later she discovered the Gurgler next door making all the noise. But at first she knew nothing. . . .

Gradually a great silence came to the annoying little room, a deep quiet in the air around her, with the Gurgler keeping mum for a while. The bees had gone, as though the whole hive was letting her rest, recuperate. . . . So one afternoon when a golden light fell across her bed, she opened the window a crack, letting the sweet breeze steal inside.

And the room stayed a room for some time, allowing her to sit up and look about. A small brown sparrow had flown in at the window; it looked this way and that, at the room and back at the sky. She wondered vaguely if the sparrow would turn into a wolf or a bee. But it simply fluttered its wings pertly, then preened in the autumn sunshine, chirping once. She fancied the chirp meant "Hello!" and she wished she could chirp back. She also found that she was hungry.

Food.

A goodbad word.

She had a cloudy recollection of meal plates being pushed inside the room by one of the worker bees and some awful, dirty animal in rags gobbling at the plates as she watched from the bed. They called the dirty animal a name: Frau Lies. . . . But all that seemed in the distant past — for now the hive put the meal plates where she couldn't reach them. Outside the door. Where she smelled the food for endless periods of time.

The savory smell lured her right to the crack in the door, snuffing and sucking and licking her lips, licking the floor right beneath the door and even the crack itself. She could just see the plate through the crack, sitting out in the hall, and she clawed the floor on her side, leaving sweaty streaks from her fingers. She heard the wolf's snarly voice outside. But sometimes she heard snatches of speech. "I've brought your *grrrrrrrr*, Fräulein. . . ."

Did the wolf know her trembling fingers were pressed to the wood of the door? Feeling the food's warmth beyond? And her lips pressed to the door crack, trying to suck the delicious stuff through the narrow gap? She was frantic, starving, on the verge of opening the door —

When the food smell vanished. They'd taken the food away. . . .

Time passed. A century? The goodbad food smell dragged her from the bed. She crawled to the door. Her trembling hand touched the doorknob. The warm metal knob turned so easily that suddenly a bar of light plunged into the dark room. She snatched the meal plate inside and slammed the door.

She gobbled down a few mouthfuls and immediately retched, vomiting them onto the floor. After a few minutes the spasms subsided. She gulped the spit-up where it lay and snatched some more from the plate. A great fist wrenched her guts around, doubling her over. She writhed on the floor. . . . Her stomach heaved and shook itself; she fought to keep the food down, then snatched another mouthful. She sobbed, choking as the sourness of her stomach rose into her burning throat. But she had cleaned the plate. She had eaten. Eaten food. Gobbled it all. Even the sourness from her insides and whatever bits came back up . . .

Before she melted into a clear little egg this last time, she heard the rumor of animal sounds in the hall. The wolf and one of the worker bees, named Zee, were speaking together. The wolf saying, "You are my witness. On the thirteenth of October, 1905, the larva consumed its first meal in five centuries, between the hours of one and four in the morning . . ."

And the Zee bee buzzed back, "Jawohl, Herr Wolfpants!"

Sometimes when Wolfpants or the Zee bee came to the door they also brought the Brass. But what was this round brass thing? Just looking at the gleaming metal made her shiver. It had a name, surely . . . a dirty name. Old Sewer Mouth? Wrong! Wrong!

She set it in front of her dresser. And slowly but surely, as she emptied her meal plates, the Brass mysteriously filled. Yet how it came to be filled she did not know. How unspeakably glad it made her to see a fresh one! Then finding herself back in bed, thanking the Brass from the bottom of her heart: a sweaty relief coursing through her limbs as though mighty hands had wrung her out. And all the while the Brass filled higher and higher.

One night a full moon rose brightly across her window. It lit the whitewashed walls, turning them to silk and the marble floors to opal. In the branches of a nearby tree perched the coal-black figure of a hunting owl. When it turned its head the moonlight caught its nighteyes, making them deep pearls, staring incuriously at her. Down below in the garden, another animal, not one of the Burghive beasts or some mutant from the glass fishbowl, stood quietly in the night.

"A deer . . . ," she said voicelessly to the window. The deer had been nibbling at the grass border of a dry flower bed. But as if hearing her speak, it raised its head and looked to her window. And one

258

of its wooden brown eyes turned to amber. Abruptly the sense of the whole world's reality struck her — its immeasurable, monumental existence — wholly independent of who and what she was. A real moon, a real garden . . . a real owl, a real deer, all occurring in this moment of time.

The deer in the garden looked steadily up at her but did not speak.

"I'm in a madhouse," she murmured softly. And this time the deer dipped its head, as though ashamed, troubled with an aching sadness.

She squatted on the floor over the Brass. Her own reflection in the window — a hunched leper, swathed in rags. The rim of the Brass felt warm under her bottom; and she bit her lips to keep from crying out in good pleasure for the love of Herr Wolfpants and the big Brass he brought her.

But wasn't he terribly uncomfortable, bringing her all those Brass and saving none for himself? After all, where did *he* go when Old Sewer Mouth called him? Down in the garden? And what about the meal plates? Did he keep none for himself? Herr Wolfpants must be starving, bringing her his meals every day and then snarling over the scraps. Wasn't he growing hungrier and hungrier, so ravenous he might burst in and devour her? How terrifying.

If he devoured her one day, she would never be born. Just gobbled down as a clear egg without a center, while the worker bees hovered nearby, wringing their hands. She knew that if she did not solve this problem for herself, one day he would gulp her down in a single bite. She must give him a precious offering, to placate him. Something of herself . . .

Her babies.

She would give him her babies to eat. Or put in the Brass if he wished. And then she might gain time to be born again. Born herself.

Her babies.

How long it took to make them. She ate only potato now, no grease of any kind, no meat. So she returned it to the Brass in the proper consistency to work with. Tearing off bits of sheet; starting each tear by chewing a pinhole with her teeth. Tear it, then chew a bit crosswise and tear it again to make a strip. Thirteen strips she cut in the darkness under the covers; thirteen times on the Brass. Shaping them in the thick air . . . chewing bits of meat to pulp so that she might wipe down their tiny bodies with a sticky paste of *food* for the wolf to eat. And lastly making the little cowled heads, using grease to harden the hoods.

When she finished, she cooed over them, caressing them, gazing tenderly down at their thirteen empty heads.

Soulless.

So that Herr Wolfpants might see any face he wished there . . . Sweet pink baby faces. Rosy cheeks, cuddly and succulent. Any face at all. Except hers. For hers had yet to be born. Thirteen she made for him. Each one a year she had been waiting — marking the time back. All the time she waited since she died.

Would Herr Wolfpants understand?

Her thirteen children lay outside the door. Waiting for him to devour them so that she might be spared and born again herself. She heard Herr Wolfpants growl softly, "Thank you, Fräulein Bee. I'll save them for later. Maybe someday we'll eat them together, you and I . . ."

The door opened, and Herr Wolfpants pushed his suit-sleeve wolf-paw inside the dark room: the paw balanced a shoe box on top. He had gone to great trouble to settle her babies comfortably. Wasn't he going to eat them after all? He was a wolf, wasn't he? He smelled like one and bristled like one. . . . Oh yes, he'd gobble them up.

The Gurgler was screaming again next door. . . .

Lying on his bed, just as she lay on hers, but he was a stump of a person, with no legs and little fleshy paddles for arms and hands. Rocking back and forth, fluttering his useless chicken wings. Soon she'd sneak into his room and throttle him. Take him by the throat and choke all the whimper right out of the helpless little turd. Wring and twist while he tried to beat her off with his disgusting little flappers. Until his beating and bleating finally ceased, eyes bulging in their sockets, and his tongue lolled out purple.

Yet why did the Gurgler shriek every time Herr Wolfpants tried to leave with the Brass or one of her empty meal plates? Why did the Gurgler carry on so?

After all, they weren't his meal plates.

Those weren't *his* Brass.

And then she understood: the helpless, stumpy Gurgler with his useless flappers knew how to see through walls and down hallways — knew when she had become an empty white egg without a center and when she had two legs just like a person. Even knowing when she planned to be born. He was warning her, yes, warning her not to let the Burghive take any of her bee self, not one scrap of her precious insides. Not a shred of food. Not a drop from the Brass. So that she might collect enough of her sacred mounds, her sacred clay, enough of herself to grow fuller and fuller. The cell tighter and tighter.

Until she, the She-Mother, gave birth to herself again.

Once, one of the worker bees, a nasty female drone, came into her room and tried to take a bit of her holy royal insides. She killed it with a blow to the back of the neck, cutting off its head entirely, and the drone flew into a decapitated rage. It buzzed mindlessly into the hall, smashing into walls and finally dying in some lonely, dark corner of the Burghive.

Herr Wolfpants had been coming every day. But since he showed no signs of devouring her, she let him enter the room. He brought her those square, oblong, leafy things — books. And it was a long time before she recalled, realized, that the books had many names; that they weren't all called *Anatomy*. And even longer before she remembered she could read.

Finally one day she had amassed enough of her precious insides to make a whole person. Now she let Herr Wolfpants take away the overflowing Brass. She had more than enough within.

Pregnant, heavy with her new self . . . how wonderful. She could feel herself moving inside, a new animal growing. Stretching, getting ready to come forth. But nine months was much, *much* too long to wait. No, she would let it grow for a little while more, but not forever.

She would give birth in thirteen days, then. One day for each of the thirteen years she had waited as a corpse before coming to the Burghive. Before she became a little white egg without a center . . .

She felt herself grow more and more swollen — swelling, filling, expanding moment by moment. At first it felt delicious, tight and warm, but as the days drew on, the warm deliciousness went away and she felt clogged with pain. Outside, the entire Burghive seemed to hold its breath. Even the Gurgler fell silent, not whimpering at all. The whole hive waited, work ceased. All eyes turning to her cell . . .

They were waiting for the Queen Bee to be born. She had become the Queen Mother, and out of her bowels the new Queen would come. She heard her expectant attendants hovering about her cell door, almost frantic with anticipation. The tenth day had come, or the eleventh — she could barely keep count. The pressure mounted in her belly. Her swollen body ready to split down the middle. Her whole being one long, stifled groan . . .

That's when the assassins chose to strike. A worker bee and a nurse bee. Holding her down with their jointed claws. They came at her with a pointed snout to puncture her abdomen and kill the Queen Baby growing inside. And it flashed through her whole being, from her tingling mouth to her dark clenched hole, who these assassins were: hirelings from a rival larva somewhere else in the Burghive. Caretakers of another clear egg without a center. And they wanted their own larva to take possession of the hive. The Gurgler shrieked like a harpy, spreading the alarm: "Help! Help! Achtung! They're raping the Queen! They're raping the Queen!" But no one came. And she knew who the helpless Gurgler used to be — with his stumpy body and useless flappers dangling at his sides. The twisted offspring of another pregnant Queen. The assassins had raped her too. Punctured her vitals with the sharp snout and flushed out the Gurgler prematurely. Now he lay forever in his cell, rocking back and forth, unable to do more than shriek his tale of woe.

She tried to fight them off, keep them from sucking out her baby Queen too soon, too soon! They were going to make another Gurgler. Stick their big pincers up her, *up her*, and tear the baby out —

Herr Wolfpants burst into the cell. He ripped off the worker bee's head with one swipe and slashed the domed eyes of the nurse bee with his bare claws. Then yanked their wings off and tossed their torn bodies into the hall, where they wriggled their thin hairy legs in twitching spasms. She still felt excruciatingly pregnant, as though her whole bottom half were filled with logs. Only the twelfth day! Her baby self still had one more day to grow, one more day for its eyes to form, its lips to bud.

Did Herr Wolfpants have less fur than she remembered? He would seem almost half human if he didn't slouch so. He had been coming into the room every day of her pregnancy to read from a book, *Anatomy*. What was he saying now? Describing the birth canal, the very route her newborn self would take. Between growls and clicks she heard him speak human words:

"What remains of the food mass are various indigestible compounds, which finally pass into the large intestine, up the ascending colon —"

The thirteenth day. Ready to split open like a ripe melon in a field. She clutched a bit of blanket over her head and gave birth to herself. Her whole body pressed into the open mouth of the Brass, squeezing out the royal sacred body of the new Queen Bee.

"— across the arch of the transverse colon and down the descending colon to the rectum — and at last to the anal canal."

Her breath came in ragged gasps as she pressed into the Brass. Herr Doktor Wolfpants's reflection in the window stared at her, his nostrils red and chapped, his nose running wetly. He held the *Anatomy* book tightly to his chest. The veins in his hands stood out as he gripped the cover. His face had broken out in a sweat. She felt a deep, rumbling shakiness in her guts. She opened and closed her eyes under the blanket, making sure they weren't fused together like the Gurgler's. She moved her arms and legs ever so gently. She wriggled her fingers and toes, counting them quickly. Yes, she had them all. Good. No flappers.

The Gurgler had saved her. To be reborn. A whole person.

Chapter 11

Strangling the Gurgler

Her memory floated in pieces. . . . Slashed with daggers of color that showed things brutally naked, then plunged them into blackness again. She even knew the name of the Brass now. Not Old Sewer Mouth. No, they called it a chamber pot. A chamber pot, for all the stuff that came out of her chamber and went into the pot. She recalled many pots coming and going; and the Bosch Bee, who was sometimes a fat pink sow and sometimes a fat pink nurse; and even Nek-Nek, who wasn't quite human. She saw meal plates full and meal plates empty. The books she read and the books she cast aside. She saw Herr Doktor Wolfpants when he wore fur and Herr Smarty Pants when he wore none. And a cheerful copper bathtub that came to stay one day and always left her spanking clean whenever she used it. And most of that was good. But not everything. What with the lingering terror of the black snout snuffing around the crack in her bottom, so eager to suck out her newborn reborn self. And then the pain of giving birth, which she sometimes still felt throbbing through her when she used the chamber pot. A clear memory of that hot expanding: an endless groan, the squeezing and pressing as the clenched fist of her insides pushed itself into the world, making her writhe in a mind-wrenching gasp —!

And so each day she gave birth to herself anew.

Yet on that very first day of her birth, before she crawled back to bed, Herr Wolfpants fled the cell, then leaped back with a piece of paper clutched in his paw, stammering:

"I forgot this."

He showed her a folded slip of paper, a letter you were supposed to call it. Which she examined carefully through her wrappings. A letter. A letter with words.

Now, wasn't that strange?

Shouldn't it really be the other way around?

Weren't words supposed to be made up of letters, not letters made of words? Because if letters could be made of words, and words made of letters — how was anyone supposed to straighten them out?

She never discovered. For Herr Wolfpants growled, "This came from your father. I'm sorry, but I wanted you to birth yourself." And he did seem sorry, sorrier even than if he'd gobbled her up. "Do you want me to read this letter to you or just leave it?" he prodded her. Read it or leave it? Leave it or read it? Her brain went clean and blank — because all she heard, all that struck her, was that F word. The word Flatter. "This came from your flatter," he seemed to say. That ugly, evil word: f-f-f . . .

She felt another birth coming on. She had given birth to her new-born reborn self — but now she verged on the birth of a twin. A twin lying just inside, waiting to come out. Sucking the life from the first-born all the time, all through her swollen pregnancy. An evil twin leeching to the side of the good one's neck, sucking and sucking un-til it bled her paper-white.

"Are you upset about this letter from your flatter and matter?" Herr Pants badgered her again. The bad twin in her belly squirmed sharply in her stomach. Crawling up her throat, right out her mouth. Talk-ing as it came. But it couldn't escape because her wrapped rags still trapped it to her face. Squirming behind the folds and swathings, bit-ing and scratching her lips and nose and eyes. She had to let it out. Let it out! She clawed a small opening in her burnoose, and it leaped into the room:

"Tell him I'm the Queen of Sparta with a hot rear end!"

Then this bad twin vanished into thin air. For it was only a sen-tence, with letters and words, and words made of letters. . . . She gave birth to more and more word babies after that; and each time one clawed its way up her throat and out her mouth, she made room for it to break free, unwinding a layer of swathings so each new group of words might show itself. But the words were always getting trapped and snagged on the layers of her covered head. And when they crawled over her face, they couldn't tell Herr Wolfpants what to do about that terrible F word, f-f-f . . .

"Make him understand. Make him. That the Queen rules the earth and the sky at night!" And as more words needed to come out, more layers of wrappings had to come away. And the face of her newborn reborn self stayed exposed for longer and longer periods: the face that bore itself out of her bottom but that now expelled word babies for everyone to see.

They came almost daily as the cloth fell from her head: some evil and some good. Nice ones, like "May I come in?" and "How are you?" But bad ones too, especially each time she played the word game, when the flatter and matter words came around again. And only the flatter and matter words made her want to scream The Queen.

Yet the Burghive stayed a human building for days at a time, with few if any bees buzzing down the marble corridors. When she let Nurse Bosch into her room, the nurse came not as a pink sow or a bee but as a large, broad-faced woman in a crisp white cap and dress. And though she might on occasion see a worker drone flit quickly past her door, that didn't bother her so much anymore. She even began to call herself Fräulein, as everyone else did when they came into her room wearing their human bodies with their people clothes on.

And she began reading secretly at night, sitting up against the cell door so the shaft of light from the viewing slit fell onto the pages. She read *Anatomy*. And another book Herr Pants brought her: *The Tale of Two Bad Mice* by a lady named Beatrix Potter. About two mice, Tom Thumb and his mausfrau, Hunca Munca, who tried to eat all the painted doll food in the dolly haus but wrecked the place when all the delicious-looking food turned out to be made of plaster. He also brought her other books. One by a man named Conrad which made her chest ache and her eyes cry at the end when the seaman hears Mr. Kurtz's last words whispered out of the filth of his dirty jungle hut, "The horror! The horror!" It made her wonder: was Herr Pants her darkest heart?

Or really the Nekken?

As she read one night, the shaft of light suddenly ceased. Then swept back and forth like a sword blade in the dark, while the Nekken peered about, trying to catch a glimpse of her. She froze, pressing her back to the wooden door. She felt the Gurgler in the next room working himself up to a scream, his first in weeks. But somehow the Gurgler held his breath, his flappers quivering. . . .

Then the sword blades of light vanished and the steady beam beat harmlessly down. She crept toward the bed.

And damn him!

His deadskin face stared dimly back from the waxy glass. He had only pretended to go. Oh, she'd know next time, yes, she would. And the Gurgler, he'd know too. She cursed the Nekken as she wrapped the swaddling around her firstborn newborn reborn self. No, he wouldn't fool Frau Lies again. Never.

A new book lay in her lap. Neurology. Fräulein had found the paragraphs accidentally on purpose.

> Dementia Praecox: that is, a chronic state of demented behavior. Symptoms include nonsensical language, delusions of grandeur, unwarranted terrors, convictions of constant persecution, and unrealistic perceptions of every kind. Kraepelin (1896) groups the various mental conditions into four subdivisions:
>
> Simple, that is having a uniform appearance. Subject outwardly normal but believes some impossible notion, such as that he is a jungle animal. The second is Hebephrenic. Subject acts in an infantile or foolish manner. The third is Catatonic, which includes states of mutism, paralysis, blindness, and depression. The last subdivision Kraepelin calls Paranoid: cases clearly characterized by intense suspicion of persons and events and widespread distrust of the world at large. It is widely recognized that these subdivisions overlap — producing disordered personalities with a wide variety of overt symptoms.
>
> Cause of Dementia: structural damage to the brain tissues. Specifically: minute cellular and nerve ganglia damage, either passed on through family traits or inflicted by trauma. This tissue damage is nonobservable by present methods of microscopic analysis, but this technical shortcoming is widely believed to be only temporary and soon to be remedied by more detailed methods of scientific observation.
>
> Recommended Treatment: Electrotherapy or Surgical Cerebral Intervention for violent cases. Hydrotherapy for nonviolent cases. This is a degenerative condition where the subject may continue to live for long

periods of time. No known subject has ever recovered from a diagnosed case of Dementia Praecox. It is commonly regarded as *incurable*.

She read these last lines many times. Especially the word "incurable," spelling it to herself, forward and backward. Incurable. The *I* meant herself, and the letter *e* at the end the sound of the Gurgler's shriek. Forward or backward — from the *I* to the *e* — no known cure. So the book said she'd never leave her Burghive cell. . . .

But she could always disappear when the Nekken's face stared in the glass. Then she closed her firstborn's eyes and traveled where she wanted. Passing through the door and the Nekken's body, to drift about the cool corridors of the hive like a thread of smoke. And whenever she came back from her travels, the Nekken was always gone. On the return from one of her trips Fräulein paused at her door. She quietly stared at her trunk, the steamer trunk with all her clothes from . . . the Bad Time.

What a huge old thing, with brass latches and sweet-smelling leather straps with brass buckles — and it seemed to her she had missed it very much. All her insides were packed there, all the things she had brought with her on the (don't say it) on her way to (can't say it) before the trouble happened and she came to the Burghive. How good to think it had been outside the room all this time, even when the room turned into a bee cell and the hospital a hive.

"You're mine," she whispered to the trunk as she slid under the crack of her door.

That night she did not read the paragraphs in her book but fondled its cover front and back. She had a new name for it, not *Neurology* — but *Newrongedly*. She found herself squatting over it, lifting up the swaddling of her firstborn and panting heavily in the shaft of light from the hall. Fräulein would show them how totally wrong *Newrongedly* was. All wrong.

"I do not believe, Fräulein," the Nekken said through the glass viewing slit, "you will ever be cured. I have diagnosed your case as dementia praecox — which, as you have read, is incurable. And degenerative. You are suffering from ancient brain damage, damage done to you before you were ever born. I want to inform you that no case of dementia praecox has ever been cured. And that yours will not be the first. . . ."

She felt the Gurgler ready to scream, starting to thump his head against the wall. The Nekken's sneering face vanished from the slit. She leaped to the door, peering sideways, straining to see if he lurked nearby. She heard the Gurgler in the next room, gasping for air —

And suddenly she knew that if he *did* scream this time, the whole hive would be down on her — every drone, every soldier, every worker bee. Now was the time — now — to strangle the little turd mouth. Go into his room and throttle him, push his face into the mattress until his skin turned purple and his tongue stuck out like a bloated turkey neck. Do it! Do it now!

She flew into the hall. The Gurgler gasped lungfuls, ready for a shriek. She flung open the door —

An empty room stared at her.

No chamber pot. No wooden dresser. No sheets on the bed. The stripped mattress had been rolled up, exposing the bedsprings. Because no one had lived in that room for the longest time . . . She felt her scalp throb and cautiously touched the tender spot with her fingers. A terrible thought came to her.

The Gurgler did not exist. Never had. The soreness: her own head where she had banged it against the wall. The shrieking. The abominable noise. All her. From the very beginning, from the very first day. And in a sickening flash, in utter glaring blindness, she saw the absolute truth of her very existence, and whispered:

"I *am* mad."

The Nekken chuckled. At the end of the hall, his long white hand kept orderly Zeik pinned to the chair. Zeik's face had turned gray, his mouth shocked open. While the Nekken's face — a green sneer, calmly pleased to be hurting her. And yet not really caring whether he did or not . . . She wanted to repay him. Then abruptly he withdrew. His laughter trickled down the stairs. A pale silence.

"I'm glad you're up and about, Fräulein," the Zeik orderly said at last. "Can I get you anything? I'm sorry Herr Nekken looked at you. You can be sure I'll tell —"

She hissed him to silence. More word babies came up her throat, one after another. But they were all the Nekken's sort of words, deformed and useless.

"Degenerate," she snarled.

"Brain damage" came right after.

She knelt by the trunk, touching its sides, then wrapped her thin arms around it. It was hers. She possessed it.

"No Gurgler," she spat down the hallway.

Yes, drag it into her room; the trunk belonged there. She gripped the latch and pulled. Nothing happened. Not even the littlest budge . . . She strained, squinting at the dirty white electric bulb suspended from the ceiling. For a second it seemed as if the Nekken's yellow face sneered down at her. She turned her eyes away and pulled harder. The trunk gave an inch. The muscles in her shoulders screamed. . . . She gripped the huge trunk and stared defiantly into the electric globe suspended from the ceiling. No Nekken. No taunting, sallow face. Just a dingy glass globe hanging from a metal rod. Out of the corner of her eyes she saw the Zeik orderly coming toward her. The air streamed from between her teeth:

"I'm not a bee anymore!" she spat. "Not an egg!"

The Zeik orderly froze. She readied herself for one more try, one more pull. Her bare feet slipped again and again on the cold marble floor. The strings in her fingers sobbed.

One more tug. One more pull. The trunk had wedged into the doorway; she cut her toe on the jamb, yanking the thing free. She threw her feet against the wall and coiled like a spring. One more pull.

The trunk slid with a slow groan that sounded like *damn them!* into the center of the room. Almost filling the whole space. She closed the door and sat on her bed.

She began to weep.

She wept because the trunk brought all the way from home had finally come into her private room, with fresh clothes inside. She wept because now she knew about being crazy. Away from home. *Alone . . .* And as she wept she thought in normal sentences, the way people were supposed to think. Wondering, Where am I? Then answering, In Zurich, Switzerland. In the Burghölzli Hospital for the Mentally Insane. Such a clear, nice, concise thought. If only she could leave all her regular thinking right there and not push on any further. But then she thought, I was supposed to go to medical school. Medical school? She had never wanted that. She must have been misunderstood. Or gotten herself mixed up with someone else.

Because I'm *crazy*, she thought. Yes, I'm crazy, and my doctor's name is Jung.

She found the book called *Newrongedly* on her bed. No, *Neurology*. She clutched it like a prayer book, like a family Bible, like scrolls of the Torah. She would take it to his office, right now, this very second. To show him what she knew. The great difference between *Neurology* and the other. God! she prayed. Don't let me forget those simple things. Those simple little things. That I'm crazy. That I'm far away from home. That I *wasn't always* crazy.

And that my doctor's name is Jung.

Chapter 12

Regression of the Laughing Horse

"Yes, sir, that's just what I saw, Herr Doktor, sir." Orderly Zeik wrung his hands and shifted from foot to foot. "I'll wager that Nekken must have been spying on her pretty regular, sir. Maybe creeping past my chair while I was dozing. But then, sir, you should have seen her drag that trunk inside. Scarred the floor, it did. Grooves cut right into the marble."

"Krantz in Accounting will have something to say about that. Probably tack the cost of repair onto her bill," Herr Doktor remarked dryly.

"But she's rich enough, I've heard." The orderly winked.

"You have been misinformed," Herr Doktor replied gravely. The payments from the parents had all but ceased. He had adjusted to the prospect of securing the girl's credit indefinitely. "And it seems Nekken wasn't the only poltergeist to pass you on the nod."

Zeik hung his head. "It's been a busy night, sir, I'll admit. First that old jackal lurking about. She drags in the trunk. Bang! down to your office. Zip! back to her room. Then you show up. Is that her book?"

The neurology text. He had found the passages on dementia she had read to death. The words "dementia" and "incurable" had been rubbed off the paper; no longer readable. Where they once appeared, now tiny holes showed, revealing the next page.

By pure chance, two new words peeked through. Where "dementia" used to be, now the syllable *proto*, as in "protozoan," appeared. And in place of the word "incurable," part of the word "cryptogenic" showed — with only the *genic* visible. The girl had rubbed out the words that condemned her forever, "incurable dementia," and in their place created another message altogether: *protogenic*.

Proto as in prototype. Genic as in Genesis.

Proto . . . genic.

The First Birth.

In her anger Fräulein had obliterated the words of her incurable madness and discovered, beneath them, a first birth. A new chance. Hope. Protogenesis commuting the life sentence of insanity. And so, sitting in his office in the middle of the night, he finally understood. . . .

She was right. He didn't know anything. Dumb as the big trunk sitting outside her door. For by pulling in the trunk she had finally taken charge of the well-made clothes of her former self — old friends long forgotten, whom she wished to see once more after strange travels in a dark country far away.

During the first chill weeks of March, Fräulein opened the steamer trunk and handled some of the things that had once been hers. Freeing the latches with clumsy, awkward fingers, glancing suspiciously over her shoulder, then going back to the trunk again. Yet it seemed repellent. Her face paled as though she were about to retch. Clutching the trunk, letting her fingers explore inside, hesitantly, as if trying to decide by touch alone . . . a blouse, a skirt . . . ?

Suddenly to grab a fistful. And sink her face into a knot of folded underthings. A ragged sigh.

Oh, to touch the silks of long ago . . .

Over the course of that week she eventually found a pale-blue cotton blouse with a high collar and frilly lace around the cuffs. She misbuttoned most of the buttons but got the garment on all the same, tearing a bit of lace that hung from her left wrist. The lace fascinated her; she gently traced its complicated weave. She wrapped her bottom half in dirty sheets from the bed. Misbuttoned blouse and sheets around her legs. Ridiculous — and yet . . .

Regal.

In the days that followed, a regression occurred. One moment she might be talking to him, really talking, and the next all her lucidness cracked like a glass ball. Enraged. Barbaric. Shouting another scrap of nonsense like "the Queen of Sparta."

Only this time it was . . .

"I can't stand it when the horse laughs!"

She twiddled when she said it, sawing her thigh; sometimes sawing the trunk, then back to her thigh. Once, she accidentally exposed her leg nearly to the hip. Her flank glowed whitely, coarse from being long abed. And red weals had risen from the twiddling, for she always twiddled when she touched some piece of clothing loaded with hidden powers. . . . Her voice rasping, "Can't stand the laughing horse! Can't stand it! Can't —"

Were the things from her trunk a catalyst? A blue blouse with fine lace. A cashmere sweater. A set of mother-of-pearl combs for her hair. A silver hand mirror and matching hairbrush, with long, thick handles. All too loaded with memories, too precious, too painful to bear?

A line from the Vienna letter came to him. He had not glanced at the thing for a long time. Odd, considering how impatiently he had waited for it and how hard it had been to write Vienna in the first place . . .

> Her acts, her fantasies, are not arbitrary. Even as they hide the truth, they seek to reveal it. Symptoms wrought to conceal their coherency, yet cunningly fashioned to relieve a great pain. A trauma from the past with no other channel of escape.

They sat together in her room once more. She had chosen to wear the pale-blue blouse again. Now buttoned more properly.

"What did you see before you came here?"

"Nothing. Blackness. I lived in the trunk."

One finger twitched on her thigh, threatening to break into a full-blown twiddle. "Coming here," she said vaguely, "sometimes I was taken out of the trunk. We were on a journey. By carriage."

Then, more firmly, "We were going to the Rostov station. We had tickets. First-class tickets for the Zurich train —" She halted as if unsure. Beyond the window, the trees shook fitfully.

"A horse and carriage . . ."

She struggled on. "Riding on a long street in the wholesale meat district. Red-brick buildings with butchers' signs. One sign read: *Fleischerei Hans Schandung.*"

Herr Doktor winced at the use of the words in the wholesaler's name. Schändung — meaning dishonor, rape, violation. Hans the Rapist

Butcher. Hans the Filthy Fleshman. Amazing how Schand also formed the first syllable of Fräulein's family name. How cleverly she brought it into her tale. Schanderein, a name that combined disgrace with the common word "pure." Disgraceful Purity. Pure Shame.

Fräulein worked her mouth. "My f-f-f . . . My m-m-m . . . Yes, they were in the carriage too. We rode in the open." She touched her forehead, troubled by some detail. "They're sitting across from me." She ground her jaws. "My f-f-flatter in his blue suit and my m-m-matter in her traveling cloak. But no faces. Like shopping-store mannikins . . . human heads but" — she searched for the words — "with no expression."

Oh, what wonderful words she used! Mannikins. Shopping store. Human heads. Describing things, how they looked, how they felt. Who cared if it wasn't perfect.

"I can see so clearly. From above, like an angel over the carriage. Glad to be coming. Coming here to . . . to . . ." She seemed to lose her way, then abruptly jumped ahead. "That's when the horse lifted its tail. His whole rear quarters jammed between Flatter and Matter's blank shopping-store faces. Its whole insides coming out right between their blank empty heads. Without even breaking stride, expelling . . . pumping . . . a huge round . . . and I saw the ring, the inner lining of the animal's —"

Ja, ja, ja. Herr Doktor knew what it looked like. He once saw an elephant go in the midst of a circus performance. The audience gasped. Then roared bravo as clowns with brooms bumbled in to clean up.

"Right between their blank empty heads!" Fräulein said loudly through her teeth. Then, with disgust, "They were laughing! Laughing as the horse shit between their faces!"

Her parents' blank dummy heads — just open mouths and painted lips, jeering laughter from empty noggins. He exulted; who cared how revolting her story was. That she *told* him. After all these months, letting it out for him to see. Telling him because she wanted to! He was winning!

A hard object struck him on the cheek, clattering to the floor. The girl had flung a mother-of-pearl hair comb at him, and now she flung another, screaming, "They were laughing! Laughing! And shit between their faces!"

275

His absurd exultation vanished. The second comb hit him square on the forehead, and he saw a bright flash. "Get down," she raged at him. "On your knees. Down for the Queen!"

She flung a book, which found its mark, and then another, and a black marble paperweight in the shape of an egg, which glanced off his forearm and thudded against the wall, cracking the plaster. He covered his ringing head, warding off the blows as they came. He had forgotten how strong insane people could be. Beaten down as the air in the room went gray. He faintly heard her shouting, "On your knees! Your knees!"

"I am!" he wailed.

"Lower," she ordered.

"I am." Pleading now.

"Lower!"

"Please," he begged. He feared she'd throw something heavy or sharp. He had a brief vision of a broken skull. The brains leaking out. What idiocy to have been so hopeful. He waited for the final blow to come. He had almost given up caring if he died.

"That's better," she said at last. "Get up."

Warily he peered at her. She sat on the bed, cold and cruel, a thin smile across her startling red lips. She had bitten them in her tantrum, and they stood out, moist and swollen. She held the silver hairbrush limply in her hand. Presenting the long handle for him.

"Come here," she said darkly. "Come sit by me. Come brush my hair." Clumsily he sat beside her, taking the long-handled brush. Her hair had grown out, thicker — a few knotted tufts but beginning to flow down her neck. He started to brush her hair from the top, getting caught in the tangles and pulling sharply.

"Ow! Not like that," she scolded. "From the bottom, and separate as you go. You'll just make a mess if you try to mash the tangles."

He tried it the way she told him. She had talked to him again, yes, just like a person. But he felt flat inside. Slowly one or two of the knots loosened. She posed demurely like a schoolgirl, swinging her legs.

"That's enough now," she said. "You can't untangle them all at once." For a second he thought she said, You can't untangle *my head* all at once, but he knew he'd got it wrong. She took the pretty brush from him, gently slapping her palm with the broad silver back. Being on the bed made him feel so tired and sleepy. He almost lay back against the wall. Would she let him close his eyes for a moment? He wished

276

he had never heard of the carriage and the horse. He leaned back against the wall, and they sat side by side in silence for a while. She let him close his eyes.

"Is there more?" he asked her.

Her hand twiddled, sawing mechanically across her thigh. She chirped gaily:

"Of course there's more. Presently we arrived at the railway station. All aboard the Zurich Express! Where is our private compartment? We booked a private compartment. No, not second class. Too many second-class people in there already. Commonest riffraff of the lowest sort."

Herr Doktor listened with his eyes closed. She went on, spinning the yarn to heights of improbability. They had overbooked the second-class coach, packing it to capacity. The passengers grudgingly shifted over to let the three newcomers enter. Fräulein's parents sat down awkwardly, hindered by their stiff mannikin bodies. Their plaster-cast heads showed painted grins, part sheepish, part wild, as if scrawled by a child. Fräulein sat between them. She was twiddling, furiously sawing her thigh near the groin, digging into the folds of her dress.

The second-class passengers stared aghast.

Until the conductor bustled in with the girl's steamer trunk. He shoved the huge thing right in with them, taking up all their legroom. But instead of becoming angry, all the second-class passengers scuffled and fought for foot room — erupting in gales of laughter as if this were the funniest thing in the world. The conductor, scandalized, huffed and puffed through his walrus mustache:

"Can't you see there's no room, young lady!" As if it were all Fräulein's fault, and expecting her to fix the situation. "No room!" he snorted.

Father mannikin's lips were now painted in a somber frown. "Can't you leave us alone?" the dummy head asked.

"No room!" the conductor insisted.

Now the plaster-cast head of her father was painted in an angry shout:

"So leave us alone!"

And then Mother mannikin cried too, with hysterical gales of laughter, "Alone! Yes, alone! By all means, leave us alone!"

*   *   *

277

Fräulein came back to her hospital room, both eyes shut tight. Her hand twitched, sore from the endless rubbing. "They laughed," she said in despair. "All they did was laugh."

She bit her lips, afraid to open her eyes. Dreading to look at him; because if she saw him sitting there wearing his favorite green paisley bow tie, but with a plaster-cast head sticking out his shoulders, she'd die. Die if she saw only painted sympathy on an empty shopping-store face. Just like her f-f-f, just like her m-m-m!

That day he wrote case notes, the first in weeks. Why? Perhaps because everything about her story was a complete fabrication. No horse and carriage. No second-class coach. In fact, no such thing as a Zurich Express from Rostov-on-Don. Obviously the girl had not been in a state of hysteric delusion all her life. At some time she had learned to read and write. Then a notable decline in her sixteenth or seventeenth year, ending in her seclusion at the "hive," as he knew she called the Burghölzli. Lucky for her she remembered how to read. Those torn-up books had been threads leading her from the maze. . . .

Was the absurd laughing horse story a similar thread? She had said, "They laughed . . . ," and those words echoed faintly in his head. Weren't they spoken when she played the Queen? With smeared menstrual blood on their teeth. He bared his lips in a gruesome smile. And she bared hers back.

"Laugh," he'd said.

She repeating it until she twiddled. Then, when he bid her farewell, saying, "Well, perhaps tomorrow," she spoke another word:

"Always."

Always tomorrow. Tomorrow always. He had taken it to mean they'd always talk about their playing the Queen, or her twiddle, or even her troubles. And that if they struggled on, there always *would* be a tomorrow in their future.

Or did the word "laugh" come from even further back? The laff and baff of their word association games? Baff, her second real word. Ach! At least he had listened to her then, considering it a serious request and arranging for a bathtub. If baff was the way to cleanliness — was laff a dirty word? He had a fleeting glimpse of the parents' blank dummy heads laughing as the horse moved its bowels, and another glimpse of the cramped passengers in the train compartment jammed in tight (like holding one's bowels?), all of them laughing cruelly at her discomfort. Laff dirty, then? And baff clean? Was the laughing horse story a clue, an image — a *symbol?*

A symbol of what, then?

Revenge.

What a leap of faith. But if you took the fantasy at face value, what had you got? Parents. And bowel movements. Literally a horse dropping its dung between their blank, dummy faces. In simple language, the story said: Shit on my parents.

But as for the railway compartment element, not so much revenge as a cry of reproach. Fräulein desired her parents to be thoughtful and caring, to see she traveled first class (didn't everyone want to go that way?). But no, they shoved her in second class, acted like perfect strangers, then jeered at her with all the rest.

Ah, now he saw more clearly how the choice of a "packed compartment" brought the fantasy situation completely under her own control — if choice it was. For a packed compartment was the same thing as a packed bowel. It proved she wasn't an animal like a horse, defecating anywhere, anytime — even between people's faces. No, it proved her better than that. What a clever fantasy! Combining the animalistic revenge against her dummy-headed parents with the accusation they treated her like a stranger, and squashing them all, strangers and family alike, under the huge contents, the locked soul of her steamer trunk.

In a sickening flash he recalled the girl's first day at the hospital. Two orderlies and Nurse Bosch had given Fräulein the routine delousing. The girl fought and shrieked through the whole procedure. She bit one orderly on the hand, and the other slipped on the wet tile of the shower. Had anyone bothered to ask the parents if their daughter was clean?

How many weeks, he wondered, did it take to unravel that bit of stupidity? The machinery of the world seemed immeasurably cruel.

When next he came to her room, she had gotten rid of the pale-blue blouse and put on a light summer frock, tugging it over her sheet. "Don't laugh at me," she said, slamming down the lid of the steamer trunk. "Don't laugh."

"I won't laugh at you," he said. "But please be so good as to tell me again, Fräulein, what the conductor said."

"There's no room."

"And your father's reply?"

At the word, "father," her lips fluttered, making the f-f-f . . . Her eyes and body took on a regal air, that inflated self-possession. He felt sure that in a moment she'd command him to kneel and play Queen. But instead her mouth worked and she said with great control, "My f-f-f, my f-f-father said, '*Leave us alone.*'" The effort had been too much; she began pacing back and forth before the trunk. She wrenched it open and glared inside. Then pulled a strip of sheet poking from her wrist, as if to draw the whole length through her narrow sleeve. But the more she pulled, the more stubbornly it held. "Leave us alone! Alone!" she said.

Didn't her parents really say those words? But not in any make-believe railway train. They'd said them in his office at the time of their interview long ago. Herr Doktor was having some trouble recalling their faces. Far, far too easy to see them as dummy plaster heads, just as Fräulein did.

But slowly the parents' faces did come back. The father with that roguish highwayman look and the sly curl of his pipe smoke . . . While Frau Schanderein sat like the Empress de la Valse, bolt upright in her china-blue dress and her bold, jutting breasts staring him in the face. Her strong red lips and mobile mouth and her eyes cold as the blue silk of her clothes. The embroidered masks of comedy and tragedy with their laughing and crying mouths. There were blank sockets in those eyes too.

"We've tried," Frau Schanderein told him. "But there's no room for this in our lives."

Her husband seemed a little softer, eyes dark with dread, with suffering — his own and the girl's. "But the way she is now, day after day. You wear out. It never leaves you alone." The man's eyes flitted weakly away as his voice dropped, plainly unsure whether what he said or thought was right or wrong. Or ever had been.

Odd coincidence, their choice of words. How remarkable the girl should pick them up, even in a different context.

There's no room.

Leave us alone.

Did Fräulein's parents drum that into her for years? Pounding it in until Mama's and Papa's own faces had mutated into blank, emotionless headpieces with painted expressions of hilarity or anger, changing with the hollow meaning of their hollow words? Herr Doktor pushed the unfinished case notes across his desk. They no longer interested him. By accident, the reply from Vienna appeared. A single page, evidently lost for some time. How had it gotten separated and stuck among his ragged pile of papers? A clever losing if there ever was one. And a cleverer finding. How annoying the page should turn up now. A sear of jealousy scorched his neck. Instantly wishing he'd thought of the lines himself:

> In the secrets of her dreams you will find the wounded demon, shrieking to escape. Find him and you'll unravel the knot of her existence. But let *her* find the demon and she may yet weave a life of her own free will. . . .

The secrets of her dreams. If only he could write a sentence like that, the secrets he would show the world! Yet what conceivable difference did it make if he found her demon or *she* did? Why such a fine distinction? He vacillated between gusts of jealousy and doubt, tempted to sweep the Vienna letter off his desk and let it lie on the floor till the end of the world. Did Fräulein dream at all? And come to think of it, did crazy people have crazy dreams — or did they dream of normal life, a confounding paradise, forever beyond their grasp?

Herr Doktor sat back blankly in his chair. He found he had been sawing his thigh with the edge of his hand for quite some time. . . .

Him twiddling.

Ach! So you've regressed to her level, my good man. Wonderful.

And that stopped him cold. Not just because of the remark's cruelty (true enough), and not just because it showed his cowardice (also true), but because it held a grain of truth. His cruel, cowardly thought had brought back the word "regression."

During the tale of the laughing horse, the girl had not merely been degenerating, not simply meandering, but regressing to something. In order to enjoy a forbidden act, indulge a starving wish. Throughout the long period of her horrid shrieking, the smearing of the menstrual blood, the making of the cowled dolls . . . these were messages, tokens, signs. But she had changed. By throwing things, by striking him and playing the Queen, she now engaged in long-denied actions. An infantile tantrum was clearly regressive, clearly demented in the common sense of the word, but also an achievement. Clawing back into her past to taste a pleasure, buried deep, a sweet revenge.

To right a wrong, administer a punishment long overdue. Flagellating the lone straw man of those relentless monsters out of the "Before Time" — throwing objects at Herr Doktor — but actually beating Empress Mother and Highwayman Father: doing the deed to Matter and Flatter.

Regression wasn't going back. But living over again what you might have done. Finally taking for your own what rightfully *should* have been. Ja, ja, a demon cutting his way out. And hers was a laughing demon, clawing anyone who held out a helping hand. . . .

Chapter 13

Last Night I Had
the Strangest Dream . . .

At first she remembered only fragments, littered like shattered glass on the bare floor of her mind. On a raw night in late March the wind gusted onto Fräulein's window in noisy blows. She quailed at the black glass, so thin and trembly, such a fragile wall against the wild beyond. She took a long time to wrap herself, so that if the black sky broke into her room, the snug cocoon would keep her safe from its snatching fingers. And as she slipped off into sleep, she saw in her mind the page from the neurology text. That ugly, deceitful page she loathed so much. With the words "dementia" and "incurable." The very same page she had rubbed to death, until she wore the damning words away . . .

Standing on the high moors of sleep, she saw once more the lovely, hidden words she found beneath the bitter page: *proto . . . genic . . .* Repeating them to herself as the drowsy heather rose to take her and the black sheets of wind slapped against the windowpane. *Proto . . . genic . . . proto . . . genic . . . proto . . .*

Fräulein found herself sitting in a green leather chair in a cozy room. A fire burned in the grate. A black briar pipe rested in the well of an ashtray standing by the chair's thick leather arm. A thread of smoke wound languidly from the pipe as if recently abandoned. In her lap lay the book from the Before Time. The book that vanished and came again during the long years of nothingness. If only she could show Herr Doktor Pants the pictures in it, so he might know how she died:

The Exegesis of Aching Dottery

No, dammit, see it right! And as if by magic, the title of the book seemed to change. Now it had another title, a more correct title. She whispered it out loud:

"The Evidence of Ancient Pottery."

What a grand book. Bound in pressed linen, its thick cover marbled in swirls of blue and green. And now she saw quite clearly a raised subtitle, printed in gold lettering:

Artifacts from the
Prehistoric Peoples
of the
Peloponnese

As she stared, the book slowly opened its covers, and the pages began to turn. She felt herself shrinking in the green leather chair. A tiny Fräulein doll, tiptoeing over the book's turning leaves. And as she skipped over the turning pages, she felt herself sliding back year after year, age after age. Back to the old time. To the time she really was the Queen . . .

The pages stopped turning.

Beneath her feet lay an engraved illustration. The lithograph showed the carved stone face of a goddess fitted into the mud brick of an ancient wall. A face of terror to ward off intruders and brigands: the face of a woman with tangled hair, lips pulled back, tongue hissing through bared teeth. A puny, stunted body dangled from the swollen head. Stout little legs pumping furiously up and down. A gigantic head, running madly . . .

Fräulein searched for some clue to explain this strange carved head fitted in the wall. Far away at the bottom of the page she spied the letters of a caption. She walked the length of the page to read it. *Talisman of a Gorgon in a village wall* was the disappointing answer.

Gorgon? What was a Gorgon?

Beneath her feet the stone head moved its lips.

The Grim One . . .

Fräulein looked doubtfully at the picture. Had it really spoken? Her head bumped against the mud-brick wall. She touched the dry stone carving. Quite dead. But the stone spoke words. . . . So dreams could have their own dreams.

She beheld a silver ribbon that wound down from the hills, watering a shallow plain. Terraced fields. Clustered trees in orchards. Beyond the fields the land rose sharply: grazing pastures of high grass, green spears waving in the wind. A dark forest cloaked the knees of the hills. Inviting woods, calling her to sit under their cool boughs, to ponder the stillness and the way of their dappled leaves. The Gorgon's Wood? The Queen's? But the leaves only danced upon the wind in answer.

Higher up, pine trees stalked the naked slopes of stone. And higher still, the bare flanks of the mountain, home of rock and sky. The glint of ice burned in the shadows of the mountain's crags. Empty but for the lonely cold and the tang of spring that spiked the air.

Abruptly Fräulein stood in the midst of a village. A mere few cottages of mud brick, bleached white from endless seasons. Some faded rags hung limply from a line strung between two huts. "Is anyone here?" she called. But only silence came. A village dog trotted past, sniffing at every empty door.

She dipped her hands into the cool depths of a wooden trough. A mud-brick kiln sat near the wall of the potter's cottage, a kiln built in the shape of a beehive. And here again, on the oven door, she saw the Gorgon's terror face scratched in the clay.

Within the hut an old man of skin and bone lay on a mess of straw. His eyes bright and sharp, but his thin mouth drawn. Above his head a tattered robe hung on a peg. It might have been purple once but now was as faded as the man. He raised a tremulous arm, his bony fingers pointing silently across the room.

In a dingy corner squatted a small figure, a naked girl of eight or nine, hands and feet bound with cords. On her face a mask of clay with the same face as the kiln's, as the stone in the wall, but painted. Black-rimmed eyes, red open lips — as if the mask itself had been feeding on an open wound. The girl wriggled and whimpered in her bonds. The old man took a skin from the wall and poured a draft of dark-red wine into a small stone cup. Red drops ran out the crack in the cup's rim, dripping on his hands. He went to the child, tipped her chin, and poured the wine down the mask's open mouth. The girl choked and sputtered, streams of wine running down her chest.

Once more Fräulein stood upon the picture book. How could she tell Herr Doktor any of this? Whatever she said sounded so stupid. Oh yes, Herr Doktor, last night I had the strangest dream. . . .
 So instead she told him:
 "Last night I went to the place where the Queen came from. To the cave where the world was born."

Chapter 14

The Cave Where the World Was Born

They sat in the Burghölzli garden, under the hundred window-eyes of the hospital. It was the first of April. Herr Doktor had been careful to wipe down the stone seat by the garden wall, for it had rained the night before, and he'd placed his topcoat under them so they might sit. A ground mist lay in the hollows of the garden; raindrops clung to the naked thorns on the vine.

The gardeners had begun their season's work despite chances of a sudden frost. Herr Doktor and the girl watched silently as the head gardener inspected a flower bed near the glass-enclosed dayroom. The headman rubbed the dirt in his palms and muttered to himself, while his young helper, a cheerful lad (rumored to have a police record), leaned on his spade and stared pensively into a sad gray sky that threatened snow. All about them the buds and shoots on the trees were swollen and ready, needing only the sun and moon of summer to set them free.

"In my dream I'm sitting in a room," Fräulein told Herr Doktor. "In a green leather chair. Then I go to another place. It's the same time of the year as now. But far away. And very old."

"Sparta?" he asked.

"No!" she snarled. "Didn't you hear me? I said *old*. Before they called it that. A village. And a Lady of the Wood. Lady of the water we drank and the mountain stone. Lady of the earth and sky. I was her daughter of the night . . ."

Before she had only sputtered in fits and starts, spitting out phrases with intricate meanings. But now she said things. Who cared if he didn't understand it all. They were finally talking — where he might say things too and she might listen. A great passion bloomed in him.

For he had led her from the solitary room into the waiting trees of springtime. Him alone.

"Where were the people? No one in the village. All gone into the hills to watch the sky and count the days. Only Grandmother Gray Face knew the time to come down, to dig the Green Man from his grave and plant him in the fields. We had other names for Gray Face. The Hag. And Moon Watcher.

"And the Lady of the Wood had many names. I saw her face staring from the village wall. From the potter's kiln. On every painted mask . . . Queen of the Mountain. And we loved them both together. Hag and Lady both. Though one was old as a grasshopper. And the other made of stone."

She called her tale a dream, but it seemed far too detailed for that. And as she spoke Herr Doktor realized the Queen of Sparta ritual they played was but one of its acts. Clearly hers was not the Sparta of the Heroic Age, of Troy and Mykonos, but far earlier. Fräulein seemed to be describing what sounded like the long-forgotten rites of season and fertility. The moment of magic, of ceremony and passage, where the extended family of rugged hill tribes gathered for the spring sowing of the land. And as she told him her dream, he ceased to notice the chill garden, even the hard stone seat on which he sat. She spoke and he listened, as when they first played the Queen. And as before, there came the insistent prodding of invisible hands, the whispered urgings of hushed voices — unintelligible, yet dreadfully familiar. The muffled sounds of people gathering in the dark. Waiting for some signal to begin. "I go to the Gathering," Fräulein whispered. "I see it in my lap, in the book. And I go there. In the dusk the people of the wood went with the old man and the girl. Gathering together under the oaks . . ."

A sliver of moon rose above the trees, shedding a faint light on the rushing stream that wound down from the hills.

Fräulein stood on a path strewn with crackling leaves. The smell of sap issued out of a thousand trunks and boughs. She heard the sounds of bells shaken, and a lone voice singing words she did not understand. She felt the press of bodies all around. And the steady stamp of feet marching higher along the wooded path. While down below, the village lay dark, all the hearth fires cold.

They went to a clearing cut in the knees of the mountain: a low cave like a toothless mouth opened on the face of the slope. Before the cave the Last Fire burned. Now the people of the wood came to seize these last red coals, to bring the village hearths to life. While she whom they called the Gray Face poked at the dying embers, sending sparks into the starry night.

"I saw another person by the rushing water. Not a person. A rock. Sloping head. No eyes. A crack for a mouth. A figure partly carved and partly left alone. When the rain fell on her, we said she was crying. Urania. Queen of the Mountain. Mother of Stone. And Hers was the birthing cave where the world was born. Where the women groped out blindly in the dark for the old Hag's hands. And when the pain came, praying with their birth beads clutched to dry, cracked lips . . . Then rubbing them against their foreheads as they soaked the floor with their sacwater and their blood, even as they chewed their birth cords free. For it was *Her* name they gasped in the moaning cave. Panting: Mother, help me. Mother, please!"

Herr Doktor gripped the edge of the stone seat. Birth beads! Now where in hell . . . Ja! In a grimy glass case in the British Museum: little bits of carved antler, or stone or coal — most no larger than a knucklebone. A faded caption card inside the display read:

Deer Beads
Aurignac Caves
Uncovered 1887

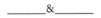

By some oversight the discovers' names had been overlooked by the museum's curators. But they called them deer beads because of their shape. Always carved in the shape of a pregnant doe's body, with the back-jointed hind leg of a running animal. Never any head or hoof, and the ripe pregnant belly looked almost human. Half human female, half female animal . . . Hundreds had been found across Europe, buried in the floors of caves with the chewed bits of umbilical cords — shreds of Motherflesh as gifts to the Goddess? They found one bead from Peterfels, Germany, still freshly carved, as though never handled, showing none of the incessant rubbing that all the others evidenced.

Had women giving birth rubbed them smooth as the pangs came on and the hours wore away . . . ? Were they magic charms, lucky pieces passed on — from mother to daughter, sister to sister — in hope and prayer for a healthy birth? And if stillborn babies came, or the mother died, were the unlucky pieces cast aside and never touched again? Were Catholic rosary beads and Arab worry beads distant relations, faded reflections of a long-abandoned practice? For a fleeting moment he saw the countless birth caves of Stone Age man. In Germany, in France, everywhere, a thousand tribes, a thousand worm-crawls, a thousand women's cries of Mother, help me, Mother, please, for a thousand years, ten thousand, more! Cries that rose and fell while the cave's stone walls slowly darkened over time. And when in the course of civilization the mute holes ceased to hear woman-kind's cries, laden with the death-life struggle of human birth, had man as well? Who really knew . . . ? Herr Doktor had given up and turned away from the dusty glass case.

He wished he could have taken notes as she hurried on, but he would have made her repeat things like Moon Watcher and Green Man and Mother of Stone. So he let her gallop forward, blurting out the rest, losing details in confusion and finally coherence:

"But our night of the Gathering was not for the birth of one child only. No. Tonight we gathered for the birth of us all. Moon Watcher kept count of the days. Knowing when to plow and when to sow. The huntsmen trapped a stag for the blooding. For the Inescapable One. Dragging it to Mother of Stone still alive.

"'Now bring him to me,' Moon Watcher cried. 'Bring him low!' And they laid the beast against the standing rock. The circle of faces wore clay masks with open, howling mouths, tangled vines and leaves in their hair. Wood people . . . The old man strode out of the circle, dragging the little girl by a rope at the neck. She stumbled to the feet of Mother of Stone. Her clay mask fell away. And I saw my face, *my* face on the little girl's head!

"The old man thrust me close to the stag's wide brown eye. 'Wish it were me, don't you? Stick me with the knife and see the blood run out. Next year, you think! Next year you'll bring me low before the stone!' Now Moon Watcher hobbled from the fire, holding the cracked stone cup for all to see. From her bony chest hung withered paps. 'My cup is dry. No son have I. But for the Green One who lies in the orchard down below.' Then, raising her arms, she cried,

"'Let the Blooding begin!'

"The huntsmen pinned the beast at every point. No, not huntsmen . . . but women. Smeared with dirt. Leaves in their hair and saplings tied to their arms. Things of water, wood, and field. Hunt-hers. One of them cut a flap from the stag's shoulder. Its eyes bulged, liquid centers ready to burst. She pressed her thumb into the vein to make it swell. Then sliced it with a flint. A fine spray sprinkled our faces. Welling into the warm flap. The stag screamed a long, thin scream as its life seeped out. . . . We dipped the rock cup into the beast's neck. Passed around the cup and drank. The stag's face streamed with tears of wetness. Or was it me?

"'It is done,' the old man said.

"'Done,' Moon Watcher echoed sadly. Then, pointing into the dark valley, 'Go down and find the Green Man in the earth. My only son. Find his growing head.'"

Fräulein's voice was harsh from so much talk, and her limbs loose like a marionette's, as if the hands that held her strings were all worn out. "The Hunt-hers tied off the stag's vein and repinned the flap of skin to sew him up alive. They carried the stag on a long pole down to the valley. When we reached the orchard, the old man forced my face to the ground.

"'Now dig.'

"I clawed at the roots of an apple tree with a stick, then with my bare hands. The old man yanked the rope around my neck. 'Faster!' The pile of dirt grew at my feet. My gritty fingers struck a body in the ground. About my size . . .

"'We buried him dead,' the old man sang. 'Is he alive?' I showed the limp thing around the circle. Not human and not dead either. A bundle of old stalks woven in the shape of a little man. Husks for hands, knotted grass for knees and elbows. Dressed in a bit of sacking. A hooded face. Inside, a handful of barley seed, now sprouting green hairy bristles beneath a shadowed cowl. Buried dead in winter. Now alive.

"The Hunt-hers snatched the Green Man and spread him across the apple tree. Pegging off hands and feet. While the people pranced around the trunk, crying, 'Alive! Alive!' They hit the Green Man with switches. They struck his vitals. Taking him apart stalk by stalk and reed by reed as they leaped around the tree. Beating him to frayed shreds that floated in the darkness till not even shreds were left."

"Suddenly the dogs bayed madly. The Hunt-hers had unslung the stag. It bounded away through the orchard, wobbling as it crashed over the black fields. I saw a dog clamped onto its hind leg. The whole gang of us howled and went after it in a pack. The Hunt-hers caught the beast by the running stream. They swarmed over it with flints, skinning it alive. We tore the stag to pieces, gobbling handfuls of its guts as it shrieked helplessly. Bones and entrails lay strewn over the ground. Food for foxes and kites. When the thing was finally limp and dead, the mob broke up and wandered off, straggling into the night. . . . In the morning there would be nothing left. Only a dark stain on the ground, soon to be overgrown by riverbank reeds.

"A silence lay over the valley. The people of the wood lay quiet in their huts. The only sound a dog slavering over its knob of gristle."

The last part of the story came out like splinters. "I took the stag's pelt back to the birthing cave for the Inescapable One. What a strange expression on the animal's face, as if still wondering, Who on earth gouged my eyes out? Moon Watcher put the stagskin over Mother of Stone's head, giving her a crown of antlers. I heard the Hag chanting:

"Who is she?
The One you know.
Who is she?
The One of Woe.
Who is she?
The One for Thee."

The girl's voice came taut as glass. "Above the fire, the moon set in Mother of Stone's crown of horns. The moon passed down, but no daylight came. No sunrise . . . The black night grew full of stars, and the moon herself rose up again to cross the sky. I am in the forever night. . . . Suddenly I'm holding an antler spike of my own. Smoothed flat on one side, as if to be carved with marks. And as each white face sails overhead, I cut a scratch upon the antler with a chip of flint.

"The moon goes faster as it flies across the sky. A brief breath of darkness, then it kneels up again in the east. Waning from old and waxing full. Across the sky it swells and dies, shooting from horizon to horizon between gaps of black. And each time the moon flashes through the dark, I scratch a mark on the bone. Moons and months pass as I scratch and scratch. The moon leaps across the arch of heaven, a white band in the black sky. I've been scratching the bone for a hundred years, a thousand, ten thousand. Frantic to keep up. The flint cuts my hand. But it's no longer a little girl's hand. Aged. My hand as wrinkled as an old woman's claw. I *am* Moon Watcher. Me all along. Gone from little girl to Hag with no life in between. Old and about to die. I'm not ready! It's not fair! Not fair!"

In the Burghölzli garden the girl shrieked, "Not fair! Not fair!" The head gardener stared at her, wondering whether to call an orderly. But since Herr Doktor gave no signal, he turned his face to the earth and forgot her existence.

Fräulein had begun to twiddle furiously, but instead of sawing her own thigh, she reached over her lap and sawed Herr Doktor's. Already the muscle beneath his trousers was getting sore.

"What does it mean?" she demanded. "Tell me. Tell!"

He shifted his leg a bit, moving the twiddle to a fresh spot.

"I don't know."

She flew into a passion. "You don't know!" The hand began to saw its way into his flesh. He tried to shift again, but she followed the same spot on his thigh cunningly. "Why not? You're supposed to know! Supposed to!"

"No, Fräulein. Only you know what it means."

She snatched her hand off him and sawed her own thigh in the V of her hips. "So why should I tell you anything? You're not my flatter, not my matter! You just used me to tell you stories. Snickering with the worker bees. Telling everyone what we did and then laughing behind my back!" He tried to deny it, vigorously shaking his head, but she wanted none of it. "Liar! You used me! You —"

She froze. As if some tight spring had snapped inside . . . For a moment he thought she'd been struck by a seizure. Her hand paused mid-twiddle in the crevice of her thighs. An odd expression on her

293

face, a sort of wonderment, as if she'd just grasped a problem that had preyed on her mind for a long, long time.

"I've seen it before."

"Seen what?" he whispered, afraid to jolt her.

"The deer in the firelight . . . the shoulder where they cut it. I've seen it before. A long time ago. In my parents' house. I — I remember now."

"You saw an animal's leg in your parents' house?"

"No . . . not a deer's. By the light of the fire in the grate . . . My brother's. *My brother's leg.*"

BOOK IV

TRAUMA

Chapter 1

Echoes in the Dungeon of Years

For a moment she sat with her head bowed, going through it all again in her mind: the veil of fire, the red embers, the book-lined parlor of her parents' house. A vision that seemed to walk straight into her mind from the outside. The way the embers fell in the fireplace grate, glowing deep and remote in the polished brass face of the andiron shovel. The whole room reflected in the shovel's flat brass pan as it leaned into the metal arms of the stand. As a little girl she liked to stare into it, as in a looking glass, seeing the big green leather chair and the books standing in their shelves along the walls.

She thought she remembered the stag, sitting with its legs crossed, smoking a pipe — the deer's haunches filling the entire seat like a side of beef. And then she winced. No, not a stag, but her flatter sitting with his legs crossed, his black briar pipe in hand, staring moodily into the fire. But what happened next? He put down his pipe and un-crossed his legs. Then leaned over the chair to pick up a deer's hindquarter off the floor, laying it on his lap. It straddled his knees and he was slapping it savagely. Raising his hand and bringing it down, and the sound of his palm striking the moist flesh rang in her head.

No! No! No! Not a haunch of meat in his lap. But her brother!

"My twin brother!" she wailed at Herr Doktor. "Right in his lap, with his pants down around his ankles. My fa-fa-fa . . . my fa-fa-flatter spanking him on his white backside, making it redder and redder. While I just stood there watching. And it was my fault," she sobbed, "all my fault. . . ."

Herr Doktor rose from the damp stone seat.

"Come," he said at last. "Let us go in."

297

But she remained with her head bowed. He did something he had never done before. Gently touching Fräulein by the elbow. She started violently, and for a long minute they stared at each other. . . . Finally he turned away and went slowly under the frowning walls of the Burghölzli. She let him go a few paces and hesitantly followed. Shuffling after him, she caught up, and they walked abreast for several paces. She reached for his hand, holding him by the fingers but not letting him take hers. Something about her taking his hand touched him deeply, making him want to protect her forever. Take her into his very home and have Emma help too. Surely if Emma could see the girl this way she would understand and want to help. Perhaps there was some way to explain, make Emma understand.

His musings came to a sudden halt. They had been stopped short on the narrow garden path. The gardeners' fully laden wheelbarrow blocked the single way leading to the stairway door. The only other entrance led through the dayroom. He wondered if they might go around the huge barrow and over the flower beds, but in a strange twist of fate, the head gardener had roped off the soft, tilled earth with pickets and twine. If they trod there, they would certainly ruin the rows of new green shoots. Herr Doktor looked for the gardeners to move the wheelbarrow, but the men were nowhere in sight.

With a growing sense of dread, he retraced their steps as she clung to his fingers. In a dozen paces they had neared the glass solarium. Fräulein tugged at his fingers for him to stop.

"I don't want to come this way," she said with a note of panic.

"But this is the way in," Herr Doktor explained. Orderly Bolzen, on guard in the dayroom, gazed at them through the glass. Not doing anything, mind you, simply staring at them in a detached way, as if at bugs in a killing jar. He felt slightly ridiculous in front of the orderly. One of the pinheads grinned at them for no reason.

"No, we can't go this way," Fräulein implored.

"But everyone comes this way when the other way is blocked." He was pushing her. He did not want Bolzen or Nekken or anyone to see them backing off, afraid. . . . Herr Tom Thumb had come to the dayroom glass and looked at them with tender sympathy, as if he read the girl's mind. The dwarf had his thing out his fly and flicked it at them.

"Everyone comes this way," Herr Doktor insisted. They had already dallied too long.

"I won't!" Her voice rose to shrillness. "Not this way!" The Bricklayer pressed his bare bottom to a glass pane. A lively crowd of Incurables had gathered by the windows. Some were openly laughing.

"Everyone does," he repeated inanely, then touched her elbow,
wanting her to trust him. She shook his hand off, glaring. "Yes! Everyone! Everyone!" She bolted back the way she had come, trampling
the flower beds and tripping over the twine. She stumbled through
the side door and up the stairs, shouting:

"But not me! Not me!"

Herr Doktor let her go. He wanted to follow her; he could probably catch her on the stairs if he tried. But instead he squared his
shoulders and marched into the dayroom, nodding. "Good day,
Bolzen." And then passed through the confusion toward the haven
of the inner doors.

Nurse Bosch had just started to change the girl's chamber pot in room
401 when Fräulein flung open the door. The chamber pot clanged to
the floor, a stream of liquid sluicing under the bed. The girl edged
back along the wall like a trapped cat, inching her way toward the
bed. A fierce light burned in her eyes.

"You're laughing at me," she snarled.

"No, really I'm not, dear."

"You are. You *all* are."

Fräulein stood on the bed and struggled with her clothes, tearing
at them. Nurse Bosch tried to lend a hand. "Can I help you, dear?
Would you like a nice bath?"

Fräulein had wound her tartan skirt about her waist. "Don't touch
me, pig! No flatter! No matter! No Doktor! No bath! Get out!"

As the nurse left the room, the girl was spinning herself into a cocoon of bedclothes. Mumbling, "I'm not a glass-house thing. Not a
sick bee. Not an egg anymore. I'm the Queen. The Queen . . ."

Herr Doktor had to sit quietly and think. Ach! Trying to parade the
girl in front of everyone like a prize cow — trying to make her go
through the dayroom and come out the other end . . . Appalling!

Her dream story floated through his head like dandelion fluff.
Hunting bands of women. A cave where the world was born. Sucking the life from the veins of a bound animal. Flaying the figure of a
hooded man tied to a tree. Marking the cycles of the moon on the

flattened side of a bone. The People of the Wood did she call them?

Visions from her past? His past? *The* past?

More like a door leading down a dark tunnel of years, where you saw things that really were once upon a time. Not in the age of Menelaus, whose name meant "Might of the People." No . . . these were the echoes of a far older time, with far older names: like that of the fair maid Helen, the Bright One. Of the Great Goddess, of her Mysteries and the Moon. In rocky Arcadia among the tribes called Pelasgoi. The Ancients, the Seafarers — though how long ago they came across the wine-faced sea, no one knew. . . .

He glanced along the bookshelves in his office, searching for some clues among the silent tomes. He read a brief encyclopedia entry on Arcadia. It called the people "pastoral" — as if all they did was collect butterflies, count their goats, and chase young maidens. He found a slim volume by an explorer back from Africa: the fellow claimed he saw a bull sacrificed by the Masai warrior tribe. The hunters opened the beast's throat while it was still alive and drank from it. Emma's odd collection of that French priest's drawings of the cave art in Les Eyzies . . . wisps of ghostly men in a hunting party, a bear bleeding torrents from the mouth, a score of spear wounds along his flank. Like children's drawings, really. Elusive and yet pointed.

The Ancient Ones had lived in the hills, just as Fräulein had said. A handful of sacred tribes hidden in mountain valleys. Tribes that met and married, loved and died — who called for blood sacrifices to the powers of earth and sky. And in times of feud, disease, or drought, lonely men fought duels on the mountainside in the stony night. And as the tides of men ebbed, invaders came up the valleys, marrying into the sacred tribes. Then more invaders, who pushed the Ancient Ones even deeper into the hills. Last of all the traveling chroniclers arrived, to search out the sacred ones and listen to their tales. But the customs of the mountain people were strange to all the latecomers. Arcadia had become a dark, backward place. The final refuge of savages clinging to their Stone Age ways.

By the time of Homer, the Ancients were being reviled in tales of family murder, incest, and cannibalism. . . . How long, Herr Doktor wondered, did it take the old stories to change, as the beliefs of one people were grafted onto the beliefs of another? How long for the reasons of ritual to be forgotten and die? Why women worshiped bees and cows? Why men worshiped stags and goats? Why men wove

300

leaves in their hair, and why women chased them through the woods? Herr Doktor tried to remember who said that bit — which chronicler? His eye fell on a row of books his father had given him in his early student days: translations of the Orphic *Fragments*, Hesiod's *Works and Days*, a dusty Pausanias, and an even dustier Apollodorus. He couldn't remember.

Chroniclers, hah! A troop of old voyeurs traipsing around the rocky fist of the Peloponnese, staggering from one drunken festival to the next and worshiping whatever god was being honored, whoever he or she happened to be. On the seashore, a dolphin cult. In the mountains, a stag cult. In the woods, a boar cult. If they reveled on a mountain above a fertile plain near the seashore: presto! a feast of the Barley-Dolphin-Stag cult. Bulls, sheep, goats, or bees — just so everyone got drunk a dozen times a year and groped in the bush with anyone's woman but his own.

The chroniclers called them promiscuous practices. Nights when the fishwives, huntwives, and herdwives all went mad, chasing their men through the brambles, along a sandy beach, or in the new-plowed fields. And then grappling in the lustful dark, until the gray dawn saw them stumbling home with red eyes, dry-mouthed and shaky — still wondering who it was they'd clutched that night.

But customs changed as the revels were taken over by city-states and turned into civic mysteries. And later purified entirely, until sober temples of chaste youths and vestal virgins remained. While only those few tribes left in the mountains ran amok. Saturnalia. Walpurgisnacht. Carnaval. Easter. All the holy days stretched back to the wild revels in the dark: the coupling in the sea waves, the rutting in the hayfields. Herr Doktor seemed to recall reading a version of Aphrodite's ways and deeds where the love goddess went from man to man and god to god, sleeping with them all and then going down to the sea — emerging clean and fresh, with her virginity renewed!

What long-forgotten rite was hidden in this tale? The promiscuity and the cleansing afterward . . . He was reminded of the maypole dances and drunk peasant fetes of early spring, which always ended with the town fool being dunked in a duck pond or a young boy and girl married by the local barber, then carried around the village in wicker chairs, while the neighbors threw corn seed and leaped around a bonfire. . . . A mob of fruity Swiss peasants drunk on May wine, and

301

before you knew it — poof! Sister Anna got pregnant, and out pops a little blond girl who looks just like Uncle Horst. Alpine meadow children, smiling, blond, and yodeling. Who wouldn't want to yodel if all you had to do was massage a cow's udders and poke Sister Anna in the hay!

He pulled an old volume of Pausanias down from the shelf, thumbing through for the part about Aphrodite and her promiscuous activities. Or was it Hera who renewed her virginity in the sea? He glanced at the gruesome print of Actaeon and the hounds that hung crookedly on his wall. Oddly, he recalled that the huntress Artemis's name meant something like "Source of High Water." The rushing mountain stream of Fräulein's dream tale? Artemis hunted stags. And men.

Coincidence? Had Fräulein read the classics too? Then she read them closer than an adolescent boy of sixteen who still dreamed of the warm place between Nanny Sasha's thighs. Might the girl have gotten this from that special book of hers? *Did she make it all up?*

Or did she see things that really happened long ago? When troglodytes changed from animal to man and back again at will . . . Seeing them through the lens of her hysteric mind? For how else could the buried past arise through her? Boiling up like lava in the throat of a volcano, with no heavy core of sanity to keep the ancient fumes from leaking out — or to keep the visions trapped inside her cells?

Maybe that's why he dragged her toward the crazy dayroom. As if asking the girl for everything at once — to be his window into the lost past and be cured as well. Let me use your mind to see, but don't end up a dayroom lunatic. . . . He quaked with a forbidden knowledge, that her dream tale, her ancient memories, were mankind's stories stored in the chemical makeup of her body, living in the nerve cells of her brain. Locked away and calling for him to tap them. How could a sane man want to cure *that*?

Halt!

Get a grip on yourself. Thinking things like mankind's stories in her cells! What next? That crazy people were primitive savages in disguise? Soon he'd be having dreams like hers himself — waking with a string of bear claws around his neck while Emma squatted by the bed rubbing sticks together for a fire.

But the details of the girl's dream story must *mean* something. Obey

302

the rules of dream interpretation. Take the old man in the potter's hut. The potter . . . the *pater*, the papa? He began a case note.

> The potter and the Hag are her father and mother. For she cannot actually say the words in context. Either disguising them (Mother of Stone) or rendering them harmless (flatter and matter). Perhaps implying that your father is a cheap flatterer; it's your mother who really "matters."

He stopped writing. All the cutting and slicing . . . An idea toyed with him.

> The flint knives, the bound child, the bound stag — all point to her personal past. An innocent victim brought for slaughter. Lacerations of her childhood, hidden wounds with the power to drive her mad.

He put down his pen again. And the antler spike at the close of the dream tale?

> The horn she marks with each passing moon *is* her childhood. A bone cut over and over — but a bone is also hard and unyielding. Just what the girl wishes she were. Invulnerable. Yet her very own hand marks the antler, becoming the instrument of her pain. . . .

A fierce headache clamped its fingers onto his brain. He heard the echo of her words "all my fault . . ." Where was Freud's damn letter? Ah — under a stupid book. The headache blinded him to all else as he held the quivering page before his eyes. It had meant nothing to him until now. The only solid piece of advice Herr Professor had offered.

> What of the number 13? These strange dolls she made. This is no coincidence. Take the number alone and see what you find.

Oh, God! How many times had he meant to do just that? Why had he never done it? Because deciphering the code of her words had

303

been his sole obsession. Forget the code, the crazy talk. Take the number alone.

Thirteen cowled infants in a shoe box.

Suppose a sick young woman of about nineteen years of age peered back along the span of her life? She would perceive herself as a child. The number 13 signified time, the number of years her torment lasted. Thirteen the long imprisonment of her illness.

Time remembered.

Time served.

Time endured.

And how cleverly the number 13 fitted into the flayed body of the hooded Green Man. That he should be buried for a year (thirteen lunar months!) and dug up again. The Green Man *was* Fräulein. Asleep in the earth . . . Yet long hoping to be woken from the prison burial of a thirteen-year life sentence. But when the People of the Wood flayed the old scarecrow to death, and flecks of his body wafted off into oblivion, the girl denied herself even this hope. Preferring to hide in the dismembered safety of madness . . .

He sighed and looked at his watch. Near eight o'clock. He had sat there almost three hours. He glanced at his notes; a single page of Freud's letter had turned up unexpectedly. The page with that matchless phrase *the secrets of her dreams* . . . The headache had left a faint graininess in the corners of his eyes. All his insane devotion, all her awkward steps, all the risks — all ending in an imaginary fire from long ago and a forbidden memory long suppressed. Had he at last caught the Queen of Sparta with the hot rear end? Or had she once again slipped away, like an echo that fled from him as he searched for her in the dungeon of years . . . ?

"Well," he said to his empty office. "I suppose it's a beginning."

How tired he was. How truly tired.

Chapter 2

The Black Velvet Dress

"A beginning . . . ," the old man said, nodding to himself. He raised his bleary eyes from the stone windowsill. Nothing had changed in the hearth room. He moved stiff fingers, then clenched his fist to bring the feeling back. So his second seizure hadn't killed him either. He felt a twinge of regret: all his fancy notions about the afterlife, seeing other people's lives and being chauffeured about by flies — just so much fluff. Too bad, too bad . . . "It *was* the beginning," he repeated quietly. He remembered everything now.

The door of his private cabinet stood ajar, the ring of keys still hanging from the tiny lock. The compartment had been pawed over, and a mess of papers lay on the floor. Old letters . . . a secret store of unpleasant reminders. Bad book reviews, hate mail he hated too much to throw away, and worst of all the letters he never intended to answer. Invariably, ones from the old Faker. And that last letter she wrote him long after her return home. A final good-bye . . .

The creased envelope lay on the stone sill. The stamp bore the stern, bold face of Lenin, handsome and indomitable, gazing into the vast Soviet future. The postmark showed it had been mailed in Rostov, January 10, 1933. Over six years ago now. A letter he had immediately sent into exile. He saw her slow, well-paced handwriting — a languorous, voluptuous hand. The script of a person who had all the time in the world. Trying to tell him an intern from the clinic might visit him in Zurich, a deranged child in tow. Could he see his way to helping them? She hoped to get away before the authorities came for her.

Christ, he had stopped taking on new patients decades ago, even for consultation. And especially not from her. Not for any reason. And so when her letter came, his eyes went blind, fierce hands squeezed his brain, and he banished it to the little compartment of unpleasant things. Yet now, as he squinted — trying to focus — he saw her words in a slightly different light. Not that she hoped to get away — but *wished* she could. So she hadn't been threatening him with a personal visit at all. Pity he didn't realize this at once; he might have received her intern, perhaps even seen the child. Or *had* he? Funny, he couldn't remember one way or the other. . . .

A pale-golden butterfly floated to the windowsill. Just looking at it seemed to ease the pressure in his head. What was that tale about butterflies? They were the souls of heroes? No, but close. Not heroes — Herakles. He had seen butterflies in the Herakleion museum. A carved ivory butterfly from Knossos, the size of his palm. The ivory a cool blue, its wing markings two circles like eclipsing moons about to touch, etched into the piece and painted oxblood red. What kind of butterfly he couldn't guess. One that flew over Cretan pastures four thousand years ago . . . The tour guide in the Herakleion museum had said that the word *psyche* meant not only soul in Greek but also butterfly. That on some ancient artifacts a young girl was shown with butterfly wings. And that perhaps this carved butterfly was a symbol for the soul.

Perhaps?

Later on the tour he had seen a royal signet ring engraved with miniature figures. The golden ring showed the goddess standing between two men. All three figures were partly insects: the men's legs barbed and jointed, their hands tapering to pincers. The same with the goddess: her arms tapering to insect arms. In none of the three could he distinguish a human face. All had small insect heads, with tiny feelers for eyes and beaks for mouths. In the sky above the goddess, two butterflies and a chrysalis floated in the air. The tour guide seemed reluctant to speculate on the purpose of the royal ring. Instead the guide praised the workmanship and left the content of the scene alone. Were these symbols for the soul?

Why *make* a symbol for the soul?

The golden butterfly from the meadow flitted to the letter, setting down with quivering wings. Whose soul was this? The old Faker's? Some lost patient's? His own?

No, he didn't appreciate his own soul staring back at him across the ledge. *"Raus mit dir!"* Scram! He shook the letter, and the golden butterfly leaped away. It hovered outside the window, then lazily dipped and soared into the blue. Her banished letter had fallen to the grass below the hearth room window. He stared dumbly at it. What did she really want from him? They both knew what the letter said anyhow. Hadn't he read it a thousand times? Hadn't it begged him through the locked cabinet door? Why was it he could never find her in real life? But if he closed his eyes and dreamt of her, he always found her waiting? Close his eyes and she was his. . . . What was she saying? Ja, ja, that he should fetch the letter. Go pick it up. And listen to what she said.

He staggered to his feet, the room gently swaying. Far below, the floorboards seemed to ooze beneath him. His left side felt numb, but he could still walk a little, dragging himself forward half a step at a time. Hours it took, hours and hours to cross the floor and pass the threshold. Outside, he sank to his knees. More hours passed as he crawled painfully around the base of the building.

He paused for a moment to catch his breath. Directly overhead, a great drop of dew clung to a bent blade of grass. The dewdrop a huge glass ball that reflected the entire world. He saw his reflection in the glistening drop and knew why he crawled so slowly. He had no face; no legs, no arms; his back was a stripe of wafting green fur, tipped with handsome black-haired spikes. He had become a fat green caterpillar. And he was so thirsty after his long crawl! So he lifted his head and drank his own reflection, drinking deep, cool swallows from the clinging dew. . . .

When he had slaked his thirst, he looked ahead through the forest of grass. Her letter lay in the distance. He plodded through the tall blades like a stubborn bug. The sun burned his back. Under the corner of the letter he saw a cool patch of shade where he might rest. He was almost there. Ah, to rest in the shade of her letter, to sleep.

He struggled into the shade and rolled on his side. Her letter lay overhead, and he curled comfortably beneath it. Time to wrap himself in a blanket and go to sleep. Yes, time to change into something else. He felt a rumbling down his body; something coming out. A fine gossamer thread that he squeezed from his tail. First he attached his head to the paper, spinning the thread round and round. . . . His bug face went first, then his neck, his shoulders, his handsome green fur. Winding himself into a chrysalis, woven right into the grainy paper. He slept long and deep, and through his long sleep the tides of her mind in that lost letter came to him like a melancholy sigh. Her whole being crushed by the fate of her Soviet Burghölzli. As if speaking sadly to herself.

"One child out of twelve. Not so good, is it?"

He tried to console her. If you save just one, Fräulein, that's what counts. *I* taught you that. . . .

At last his black sleep came to a close in a ravenous hunger. He chewed a large hole in his cocoon and began forcing his way through. The silk thread slowly split apart. His wings were wet, and he spread them out to dry. Not the sturdy practical wings of flies, but gauzy paper ones. Fragile rice-paper wings covered in gold dust, too thin for flying in strong winds but just right for tumbling toward a run-down town house in a damp part of town . . . Across the yawning darkness Fräulein's school took shape; it pulsed with a radiance that made his body thrum with strength. So he circled and dipped and soared, always swooping closer to its alluring glow. Then Frau Direktor's clinic opened its front doors, taking him inside. . . .

Petra had just helped Madame put the children to bed. Now she too could rest. . . . Madame watched as the housemaid lay on her cot in a wandering doze. She should take a turn herself. The waiting seemed like Christmas Eve, not being able to sleep or close your eyes. The wind outside moaned its troubles, stealing about the eaves and making them groan. The house, too, slept uneasily.

But not all the children had gone to bed. Marie, their sugar-eater, stoutly refused. Maximilian had failed to coax her from her wooden desk, so he let her sit up late, with crayons and paper, in the empty common room, finally slumping down himself at a desk nearby.

Head resting on his folded arms, he saw the eternal Nile. A basket of woven reeds floated along the sheltered bank. A lazy crocodile gazed with jasper eyes over the mudflats and blinked. Maidens washing their clothes waded in the shallow bay. They brought the woven basket to the reed-hidden shore. The crocodile smiled widely at the sun. When the dripping maidens hefted the basket from the blue Nile water, Max awoke and murmured, "Moses in the wombrushes . . ."

He rubbed the sleep from his eyes. Marie had finished the last touches of a drawing. "Can I see?" Max asked. The girl had titled it in a scrawl of letters: *The Deth of the WreckShip.* It showed what looked like Noah's Ark but with many more windows and gables, much like their own town house. Sad children's faces peered out. One small child clung to the prow by a single finger. The dangling child was crying, his tears becoming big teardrops, which turned into pools and the pools into oceans.

The butterfly found Frau Direktor alone in her office, writing in a cone of light. He settled on the warm green lampshade and let the sense of her surround him. The black velvet dress enhanced the whiteness of her throat and bosom. He felt the heavy calmness of the woman now — the asthma attack a dim event, as if all her troubles had been honed away. Her hand slipped across the paper in that steady, graceful script:

> Mein Lieber Herr Doktor. You keep silent well. But it's too late for reproaches. Doubtless you know of conditions here. The children have finally grown to like the place, and just at the moment when we're coming apart. Madame, my oldest intern has chosen to remain. If my friends reach Zurich, do what you can for them — and I'll always be grateful. . . .

No, those weren't her words! She'd written in some silly code. Escape. Sick kid. Therapy. Help. What was this, an early draft? He couldn't stand any more. What right had she to burden him? All about, he felt the blasting cold lurking beyond the walls. "A butterfly in winter," she sighed. She meant that they were both doomed. So fragile — existing in the same bubble of time but never coming together now that he might finally tell her things to make a difference. She rose from her desk. The window creaked and the cold stabbed in. "Go on," she said.

Oh, God! One gust from the open window and he'd vanish like the school itself! She waved her arms and he sailed helplessly out of the warm light. He grappled on the window ledge for a moment, trying to hang on against the bitter wind. "Good-bye," she said. He beat his way back to the window, crawling on the ledge. Trembling in the cold, he pressed himself to the warm glass.

"Let me explain!" he cried. "Explain!"

But his small voice perished in the air. A staggering gust came and swept him into the icy, agonizing sky.

He saw now that in buying the black velvet dress for her, he had committed an improper act that he could never set right. For it was both a secret promise to a young woman that no young woman could possibly misunderstand, and a secret betrayal of his wife that no wife could ever forgive. But he could not help himself. God, how he *loved* buying her the black dress. Doing it, he felt more tenderness, more passion than any lover.

He'd gone crazy. . . .

Day after day, hour after hour, a powerful sexual pressure building up in him. While they merely talked in the garden below her window or sometimes just sat in silence, gazing up at the April clouds gliding high above the Burghölzli turrets. Their talk made him a teakettle on a slow flame, coming to a boil with little wisps of steam escaping from the spout. When he bought the dress one of those little wisps escaped.

But in the meantime the ravenous lust ate him alive: an appetite for women, all women, any woman but his wife. Didn't Emma satisfy him? Or was there simply too much of him to draw off in one bed alone? Sudden opportunities presented themselves at every turn. Often starting in some innocuous way, then darkening an innocent encounter with a knowing laugh. The way a flower girl picked out buds from her bucket of tangled stems, or the way a laundress walked with a load of folded linen on her hips, deigning him a smile in her unhurried way.

The mounting steam followed him through his waking hours like women's eyes. On a street corner or when he picked up a fallen umbrella in a trolley, knowing eyes met his with silky words: "Why, danke, sir . . ." Making him hear other words in their place: "Come home with me," or simply, "Come along. . . ."

The pressure flowed in and out of his daydreams until he saw a constant parade of women offering themselves. A young nurse lifting her dress for him as he passed in the corridor, while the toothless old charwoman cackled as she mopped the marble floor. No escape, not even in his sleep. For in the deep middle of the night, he imagined ragamuffin Fräulein bending over his sleeping body, putting her wet lips to his mouth, panting over their first midnight kiss.

When she came to him this way, Herr Doktor always felt he should protest, stop her somehow, and he would wake feeling shameful, Emma's warm body beside him in bed. Why didn't he just grope for it, spread her apart and let the pressure flow into her?

Because he saw only the black velvet on the mannikin in the window, the sparkling crystal buttons off its left shoulder — and later the youthful expanse of bosom that pressed toward him when he first saw her wearing it. . . .

The shop was called Scheherazade. The dress glittered in the window as he passed the tiny boutique on the narrow Lindenhof Stairs, glittered the way beautiful fabrics do when they are very expensive, revealing remote depths in their color and texture. How many nights had he wandered out of his way so as to pass the narrow display, how many nights glancing furtively at it before mounting the courage to charge in and look? How many nights before he worked himself up to grip the cold metal knob and plunge inside? Then was shocked to discover the doorknob in his fist not cold at all — but warm. Heated from the room within.

He plunged into the gold and silver light. The shopgirl smiled coyly. "How do you do?" Her words searing him as he rubbed his frozen hands and wondered what to answer. He had imagined actually buying the thing would be nothing, but now he seemed to have lost all power to act.

"The dress in the window," he stammered. "I'm the gentleman who put a deposit on it, by private messenger. I'd like to pay the balance and have it sent."

"Oh, so you're the gentleman . . . ," the shopgirl said. The flicker of a smile. "We were wondering when you were going to stop staring and decide to come in."

"Yes, I decided." His hands were warm now, but he kept rubbing them. The awkwardness seemed to cling even as he shed his overcoat across a chair. Still, he felt smooth and happy all over, ready for anything.

"When will Madame come and have it fitted?"

"She won't."

"Ah, then," the girl concluded a little doubtfully, "you'll want us to come to your home for a private fitting."

"No, I don't think so. You can wrap it just as is."

311

"But what of the length?" the girl protested gravely. "What if Madame does not like the style?"

"Not like it?" he blurted. The pert shopgirl cast him a guarded look but agreed amiably. "Certainly, Monsieur. Madame would have to be quite mad not to love such a thing." Then in a businesslike manner she found the shop's deposit stub, took up a pen, and poised over the bill of sale. "May we have Madame's name and address?"

A damning blank descended over Herr Doktor. The shopgirl waited. He groped for a suitable answer, completely at a loss — until the proprietress rescued them both, summing up his predicament in a single glance. Ah, for the gentleman's mistress! Gently dismissing the shopgirl with "Thank you, Sabrina. Please fetch us the tissue and the box." Then to Herr Doktor, in a quiet, accepting way, "My seamstress will do the fitting at Madame's convenience, of course. A fitting here at the shop, or as you please."

"Thank you." Herr Doktor sighed, most relieved.

The shopgirl busied herself with the purchase, peeling the black dress tenderly off the display mannikin. She stuffed it with pink tissue paper, then hung it inside an elegant green upright box. She pressed her pretty hands around the body of the gown, crumpling in more pink tissue paper to keep it snug. How expensive and rich it looked; she ran her finger along the edge of the shiny green package.

"A fine lady's dress," the shopgirl said with a touch of envy. "She must be beautiful to wear it."

"Exquisite." He had never used the word "exquisite" before. Now it sounded so right to him. The proprietress dutifully took down the address of his office at the Burghölzli. At once Herr Doktor realized all the pressure in his head had gone. And among the three of them a delicious understanding blossomed, an air of gay conspiracy. They all knew the black velvet dress wasn't for Monsieur's wife. The shopgirl's eyes fairly glistened as she slipped the bill of sale into a gold-edged envelope. The proprietress delicately savored the final wrapping of the gift box: binding it with lengths of dark-red ribbon from a spool. Lastly, she tied a six-pointed bow and licked the gum of a glossy black opal seal embossed with the name of the shop. Every little act so skillfully performed. And Herr Doktor saw how the women silently approved of his buying the gown. Of the secrecy. Of an *affaire d'amour.* Both women wishing such a man as he would purchase such a gown for them . . .

The shop door clicked behind him. As the fresh air stole sweetly into his head, he thought about Emma lying silently beside him at night. He wanted to press himself into her now, press against her clenched thighs, forcing them to rub against him as she liked to do. Rubbing them back and forth until they warmed and opened, and she began to say things like "Come touch me . . . Touch me now."

The gown arrived at his office at 10 A.M. the next day. Fräulein had gone down to the garden to sit. From his office chair he saw her on the stone bench in front of the ivy-covered wall. Overhead, a cloud unfolded into a mountainous gray ceiling and the wind picked at the ivy leaves.

Upstairs, he opened the door to 401. The bed had been made, the sheet neatly turned over the blanket. Her trunk dusted. The copper bathtub shined. He sat the elegant green gift box in the chair by her window. Then slipped a note under the red lacquer ribbon.

From Me to You
For Everything

When Fräulein came back upstairs, she paused at her room door, suddenly wary of Zeik and Herr Doktor standing expectantly at the end of the hall. "If you're waiting for me," she said, "don't bother." And without further ado vanished into her room.

The minutes passed. . . . No sound of tissue paper tearing. No cry of delight. Herr Doktor and the orderly stared at each other. Zeik shrugged, confounded. They had imagined her ripping off the ribbon, laying open the box, and reaching inside. A fine swooshing, crackling sound. Then holding the gown to herself, waltzing one-two-three! around the tiny room. But no — only obstinate silence.

After ten minutes, Herr Doktor's curiosity got the better of him. He went to the door and knocked.

"Come in."

She held her palm against the shiny green box as if silently worshiping its beautiful, perfect form. His note lay on her lap. "Why don't you look inside?" he asked. A chasm of hurt had opened at his feet.

"Not now," she said softly. "I will, though. I promise I will."

An irresistible force urged him to push her, make her open the thing, acknowledge his buying it — as when he marched her to the dayroom. But this time he swayed at the lip of the chasm and held back. Asking, "Don't you want to know?"

She gingerly touched the black opal seal with Scheherazade engraved in raised letters. "It's a dress from a dressmaker's," Fräulein said in a husky whisper. "It's a beautiful lady's dress. One I have to take care of. One to go to the theater in. And to dinner. And act normal in. You're saying you want me to put on a dress and act like a lady."

"You are a lady," he told her.

She examined every crevice of his face to see if he lied, had any doubt, betrayed any jest in his words.

"I'm not a lady yet. But you want me to be, don't you?"

"Is it such a bad thing?"

Her hands roved over the box, feeling the smoothness of its top, the fine construction of its sides. Her fingers glided over the long expanse, tenderly petting it with love and pain and sadness — not daring to believe the magic glory of it all. "Scheherazade . . . ," she whispered into its green depths. "I'm so scared."

Chapter 3

Cinderella

They had invited her to a dinner party. A party for her! The engraved invitation came on Herr Doktor Frau's personal stationery, hand delivered by Orderly Zeik. A creamy white card with blue piping around the border and a watermark on top, back-to-back capital J's with given-name initials on either side:

ꙫ𝖩𝖾

Fräulein replied at once, in her neat, careful handwriting. She gave her RSVP to Zeik, who waited like a footman in the hall. After he left, she stood in front of the dresser mirror. Her hair had grown since winter. Falling in thick, lustrous tresses to her shoulders, by May it was long enough to braid in a twist.

On her dresser lay the silver hairbrush and matching mirror from home, long buried in her trunk. They were made of solid sterling, their long fluted handles molded in fruits of the vine, with bunches of grapes and other berries growing among the leaves. Each handle ended in the knob of a ripe fruit: the brush in a peach, the mirror in the plump bottom of a pear.

Fräulein picked up her brush and put it down. In the corner sat the gift box, the seal unbroken. She had not dared open it. Each morning she said to herself, "Today I'll do it. I'll open it today." Sometimes she'd even get as far as plucking the red ribbon with her finger, but finally she always shrank from it, saying, "Not now . . . later." And went to the window, staring below. Before long, sitting on the stone bench in the garden, promising, "I'll open it when I get back to my room. This time I really will. . . . Maybe tonight."

The day of the party came, and the box remained unopened. As she climbed the stairs from the garden, all the strength and courage went out of her. *It's too late now,* she thought.

In her room, Nurse Bosch had gone to her trunk and laid out some underthings. The big woman looked at her with soft, dismayed eyes. "Bless me, child. You haven't even looked inside!" Just like a fairy god-mother, come in her hour of need to help her dress for the ball. Only, Fräulein knew no handsome prince waited . . . no glass slippers. She felt light, and a dizzy pain went through her head.

"I'm not going," Fräulein said, braver than she felt. "You can't make me." For a moment she expected Nurse Bosch to turn into a bee or a pig. But the woman merely pulled a silk slip from the trunk and shook it out in the direction of the elegant gift box.

"Open it, child."

"I won't."

"Open it."

Fräulein stamped her foot. "It won't fit."

"How do you know?"

"He doesn't know my size."

"How do you know?"

"I just know!" Fräulein wrung her hands. She began to weep. "It'll never fit. Why did he buy it? People will laugh."

In the end Nurse Bosch opened the box and peeled back the rustling pink tissue. She held the black velvet gown against her stout body. Her huge breasts plumped out the bodice, making the dress look even more slender and willowy. The four crystal buttercup buttons twinkled fitfully in the light from the window.

"It's the new style," Nurse Bosch said knowingly. "Off the shoulder and no more bustles. If you have a buttocks you show it. If you have a buttocks like me, you don't wear this style."

Fräulein looked doubtful. She had never imagined owning a dress like this, one she could go places in and be seen. Her hands strayed to her behind, speculating on the fit. In a moment she forgot her fears. "Let me see! Let me see! I want to try it on!"

Alas, when poor Fräulein pulled it over her head the bodice proved too loose in front and the backside too tight by far. Nurse Bosch almost had to yank it over her derriere before the dress squeezed into place.

"I told you so! I told you!" she cried, her tears spotting the velvet.

Now Nurse Bosch lost her temper. "Stop it this instant, you silly goose! Didn't your mother ever teach you anything worth knowing?"

"Nooooo!" Fräulein wailed mournfully. "Nothing. Never!"

"Then stop crying and listen. You may be crazy, but you're not a fool. No dress fits at first."

"None?" Fräulein sniffled suspiciously.

"None. Now, there's no time for the dressmaker's, but we have some laundry girls who can sew you up in a sack before you've said Hans Christian Andersen! Just peel yourself out of that." Nurse Bosch was gone before Fräulein thought of protesting the idea of strangers seeing her without clothes — when the woman scolded from the hall, "And don't you dare cry on the fabric!"

Fräulein worked her way out of the dress and glared resentfully at the closed door. "Sew me up in a sack," she muttered. "Well, they didn't invite you to dinner, did they, Nurse Fatso?"

The laundry girls oohed and aahed so appreciatively, Fräulein let them admire her in the dress and *out* of it as well. One of the girls had been apprenticed to a seamstress. "At least the length is right," she said. "And that's a help. But you'll need a quarter inch at the bosom and half an inch at the rear." For a fleeting second Fräulein wondered how to grow a quarter inch on such short notice. But the two laundry girls looked at each other and giggled. "Begging your pardon, we don't expect Fräulein to grow it herself. We'll take it in and out as needed."

"Have it ready in an hour," commanded Nurse Bosch.

"Yes, Ma'am, but we'll need another half hour to steam out the creases."

"Don't explain it," Fräulein pleaded. "Just do it. We're almost late already."

"And whose fault is that, missy?" replied the nurse.

"Oh! Please don't be angry. Just help me do it. Help me now."

The laundry girls stood dumbly at the door. "Well, be off!" Nurse Bosch barked. They vanished in a swish of the gown. Then, more gently, "All right, young lady. But you have to promise me, no more crying. Save your red eyes for the end of the night, not the beginning."

And so with that, the nurse sat Fräulein down before her dresser mirror and began to put up her hair. Suddenly the girl realized just how foolish she'd been to delay. "What about shoes?" she despaired.

"Show me your feet."

Reluctantly the girl revealed her paper-white feet; long gray toe-nails grew out like dragon claws. Cracked nails, the skin around them chapped and flaking. "Narrow . . . ," the nurse muttered. And, as she left the room, snapped, "Clip 'em! You're not Puss in Boots, y'know."

In a few moments she waddled back into the room with a pair of black satin ballet slippers. To Fräulein's delight, the slippers fit. "Fine," Nurse Bosch remarked. "Frau Horst will have to dance *Swan Lake* without them tonight."

Frau Horst was an elderly woman, rich as sin, in a private room nearby. "Does Frau Horst dance *Swan Lake* every night?"

"No." Nurse Bosch calmly finished pinning Fräulein's hair. "Once in a while she wears white slippers and does *The Nutcracker* with the Bolshoi."

Fräulein's pinned hair swept up in a wave, curling into itself at the base of her neck. But she didn't notice any of that. Instead she saw a sallow, yellow face stuck in the dresser mirror like an old cheese in a cupboard. She gaped at her horridness, realizing the worst: "No pow-der, no rouge, nothing for my eyes . . ." Her hands rose to tear out the pins, fingers working like spiders' legs.

Nurse Bosch's heavy face appeared in the mirror. "Don't you dare touch that, missy," she scolded. "Don't you *dare* undo my work, or I'll really show you Tragedy!"

Fräulein's hands hovered about her head, not daring to pluck at the pins. "You can't talk to me like that — you're not my m-m-m! You're not my f-f-f!" Shouting, "I'll tear them out if I want to. Tear out the pins and cram 'em down your fat throat, you —"

Just then the laundry girls returned with the dress.

"Won't need it," Fräulein snapped savagely. "Nothing for my face. Take it away."

"Don't be ridiculous." The first laundry girl took a small pot of kohl from her skirt pocket and put it on the dresser. "You don't think we'd let you go out looking like a dayroomer, do you?"

Fräulein stared dolefully at her reflection, but her spidery fingers had fallen from her perfect hair. "Are they laughing at me?" she asked meekly.

"Put on the gown," the big woman told her softly. "While I fetch some rouge for your face. And as for you two imps" — she scowled at the laundresses — "lend her a hand if you're not too fey."

Nurse Bosch borrowed a purse full of cosmetics from one of the young women in Accounting. After a little skillful application, Fräulein gazed at herself in the dresser mirror. Her hair and face and shoulders emerged from the black velvet gown like a lily from a dark stem. Nurse Bosch fished a string of pearls from her uniform pocket and clipped them around the girl's neck.

"They were my mother's. They're real. Don't lose them."

The laundresses gawped at Fräulein with open mouths. She was so radiant, so . . . When she touched the pearls around her neck, tears started to her eyes. How was this possible? She hid her face, unable to look at her reflection. "I — I don't know what to say," she stammered. "Everyone at the party will stare at me. And I won't know what to say."

Nurse Bosch stepped back, quietly admiring her work.

"Say nothing, then."

The time had come.

Zeik cleared his throat, announcing the arrival of the carriage. "Ladies, the coach awaits. . . ."

They wrapped a light cloak about Fräulein's shoulders and took her to the carriage in a sheltering flock. A stranger might not have recognized the looming hospital but seen instead a fairy palace, with countless lights winking behind high windows in the gathering dusk. Seeing not the inmate of an asylum but a young countess stepping daintily down the wide marble steps, while her footman and ladies in waiting helped her into the carriage, and the horses stamped their feet and their silver breath wreathed the coach lamps.

The whip cracked over the horses' heads; carriage wheels clattered away down the drive. Was the beautiful countess but a dream? Who could tell? Only the four servants remained, like mice at the huge palace door, waving the young lady farewell. . . .

Chapter 4

A Dinner Party

Herr Doktor's house was made of white stone. Rain had left damp streaks down the window casements like tears on a pale face.

In the entranceway the maid took her cloak. A marble stair climbed to the upper floors, with veined steps and a gleaming black ebony rail. French doors opened onto a parlor. She heard a music box playing, Borodin, his Gypsy rhapsody or *The Steppes*, but the music box had none of the throaty horns and mournful winds, so it played its Gypsy dance a touch too brightly. She also heard Herr Doktor's voice, then a deeper note she didn't recognize, and last the gay splash of a woman's laugh.

Getting dressed was well enough, but what now? What if she went inside the parlor and saw bees hovering over the carpet with drinks in their claws? What if Herr Wolfpants turned on his hind legs and growled, "Can I offer you a cocktail, Fräulein?" It seemed easier to turn around and never look back. Flee to the hospital, to her room, right into bed. But the sound of the carriage rattling off into the night left her stranded where she stood.

"This way, please," the maid said, as if unsure how to bring the girl into the company. Fräulein moved stiffly toward the French doors, her hands growing cold. She paused before a long gilt mirror in an ornate golden frame. A frame carved to show woven thorny branches, like a secret doorway to an enchanted forest. As if all you had to do was make a wish: *Mirror, mirror on the wall* . . .

The stunning figure of a woman stared at Fräulein from the glass. A lithe and elegant creature in a black velvet gown that clung to her body like a handsome serpent's skin; and each time the beautiful figure moved, the row of crystal buttons flashed along one shoulder. While the other shoulder lay exposed, bare and pale as living alabaster, altogether perfect. And the face that stared back at her, stared with dark and knowing eyes. Assured. Self-possessed. The eyes of a woman.

"*Me* . . . ," Fräulein whispered.

Someone touched her softly on the wrist. She recoiled, obliterating the vision in the glass.

"Welcome, Fräulein." Frau Emma wore a burgundy satin skirt, its narrow pleats seeming to make her rise out of the floor like a pillar. As if part of the hallway, the stairs, the rest of the house. At her throat she wore a green agate brooch. A faint chill seemed to flow from Frau Emma, a river of cool nobility, making Fräulein immediately think, *This is his wife.* Thank heaven the woman wasn't an insect or an animal, that the fingers on her wrist weren't paws or hooves or claws . . .

"Won't you come in?" she asked.

Fräulein's first impulse was to curtsy. Which she did once, smartly. But that only made Frau Emma smile in surprise, saying, "Am I as daunting as all that? Just come and meet everyone."

"Thank you. I will." If only Fräulein could tell Frau Emma how magnificent she was. But she never found the words before the woman led her into the parlor. Conversation stopped. Herr Doktor turned from the mantel and, with a graceful flourish, presented a distinguished elderly gentleman. The hospital's Direktor Bleuler. The elderly man seemed to have been struck dumb, speechless. And then suddenly she felt both men's eyes rove over her like angel's fingers touching the string of pearls. Was she blushing? Her hand rose shyly to her throat.

She liked Direktor Bleuler. She liked his rosy cheeks, his white beard; she liked the way he looked at her with that crisp twinkle in his eye. Like meeting Father Christmas in formal dinner wear; how becoming in frosty black and white.

"Enchanted," Herr Direktor said, taking her stiff fingers in his soft monkey's paw. She fought the urge to jerk her hand away. He clicked his heels in a short formal bow, saying kindly, "I never would have believed it, Fräulein. I never would have."

"Never believed what?"

The group of them, considering her with an odd look in their eyes, as if seeing for the first time . . . A slender young woman in a gown that sucked the very light from the room, leaving the sight of her alone. White shoulders and throat rising out of a black sheath. The feeling of power restrained, as though her whole body threatened to emerge from the black velvet gown entirely on its own. When several long moments passed and Herr Direktor made no answer, Fräulein did the only thing she could think of. She pressed the soft monkey's paw back.

"I'm pleased to meet you also."

The old man relaxed and sighed as though some bridge had been crossed. He groped with relief, trying to explain. "What I can't believe, my dear Fräulein, what I can't believe is that you are finally . . . that you are really —"

At that moment the front doorbell rang. A common shiver seemed to run through the room. Bleuler never finished what he wanted to say. Really what? Not a freak? A little egg without a center? Herr Doktor had just put a glass of sherry in her hand but glanced guardedly at the door.

"Ah, that must be Nekken."

Fräulein thought of an ice pick going through her liver. And of the words *You'll be crazy for ever and ever.* She seemed to be looking at her hands from a protracted distance, the fingers holding the sherry not really her own. The liquid in the glass trembled, but what of it? The doorbell! That's what everyone was thinking about. And oh, yes, a newcomer had arrived. Surely she knew the late arrival's name. It clung to the tip of her tongue. Very soon she would scream it.

The maid went to answer the bell. Fräulein frantically wanted to shout, Wait! Wait till I've remembered the *name* of the newcomer. If only she could whimper, Please, maid, come back, maid . . . At a sign from Herr Doktor, the maid stopped in her tracks. Did Fräulein catch Frau Emma frowning?

"Don't you like the sherry?" Frau Emma asked.

Fräulein sipped its sweet nothingness. "Yes, it's delightful. When it's done, I might even have another."

The doorbell rang again, a long persistent chime. As if the person hanging on the bell had all the time in the world to go on asking for admittance. Fräulein steeled herself for the inevitable. . . . And with a nod, Herr Doktor freed the maid from her post by the stairs.

After a moment Herr Nekken came into the parlor with his overcoat draped on one arm and a gold-headed cane held nonchalantly between two fingers. He palmed them off on the maid and turned his attention to the group. At first his eyes passed indecisively over her with a sort of vapid anticipation: an eagerness to examine this unexpected face in the crowd but first having to deal with the social amenities. "Good evening, Herr Direktor," he said. "And good evening to you, Herr Junior Physician." But then he was drawn back to the rich blackness of the gown, the glint of pearls, to the woman calmly poised by the mantel. Still unknowing, but with a sweet touch of suspicion in his voice, he asked the company, "Won't someone introduce me to this charming creature?"

Direktor Bleuler made a deprecating smile into his whiskers and coughed softly. "Ahem, surely the young lady needs no introduction . . ."

No one spoke, leaving Nekken at a silent disadvantage. He seemed to waver.

"Allow me," the girl said at last. She stepped from the mantel and held out her long white hand. "Fräulein Schanderein. Room 401." Her hand floated in the air before Nekken, waiting to be kissed. The faintest gasp of surprise escaped him, but his composure was a mask and he spoke with no trace of unease. "Yes, of course. How silly of me. Forgive my rudeness." And then he took her outstretched hand, kissing it with profound gallantry. He seemed completely intrigued, as if suspecting some trick involved, a secret, and he watched the young lady under his eyelids as if admiring a rare species of trained animal.

"Let me congratulate you on your recovery," he said, letting go her hand. "And let me compliment you on your exquisite gown. I wouldn't have recognized the devil herself. Where did you get it?"

Was there a flicker of fear in Herr Doktor's eyes? Did Fräulein hear him catch his breath . . . like a wisp of steam escaping from an overheated valve? The Nekken waited for an answer.

"It was a gift," she told him. Nekken smiled vapidly at the sound of her voice, as if her answer confirmed what he already knew. Yes, a trained poodle who jumped through hoops, a pretty tropical bird who chirped clever things.

"Will you indulge in another sherry?" he inquired, taking her glass from the mantel. "Let me get another for you." He went to the small table where the decanter sat on a silver tray, his eyes never leaving her as he poured the flowing sweetness. She saw how each moment

he was hoping for her to slip up. He poured the liquor without looking, knowing just the right moment to break off and put the decanter
down. All the while chatting with his colleagues:

"She reminds me of that new soprano at the *Oper*. What's her name,
now? Carl, do you remember?"

"Afraid not," Herr Doktor replied. "I let my season ticket lapse this
year."

"Herr Direktor, do you recall?"

"Let me see now, let me see." Bleuler pondered the diva's name,
stroking his whiskers. "Lili something. Played Salomé. Danced the
dance of the seven veils around John the Baptist's head."

How wonderful to watch them talk, even over something she knew
nothing about. They thought she looked like a girl in the opera. *Die
Oper!* My God, what a world outside, beyond 401, beyond the cold
marble walls. A world where women danced onstage and sang before
an orchestra and didn't drool or twiddle or hide under filthy rags. A
world of light and beauty, of self-possessed creatures and all who admired them. And for that moment, with the sweet-nothing taste of
sherry fading on her tongue, how Fräulein longed to be out in that
glorious world, if only to sit in the audience and be part of the throng
of normal people, who sat quietly and watched.

"No, gentlemen," Nekken said. "I know whom she really resembles."
He gave Fräulein her sherry with a hint of a smirk. "She looks like the
Frenchwoman — Madame X — in that Sargent painting."

"Who is Madame Eeeks?" asked Fräulein.

"Madame *X*," Herr Doktor explained. "*X* — as in the letter. A great
Parisian society lady. Sargent painted a portrait of her in a revealing
black gown. It caused a sensation. The artist hid her name to protect
her from rumor and scandal. Her real name was —"

"Excuse me," Emma interrupted, her sharp fingers clutching the
girl's elbow. Fräulein fought the urge to wrench her arm free. No, she
thought, it would definitely not be proper to slap Frau Emma across
the face. They're allowed to touch you in the outside world: people
sometimes *touched*. . . . "Come along, Fräulein," Frau Emma insisted.
"Come help me in the kitchen." Fräulein reluctantly let herself be led
away. Frau Emma's fingers dropped from her elbow of their own accord; she shuddered in relief. Nekken's eyes followed them intently.
The last thing Fräulein noticed was Herr Doktor standing incon-
spicuously by the mantel, just as she had. A shade seemed to be pulled

over his eyes, blank shutters against the people in the room. But she felt him writhing, simmering with an incredible effort not to show anything. Then their eyes met for an instant, the shutters opening so she might look inside, and ja, she saw his eyes were wet, blinking back his pride.

On the way to the kitchen Fräulein drew close to Emma and spoke politely in her ear. "Please don't grab my arm again, Frau Doktor. It makes me giddy. If you do it again, I'll have to slap you."

The stately woman caught the hem of her dress, breaking her graceful step. She shot the girl a terrified sidelong glance.

"I mean it," Fräulein said.

Once in the kitchen, Frau Emma gave orders to the hired cook. The maid bustled about, getting the service ready. By the hearth, a large orange house cat stared indifferently at all the ruckus, glancing once at Fräulein with precisely the same degree of attention, which was rather slight. Fräulein felt awkward and stupid . . . so she went to the cat and stood next to it. The cat rubbed itself up against her gown, leaving a streak of fur. She didn't bother to brush it off — it seemed somehow a compliment that the orange house cat paid attention to her.

She wondered if Frau Emma gave many dinner parties. Apparently the table hadn't been set or the silverware counted out. Two heavy candelabras were thrust into Fräulein's hands and she found herself following the lady of the house to the dining room. "I'm simply awful at this," Frau Emma confessed. "I've never done it right."

"I think you're fine," Fräulein said, putting the candelabras on the white tablecloth. The lady of the house laughed darkly and thrust a box of matches into Fräulein's hands. "Here, why don't you light them."

She stared at the box of matches. How very familiar, but what were they for, now? The candles. Strike the heads on the box. She did it slowly and deliberately; the tiny flames danced brightly over the shiny plates.

The company was called to table. A reflection of Nekken's long, horsey face swam in Fräulein's water glass. She drank the glass of water down. Straight away, the maid filled it again. Were you supposed to drink each glass down as they poured it? She caught a panicked look in Emma's eye and decided not to drink the water right then.

How strange the conversation sounded. Everyone seemed to be speaking in blocky, mechanical phrases, like paragraphs cut out of a book. One stilted block of speech after another. First Frau Emma:

"More wine, Professor Bleuler? More wine, Herr Nekken?"

Both replying: "No, thank you, Emma. No, thank you."

Then Nekken: "I say there, Carl, after all your recent experience, you should really write a book. The Curable Incurable Dementia. Send it to that man in Vienna, that one you know, I can't remember his name right now. Do you think he should write a book, Emma?"

"It's not up to me at all."

"Fräulein, do you think he should write a book?"

They all looked at her, waiting for an answer. She went from face to face. Their skin had taken on a waxiness like the painted plaster flesh of shopstore mannikins. And yes, like her parents in the carriage dream. Was Nekken's horsey face going to turn into a horse's ass any second and have a bowel movement on his plate? If that happened, Fräulein decided to say nothing about it.

"If he wants to write a book, he'll write one," she answered. "And if he wants my help, I'm sure he'll ask."

They all reached for their wineglasses with a general sigh, as if some great labor had been done. They drank deeply. She stared at the wine in her glass, untouched. How much easier talking with Herr Doktor in the garden alone. Just them and the clouds passing overhead, and once in a while the occasional scrape and clink of the gardeners' tools in the ground. But here at the table Fräulein felt slightly removed, dizzy, as though standing on a high, shaky platform. Observing the company's nodding, waxy heads and the blocks of conversation coming out of their mouths in lifeless chunks. Was it time to drink the water or the wine? Which fork to use? Achtung! Be careful! The maid is at your shoulder, serving you the soup. Remember to say thank you, and don't spill it.

She dropped her napkin to the floor. Should she pick it up?

"Thank you," she said to the maid. "May I have another napkin?"

"Take mine," said Bleuler. "No, mine," said Nekken. The maid brought a fresh napkin.

The soup was a blood-red borscht; it filled a white china bowl. Bits of onion and stewed meat floated on top. Fräulein dipped her spoon into the broth: a little white nub rose to the surface and sank again, while the stilted conversation went on around her.

"Why, Emma, this is wonderful soup," Herr Doktor said.

Then Direktor Bleuler: "Yes, yes, I agree. It is wonderful soup."

And Nekken: "Yes, borscht is wonderful soup. My absolute favorite. Tell me, Fräulein, is borscht *your* favorite soup?"

She swirled her spoon, and the little white nub appeared again. She saw pale, puckered skin, the bone and flesh of a boiled pinkie finger. A shiver came to her limbs, as if the very hand that lost its pinkie were stroking her thighs. She swirled the spoon again, praying, Please, God, no, don't make it a finger in my bowl. Then I'll have to show them, get them to take it away, oh, please, God, don't make it a boiled finger in my bowl —

The nub of a white onion floated to the surface and sank again. Only a mistake, a mistake. An onion, not a finger. Couldn't anyone make a mistake like that? Fräulein brought a spoonful to her lips. She swallowed.

"Yes," she said clearly to the company. "This *is* very good."

Again, a wee sigh rippled around the table, and the glasses were drained. Fräulein wondered if you were supposed to drink a whole glass each time? When she dipped her spoon into the bowl, the nub of a white pinkie rose to the top and disappeared below. . . . The spoon dropped to her plate with a sharp clink. Did anyone see? Did they know the cook was a cannibal? She glanced at Herr Direktor's plate; the shred of what looked like a white knuckle floated there. . . . Bleuler dipped in his spoon and scooped it up. He smiled at her as he swallowed it down.

"Will you have some sour scream, my dear?" Bleuler suggested. "Borscht is always better with sour scream. Emma! The scream for Fräulein."

Sour scream . . . ?

A bowl was brought. Sour *cream*. A huge bowl of it, a peaked white mountain.

"Be sure to give the girl plenty," said Nekken. Then Bleuler again, "Yes, by all means give the girl plenty. Be sure she gets enough."

The maid pushed the bowl almost under her nose and began dolloping it into her soup plate. "Yes, Fräulein, tell me when you've had enough. Just say when . . ."

Fräulein went far away. A startlingly clear vision appeared in her mind. Also at a table. Also eating. But she could not move her arms or legs — they were made of lead. She was eating and eating, gagging and choking, and still the food kept coming.

"Essen! Eat!" a harsh voice scolded. "One more bite and then you're through. One more bite and that's enough." A huge spoon came toward her. She opened her mouth to swallow this last bite. If only she swallowed this last bite the huge spoon would go away.

"Open your mouth. Wider!"

Her mouth yawned open.

"Now swallow."

Slowly . . . the food crept down.

"All right now," said the sharp voice, "just one more bite."

The voice had lied!

And in that moment, Fräulein saw the spoon frothing over. Endless mouthfuls from a vile bowl of steaming broth, with boiled toes, scum and shreds of purple tongues, rolling eyes and swimming hair. She set her jaw, but the spoon crammed through her tight-clenched lips.

"Just tell me when," the maid chirped brightly. "Just say enough."

Two dollops of sour cream floated listlessly in the soup, sending out ghastly swirls of pink. The maid hovered; a third gob of sour cream quivered suggestively on the lip of the serving spoon.

"Enough!" Fräulein whispered politely. "Thank you, enough."

The final gobbet of cream slid abruptly off the spoon, splashing clumsily into her borscht. Drops of soup splattered like blood across the white tablecloth. The company stared in silent shock. She glimpsed a warped reflection of herself in a wineglass: drops of bloody soup across her exposed throat and breast, angry red against the pure, snowy powder.

"Oh, I'm sorry. So sorry," the maid repeated in dismay. She dabbed at Fräulein's throat and breast with a cloth. A dark drop of borscht clung to a white pearl.

Fräulein feared she'd start twiddling at the dining room table. Spastically twitching her hand like one of those dayroom idiots.

Twiddling.

She'd heard that word before. . . . But never thought it applied to *her*. Rather to the little egg without a center, to the Queen — or the drooling Gurgler in the empty room next door. But never, never to Fräulein Schanderein. And she perceived quite clearly how this twiddle was an act, like eating or washing or sitting in the garden. What made her relentless hand want to go like that? Could she control it if she wanted? She had never tried. Amazing! Herr Doktor must have watched her for months on end. And now she formed a clear sentence in her mind: I have been doing this spastic thing for years, twiddling in public like one of Nekken's demented idiots in the big glass room. But the words were stopped in her throat by the ring of hard faces around the table. Numb shock in their confounded looks. Fear that at any moment she'd let loose, wipe food all over herself, pee in the chair —

They're staring at me.

They still think I'm crazy.

The maid ceased her dabbing and carefully backed away from the table. The girl felt her fear radiating like heat. Not of her mistress for the blunder of spilling the soup, but of Fräulein herself. Frau Emma clutched the edge of the table so, the blue veins in her hands stood out. Nekken's face wore a mask of sympathetic concern. He dipped his spoon into the soup and carefully took a sip. Direktor Bleuler looked immeasurably sad, as if some cherished hope had suddenly crumbled before his eyes. Hope in *her.*

Fräulein met Herr Doktor's gaze across the table. What fathomless light in those eyes. Expectation. Acceptance. Affection. No trace of sadness. No pity. No cowardice or cold revulsion. Fräulein cringed at the thought of her spastic hand. A wave of shame struck her: for all the months of twiddling in his presence. What a beast he must have thought her. Yet he never punished her, never slapped her hand, or tied it to the bed.

Tied her hand —

Tied her —

In the kitchen of her childhood house, pale-blue paint on the walls. A cuckoo clock in the shape of an Alpine chalet, with little white rocks on the roof and flower boxes at the windows, ticking away in the corner. Both her hands were tied. . . . Everything had frozen in time. The dining room table, the faces. One of her fingers threatened to tremble. The verge of a twiddle. Fräulein moaned inside. Don't care about them, what they think, what they do. Care about yourself.

Your power. You. She glared at the trembling finger, commanding it to obey. Slow . . . Stop. *Now*.

She was *not* going to twiddle.

The finger flickered, threatening a full-blown spasm.

She was *not* going to clutch the table.

Not going to crack wide open.

The finger quivered insolently for a second. Then ceased moving completely. It lay innocently on the white tablecloth. Time began flowing freely again. Fräulein glanced from the spilled soup to the company.

"Oh, the poor tablecloth!" she said in genuine dismay. "Those awful stains. How will they ever come out?"

And with that simple remark Fräulein released the company from its strangled limbo, bringing them back on her side in one swift blow. Nekken clumsily dropped his spoon in his lap. Bleuler upset his wineglass into his soup plate. Frau Emma's death grip let go.

"You mustn't fret, Fräulein. We'll put a pinch of salt on the cloth and later a cold wash. Helga, dear," she said to the maid, "a little salt, please. Here, Herr Bleuler, let me get you another glass. My, how clumsy we are today. See, there's my fork on the floor."

The awkward moment ended. Fräulein could rest now. Neither hand showed any sign of twiddling. A deep, consuming tiredness swept over her like a warm wind, making every movement labored and pointless. She closed her eyes for a moment. No one really mattered any longer. Only the bleak victory of remembering her childhood kitchen mattered. And now she knew she would recall all of it, everything she had to know. She mustn't forget to thank Frau Jung for a lovely evening. Yes, and meanwhile remember to be polite, by all means polite.

The dinner went on splendidly. Fräulein had a second helping of chocolate mousse for dessert. The company had a grand time. Nekken seemed a trifle quiet, lost in the thread of some deep calculation. But Direktor Bleuler emanated a rich flow of approval. Tangible results were something he appreciated.

Over brandy and coffee in the parlor, he took Nekken quietly aside. "You know, this requires we look into that Austrian fellow again. The one he's so keen on. Get his books somewhere. Let's not be the last to discover him."

Nekken raised his brandy in a private salute. "Hardly a chance of that, eh?"

Before the end of the evening even Nekken warmed up. He told a very funny tale about a stud horse and a rabbi's wife. The short of it being the rabbi's wife buying the stud horse, rescuing it from the glue factory with every intention of serving it at table. Then leading it to the kosher butcher to be slaughtered. After long arguments and debates over the propriety of eating such treyf, the butcher throws up his hands in exasperation, crying, "I'm a kosher butcher, not a mohel. Take my word for it, circumcised or uncircumcised, horse meat is horse meat!"

The company roared with laughter, Herr Doktor more than anyone. He kept saying, "Horse meat is horse meat!" until tears of laughter ran down his face.

Bleuler and Nekken left together in the Direktor's carriage. At the door, the elderly gentleman took his host's hand in both his own. "Lovely dinner. Charming girl. I congratulate you, Herr *Senior* Physician."

When they had gone, Herr Doktor returned to the parlor. The clinking sound of Emma and the maid clearing mountains of dishes drifted faintly in from the kitchen. Fräulein lay curled on the couch, eyes closed, wisps of loose hair circling her face. Her gentle breathing filled the room. He wished he could touch her. Carry her upstairs in his arms; feel the velvet dress against his skin. Lay her down on the carpeted floor of his bedroom and take the dress away.

She woke as if she felt his thoughts upon her, baring his insides with silent, inviting eyes. . . . "Do you want to play the Queen with me?"

He groped for an armchair and sank down. He saw it all. The orgasmic kill. How she put her hand over the dagger's hilt, helping to drive it in. Wiping off the dripping blade. Touching her wet fingers to her lips. His head reeled. Did he want that? Playing the Queen in the bedroom — while unawares, Emma and the maid cleaned the remains of dinner down below.

"Isn't that only between us?"

"We can go upstairs," she replied.

Herr Doktor glanced doubtfully in the direction of the kitchen. "They'll hear." But the girl dismissed the idea with a naughty toss of her head. "They won't understand. We'll just be noises in the dark."

The faint clink of plate and silver grew; Herr Doktor felt the impending event of someone coming in. His hands were damp. "Not now . . . ," he said in half a voice. Her eyes darkened with disappointment, but she didn't argue. "I hear your carriage," Herr Doktor told her. "Best not keep it waiting."

The carriage driver had been off drinking and sat nodding in the rig, flicking his whip at the toe of his black boot. He peered dreamily at Fräulein and Herr Doktor as they came out of the house. "Ah, the princess," he muttered under his breath.

"I did well," Fräulein said to Herr Doktor.

He took her hands. "You did. Very well."

Fräulein wanted to take his face in her hands and touch her lips to his hard mouth. But the cold presence of Emma descending on them flowed like a chill breath of warning. They paused, and the echo of their urge to kiss fled under the soft lights of the house. . . . Herr Doktor stood stupidly by the door as Fräulein handed herself into the carriage. She waved good-bye to him and the watchful Emma as the carriage rattled off. Soon the fleeing wheels rang dead on the road. The evening over.

Chapter 5

Noises in the Dark

He helped Emma clean up, following her silently about and seeing what needed to be done. In half an hour the party debris had been washed and dried and stacked away. He waited for her to say something, but when Emma had still not broken the silence, he broke it for her.

"It went really well, don't you think? I mean the girl's really come along, hasn't she?"

"Yes, she's splendid," Emma said in a coarse, black way. Then turned abruptly and went up the stairs, kicking Geschrei off the top step in passing.

"Why are you acting like this?" he shouted.

Ja. Why did Emma resent the whole business so much? Everything should have been all right. Fräulein had been a perfect guest. The Method proved — the girl even curing herself! Soon they would know what drove her mad. Look how much had happened.

She's just jealous.

There, he'd said it. But the jaundiced words did not lift the crushing weight from his shoulders. A thick sense of foreboding grew upon him; the bedroom door ground slowly open, as if reluctant to let him enter. Emma lay in bed already, a lifeless lump. He hated her for going to sleep so effortlessly, without thinking or talking or even saying good night.

Geschrei crept in at his heels and circled his calves in the dark. The cat going round his legs had a comforting animal touch. He slipped off his satin robe and slid gingerly under the covers. How odd he never dreamt of Fräulein. Or did he once, lifetimes ago? What difference did it make? He yawned and stretched. . . .

She'd be crazy in his dreams too.

He woke in the deep middle of the night, got out of bed, and put on his blue satin robe. When he gently opened his bedroom door the cat followed his steps. This time the door didn't seem heavy at all; a light touch, and he glided through as if the whole room were wishing him away. "Come on, Geschrei, let's go see her," he said to the cat. "Let's see if she got back safely."

"Meow," said the cat, agreeably.

He brought Geschrei to the hospital. She purred in his arms the whole way. When the carriage let him off at the iron gates, he set the cat down in the cobblestone drive, where it trotted off toward the main doors. He had expected to be alone, but under the light of the spiked lamps he saw a distinguished man in dark traveling clothes arguing with Francis, the porter. Francis was refusing the gentleman admittance.

"Please tell him I'm here," the man said. "I know he'll want to see me."

"But he's not here now," the watchman replied wearily.

"Can't you send a message or tell him I've come?"

"No, certainly not," the porter whined irritably. "I can't send a message this time of night. Doktor Jung will be here in the morning with the day staff. Now good night!"

Herr Doktor trotted anxiously up the curved drive. It became terribly urgent to set this straight. "But I'm here, Francis! I'm here — who wants me?"

Francis the porter poked his head out into the night chill. "Why, bless me! Herr Doktor himself. I have a gentleman to see you, sir. Herr Professor . . . ah, Herr . . . Terribly sorry, sir, didn't catch your name."

Geschrei rubbed against the man's dark trousers, a fine charcoal twill. The gentleman turned from the door in surprise. "Oh, there you are," he said, holding out his hand. "I've been asking after you."

They shook hands in the damp night air. What a wonderful way to meet, so unexpectedly. The gentleman looked a bit rumpled, as if he had slept sitting up in the train from Vienna and come from the station without brushing the sleep from his eyes.

"Well, come along, then; let's not stand out in the cold." The porter held the door. "Thank you, Francis. Does Herr Professor have any bags?"

334

"No bags, sir. He came just as he is."

They walked down the long marble entrance hall. "You see," the elder man explained, "on these sudden trips I find it simpler not to pack. Just wear an extra set of clothes under the first. Put a tooth-brush in your pocket. Who can tell? Get to the hotel, borrow a fresh pair of underwear from the concierge, hang your second suit in the closet, and *voilà!*"

"But what about hats?" the younger man wondered. "How do you wear two hats?"

"Two hats! Two hats!" The elder gentleman shook with laughter. "I say, my head is big, but not big enough for two hats!" They both laughed so raucously the duty nurse had to come out of her office and tell them to be quiet.

"What do you say," the elder gentleman wondered, gently taking his younger friend's arm in a confidential way, "what do you say I share my extra hat with you?"

"I don't think it would fit," Herr Doktor replied, suddenly disen-gaging his arm.

"Are you worried your head is too big — or too small?" the older man asked wryly. "Either way, it doesn't matter. We'll *make* it fit." And once again they both laughed until a nurse came along and hissed at them for silence.

"I hear she came to dinner this evening," the elder man whispered in his colleague's ear.

"Why, yes . . . yes, she did. . . . I suppose I should have invited you."

"I wouldn't have been able to come in time." Herr Professor sighed. "In any event, it's best I wasn't there to distract everyone."

They had reached the fourth-floor landing. Orderly Zeik snoozed in his chair, the cat curled in his lap. "Zeik," Herr Doktor said, gently waking the orderly, "I'd like you to meet a good friend of mine. A very knowledgeable gentleman who has come for a brief visit to see the results of our work." But when he turned to present Herr Professor, the older man had vanished from sight. Then Zeik too, leaving only the cat in the chair, flicking her tail. Uncertainly, Herr Doktor began fingering the rope tassel of his satin robe, suddenly ashamed of padding about the hospital wearing nothing but his nightclothes. Perhaps Herr Professor had dashed on ahead to visit the girl in her room. "Herr Freud?" he called down the hall. "Are you there?" The nerve! Going off to see the girl without her own physician present.

He became very angry and hurried on after him. Geschrei scampered ahead. The large orange house cat stood on her hind legs, pressing her forepaws against the door of 401. The door eased open, and the cat slipped inside.

Fräulein sat on the bed in the dark, as if she'd been waiting for him. Geschrei purred quietly in her lap.

"I came . . ." He felt really foolish now. "I came to see if you got home all right."

"Thank you," she said. "I got home quite safely."

"Did you see my friend? An older gentleman. He came to see us."

"Yes, I saw him," she replied. "He came through just a moment ago." Her eyes drifted to the window. "He's out there, I think. He wanted to see the place where we did our most recent work." Then, casually, "He's not your friend, by the way."

"No? What is he, then?"

The girl smiled as she stroked the cat. Geschrei flicked her tail in saucy silence. Why had the man come at all? To see how well his holy Method got along under his disciple's hand? No! The old Faker came to steal . . . to graft his prize student's technique upon his own. For the feat of saving a demented girl in under a year. Go snoop in the garden all you want, old man! You're just groping in the dark.

Now through the window came the soft and lonely sound of a flute being played. Not a flute he recognized, nor any tune he'd ever heard . . . A song of river reeds and mourning doves, of tree frogs and loons catching wriggling fish in their sharp beaks, a song of children playing by the slow current of a sandy bank . . .

"Go on," Fräulein taunted him. "Look while he's still there."

Out beyond the window he sensed things he had never known before.

Things he never dared to feel. Blind lust. The death rattle of a strangled man in his hands. A woman's pleadings as he took her on the ground, fighting him, crawling on her hands and knees . . . A way to find her, to be together in the dark. All out there waiting — in the prissy Swiss garden — if he dared to seize it for his own.

He floated to the window and pressed his face to the glass. No garden. Instead a great grove of trees rose into the starry night. And he, as if on a cliff, looked out onto the broken face of a mountain. A stream fell at the edge of a clearing. A black stone stood by the lip of the water. The mouth of a cave. Of course! It was *her* dream he was dreaming. Mother of Stone, the birthing cave! The girl's sacred wood . . .

Herr Professor stood by the clearing's small fire, playing his lonely flute. He looked completely at home down there, even in his traveling suit, top hat, and polished boots. His white fingers danced over the tone holes; he blew a long melodious sigh, lilting away to silence.

The flute dangled loosely in his hand. He glanced at it, the hollow instrument no more assuming than a dried stick lying on the ground. The elder man turned it over in his fingers as if wondering what his song had meant. And who he played it for.

"Just noises in the dark," the younger man murmured. He saw a score of bodies slipping quietly through the trees, like the Gathering in the girl's dream. The loose throng filtered steadily into the clearing until they surrounded the elderly man. Herr Professor looked inquiringly up to the window. "Herr Jung, do you know these people? Have I met them before, at a concert or a lecture? Am I supposed to know them?"

"Tell him at a lecture," the girl prompted.

No, that wasn't right. For suddenly he knew exactly who the people were. A mob, a gang of ingrates. They were patients the man had failed and people he owed money. There were pompous committees who banned him and a man who had picked his pocket in a department store on the Ringstrasse. A furtive lad who sneaked after him in a Parisian pissoir, hoping for a romantic liaison, and a buxom waitress he tipped badly the day before. People who hated him for no reason and a sad girl with blue eyes he once mistakenly thought he loved. There were even some dead people, come back to say one last word before going off once and for all.

"They're all your old friends," Herr Doktor said quietly. "Come to say hello."

A murmur of approval ran through the crowd.

"Are you sure?" the elder man asked doubtfully.

"Of course," Herr Doktor reassured him. The mob was moving now, wading over the shallow stream, closing in around the edge of the clearing. Herr Professor dropped the flute and backed away from the dying fire.

"If they didn't like the music, they didn't have to listen," he called up to the window. "It's the only song I know how to play!"

It was too late to be sorry. Already an arm of the mob had cut off the elder man's escape. He turned round and round like a wobbly top. His burgundy cravat fell off.

"Help me, Jung!" he cried to the window. "Only you can stop them. Only you!" But the old man's plea died in a muffled shriek as the ring closed in. Twenty hands tore at him; pieces of his top hat went flying. Shreds of his coat and shirt flew off. The bodies pulsed over him as bits of his pants came flying out. And then, as suddenly as the tearing started, it stopped.

The gentleman huddled whitely on the ground, stripped and naked, with red weals along his flanks where the mob had torn the expensive suit from his limbs. His body was hideous: middle-aged legs like stringy old meat, belly sagging from too many dinners, his buttocks wrinkled and pathetic from a sedentary life. A faint stripe of black hair ran down his jutting spine. A body better clothed, better sitting behind a desk.

Beside him lay the discarded skin of the devoured stag. The mob had yanked it from the standing stone and left it on the ground like the scab from a cut. The elder man hugged it over his pitiful nakedness. Rain began to fall . . . fat drops that puffed the pile of coals. Soon the rain came harder, gray sheets turning the clearing to muddy milk. The last thing Herr Doktor saw was the bony white legs crawling across the clearing. They vanished into the black mouth of the cave as the heavens poured down.

Back in Fräulein's room, the raindrops thundered against the glass, obliterating everything from his head. She had dressed like the Queen of Sparta, winding a sheet around her hips, and painted her lips very red: they glistened as they parted to kiss him, opening to devour him. But-but-but, he stammered, what about Herr Freud in the cave? He tried to hold her off with all his strength, but her arms encircled him, touching here and there, her eyes commanding him to silence.

"The old man's finished," she whispered in his ear. "Now there's only you. . . ." She pressed into his arms, limbs molding along his length. And her mouth came. She was kissing him, kissing him again and again —

*   *   *

"Carl?" A rough hand yanked his shoulder. "Carl, wake up."

Emma leaned over him in bed with an annoyed expression on her face. "You were shouting in your sleep. Shouting and —"

He grabbed her by the arms and drove her body into the mattress. "Never wake me again. Never!"

The woman frightened to silence. A bead of sweat ran down his face.

The drop fell on Emma's throat. There was a pause and a waiting. Her thighs rubbed together, pressed along his flank.

"Can't help it . . . ," she said meekly.

Gray light came in the window. Geschrei sat on the sill, looking calmly at them in bed, while the sound of rain on the roof pattered over their heads. A green glassy sheen had come into Emma's eyes; she wriggled deliciously under his hands. He held her elbows close, feeling her move beneath him.

"I just can't help it," she repeated sullenly. She made a tiny, futile effort to escape. But the gesture only made her seem more vulnerable, exposed. Her eyes were heavy-lidded. The corners of her mouth turned down in a mischievous way.

"I just can't . . ."

They were on the verge — she wanted it. The blood coursing through, a mindless insane heat. He knew she'd spit and claw, but she'd take it any way he chose to give it. Fast and rough or long and easy — like a duchess or a slut — just so long as they couldn't help themselves, so long as it was soon. She parted herself for him, presenting herself, guiding him, melting all around. She was ready.

Ready *now*.

Chapter 6

The Master of Her Face

Herr Doktor did not manage to arrive at the hospital in time for rounds with Bleuler and company. As he often came late, no one remarked upon it. So the workday began without him. The act of spreading Emma and making her shout into the pillow had devoured him. Afterward, he dozed for half an hour and woke ravenous.

In a café near the hospital, he sat under an awning in the bracing May mist, plowing through rolls and coffee, three soft-boiled eggs, and four slices of ham in ten minutes. He even made notes on the napkin about his wonderful crazy dream. A rivalry between him and the old man — what delectable nonsense! No, the message of the crazy dream lay in his own prehistoric childhood. . . . Nanny Sasha scratching red weals down his father's back. Prehistoric childhood. Damn good phrase, remember it! Besides, if he had nutty dreams after wild dinner parties, whose fault was that? He and the girl had essential things to talk about today, whatever his nightmares.

High time she moved out.

Fräulein woke in the cold gray light. Her bare feet touched the floor and she shivered, a wave of creaky cold passing through her. . . . What had she dreamt last night? Her bed still bore the warm imprint of her body. If only she could read the mute riddle of the wrinkled sheets. But no, her sleeping brain had been wiped smooth, and soon so would the bed.

A strange, forlorn sound rose from the garden: a low musical note, rising and falling and tapering off. The player played a kind of flute. Something primitive, like a Jew's harp, only with a hollow, haunted strain. A dreadfully familiar melody, which tugged you to stop and called you to its song.

340

She knew the music, had heard it before. A composer named Bee — no, but . . . She faintly tried to carry the tune. Flashes of last night's dream came to her, all confused with the dinner party. A mountain outside her room. Herr Doktor wearing a bathrobe. An orange house cat. Or had she simply seen the cat sitting on the parlor chair as she lay exhausted at the evening's close?

The playing stopped. She gave the window a shove, and it opened with a groan. "Keep playing!" she called out. "Play more!"

No one answered.

She drew her head inside with a defeated sigh. . . . To sit by the window in silence, to wait for the player to play again. The tune wove in and out of yesterday: getting dressed; the way the crystal glittered on Frau Emma's table. Even the loathsome borscht, the dollops of sour cream, the bloody drops splattering her neck. How everyone talked with blank, empty phrases. The hand that nearly twiddled —

Yes, she had been very lucky to escape without doing anything crazy. Very lucky. Then remembering the blue paint in m-m-m's awful kitchen. The ticking cuckoo clock. The gag spoon. The frothing bowl of gizzards.

"It's not the clock that's cuckoo! It's me! It's me!"

She shut the window. Clouds like floating mountains hung in the sky. She couldn't recall the song at all now.

"Enroll in medical school at the university," Herr Doktor told her. "I'll write you a recommendation. And you can move into town. The rent on an apartment is considerably cheaper than your room here. What's more, the hospital is doing nothing for you that can't be done better on the outside. You won't have to move immediately. I've paid your bill through the end of next month."

Fräulein sat in the chair by the window. Her hand began to twitch on her thigh in a halfhearted twiddle.

"And cut that out!" Herr Doktor said harshly, a little surprised at his fury. She winced at the hardness of his voice, but she had controlled it before and did so again. The twiddle defied her for a few seconds, then frittered off to nothing. Fräulein looked dismally about her room. A sort of sorrow came to her eyes, as though she would be saddened to bid the room farewell. The clean brass chamber pot. The copper tub. The flowers on the dresser and the icon of Christ on the wall, with bits of leaves and sprigs from the garden tucked in the frame.

"Take it all with you," Herr Doktor told her. "The bed, the dresser, everything. It's a start. A way to begin."

She clutched something close to her, wrapped in a scrap of sheet. One of her books. The one from home? The one hidden in the trunk all this time? The way she stroked it reminded him of Geschrei the cat and the ancient mountain dream. He wished she'd stop petting the book like that, almost sexually. The edges of the cover were frayed and worn: she must really have loved that book, poring over the pages until finally they fell apart. What subject? What title? She noticed him staring and ceased to stroke it.

"I still want to see you," she implored.

"At home. You'll come to my house. I have an office there too."

A cold look came into her face. She carefully wrapped the bit of sheet around her precious possession, then thrust it inside her steamer trunk, stowing it away with a firm, bold movement like a rejection and a reproach all in one.

With shocking bluntness she said, "You're afraid of what people think, afraid of how it looks between you and me. At first it didn't matter; I acted crazy all the time. So if you came to see me ten times a day, who cared? How could there be an affair between a wolf and an egg? There can't. But now I brush my hair. I sleep in a bed. I wash out the tub. I eat my vegetables. I go in the pot and clean it out. I'm respectable again. And so we've got to be respectable. You've got a position to think about. A reputation. How does it look spending day after day with a young lady in a garden?"

He had no answer for that. Struck dumb like a big ox. For long moments they sat together, just staring.

It began to rain, and as before, the forlorn sound of the strange woodwind floated up to the window. Herr Doktor stiffened with a growing dread: the very sound of the flute in his mountain dream now haunting him in broad daylight. If he went to the window, would he see a clearing? A cave? Gentleman Freud in traveling clothes, playing the lonely flute? Telling him, It's the only song I know . . . ?

The girl struggled with the window. He wanted to warn her off, but he felt nauseous and woozy. "Just like last night," she hissed, straining at the sash. "He came into my room."

"A gentleman?" Herr Doktor choked.

She wrenched the stuck window. "Yes, with a beard!"

Herr Doktor shrank to her bed; her dream in his dream, his dream in hers . . . "In fine traveling clothes?" he whispered. She struggled frantically. "Yes! I told you. He came through and went down below. He played the music!" Herr Doktor sat weakly on the bed, marrowless. Impotent to stop her. The girl groaned with a final effort. The window rattled open. She flung herself out to the waist. The tune broke off.

"Oh, that's you," she said, a trifle disappointed. A muffled reply rose from the garden. "No, I like it. It just reminded me of something. What did you call that thing? Oh . . . I see."

He wiped his damp neck. A wave of relief flowed through him. How could two people have the same nightmare? Maybe one day he would understand, but not now, not now. Below, the gardener's young helper stood on the muddy sod. He held a wind instrument in his hand, about the size and shape of a sweet potato and nearly the same color. He put it to his lips and began to blow. The sound in the damp air was simple and lovely and sad. Much like the older man's call-song in the dream, a melody of broken love, lost forever.

Fräulein rested her head on the window frame. "He's playing an ocarina," she said softly. "The street musicians at home play them for kopecks in a hat. But I never knew what it was called. An ocarina . . . playing Bizet. I was right. A composer named B! Suite number two, 'L'Arlésienne.'"

"He told you that?"

"Just the suite. I saw the name Bizet on a tin phonograph cylinder. F-f-flatter used to wind up the machine and play the thing until he wore it out."

The gardener's helper played the melody again. Fräulein touched the window. "He told me he likes to play for the flowers in the rain. He says they hear the music and come up out of the earth to see what's making such sweet noise. So he always plays them something sweet when they drink and something sad to make their petals brighter. Do you think that's true, what he says — a sweet song draws them up, a sad one makes their petals brighter?"

Who knew if it was true or not? Just as true as you wished.

"I never told you, Fräulein" — the words so difficult to say — "how very lovely you looked last night."

After a few days Fräulein asked Nurse Bosch to help her find an apartment in town. Several trips proved fruitless. The apartments were either too expensive or too dreary. In one case she found a place with bay windows, a cushioned love seat built in, and hooks for hanging plants. The bathroom had clean black-and-white tile on the floor and up the walls, and a porcelain sink that sparkled. She liked that apartment. She could have been happy there, but it was not to be. Fräulein became so excited she began to twiddle. The landlord saw her and immediately refused to cooperate. As he explained to Nurse Bosch in private, he had a good reputation and genteel tenants, and he intended to keep it that way. No one could be expected to house diseased people.

Fräulein sat silently all the way back to the hospital, twiddling half the ride. Once in room 401, she refused dinner and went straight to bed. Later Zeik brought her a slice of chocolate cake from the kitchen. "Put it on the floor," said the huddled lump. Another week passed before she ventured out again.

But behold! a few days later, at the warm end of May, they did find a nice apartment, a place on Fesselstrasse, street of the chainmakers. Zeik helped her with the move. But just as she had to learn about her hospital room, Fräulein had to learn about life beyond. How to talk to people she knew slightly and ones she hardly knew at all. How to pick fruit off a stall in the marketplace and choose meat out of a butcher's glass case. How to count her change and wait politely for the churlish shopgirl in the coffee shop — all the while revolted that people never wore their truthful faces in public and trying not to see them as blank dummy heads speaking in blocky phrases.

There were some failures. Vegetable sellers who barked irritably for no reason or shopkeepers who habitually counted out the wrong change, then refused to recognize their error. And after trying times like these, she went home to her flat and crawled into bed. Staying there as the day blurred into night. But Zurich was a big city, with plenty of shops. . . .

And now she had friends.

Nurse Bosch came to see her. Zeik also. Even the gardener's helper. He always brought his ocarina to play — and one day, in a burst of pink embarrassment, the fellow admitted he didn't know how to read. So twice a week she taught him his letters from a children's primer she found in the bookstalls near the Limmat.

Her apartment had one room with its own private toilet, a bathtub, and a narrow bathroom window looking out over the roofs and chimney pots. When she poked her head out the tiny window, she saw the blue sky rising to infinity and off in the far distance the spike of a black church spire. In the main room she put her dresser, the hospital bed, and her steamer trunk. She also bought a four-franc table with wobbly legs from a one-eyed junk seller. On the top a pair of lovers had carved their initials in a rude heart with an arrow: *K & W.* She wondered whose names the letters stood for. And if they loved each other so terribly much, why had they carved their vows on the corner of a table now lost and belonging to a stranger?

A black gas range was crammed in next to the kitchen sink, and nearby stood a squat icebox. The iceman came every day if you wanted: four centimes a chunk to keep the milk sweet overnight. Her front windows looked out onto a flagstone courtyard. She could see carriages rolling by in the street through a low, arched passage. Tenants were expected to take their garbage out onto the sidewalk and leave it in barrels by the rain gutter. She bought her first pack of cigarettes in a wood-lined tobacconist's shop and learned how to smoke.

When the gardener's helper came he brought her a bottle of May wine but drank most of it himself. In this way, he studied his letters well at the start of the visit but played his ocarina better at the end. She could see he had an immature crush on her, but she never encouraged him, and for his part he never said a word. Herr Doktor saw no harm in it. No one saw any harm in it. What could be more natural for a young man taught his letters? Stranger by far was a young woman of twenty living alone. But with the university so near, such things were not totally unheard of; a few university ladies might be in similar circumstances. Though none, certainly, fresh from a private room at the Burghölzli.

After a few days on her own, Fräulein traveled to Herr Doktor's home for her first private session. The maid let her in as on the night of the dinner party. She learned many things that first time: first, just how deeply her personal situation with him had changed. Herr Doktor now saw other patients at his home, making appointments for two or three a day.

As for Fräulein, he gave her several hours of his time to start, less later on. But even these hours a day seemed much less than what she was used to. Those limitless devotions of the Burghive. Now he spent half the day at the institution and half the day at home, and Fräulein spent as much time traveling to and from his office as she did actually sitting in his presence.

She had never realized he lived three miles down Lake Zurich in the town of Kusnacht. The night of the dinner party, she hadn't known where the carriage had taken her. But since carriages were too expensive for everyday trips, she learned the ways of the tramcars, mastering rail schedules and buying tickets from mean, wizened men in thick spectacles behind dirty wire cages, then not missing her stop or losing her way to Herr Doktor's house. All intricate, all difficult, all the time fighting the desire to creep into some cakeshop for a huge slice of torte, to gobble it down — then sit for an hour, twiddling like a leaf, shaking herself to death while the sugar raced through her veins.

So she learned to use the tramcar. And once in every dozen visits the sun would show itself promisingly out of a cloud bank, and Lake Zurich glittered like fish scales. And there she sat, alone in the coach, except maybe for a cheerful, toothless old granny and the driver ring-ringing his bell. And in those times she felt the worth of what she had done. For she had become her own keeper, not a clear egg without a center or a dayroom Gurgler in the zoo of the Beehölzli or a paralyzed twiddler listening to the talk of blank dummy heads, but a truly independent young woman sitting alone in the tramcar while her pale reflection flashed in the window. And she knew that splendid young woman.

Anonymous no more, but the master of her face.

Chapter 7

A Wolf at the Door

She dreaded talking. Wretched words, where anything she said might bring on a sudden fit of despair or inarticulate gagging as she choked on a spoonful of gristle out of her past.

At first Fräulein found ways to procrastinate and overstay her two hours . . . using spells of faintness and begging harangues, pleading on her knees, even threatening to play the Queen in the public street beyond Herr Doktor's door. But such ploys did not have the power over her they once enjoyed. She began to see her aberrant behavior for what it had always been: a scream of defiance from behind her fortress walls, a bestial bellow of Me — I — Me — I —! So if she stooped to smearing menstrual blood on him again or peed in the hall as the maid showed her to the door, such an act felt below her standing.

In her Burghive cell such behavior had been the sacred expression of her mortal soul, the battle of protogenesis versus dementia to birth herself anew. But here in his house she cringed at the childishness of it. At how blatantly she tried to project her power over him and their precious time. For the facts of life had changed — she'd already been reborn.

And *now* was growing up.

Describing her past took monumental effort, and crying was tiring work. Too much as bad as too little, draining her heart empty and dry. An hour left her exhausted, and the second hour so wilted that she simply rose from his couch without saying good-bye, nodding off fitfully in the tramcar all the way home. She said the word "Father" now, calling him by name with only a moment's hesitation.

"F-father."

But M-m-m still too difficult to say.

347

One day in late June she set the matching silver hairbrush and hand mirror on his desk, the ones he brushed her hair with long ago as they danced the ritual of the Queen. Touching them one last time as if their molded handles might help tell her tale. Then composing herself on his stiff leather couch. "You wanted to know who my parents were. It started with that brush and mirror. They belonged to M-m-m, and sh-sh-she always kept them on a glass table in her bedroom. At night I used to sneak from my bed, standing in the dark hall at the crack of her door. Watching her brush her beautiful long hair."

As Fräulein told it, the words rose into her mouth unbidden, but she hardly paid attention to what she said. For Herr Doktor's couch, so strong beneath her, melted away like soft wax . . . and she walked again in her parents' house as a little girl of five or six. Her home came to her all of a piece: not in the bright flashes of her ancient dream tale, but the way it really used to be. A town house in Rostov on a quiet tree-lined street, in a German part of the city.

Her parents' rooms smelled of must, as if an old person lived there, hardly breathing any oxygen or stirring the air. A clean old person, dry as a stick. Maybe it smelled that way because M-m-m rarely opened the windows. The halls bare, unlit and gloomy. Her own bedroom painted a sickly off-white. Its curtained window gave onto another building, a few yards away.

She had toys, though . . . a tiny silver-plate tea set and a small grand piano that really played. But her grandest was a Georgian-style dollhouse with two chimneys and rooms on either side of a central staircase. The dollhouse dining room had a real glass chandelier and the kitchen an eight-ring cook stove. The water closet even had a two-seater with wooden toilet seats. She remembered the tiny dolls as they sat propped at the dining room table — miniature mama and papa, brother and sister — all wearing their Sunday best. Also two servants, a maid in black and a fat pink cook in white, bent over the fancy stove. Their blank faces painted skin tone, with red lips, blushing cheeks, and vapid, sightless glass eyes.

She also had a stuffed rabbit with long silky ears, which she took with her to bed. Herr Wilhelm Schnitzel, but she mostly called him Herr Wilhelm. And a beautiful dolly named Püppchen, with long, dark tresses, just like Mother's, which she combed out and tied in braids. But her toys weren't really hers. Mother was always popping in to see how she got on with them. With rules on the proper way to play. *Only one at a time,* "because you'll get tired and break them." *Never more than one.*

So Herr Wilhelm never talked to Püppchen or the dollhouse family. And Püppchen never went on visits to the dollhouse or had tea picnics on the floor. For the toys had to play alone, and the minute she was finished, *put away right away.*

Mother had pocketsful of rules. They were her beginning and her end. Her be-all and end-all. "Do one thing and then the next," Mother always said. And so Little Fräulein never ate cookies while she played. Or paused in the midst of her things to go potty. Just get up and put back. Take down from the shelf and put back. Play for a while and put away. With Mother always saying, "Don't start what you can't finish. And finish what you start."

With Mother's most important rule being:
Never touch the horses.

On a high shelf in Little Fräulein's room stood Mother's china horses. Dozens of horses, of every color and breed. But these were never taken down. And only dusted once a week by the maid. The most lovely was a high-stepping pure white Arabian gelding marked *Lippizaner* on the base. One day Mother found this special horse with its proud tail cracked off. The maid would not be blamed and glowered darkly in the direction of the hated room, insisting in a low voice, "It's the girl's room, you know. I don't keep an eye on her all day long."

Fräulein didn't remember how it all turned out, but she did recall a sense of high tragedy, that something had happened that could never be set right. She glimpsed her face in the hallway mirror, papery white. . . .

Under the bedroom window stood a steam radiator with a metal cover painted a vile shade of pink. The metal cover made of die-cut tin, the cuts in the shape of fleurs-de-lis. It had been painted so many times the fleurs were filled in with drips, giving it the look of a leper with pockmarked skin. The radiator got fiercely hot when the steam came knocking on the pipes, but it never seemed to heat the area near her bed. Perhaps all the warm air went out the window. She felt her feet turning into painful wooden blocks. Her toes icy glass beads — afraid if she stubbed them they'd crack off.

Sometimes Mother read her the story of Little Red Riding Hood with her warm red cloak, trip-tripping carelessly through the woods to Grandma's house. The picture book had a page showing Grandma's table laden with steaming meat pies and cozy nooks by the fireplace, with wooden stools for you to cuddle close. But seeing that only made the cold more bitter. In the long night she hated Little Red Riding Hood for living in such a comfortable picture, hated her for sitting by the fire in the great stone hearth, with hot cocoa by the hob and mince pies on the table. If only she could be Little Red's long-lost cousin from the city, her poor forgotten sister . . .

So through the long, dark night Fräulein became Little Red's poor freezing sister in town, Ninny Blue Toes. Worse off even than the Little Match Girl, who at least died and went to heaven.

Ninny Blue Toes.

Suffering all because of Mother's ninny rules: no socks in Ninny's nighttime bed. Mother said lacy socks were for morning walks in the park, and daytime standing in the department store aisles, and sitting up late evenings in the theater. So no sneaking out of bed to steal them from the sock drawer. No, Ninny Blue Toes, no socks all ninny night long! No matter how she begged and begged.

"Kiss Mother nighty-night now."

And so Mother was kissed and the blankets tucked around Ninny's chin. Minutes passed. Maybe hours. Ninny drifted off to sleep. . . . When suddenly the door swung open. Mother!

"Off with the covers and show me your feet. Quick now! Show me your feet!"

Naked blue toes wiggled on the sheets. No lacy socks.

Letting Mother sail away once more, smiling, to her room.

"Did my p-p-parents hate each other?"

Fräulein jammed her fists into Herr Doktor's leather couch. "They never slept in the same room. If M-m-m was asleep, I'd sneak the socks on. Then wake up early to slip them off again into the drawer. But if M-m-m was prowling about the house, I crept back shivering into bed. . . ."

Ninny's feet slid over the floor like blocks of ice. A warm glow came from Mother's room. She pressed her face to the crack in the door and saw Mother at the vanity, brushing her hair. The table had looking-glass wings so you could see yourself from three sides and glass legs with frowning lions' heads supporting the top. The lions' heads stared out like soldiers on guard. Ninny sometimes tiptoed into the room to talk to them.

A wave of warm air flowed into the hall — so, so much warmer than Ninny's bare, dark hole. How she longed to snuggle in the bed as Mother sat before the mirror brushing her long, lustrous hair. Stroking with the long-handled brush she always used.

Ninny often thought Mother's face was sharp and bright like a bird's. But now it seemed soft and slack. Her eyes dreamy, her body loose. Seeing her made Ninny think of strawberry jam on hot buttered toast, and she thought, *Mother has lost something*. But what Mother had lost she couldn't guess.

Mother took the stopper from a perfume bottle: frosted glass in the shape of a dove, called Lovebird. She dabbed the stopper behind her ear, on her throat, then lower to the opening of her silk dressing gown. Following the cord that plunged down the shadow between her legs. Mother touched the stopper there.

Ninny Blue Toes smelled the scent of Lovebird welling through the crack. She had never seen Mother's dressing gown hang so open. In the room the candles flared brighter. Mother turned the long-handled brush over in her fingers, the silver flashing in the flickering light. She leaned back in the chair and carefully parted her long white legs, propping one foot on a frowning lions' head. Then softly rubbed the smooth silver back of the brush along the inside of her thigh. First lower, then higher, then lower again.

What was Mother doing? Hurting herself?

Ninny pressed her face to the crack. Mother stroked the silver hairbrush along her long white thigh, the other hand slipping down to the shadow and back to the candlelight again. She touched her fingers to her lips. The fingers moving, lower and higher, then lower again. The tiny candle flames stuttered.

Now the hands went faster. Tongue — shadow — tongue. The brush fell mutely on the carpet, but the hands kept going. Mother's naked toes clenched the lion's face. Tongue — shadow — tongue, more frantic now. Ninny shuffled on the hard wood floor. Her own fists clenching. Open — closed — open. Should she go for help?

Tongue — shadow — tongue.

Ninny Blue Toes fled.

The tin-cylinder phonograph played softly in the drawing room. Ninny stood in the doorway. Father had lit a fire in the grate. He sat in the green leather chair, smoking his pipe. Soft sucking sounds as he drew on it . . . then a quiet hiss as he blew smoke into the air. He looked up sharply.

"What now?" he murmured. "Can't you sleep?"

She always loved the way his gleaming hair swept back off his fore-head like a cresting wave. It made her want to stick her fingers in the curl. He held out his hands, beckoning her to his lap. "Come on, then."

She climbed over his knees, curling into him.

"Eh, what's this?" He held her frozen feet. "They're cold as ice!" He rubbed them in his big, warm hands. And the red embers of the fire seemed to go into her toes. If only she could sit all night in his safe lap, if only —

"What's *this* now?"

Mother towered in the doorway, tall and grim, her silk dressing gown wrapped tight about her waist. Her face no longer slack, but bright and sharp again.

Father clasped Ninny to him. Couldn't she just stay in his lap and never leave? She felt him tremble. Father *afraid?* Was he going to hand her over? "Her feet were cold," Father explained. His voice sounded doubtful, as if he didn't really believe it. Then glancing feebly at the fire as if the truth lay there. But no, just embers crumbling to ash. Ninny heard his belly rumble, arguing with itself. Then, with some resolve, "What of it?"

The man and the woman took the measure of each other. After a pause, the woman said at last, "Nothing. It doesn't matter." She held out her hand. "Come along; it's back to bed for you."

Father's large hands seemed sad to let her go. Ninny went into the hall's dark tunnel, hearing the soft sounds of Father drawing on his pipe. The tin-cylinder phonograph now still . . .

Mother pulled down the chill bedcovers. "Get in." Ninny's bare feet rubbed together, two numb blocks of ice. Mother went the round of the room: checking the china horses, feeling the radiator, seeing all the toys were put away. Finally Mother's grave face rose above the bed. Ninny Blue Toes clutched Herr Wilhelm to her chest.

In one rash stroke Mother plucked the rabbit by the ear and flung him across the room. He sailed through the air as if his floppy ears were limp wings and fetched up against the radiator. Mother's prodding fingers searched her skinny body.

"Did you go in the sock drawer?"

"No!" Ninny cried.

The bird face came closer, became harder, whiter. "That's a lie!"

"It's not!"

"You were watching me so you could get some socks. I heard you in the hall, spying."

"No!"

"What did you see?"

"Nothing!"

Mother held up the long silver hairbrush. "Did you see this?"

"No . . . ," Ninny whispered.

For a moment Mother looked like she might go away, for she seemed to rise. . . . But then bared her teeth. "Don't call for help. Don't move." The hairbrush struck the bed by Ninny's arm.

"Not a sound."

The silver hairbrush hovered in the air. Ninny held her breath. Don't cry, Ninny. Don't move. Just stare at the brush floating in the air. The silver brush . . . hovering for ages near Mother's face. Or look at Herr Wilhelm rabbit on the floor by the radiator, with his head bent sideways. Oh, poor Herr Wilhelm with a broken neck. Finally the brush disappeared into the silken folds of Mother's dressing gown. For some moments she paused in the doorway. The rabbit's eyes gazed disconsolately at the ceiling.

"Mother, I'm cold. Can I have some socks, please can I —"

"I'm sorry, Fräulein, but our time is up."

She gawked at Herr Doktor incredulously. He couldn't possibly end it now. He stared down at his desk, making notes on a pad.

"But why?" she demanded. "Why did sh-sh-she make me lie to her? Why couldn't I have socks when I was cold? Why?"

Herr Doktor ceased his note taking. In a very sensible voice, he told her, "We'll continue again tomorrow. At your regular time. Telephone me if there's any change in your plans."

She staggered up to go, too dumbfounded to believe he would actually make her leave.

"Did you bring your umbrella?" he asked.

"An umbrella . . . ?" she said uncertainly. "No, no umbrella." She groped out. Downstairs, the maid helped her with her coat. In five minutes Fräulein rattled homeward in a tramcar. Her underclothes were totally soaked with perspiration; she had a splitting headache. Exhaust from a truck blew into the coach and stayed there, sickening her the whole ride. When she climbed the stairs to her apartment, the headache grew so bad she could hardly see. She fell into bed at once, sleep stunning her like a club.

But the session went on in an ugly dream. Fräulein sat at the dining room table of her Georgian dollhouse. Up close the tiny knives and forks looked crude and rough. The mama doll and papa doll sat beside her in rickety chairs, their cloth faces painted in broad quick strokes of blush, with dots of blue and white for eyes. The oaken dining room table was really made of varnished balsa wood. And the crystal chandelier merely a loose collection of dingy cut glass.

Through the grimy French windows she saw her vast room. Püppchen and Herr Wilhelm rabbit sat on her narrow bed like giants. They were in animated conversation, Püppchen saying, "Did Mother really sneak in and slap the bed with the brush?"

"Oh yes," Herr Wilhelm assured her. "Take my word for it — I saw the whole thing with a broken neck."

"How savage!" Püppchen gasped.

"Yes, savage — that's just the word for it," agreed the rabbit.

"Did it hurt very badly?"

"Why, no . . . ," Herr Wilhelm confessed. "My neck is flexible. No bones, you know; stuffed with cotton."

"I'm hollow inside," Püppchen confided earnestly. "But my hair is real."

"And lovely hair it is too," the rabbit complimented her. Herr Wilhelm had M-m-m's silver hairbrush in his clumsy paws and was trying to brush the doll's long tresses.

"Oh, leave off with that," she chided him. "We'll do you first. I think your ears would look charming in a bun." The doll gathered the rabbit's ears, braiding them to see how they looked. "No, that's not my

354

style," Herr Wilhelm told her. "They've always looked better hanging down."

Fräulein felt so glad the two of them had finally learned how to talk. She had so much she wanted to tell them. She rushed to the front of the dollhouse, but before she reached the door the rabbit and the doll ceased their chatter, then clutched each other in silent fear. Frozen, waiting . . .

A large wolf bounded into the room. In one swipe he tore Püppchen's head clean off. The head shrieked through the air, thudding mutely to the floor. In one huge gulp the wolf swallowed Herr Wilhelm whole. The rabbit said, "Oh my!" in surprise as he vanished down the beast's throat. The wolf stalked about the room on his hind legs. Loops of saliva hung from his jaws, which he wiped with a handkerchief. His red eyes looked hungrily for her. He sniffed the sterile row of china horses, snorting at them in disgust.

Then sat on the bed, crossing his legs. He picked up the silver hairbrush, curled his tail around to the front, and began to brush it lovingly. "Now, where oh where could a little girl be?" he mused out loud. "I'm sure I was told a little girl lived in this room. . . ." He held his tail in his paws, brushing it thoughtfully. "Now, where oh where could a little girl hide? Under the bed? No, too obvious . . . In the sock drawer? No, not allowed in there."

His red eye fell on the dollhouse. "Come out, come out, wherever you are." He left off brushing and slunk from the bed, one slow paw padding in front of the next. "Come, come, Fräulein," he coaxed. "Don't be silly. Come out and we'll brush your hair. Didn't your mother give you the brush? Wasn't it her favorite? Isn't it your favorite too?"

The wolf's black nose pressed against the dollhouse door. Fräulein crept to the safety of the stairwell and clung to the banister. The wolf pawed the house off its foundation; the chandelier swung wildly. Mama and Papa were thrown from their chairs. The brother and sister dolls tumbled from their beds. In the kitchen the terrified cook tried to stuff herself into the oven.

The wolf's paw broke through a French window and clawed the front hall carpet. Fräulein held fast to the banister and prayed. "Oh, thank God he's too big to get in." But to her dismay the wolf began shrinking. Soon he had shrunk to the size of poor Herr Wilhelm. His narrow jaws stabbed into the dining room, splintering the table to matchwood. "Come, come, my dear. Come out and let me brush your hair!"

She wrung the spindly balusters and wept in terror. "Oh, please, Mr. Wolf! I didn't see anything in M-m-m's room that night! I don't want the brush! *Please*, Mr. Wolf!"

Chapter 8

The Inescapable One

Fräulein awoke in bed in her apartment on Fesselstrasse. Outside, night had fallen. Her splitting headache was gone. She glanced apprehensively about the darkened room. Nearby, the reassuring hulk of her steamer trunk slumbered against one wall. The icon of Christ on the cross hung over her bed, just as it had at the hospital. In the center of the room stood the four-franc table she bought from the one-eyed junk seller. Feeling slightly ridiculous, she peeked under the bed.

Absolutely nothing.

Why, then, did her bed pillow look so much like a rabbit thrown against a radiator? Fräulein peered about more closely to set herself at ease. Her winter coat hanging on a peg. The dirty dishes in the sink, just as she'd left them that afternoon. Püppchen lying on the floor with her dress askew, one of Ninny's frilly white socks on her foot. Poor headless Püppchen. A thread of blood ran from her neck.

"This is my a-parents!" she stammered, meaning, This is my apartment!

Moonlight fell on the courtyard, turning the flagstones blue. Down below, the wolf walked across the flat stones on his hind legs. She tried to shout for the old woman who lived across the hall, but all that issued from her mouth was a choking bubble of silence. He knew where she lived. . . . Püppchen bleeding on the floor. My God, he'd been there *already*!

His red eye pinned her at the window. He held up M-m-mother's brush in his paw. "I've come for your hair, Fräulein. Shall we brush your hair?"

A moment later his hind legs creaked on the landing. The brass doorknob turned. His black snout snuffed at the widening crack.

357

"Let's brush your hair, my dear." His tail clicked eagerly inside. "Come, give us your hair!"

No! No! No! she cried, throwing her weight against the door. She pressed it closed with all her strength. How incredibly strong he was! The animal snarled as the lock snicked shut. She sagged to the floor. The frustrated tick-tick-tick of his pacing paw nails came from the landing.

And then an evil silence.

The bathroom window! She'd left it open. His claws scrabbled at the narrow window ledge. She slammed the window shut, fastening the latch against the snarl of rage beyond the frosted glass. But even as she flew from the bathroom, the front door began grating open once more. The wolf had his whole head in, grinning at her. "Come, come now! All I want is your hair!"

She threw her weight against the door, but still it inched open. In desperation she snatched her big black winter boot from beside the door and raised it over her head. She struck him on the snout with the heel. A yelp of pain. She struck him again. He yowled louder. She stomped and stomped. Again and again she swung the boot, the wolf's jaw becoming a bloody mangled mess on the wooden doorframe. He whimpered weakly. . . . A fire raged through her. How beautiful to smash his face with her big black boot.

"Aaaaaaaaah!" she bellowed in triumph. She was winning!

Fräulein woke up, mumbling, "uhhhhhhh . . ." She meant to say, "I've won!"

This time not a fake waking, but she glanced involuntarily at the floor to see if poor decapitated Püppchen lay there. No, only bare floor. Her blood still ran hot with exultation, joy, rage — feelings much, much better than being a little clear egg without a center. A lick of fear, a taste of power. What profound changes had come over her since the night of the dinner party. The Burghölzli time over, a new life begun. Now she fended for herself, shopped, cleaned, went to Küsnacht by train, and traveled home again. But not alone. Ages ago, the wolf first came to her in Herr Doktor's suit and tie. Then in the dollhouse dream like crazed M-m-mother with the brush. Yes, even now the wolf sat beside her. At her four-franc table as she studied, in the shower, or when she slept. Out of the dollhouse and into her room. No waking from the nightmare, no escape from Herr Doktor's sessions, where she confronted the old wreck of herself. Then crawling home after every bout with the wolf — only to recover, rouse herself, and struggle with him once more.

She heard a noise. The white curtains blew in the open bathroom window. In the far distance red lights burned from within a church spire. A pair of black silk stockings hung on the shower rod to dry. She almost closed the window but listened instead to the wind moan in the sky. Her eyes gazed at the red lights burning in the far-off spire. Wolf lights she would call them — for they were red like his eyes. And leave the bathroom window open from now on, for always. To see those lights glaring in the distance. Wolf lights in an open window.

God, how far she had come!

Fräulein sat herself down at her table with a lined writing pad and tried to recall everything: the quaking dollhouse, the fake waking, headless Püppchen . . . But soon all the copying became tiresome and she left off. On a scrap of paper she had made a sort of list, all her empty heads:

    Cowled Infants
    Carriage Mannikins
    Masked Wood People
    Mother of Stone

Everywhere an empty face. Everywhere she looked, blank eyes staring back . . .

"Yesterday, Fräulein, you were telling me about your family." Another analytic session had begun. "About how you went to your mother's door. How you watched her secretly. How you saw her —"

"Yes, yes — I remember," she said irritably. A headache came on, squeezing the light from her brain. "Don't you know any good words for what M-m-m did? Aren't there any nice words? M-m-m was touching herself." Touching. Such a nice word. How gentle, how sweet. Not the brutal, ugly sex words people used. Oh, the pain in the side of her head! She rubbed her temples, her voice thin and feeble.

"I told you how I saw M-m-m touching herself. How she caught me in F-father's lap. How she took me to my room and questioned me. The next morning I woke to see M-mother still standing there. Like a statue. Like a . . . Mother of Stone."

The room slowly turned; an eyelid over one eye fluttered wildly. What had the People of the Wood called her? The Inescapable One. What was that rhyme? Who is she? The One you know. The One of woe. Fräulein held her head to keep it from cracking. "Mother put that sock on my foot while I slept. To prove I spied on her."

Ninny Blue Toes awoke in the cold morning. Mother stood over her as though she'd stood there all night. Then slowly drew back the covers, exposing Ninny's poor bare feet. But on one icy foot she wore a frilly white sock. A sock in bed! How had the sneaky thing gotten under the covers and on her foot? Mother held its mate in her hand. "You lied to me," she said. "I found this on the floor. Outside my door." Mother's voice pure silk. "Deplorable," Mother said. "Simply deplorable."

She held the deplorable sock at arm's length as if it were a soiled rag. "I told you. If Little It can't wear the socks correctly, Little It won't have sockies at all. Mother will take every pair away."

Who was Little It? No, her name was Ninny. Ninny Blue Toes. A potty pain started in her tummy, warm and uncomfortable at the same time. She wriggled to ease the pressing. What if she went in the bed very quietly, just opening her legs and letting go?

"My name is not Little It. My name is Ninny Blue Toes. Ninny Blue Toes because my feet are cold. Because of all your ninny nighttime rules. Ninny play rules. And all your stupid things." She looked hatefully at the row of china horses on the shelf — colorful, pretty things she was never allowed to touch or play with. "I hate those horses. Why don't you take them away? I wish they'd break and be gone." The pee feeling washed over Ninny, making her eyes water. "And Ninny has to go potty."

The hand holding the deplorable sock fell to Mother's side. Now her face came close, white as when she slapped the bed with the hairbrush. "Stay there!" she hissed.

Ninny's leg dangled awkwardly over the side. Inch by inch she shrank back under the covers. Any second, she thought, any second she'd open and let go.

"*Who* has to go potty?" Mother asked quietly.

"You know . . ."

360

"Not unless you tell me. Tell me and you can go."

"Me!"

"Who is me?"

She no longer looked at Mother's face. Crossing and uncrossing her legs, the potty-go feeling making her shudder. Hold on, Ninny! Hold on!

"Nin-nin-nin," she sobbed.

"Tell me. Tell me and you can go."

Give her the right answer. There had to be an answer.

"Just say it! Say it and you can go!"

"Little It!" she shrieked. "Little It has to go potty. Please, Mother, Little It has to go!"

Without answering, Mother knelt before Little It's narrow chest of drawers. Clothes and underthings came flying out. All the while muttering, "Mother told Little It. If Little It can't wear sockies correctly, there'll be no sockies at all. Mother told Little It . . ." In the end she got every pair. When empty drawers hung from the dresser, Mother surveyed the mounds of scattered skirts and dresses, slips and smocks, that lay about the room in small heaps. A queer expression had come to her face: bland tenderness. . . .

"Well, what are you waiting for?" Mother asked kindly. "The potty is right there. Why don't you go?" And with that Mother left the room with every pair of socks.

The brass rattled noisily as it all came gushing out. It hurt it felt so good. As she squatted she saw Mother had forgotten one frilly sock, the deplorable sock that started it all. Snuck under the covers and onto her foot. She swept Herr Wilhelm off the floor. The rabbit's head lolled stupidly.

"What did you see?"

But the rabbit said nothing, just smiled at her with his sewn mouth. She threw him back on the floor, head to the fierce radiator pipes. "Stay there till you can talk," she told him. "I don't care if your face burns off."

Back in Herr Doktor's office the room stopped revolving. The summer heat of early June poured into the stifling office, the light from the windows unbearably bright.

"Shall I draw the curtains?"

He pulled a cord, and the drapes rustled across the window, throwing her face into shadow. Her soft voice came out of the gloom.

"The three of us existed alone in the world. Separate even from each other. Except for breakfast, which we ate together. A silent breakfast we ate day after day. Even at breakfast, my p-parents never spoke. . . ."

"Was your brother at breakfast too?"

"No: he ate alone in his room."

"What was the matter with your brother?"

"I don't know. My p-parents never talked about it. They hardly ever let him out." A horrible nauseous feeling came over her whenever she thought of her brother. Never at breakfast. Alone in his room. Never seen. Never heard . . .

Mother had put all the deplorable socks on the high shelf of her closet, far out of reach. Little It had no socks at all. She wore her hard leather shoes with bare feet inside. The skin between her toes cracked into thin red lines that rubbed together and never healed.

In the mornings they all sat together in the blue kitchen. Every morning they ate the same thing: one soft-boiled egg, one piece of rye toast, one pat of butter. The meal passed in slow, silent mouthfuls as the cuckoo clock ticked steadily in the corner. When the hour struck, the painted wooden cuckoo bird flew out his door and cried, "Little Red Toes! Little Cracked Toes! Soon you'll have no toes!" Then slammed the door bang. Only Little It seemed to hear him.

She hobbled from bed to kitchen and back again on cracked red toes. When her feet grew too swollen for hard leather shoes no matter how loosely she undid the laces, a pot of ointment appeared at her bedside one night. She smeared it in the red cracks and on the white flaking skin between her toes. The open cracks finally closed; the dried white skin flaked away. Her feet fit into the shoes again. Father must have taken pity on her. Mysteriously, the socks reappeared in her drawer. . . .

Fräulein shut her eyes, searching her mind. "When I think of my F-father, I always see his foot. Did he have a clubfoot? A toeless foot? When he came to Zurich, did you notice anything unusual about him?"

"About your father's feet? No, nothing strange at all. His feet seemed perfectly normal."

She lay back, one arm thrown over her eyes, quietly disappointed. "Yes, of course. But I swear there was something about F-father's foot that M-mother hated more than anything. You see, when I saw M-mother with the hairbrush, loving herself with it, I wanted the pretty thing to love me too. It wasn't hard to steal. But all that was just the beginning. . . . It got worse. Father used to watch me in my room."

"Watch you how?"

Little It sat on the bed with Püppchen tucked under her arm, waiting for Mother to leave. She glimpsed long black gloves and hat swishing through the hall. Had Mother really gone? She found the hairbrush in its place by the crystal perfume bottle of the dove. She greedily took both. In her room she brought out the dollhouse family so they might watch. First Brother from the toilet. Then Mama from the dressing table, so she wasn't gazing at herself all the time. And last she sat Papa in his armchair with Sister in his lap. . . .

Suddenly she decided Mama shouldn't see; after all, hadn't she just gone out? Then Brother fell off his chair. Good riddance, then: if you can't sit straight go back in the toilet. Now only Sister and Papa were watching, Sister doll on Papa's lap, as it should be.

She unstoppered the perfume bottle and did what Mother did. Going under Püppchen's dress and underneath her own. Then touching with the handle of the brush. A pleasant tingling weariness came over her; the long silver handle felt better on herself than on the stiff lifeless doll. She rubbed her thigh, higher up and deeper, until there came a long, sighing ache. She glanced in her dresser mirror, but it seemed clouded over in mist. A silvery, shuddering, slippery wetness lay over everything. Oh, Püppchen, dear, how sweet you are! The doll's brown eyes glistened, and her long hair was splayed across the floor. Oh, Ninny, dear, how nice it is when you brush my hair. . . .

Now she did it for Papa doll to see. The silver handle going up her smock, the tender itch growing safe and warm all over. The brush handle went on, turning the room into a creamy soft mitten. Vaguely she noticed Papa Doll wasn't sitting in his chair by the dollhouse. The odor of his pipe drifted through the air, smoky and reassuring. He stood in the empty hall, looking into her room. Papa Doll had become the real Papa. . . .

Watching her as smoke rose in wisps from his pipe.

Little It gave him a smile and he smiled back, his eyes blessing her.

See! He *did* want her to take the brush, to be like Mother, soft and loose. . . . When she looked up through the soft mitten haze, he just smiled and she kept on. Did he want to use the handle too?

Downstairs, the front door slammed.

Mother! Back so soon?

Father plucked the brush from her hand, right from between her legs. His face, even his lips, were gray. He put the brush on Mother's dresser. No, not the dresser! On the vanity! But Father caught her at the door, whispering brutally, "It's all right! All right!"

But she knew it wasn't.

Mother came into the hall. She stared at them for a long time, till Father slowly lowered Little It to the floor. "I can hold her, can't I?"

"If you wish," Mother said dully.

For a few moments she looked over her things: the bed, the nightstand, the glass vanity . . . sensing the ripple of some disturbance. She went to the dresser and touched the silver handle lightly, almost caressing it.

"I'm tired. I want a nap," she said.

And closed the door on them both.

Another day. Another hat and gloves to the door. Mother paused before she left. "Now promise me you'll be a good girl while I'm gone."

And Little It said back, "I promise."

The front door slammed. Father brought the brush. Somehow he always knew when Mother had really gone and how long they could play. Then he'd say, "That's enough," coming from his place by the door to take the long-handled brush gently back. But after a while, just the words "That's enough now" made her cool and stop. And he knew the brush's proper place — on the glass vanity, near the stoppered bottle of the dove.

When Mother finally came home, Little It was playing safely alone in her room, while Father kept away, sitting in his green leather chair. Reading from the book he brought down from the shelf. A large picture book that he wandered through, turning its pages . . .

But one day when both were out, Little It took the brush alone. She went on for a long time, until she was very sore and tender. Then quietly as a mouse she slid back to the glass vanity.

364

A floorboard creaked. Mother.

Little It snatched her hand behind her back. But Mother smiled kindly, as if everything were right and good. . . . She lifted the brush from its place on her table. Yes, offering. "Would you like this, darling? I'll let you have it if you show me," Mother tempted.

Little It wanted it. The silver brush should've been hers. Ought to've been hers. "No," she told Mother.

"But why won't you show me, darling?"

"I'm not darling. I'm Little It."

"But why won't Little It show Mommy?"

"Because . . ."

"Because why? Because you only show Daddy? Because you think I'm angry? I'm not angry. Show Mommy how you show Daddy. And I'll give you the brush. Don't you want the brush?"

She did. She did. She did.

"No," she told Mother.

But then Mother fetched Püppchen, offering the dolly and the brush. "Show Mommy on Püppchen. Show me on your dolly." That seemed easier; reluctantly Little It took the dolly and the brush. Going up the dolly's dress. And then her own, saying, "Now it's my turn. . . ." The hazy mist curled from beneath her smock, weaving in the air. Distantly she heard Mother say, "Oh, I see. I see. You saw me. You saw. . . ."

Little It nodded in agreement, not meaning to, but nodding.

Mother took the silver brush, laughing through her teeth. Little It giggled in the cottony haze. She found she didn't need the brush handle at all, that fingers were good enough. Better, even. Püppchen slipped from her arm. Mother pushed the silver handle under the dolly's dress; laughing, always laughing. She brushed the dolly's long, thick hair. "What long, thick hair she has. Just like yours. So pretty. But don't you think Püppchen's hair needs cutting? Just a snip-snip here, a little trim there?"

A pair of scissors clicked in her fingers.

The soft haze was breaking up. "Oh, Mother, please don't. Don't cut Püppchen's hair!"

"But Little It, darling, just a little trim." Snip-snip went the scissors. A few locks of the dolly's hair fell to the floor.

"I don't want the brush."

Snip-snip went the scissors. More hair fell. One side of Püppchen's head all bristles. "But we have to even her out. We can't have her walking around like this." Snip-snip went the scissors. She trimmed the other side of the dolly's head. Wisps of hair clung to Mother's white hand. "So you see, darling, Püppchen doesn't need my brush so often now. And so we can leave it on the table." Little It looked at the dolly, feeling the hard bristles on her scalp. Mother toyed with Little It's hair. "And so if the scissors go snip-snip on you — then you won't need Mommy's brush either. . . ."

"But M-m-m, you promised —"

Mother raised the brush, calling for silence; then quietly explained: "If we do this" — the brush stroked the inside of her own thigh as Little It had done — "then we do this!" Mother struck herself. "If we do this" — she stroked Little It's bare thigh under her smock with the flat side of the brush — "then we do this!" She smacked the naked thigh, the mark glowing from white to red.

"If we do this" — now back to stroking her own thigh — "then we do this!" Mother struck herself again.

"If we do this —" The brush stroked Little It's red thigh.

"Then we do this!" Smack went the brush!

"If this — then this!" Smack! Smack! "If this — then this!" Smack! Smack! Little It crawled to the farthest corner of the bed, cowering. "Stop! Stop!" Then Mother flew into a rage, striking her own thighs, her breasts, her throat, the place between her legs, crying, "This and this and this! I hate them all!"

A silence fell. The brush waved slowly in Mother's hand. "Do you want it now?" She asked. Little It clutched Püppchen to her chest, shaking her head no. "You said you did. Say you want it. Say it now!" Little It scuttled under the bed, dragging the dolly with her. "So you want the brush? I'll give you the brush! Here it is!" The brush was flung against her back. Fingers snatched her ankle. Little It wrenched away, banging her ear against the bedframe. A sharp light went through her head. She was going to throw up all over poor bald Püppchen. But Mother dragged her out instead. She hit her head again, trying to break free. Mother towered over her like a great mountain, looming into the clouds. The silver brush sailed like the moon in a dark sky, and Mother's voice whispered far away. "Do you like the brush . . . ? Do you want it now . . . ?"

The sky above went blacker and blacker.

"I'm sorry," she mumbled to the dolly. "Sorry. Sorry . . ."

Little It woke up in bed. The same day or another day? Her body felt stiff and sore. She took Püppchen off the shelf. "Are you all right?" The dolly said nothing, its glass eyes glistening as though filled to the brink. She tried to comfort poor Püppchen, petting her bristly head. Then taking her to the dresser mirror, saying nice things to make her feel better. "See, you don't look so bad. It'll grow back. Really it will." The doll examined herself carefully in the glass, then turned white in the face with rage. The dolly began to shake all over, wailing:

"Look, Ninny! Look!"

Hair lay all over the room. In the bed. On the pillow. The floor by the dollhouse. Cut and lying like dark hay. She felt the skin along the top of her head. Patting it made a flat sound like cardboard. No hair to brush. No hair. No brush. Her eyes filled to overflowing. The mirror sparkled; she saw hot tears running down Püppchen's cheeks. "We have no hair," sobbed the doll.

"No hair! No hair!"

Herr Doktor leaned back in his chair, peering through a slit in the blinds. A narrow band of light fell on his face, making him look like a hawk. "Your twiddle is left over from masturbating," he said matter-of-factly.

Oh, God — what an ugly word. Not touching. Not loving. But that ugly, ugly word. Mustardbeating.

"It's not like my t-twiddle. Not like it at all!"

She was lying.

Of course it was.

Her twiddle just like Mas-Turd-Bating. Monster-Biting.

Just like it.

She left his office and went out into the heat, twiddling in the tram all the way home as drops of sweat ran down her body. If only he could see her now. Doing it in public. On a crowded tramcar with

367

people staring at her. She didn't care. She twiddled as she walked down the street. In front of passing carriages, in front of shop windows, in front of a dog lifting its leg against her building, even as she clomped up the stairs past melting doorways — all the way into her suffocating bed. And there she pulled up damp sheets, twiddling, twiddling. Then using the long-handled brush just as she had as a child. Once, twice, thrice, till her hand went numb.

Chapter 9

The Queen of Sparta with a Hot Rear End

Fräulein wanted Herr Doktor's office always dark now. The July heat lay like rank grass in a field. Through the darkened room came the sounds of horses in the street and the faint bell of the tram as it went down the rails. Nice sounds, comforting. Echoes of the larger world; a place of escape when the sickening tale of the day was done.

"What made M-mother like this?" she pleaded into the gloom. "Why didn't F-father take me away? Didn't he love me?"

Herr Doktor made no answer.

"Don't you think I know the truth?" Her voice sank as though telling him a dirty secret. "Of course Father loved me. But we couldn't go away because of the problem with his foot. Remember when I told you that? The problem of his foot. So we sat at breakfast. Me, mostly bald. My head itched. But Mother never let me scratch. . . ."

The cuckoo clock ticked stolidly on: tock-tock-tock. The hour struck. The cuckoo bird had been plucked clean. Little It thought he looked ridiculous with yellow nubs, but she was the only one who noticed. "Everything's cuckoo!" he croaked and shut the door. Mother held a long tress of hair in her fingers and wistfully brushed the tips with the silver hairbrush. Father sat staring silently into his egg cup. Mother hummed the melody from the tin-cylinder phonograph. Between bits she said:

"I know you watch her."

"That's a lie," Father said into his egg cup.

Mother taunted him. "No lie, no lie. She told Mummy, didn't she?" Father's face went papery. She went on taunting him in a flat singsong. "I know you want it from her, but Papa's not going to get it. I know she'll give it to you, but Mama won't let her. Mama knows she's just

369

a little slut just begging for it all the time. And you'd take it from her, wouldn't you? You're nothing but a little-girl-licker. A little-bitch-kisser. Nothing but a slit-tickler!"

Singing scornfully:

"Nothing but a Ped! Ped! Pederast!"

"The reason we could never go away," Fräulein Schanderein said into the gloom, "was that my father was a pederast. Ped. Greek for foot, understand? The problem was his dirty foot. He used little girls. So how could we go away?"

Herr Doktor sat silently in the shadow. She felt him watching her, scrutinizing her through the dark room. "Well, why don't you say something?" She was sure he was about to call her a liar or an idiot. But instead he cleared his throat and said quietly:

"*Pod* is the Greek word for foot. The word 'Pederast' comes from a different root altogether. *Paiderastes.* Specifically, however, a lover of boys. Not little girls. You've got your genders confused."

Fräulein flew into a fit. "Genders!" she shrieked. "Who cares spit if I've got my genitals confused? Ask my brother. Father was doing it to *him.* That's why they never allowed him out of his room. That's why Mother always beat me. To keep me good. That's why she and Father never spoke. Father was going into my brother's room every day. Twice a day! And I was next. Soon my brother would be all used up, and I was *next.* . . ."

Fräulein broke off. She pulled a handkerchief from her sleeve and began to spit into it as if to rid her mouth of dirt. Indeed, her mouth tasted bitter and soapy and completely revolting. She had the distinct impression of a stranger's hands probing roughly up her dress, pawing feverishly at her underthings. She felt the horrible sticky sweat between her clenched thighs and the man's thick, dirty fingers.

"How do you know your father molested your brother? Did you ever see them?"

Fräulein ground her teeth. "How did I know? Do you think I remember every dirty little thing?" She pressed her fingers to her head. A vision appeared, herself as a little girl. She was reaching for the shelf of china horses. "Yes, I saw them," Fräulein told him. "I saw them the day the horses died. All Mother's horses died together. . . ."

*　　*　　*

370

The herd of Mother's precious china horses pranced across the high shelf in a frozen imitation of life. Little It picked up one horse. A fiery American Indian war pony at full gallop. She had the delicious feeling of holding on to her potty-go. Holding on and knowing she could release it anytime. Squirming and crossing her legs as she reached toward the shelf. Seeing the brass pot in the corner and knowing it was there. How grand Mother's face would be when she opened the door. Just like Little It waking up bald. Surprised.

And wonderful.

The morning passed slowly. Little It broke every horse. Snapping the hoof off one. Cracking the head off another. She stepped on some with her leather shoes until nothing but colored glass fragments remained. She even dropped one out the window, watching it skitter down the brick wall and shatter on the pavement in the narrow gap below. Horse after horse. Soon all the horses were dead.

When Mother came in to say, "Now promise me you'll be good —" her shoes crunched on the broken glass. She had stepped on the head of the white Arabian gelding, which had been neighing fiercely at the sky. All around lay bits and pieces. A hoof. A tail. A glass base of painted turf with a snapped foreleg. The rounded shard of a thundering flank —

Mother came for her, white-eyed, her mouth dripping. How odd to see Mother's sharp fingernails straining through the thin leather of her black kid gloves. A long wail filled the room. Little It fled down the empty hall, calling, "Daddy! Daddy! Daddy!" as the wail pursued her.

Father sat in the parlor chair by the fire.

But not alone.

Instead she saw the shamed face of her brother, pink and sweaty from the heat. Father had yanked down the boy's pants and was slapping his round white bottom, turning it redder and redder. Brother whimpered, eyes glistening with tears. And his round behind showed glowing handprints with each slap. Suddenly Father hauled him around so Brother sat, his bare bottom on Father's thighs. The boy wriggled and squirmed as Father's hands milked his body, and every so often Little It saw the oily worm vanish as Brother whimpered, "No, Father! Please, Father!"

*   *   *

371

"Fräulein!" Herr Doktor cried angrily. "Stop this at once! Do you hear me? Stop it now!"

"It's true! It's true!" she shrieked back.

The drapes flew apart with a bang. Sunlight streamed into the dark room. Fräulein hid her eyes. "True! True! True!" she screeched through her hands. Herr Doktor tore them from her face. The blinding light streamed into her head, the shock shutting her mouth. She wrenched her body from side to side in the awful silence.

Herr Doktor's hard voice filled the room.

"Fräulein! Listen! You are an *only* child."

She choked on a sob. Yes, yes, the simple, dirty facts.

"You have no brother."

Herr Doktor closed the drapes. Fräulein sank into a corner of the couch. She buried her head, muttering, "Yes, alone. My own alone. No brudder. No fahder. No mudder. Just my own alone . . ." She weakly lifted her pasty white face, imploring him. "Excuse me. I'm very — I have to —"

She never finished.

Lurching from his couch, she threw up on his desk in a great bubbling rush like a heaving fountain. Herr Doktor leaped from his chair, barking, "Good heavens!" And at that moment the maid knocked on the office door, informing him that the hour was over and another patient waited in the dining room.

Fräulein stood before his desk, shaking like a leaf.

"Wipe your mouth," he told her. "Go out the side door. Helga will show you where to wash, or rest if you want. I'll see you tomorrow."

Fräulein stared vaguely at him. At the mess of his desk with her vomit settling over it — reeking now. "Tomorrow," he insisted. She turned meekly and left. Gray in the face. Too weak to argue. Helga the maid showed her where to wash up, without so much as a raised eyebrow. She rested for a while on the same divan as on the night of the party. After fifteen minutes she stopped sweating and went home. How Herr Doktor managed the mess on his desk she didn't know and didn't care. At home she put on tea and made toast. She swept a pile of university preparatory books from her table and sat there drinking tea and eating toast, the crumbs going everywhere.

Once upon a time I knew how to study, she thought. Did I actually sit in a classroom with other children, at a wooden desk, with books and pencils, and a teacher standing at the blackboard? But with gravelly toast in the corners of her mouth, she didn't want to think how far off that had been, in what lost lifetime. And she didn't feel like studying now anyway. She could still taste the sour tang on her tongue. She reached into the pile of books, into the mess of papers, searching for the ugly picture book. The book of the Black Time. Would she see its title correctly now? She had, once upon a time. . . .

Why couldn't she have just stayed a safe little egg without a center and never given birth to herself?

Why?

Because seeing things clearly was what being sane meant. That's why she never saw her precious book's title right. Because she herself was still not seeing right. And when she saw it long ago, first as a bee egg and then in her ancient dream tale, she had stepped into a sealed room in the mansion of her mind, where she found the stored belongings of her past life under sheets and cobwebs. Now she knew for certain no Burghive Bee Hospital existed. No Gurgler to strangle in the room next door. No horses having bowel movements between her parents' dummy heads. No people talking in blocky, hollow phrases at dinner parties. No ancient dream time where the People of the Wood tore a stag to shreds. No Hunt-hers. No Hag. No Mother of Stone. And no brother buggered on Father's lap.

Mere shades on a cave wall in the hospital mountain. Dayroom faces in the People of the Wood. A bloody sacrifice in the remnants of Mother's china horses, cast down long ago. Dummy faces in the dimly remembered conversations of a lonely little girl named Ninny Blue Toes talking with her dolly and velvet rabbit.

With a deep sigh that sounded like *I'm almost sane,* she tried to see that last memory as it really happened. Little It had smashed all Mother's china horses. And Mother meant to kill Little It, stomp her and mash her for the terrible thing she had done. Once again she was a little girl and fled down the empty hall, crying, "Daddy! Daddy!"

Father was reading from his favorite picture book, with the pretty color drawings inside. Looking up, surprised, he caught her as she leaped into his arms. Then kissed her, cooing, "There now, there now . . ."

His voice trailed off. Little It tried to burrow into his big man's body. Mother's sneering face floated in the air. Then, contemptuously:

"Why, if it isn't my dear Herr Küssen. Herr Kiss-Kiss and his Kitty Kat." Little It felt a bubbling gas pain inside — not the delicious hold-on-to feeling but a cold and hungry pressing, crawling around the slow corners of her bowels, forcing its way out. She held on tight as Mother glided into the room, reaching with both hands to take her away. "Give her to me," Mother said politely, as if nothing were wrong. "Now, if you please . . ."

"What do you want with her?" he snapped. But suddenly, as if Mother knew his very thoughts, Father's arms began to tremble.

"You *will* hand her over," Mother said with a smile. "Because I know about you two. I'll tell our maid. I'll tell the shop people. I'll tell your business associates. And if only one person believes me, you'll still be ruined. The police will come to the house. With their questions. I'll give them the hairbrush and say I saw you doing it to her —"

Mother licked her lips, savoring the sick taste of her words. "I own you. From the second I let you touch her, I *owned* you. And the little beggar too."

Father's arms squeezed tighter and tighter. She struggled to break free, but the more Mother sneered, the stronger the arms held on. She felt the slow fear bubbling in her guts come pressing out. She was letting loose, going all warm and juicy down Father's leg. And when Mother saw, she clutched her sides and leaned weakly on the doorframe for support. There was only the warm juice, Mother's terrifying soft laughter, Father quaking with rage. And Little It alone. Ashamed . . .

Rough hands hoisted her in the air, then threw her across the big man's knees. Panties ripped down. The hot strike of pain. Father spanked her wet, runny bottom, while deep inside a clutching mouth spastically opened and closed. Silently screaming each time the burning hand struck. The smell of her potty-go everywhere. While the man cried, "You don't own me! No one owns me!"

She thought it would never end. Sweat ran down her face as Mother snarled gleefully, "Go on! I'll tell them anyway! The whole neighborhood! The world!"

Father's hand came and came. Her behind turned into a warm, wet throb, growing larger and larger, swelling to the size of a pumpkin, then the size of a horse, then filling the room. Little It thought it would never stop. She did not feel her Father's single slaps any longer but only the dull hugeness of her behind. Yet when he struck she felt a distant pulse, throbbing like the beat of a muffled drum. Mother's face had turned into that of a donkey, braying, "Herr Küssen and the Kitty Kat! Herr Kiss-Kiss and the Kitty Kat!"

What did those silly words mean? The last thing she saw was Father's picture book, which had fallen on the floor. The open pages calling her. Beckoning her to leave the awful room and vanish safe inside. And then her huge rear end finally filled the universe, throbbing into infinity with a light of its own.

"Behold the Queen of Sparta with the hot rear end!" Fräulein sat once more in Herr Doktor's dark office. "Really two people all along. My M-mother as the Queen. And I . . . I the hot rear end." She pushed her precious book across his desk. She saw the title clearly. No mutations. No mistakes:

THE EVIDENCE OF ANCIENT POTTERY
Artifacts from the
Prehistoric Peoples
of the
Peloponnese

Herr Doktor looked silently at the cover.

"Inside is everything we talked about. The Queen who rules the earth and the sky at night. The killing and the sacrifice. How they lay with their women in her temple under the moon . . ."

Clearly the book had seen much wear. The corners were frayed, ragged edges along the binding. Slowly, he opened it. Inside even worse. The title page gone. The frontispiece in tatters. Page after page: contents, introduction, the first few color plates. Herr Doktor flipped faster and faster, looking for something to lock his eyes onto. But the book contained nothing but ribbons.

The entire volume, it seemed, had been ripped to shreds.

Chapter 10

The Abyss

"But I wasn't crazy then. Not yet." Fräulein took a handkerchief from her sleeve and patted her damp face. "Mother created me. Like a story or a painting. And it took all her ingenuity and effort. She never quite terrorized me into blind obedience. I was terrified, yes — but never obedient. And time passed. . . ."

Her younger childhood and middle childhood. They tried giving her an education, as parents were supposed to do. On many days the maid dressed her for school, brought her to the schoolhouse, and sat her at a wooden desk. The other children stared at her but kept away; they seemed afraid. And the teacher who stood at the front largely ignored her too, approaching her desk only to open her workbook to the proper spot. Little It managed to turn the pages and follow along, closing her workbook when the lesson had finished. But she rarely spoke in class, and the teacher seldom asked her questions. At the end of the day the maid came to the schoolhouse door to bring her home. . . . Years dripped by like drops from a rusty pipe. . . . She grew too big for her clothes, which she wore till they faded, became tattered, then fell apart. Mother never bought her new ones to wear, except for appearance's sake, so as not to arouse the attention of her schoolmates or strangers on the street.

"Until I was nine or ten, she crammed me in a beat-up high chair." Little It towered awkwardly over the kitchen table. Having to lean down to reach her food. Never eating enough. Too cramped. Too crushed to run away. A mannikin. "But always a secret part of me safe from her." Fräulein lowered her voice. "What I did in private."

She touched the handkerchief to her mouth in dread, then kneaded it into a ball as if to wring some strength from it. Time and again she stole into Mother's bedroom to steal precious moments with that lovely hairbrush and its lovely handle. And when Mother caught her, which was often, she chased her, dragging her by the hair, slinging her into the high chair, where she tied her down with cords. And when Mother left the kitchen, she forgot Little It existed. In time she learned to wriggle free. Fleeing to the toilet, locking herself in. Then sitting in the dark for minutes or hours until Mother tired of her shouting and left Little It alone. Then later, in the safe and quiet, she would come creeping out.

"She used to do something to make my bottom sore. Concoctions spooned down my throat while I sat strapped to the chair." The spoonfuls gagged her and burned their way out as she shivered over the chamber pot or the toilet.

"Delicious brush. Slapped thigh. Gagging on the choke spoon. Sore red bottom. Pleasure and pain all mixed up between my legs until I didn't know one from the other. Then hiding in the pages of the book. Forgetting who I was. Or where . . ."

Fräulein unwound the knotted handkerchief, searching its folds for answers. "Father's picture book was my escape. Begging the pages to take me away. I found a place to be alone with the book, where no one could find me. . . ."

Little It found the iron stove in the kitchen. The oven was the safest place she knew. Crouching in the dark for hours at a time. Making it a big, soft nest with pillows. Keeping the door open a crack, so light shone in. And there studying the book, asking it to let her in and let her stay . . . Once, she must have fallen asleep. For she awoke in the warm dark. The maid had shut the door and lit the broiler underneath. At first she kept quiet, listening to the hissing of the gas below. But as the heat filtered through the pillows, she struggled to get out. The door jammed; she pushed and hammered. No use . . . She must have screamed, because the maid yanked open the door and the pillows billowed with smoke. Her dress parched, the skin on her legs red. "'Are you roasting me for dinner?' Little It asked. The maid got so mad she spat, 'Shut your filthy mouth! Or I'll cook you with those pillows!'"

The book went back to the drawing room bookshelf and she to her room. But Mother found out about the pillows. Mother always found out. . . . From the awful time she broke the china horses, it all became blacker and blacker.

"I never really knew the time or where I was." Except that she seemed to be standing on the ledge, looking out over a great chasm. And when the ledge finally gave way, she slipped. Falling forever in an abyss without end . . .

She had been staring at the wonderful pictures in Father's book. The Water Jug. A red clay jug, the naked figures black. A fierce man with a sword was slaying his brother. The fallen one bled from his belly. He wore a deer pelt, with antlers in the skull. The Slayer loomed over him, sword arm raised for the final blow.

Another picture showed the jug's back side. The Slayer chased a beautiful Lady in flowing robes. She fled, laughing in his face. Her body shone through thin veils. She held aloft the deer pelt, tempting him as she ran.

Around the top of the jug a line of men and women danced. The dancing ladies had needle faces like insects, or open yelling faces like Mother. The needle ones looked as if they would suck your insides out, the shouting ones as though they'd chew you up. The dancing men had serpents rising from their bellies, like tails in front.

Little It touched the dancing ring.

Like F-father, she breathed in awe. . . . Just like Father standing in the shadow of the hall. Father's secret pet, which he showed her when she paused with the lovely handle. Father's pet servant. Pet serpent . . . Then put away. Did she really see it?

A wisp of flowing veil brushed against her face. The fleeing Lady beckoned. "Come with me! Come!"

Little It wept. If only she could go with the beautiful Lady inside, if only —

Clop-clop-clop came Mother's hooves in the hall. Since the horses died, Mother's feet had turned into hooves. Rough horses' hooves that grew at her ankles. Little It shoved the book onto the shelf. Then Mother stomped in the parlor, flopping back and forth.

"What are you doing? Reading that book? Stealing my brush?"

Little It backed away, silently shaking her head.

"You lie," Mother told her.

She shook her head harder.

"To the chair," Mother brayed. "To the *chair!*"

No, Mother. No! she pleaded, but no words came out. Dragged by the hair to the kitchen. Strapped to the high chair. Mother had the large brown bottle, the thick wooden spoon, and she was pouring out her home brew. It smelled of red pepper and linseed oil, of stewed socks and toilet sweat, of garlic paste and soap. The spoon thrust into her mouth. Dose after dose burned its way down her throat. Where was Herr Kiss-Kiss, to hold her in his arms? The home brew wrestled in her stomach, climbing back up her throat —

"I think that's enough."

Mother always knew when enough was enough.

"One leg! One leg!" Mother was shouting.

Little It stood in the hallway by the water closet. Her clothes half gone: a tattered gray chemise over her shoulders, underpants off, chill air striking her bottom. The dark wood door to the water closet stood open. Inside she saw the narrow, gloomy room, the white porcelain bowl gleaming dully, crouching like a dwarf. For some reason Mother had brought along her old brass potty.

"One leg! One leg!"

Little It strained to stand on one leg. The burning home brew burdened her guts, but she held on with all her might. She pictured a large balloon hanging off her behind like a bustle, a heavy, expanding bag like a cow's udder, filled with liquid, which shook and quivered and threatened to break, gushing forth.

"Do you promise not to use the brush? Promise not to look at the book? Promise me! Promise!"

I prumse, prumse, Little It tried to say, but her tongue was so thick, too hard to talk. She trembled, the balloon ready to break. She couldn't hold it any longer. She was letting go —

Just as Mother relented in a bored voice: "Well, what are you waiting for? Go on, then. Go . . ."

Little It went for the dark, narrow toilet. "Not there!" The dented brass pot was shoved under her behind. The balloon exploded and the burning came and she was mumbling, "Prumse, prumse, prumse . . ." Her bottom stung, and still more came gushing out. The reek everywhere. She gazed down the hall. Past Mother's room. Past Father's room. Past her room and to the landing of the stairs . . . A figure stood there. Long-lost Herr Kiss-Kiss. The figure wavered and was gone.

She crouched in the water closet for hours. The home brew had long run out. Later Mother took Little It to the tub to wash her body. She brought out new clothes. The old rags were thrown away. So much easier just to let it all happen — not to fight or make a fuss. Mother fixed and combed her hair. Trimmed her nails. Rubbed cold cream into the sores around her wrists. "There now," Mother said as she buttoned the pocket flaps of the pinafore. "A little princess, all done up." Mother brought her to the kitchen, but she wasn't hungry. She fell asleep tied to the chair while the cuckoo bird nodded on his perch.

"How many times did I steal the silver hairbrush?" Fräulein said into the gloom. "How many times did I touch myself in secret? How many thousand times did I wander over the pages of the pottery book, coming back to the picture of the Water Jug? How many times did she catch me? Strap me to the chair? Gag me with the home brew?"

She did not wait for Herr Doktor to answer, suddenly shouting, "How many billion times did I stand on one leg till I shat on myself while Father just stood there, stood there and did *nothing?*"

She broke off to catch her breath. "And always the sound of Mother going clop-clop-clop in the hall. Just the sound of her sent me shrieking to the toilet. Where I sat for hours, shivering and shaking. Even now when I hear stupid horses going clop-clop-clop in the street I need to hide. In some dark, small hole. In some dirty toilet. When will it go away? Tell me!"

Herr Doktor shifted uneasily in his seat. Her voice sank to sadness. "Will it ever go away?"

He made no answer. No one knew.

There was no answer.

Little It was dreaming her favorite dream. In the empty parlor, her precious book inched from its place on the shelf. It floated out the door and down the hall, coming to visit her. Drifting gently to her room . . . Then opened to the page of the Water Jug. And there Little It saw the Lady of the Veils. Yet even as she stared at the picture, the beautiful Lady rose from the page and sat by her bed.

The beautiful Lady of the Veils had become her fairy godmother, just as in the stories she remembered from long ago. And though her fairy godmother rarely said a word, still, through the silent touching of their eyes, they told secrets back and forth. How Little It loved the Lady, and the Lady loved Little It back. How very soon the beautiful Lady would take her away to a wonderful place where there was no prumse-prumse, no standing on one leg or home brew in the gag spoon. Soon, soon, they would go together. Hand in hand to a warm place where the Lady of the Veils would take care of her forever.

And whenever Little It woke from this dream she ran straight to the parlor to see if the beautiful Lady was still there.

In one corner of the fireplace lay the torn cover of the book, its veined marble edges charred. Pages ripped out. Some burned. A crumble of black ashes nearby filling the grate.

She fell to her knees, gently taking the empty cover. Scrap by scrap, she collected the torn pictures in it. Her heart was crying: the beautiful Lady of the Veils had prumsed, prumsed, prumsed to take her away. How could they go away if Mother had torn the beautiful Lady to pieces?

All through the night she stared at the shredded pages in the book. All through the day. Just staring at the cover. Seasons passed. Summer changed to fall, autumn to winter. . . . She found shreds that fit together. A torn piece, another. She stole some paste from the cupboard and white paper. She pasted the scraps in place. *There.* The beginning of a page. Months and months, a scrap here, a shred there. The Water Jug picture came together even though it had been badly slashed. The fallen deer man and his slayer were almost totally missing. When she could find no more, she left them unfinished.

She found nearly all the beautiful Lady, but some pieces were mere slivers, as particular attention had been taken to tear and slash and mutilate her image. Her beautiful breast, which shimmered through the veil — entirely gone. Little It carefully drew it in. . . .

Little It talked to her redrawn picture, talked to the beautiful Lady the way she used to talk to Püppchen, saying things like: "I've remade you. Reborn you. So we can live together. So you can take me away . . ." Whispering to the picture in the dark, whispering her own life into it until she fell asleep. And the Lady of the Veils came to sit on her bed, cooing softly: Soon, soon, we're going soon. . . .

The lights came on. Caught! She tried to hide the book under the mattress but never made it. Mother held the Brass, waving it around. "What's this, eh? What's this?"

It's the Brass, she tried to say, but all she could manage with her stiff, awkward mouth was: "Iddah bah."

"Bad. That's right, it is bad."

No, no, no — not right — but too late.

"Herr Kiss-Kiss, fetch the syringe!" Mother ordered. But the man seemed reluctant to do her bidding; he stood at the door uneasily, shifting from foot to foot. "Now, I say." With a crushed sigh the rubber syringe was brought, the man looking away, handing it to Mother without meeting her eye.

"Hold her down."

Father stiffly came for her, laying his mechanical hands upon her jointed body. Nightdress peeled off. Mother held the snouty end of the syringe in the air. She squeezed the big pink rubber bulb. The pointy black spike spat a stream of water. She could feel it enter her, fill her up, like a bloated tongue going round and round inside. Mother's face came close. "Don't you *dare* let go! Don't you dare!" An immense pool of water gathered deep inside, pressing to break out. She was ready to pop open, the dam ready to crack, explode —

On the bed. On her self.

A scream danced in the air of the room, a scream that never died. The brass potty filled as the water kept gushing out of her, flood upon flood. And the Brass itself kept growing. Now the size of a coal scuttle. Now a soup pot. A bathtub. A huge cauldron. She sank into it, the cauldron walls rising higher and higher.

And she was falling —

Plummeting into a lightless cavern, down an abyss of no time, no pain, no tears. Only the rush of air sounding strangely like the Lady of the Veils —

Cooing:

Soon

Soon

Soooon

BOOK V

WISH FULFILLMENT

Chapter 1

Shock Treatment

When the falling finally stopped, Little It had turned into a mannikin, packed in the steamer trunk. A dummy they took out of the dark occasionally and sat in a chair by the corner. The dummy did not wish to be disturbed.

Daylight dawned at the Nunatorium.

All through the long day the mannikin watched the beams of sunlight crawl across the gray stone floor, listening to the faint rustling of the Sister Nuns as they drifted to and fro among the high stacks of books. Often a Sister Nun settled into a chair by a small writing table, turning the pages of a book that she read out loud to the dummy, her dry voice floating into the high stone vault:

> In the beginning God created the heaven and the earth. And the earth was without form, and void; and darkness was upon the face of the deep.

Sometimes the Sister Nun moved the mannikin's pale wooden hand across the print, touching the letters to see if they would speak. Trying to get the dummy to read along with her. But the words from the Sister Nun's book never took form in the dummy's empty head. The Sister Nun droned on, regardless:

> And the spirit of God moved upon the face of the waters.
> And God said, Let there be light: and there was light.

At the close of the reading the Sister Nun looked over the mannikin's face to see if it had been following along. But no flicker of life. "Ah, well." The Sister Nun smiled. "We'll try again tomorrow. . . ." And put the dummy away in the trunk for the night.

In the world beyond, snow and rain fell. There was a time of gusty wind. A time of ice and a time of melting. A time when leaves plastered their dead hands against the windows and a time of still emptiness. The limp mannikin sat in a corner of the high-vaulted room. Upon the desk lay a large black portfolio composed entirely of blank white sheets. The mannikin's pale wooden hand held a pen. Thick leather tomes grew at its feet. And when the mannikin finished copying from one book, they put another in its place. If the inkpot ran dry, a Sister Nun came with a fresh one. The wooden hand copied histories and biographies, treatises and forgotten alchemies. They were copied for the mannikin's education, or simply because they were old and rotting, or just to give the mannikin an occupation. It did not matter. The wooden hand traced down all set before it. And the words issued into its hollow head like the sound of wind moaning in an empty cavern, rising and falling and then dying away without a trace. A moan like the faintest echoing coo from the Lady of the Veils . . .

The mannikin's pen dipped to the inkwell and poised over a clean page. Hesitantly the wooden hand began to draw. At first the hand felt awkward, but soon the fingers grew surer and surer. Slowly a picture emerged . . . the beautiful Lady of the Veils. She was running as she had on the water jug, the wisps of thin gauze clinging to her body, her thighs, her breasts. . . .

A Sister Nun plucked the pen from her hand.

"What's this, eh? Pictures in the copybook? We can't have that. No, no, no, we can't have that!" The Sister Nun slipped the copybook under her arm and marched off.

The mannikin watched her go with a terrible longing. The word *Stop!* surged up her throat, right into her head. The first living sound in that empty cave in so long. She tried to speak, to call out, but alas, the only sound was her fingers' dry tattoo as they pattered on the wooden desk.

She rose from her seat. A halting step. And then another. She hobbled over the stone floor, blundering down the long vaulted hall, wanting to cry, Sister, come back, bring the Lady back, please come back! But she had been a mannikin too long to talk, too long for words — and so the Sisters grabbed her clumsy puppet body and returned it to the trunk.

A semicircle of seats rose in tiers like polished wooden sentinels. The mannikin dimly saw strangers' faces gawking down or whispering among themselves. A pleasant voice came out of the light and said:

"Students! Let me thank you for coming. I think we can all agree the Odessa Sanatorium is lucky to have procured this subject from the Convent of Saint Agnes for our demonstration. The convent sisters claim our subject knows how to both read and write — but the manifest evidence does not bear them out. Shall we proceed directly with the demonstration? That's right, gentlemen, wheel over the galvanic . . ."

They lifted the mannikin onto the black table. The speaker showed a leather thong to the crowd. "We place this leather thong between the teeth so no damage occurs to the tongue."

Dots of grease were smeared on the mannikin's head. "We apply graphite petroleum to the subject's temples to promote conductivity from the terminals to the nerves. Do not be alarmed if the lights dim at the moment of charge. Are we ready? Very good. On three, then . . .

"One —"

The mannikin saw Mother sitting in a wooden seat, brushing her hair.

"Two —"

Then the beautiful Lady of the Veils sat there instead.

"Three!"

A soft blow clubbed the dummy's head. The amphitheater vanished, strangers, Mother, beautiful Lady, and all.

Then one afternoon a few weeks later, they packed the mannikin's limp body in the old steamer trunk. Once more sent back to the hands of her family. With deep regret, said the director of the Odessa Sanatorium.

Subject unresponsive.

"And so in the end you came to me. . . ."

The tattered remains of her old book lay on Herr Doktor's stiff

387

leather couch. "But how did my book stay with me all this time? Through all those years — my old book and Mother's silver brush. How?" Fräulein pondered the frayed binding as if it had further tales to tell.

"Open the curtains," she said. "I want to see the light now." It was an overcast, stormy day. Fräulein shielded her eyes for a moment, then rose from the couch to stand by him, one hand resting on the back of his chair. "Someone must have stowed the brush and book in my trunk. Hidden, so I always had them with me."

"Someone?"

"*Father,*" Fräulein answered. "Father hid the book and the brush for me. He put those precious things where I could reach them, when all else was gone. His last effort to save me. Funny . . . ," she mused sadly. "I don't really feel like thanking him."

Herr Doktor snorted. "Can't say I blame you."

She struck his face with her open palm. "Stop laughing! How dare you laugh at me!" A handprint glowed on his cheek.

"I wasn't laughing —"

"And I say you were." Her face had taken on a dark, threatening cast. White heat curled inside him, an urge to strike her back, yank up her black wool skirt, spread her legs, hold her by the hair as he —

Ja! The act of Ritual as they played the Queen: the hunting and the killing, the stalking and the bloody death, and then, at the very end, Fräulein as she lay prostrate before him, open and willing, spread among the pillows he had slain . . . Yes, God, he wanted her then. To think he tried to cauterize that red desire with a black velvet gown and a dinner party! What a fool!

"Don't you wonder why I never laugh?" she demanded now.

Mother laughing as Little It's diarrhea ran down Father's leg. As the home brew poured down her throat. As the rubber snout jabbed in. As the little girl's bottom exploded in the brass pot.

"I never thought you had anything to laugh about."

A shadow fell across his desk. Suddenly she knelt beside his chair. She took his hand in hers and petted it like a child. Touching it to her cheek and pressing it to her skin. Waves of light and warmth flowed into his lifeless fingers. How could it be so wrong if she made him feel this way? Why so forbidden when they both were aching for it? To flow together, to mount and crash, sinking again like the

388

ocean on a strip of sand while sandpipers danced along the brink. Finally he knew what she was supposed to look like. All through the times of starvation and the skinny shrieking filth — she was really this ripe, blossoming face, a sullen fruit that parted and took you inside the sweet flesh.

"Sometimes a man laughs when he enjoys a forbidden thing," she told him. "But when a woman laughs, she doesn't laugh through her mouth or throat." Her voice grew low. "Sometimes she laughs through the dark place between her thighs. . . ."

Here, she gripped his first two fingers, holding him in the warm fold of her fist. She gave his fingers a brief squeeze; the pulse of it ran into his arm and down his spine. A coupling of hands, a fleshy palm and strong fingers doing what a man and woman were supposed to do. Only holding hands. Just hands. And as she spoke their hands made love again. "So when I laugh, my insides laugh too . . ."

The pulse of her flooded through his arm.

"But I haven't laughed in a long time. Not since Father watched me through the open door. Since I played on the floor. Not since the Black Time." Her eyes glittered darkly. "Don't you like it when I laugh?"

His fingers fused to a single root. Her relentless fist pressed once more, and the pulse of her hurled in. Was she feeling any of this — or was it all him, sick and depraved?

So innocently. "Don't you like it when I laugh?"

"I like it," he said hoarsely. The office slipped away and the dark came to his eyes, the dusky place between Nanny Sasha's thighs. There came the faintest rush of air as Fräulein whispered:

"Doesn't Frau Emma laugh?"

Again, the pulse, as she worked her fist around his thick fingers. "Emma . . . ," he said vaguely. Those times with Emma seemed shallow, jerking spasms — not the sobbing convulsions he knew were coming. "No," he whispered. "I don't think Emma ever laughs."

"Not like this," Fräulein teased. The pulse pounded in his chest. She gazed at him through heavy-lidded eyes, rocking on her knees. Now eyes closed, her mouth slack, purring:

"Not like me?"

"Not like you."

She clung to his arm, her voice satin and breaking. "When I laugh it means I want someone. Want him badly . . ."

389

He touched her swaying head, spreading her hair. His cuff link unfastened and fell on the floor. She swayed, going rigid and slack. Her free hand clawed his arm as her coupling fist sapped the life from him.

"Don't all women laugh?" he demanded.

But she made no answer. So he held her hair, forcing her eyes into his. "Don't all women?"

"I don't know," she moaned. "Don't *know!*"

Hot tears gushed from his eyes, blinding him. She tore her head from his grip. The coupling of their hands broke. She panted and hung her head. In his lap, his pale, weak fingers stared up at him. Damp and limp. It was over.

She feebly straightened her clothes. Sometime during it all, he had pulled down the shades. He could not see her face. They let the hollow silence of the room protect them for a while. Neither met the other's eyes. She made ready to leave.

"Don't forget your umbrella," he said stupidly.

At the door she stopped, then asked the dark room:

"Shall I come tomorrow?"

"Please . . . ," he whispered fiercely. "Tomorrow. Always."

And when she had left he fell asleep at his desk, a dead black sleep until the maid knocked on the door, announcing the arrival of the next patient.

Chapter 2

The Sleeper Must Awaken

That night as he lay in the darkness, Herr Doktor had the strangest sensation — that the girl had entered his bedroom and was standing quietly in the shadows, watching as he lay in bed with Emma. So beautiful, the Lady of the Veils brought to life . . . While beside him Emma kept groaning in her sleep, as if she sensed something amiss. At last, weary of his wife's restless slumber, Herr Doktor drifted off into a troubled doze. Yet with half-closed eyes he still saw the dim white figure standing in the shadows. Slowly a bit of her shroud fell from her. Then more, as from a statue. She unwound, unraveled, lengths of drapery falling to her feet. She was spinning like a top, like a spindle, she was twirling round and round. . . . And her voice said, "I will come to you tonight. Tonight and every night. In the place where we can be together. You know the place."

Fräulein opened her eyes. She felt a dampness between her thighs. A kind of sorrowful ache that had no name. She was sure he was dreaming of her now. Through the window she saw a great summer moon sailing above towering clouds, thunderhead clouds in the dead of night. She found the silver-handled hairbrush on her dresser and gently touched its smooth, long silver handle to her thigh. . . . How *telling* Herr Doktor's fingers had been. The great faces of the clouds loomed down upon her; they opened their mouths to speak. A shiver of lightning came from their eyes. The smooth handle of the brush ran up and down and deeper down again.

After many heartbeats there came a distant thunder.

Night lay over the valley. Herr Doktor had come with Herr Vienna Professor to their little village, come to celebrate the sowing of their fields, to cast seed and sprinkle watered wine upon the earth. They had been drinking from dawn until dusk, and he had lost the old codger somewhere. But that didn't matter so much, for he was drunk too. And Herr Freud should be man enough to hold his liquor. Ah, what wine, he thought, as he swilled from the jar. A picture of a running naked woman had been drawn on the clay. He patted her lovingly. Nice bottomless jar, nice Lady . . .

In the furrowed fields a fire leaped up from a pit. He cradled the jug and stumbled toward the leaping light. Maybe he'd find the old sot down there.

But instead he found the women.

Emma and Fräulein knelt by the wavering coals in the fire pit, their heads bent together, tittering and whispering secrets. Emma lifted her flinty eyes to him. Fräulein smiled knowingly. They beckoned him, and his mind burst into flames. Ja, here and now. "Both of you," he cried. "I want you both!"

The women straddled him in a furrow, one upon his hips, the other upon his face. He tried to squirm, but they pressed him down, his greatness rising up for them. But which one? Sweat ran from his eyes. He wanted to laugh, to scream, to shout, as the life gushed out of him. While high above, great thunderheads boiled over the mountains. Gods making love, he thought. . . .

The raindrops began to fall; Fräulein crawled from the trench, leaving the two of them wound together in the muddy furrow, slimed over with sweat and wine. In the orchard she crouched under the shelter of some low-hanging branches. They had tied the Green Man to the tree, but now they used a living man, Herr Vienna Professor — bound hand and foot. The old withered body shone in the slippery rain. He peered blearily into the wild dark, sniveling, "Help me. Help . . ."

"All right, I'll help." Herr Doktor had suddenly appeared. He held a sapling in his hand, which rose and fell. Old Herr Professor cried out with each blow, the welts erupting on his white skin. The sapling lashed and lashed until the blood ran down the bark, lashed and lashed until the old man's limp thing stirred like a waking animal, lashed and lashed until it rose for them in a pain of ecstasy.

Fräulein found herself kneeling at the old Professor's feet. She was fighting with Frau Emma, fighting over the old man's risen thing, taking it in their hands and mouths, pushing and shoving until at last they brought him off — and with a great cry he sprayed over their furious faces and onto the damp bloody ground. While the mob sang their praises, rejoicing. "You — you! . . . You — you!"

Fräulein sat up in bed. Outside her window gusts of wind pelted the curtains. Fat raindrops fell recklessly on the open sill. She wiped the dampness from her chest.

Herr Doktor shuddered. Geschrei the house cat leaped to the floor. He felt the body of Emma in bed. Did she know? Or sense the change in him? He felt transparent. Ravenous. He thought of foods, of beef roasts with a crackle of burnt fat around the bone. He thought of candies in silver paper and puffed potatoes and baked pies, of tomatoes and wet, leafy salads, shining with droplets of vinegar and oil. . . . He saw melons for breasts and hard ripe strawberries for nipples. He saw open oysters, succulent and quivering, for the dark place between Fräulein's thighs.

Once more he looked at the body of Emma beside him; he groped for the roundness of her behind. She grumbled and snuggled in bed; but also lifted her bottom for him. Yet when he pressed her for it, she shrank away, clamping down on herself. He insisted. She refused. He yanked her nightdress, ripping it, shoving into her. She bit and cried. She scratched his face before the end. While the cat watched, with yellow eyes.

He awoke late in the morning. Emma was up and about, whistling like a mockingbird as she picked up strewn clothes scattered around their bed. She smiled as if she knew his secrets, a knowing female smile. "I bit your neck," she warned him. "Wear a high collar today."

He didn't care. All he could think of was Fräulein coming for their early afternoon appointment.

Chapter 3

Torn Apart

The girl failed to appear. In the few moments of waiting he completely lost hope, dreading the imminent ring of the telephone with the message she could not come. Ever again . . . At last she arrived, after ten minutes, bedraggled from a sudden shower; she had forgotten her umbrella and been obliged to take shelter in a doorway in the street.

Now at his office she stood on the threshold, reluctant to enter. What was there to say? They let the aria of their eyes run together like a song. Did you dream my dream last night?

"It was raining," Fräulein said.

Ah yes, the answer . . .

"We were both wet," he sighed.

At once she moved boldly into the room. They met on the couch. He searched the soft valleys of her palm, the fertile plains, and traced the river lines, how they wound around the smoothness of her wrist — all in the quiet of his office, with Emma and the maid downstairs and the birds in the yard chirping bravely in the dappled, damp leaves.

Since the beginning she had been ready to burn, purring under his hands as he petted, unbuttoned, undid her. So ready now, open and waiting. For all along she had wanted him to search her out with tongues of flame and burn her into ashes — taking her completely in that low place in the deep dark. She melted, warm and supple, across his limbs, soon helping his trembling hands under her blouse, laying herself open for him throughout the soft silence of the hour, while the business of the house went on below . . . and the time for the next patient's appointed hour drew steadily closer.

Could it even be explained? No . . .

Not the unbuttoning, not the entwining. Not those hours in his office with the girl — or the nights when he came home to Emma in his heart. For Emma was still in his heart — more, it seemed, than ever before. He took her every night and saw her wonder at the change.

He rutted Emma as she came from the bath.

Rutted her on the dining room table among the rumpled linen and dirty china. He had her standing up in the yard on a moonless night while a tomcat yowled for Geschrei to come out and play. And down in the cellar among the cobwebs and old casks as the inky darkness devoured her moans.

Morning and night.

Office above and home below.

He would bring Fräulein to quivers and trembles, her dress hiked up, his hands wet, but he himself still contained — until she peeled off her white gloves and did him to the end. Yet when Fräulein had gone quietly home, he craved a deeper release. A gnawing hunger at the total impossibility of having the girl completely, as she so needed to be done. And a strange, consenting satisfaction in Emma's passivity as she allowed him her body whenever, however he wanted. The ravenous hunger for Fräulein was gorged on Emma's open flower. Feeding the insatiable delusion that he could go on like this forever, for the rest of his life.

So he ran to Emma. Catching her on the stairs, or straddling her over the balustrade while the servants were busy in the kitchen. Many evenings they laughed and got drunk at dinner. Woke up with headaches. And told no one, like children with their private games.

In the middle of July a letter came from Freud, inviting him for a special Wednesday Society meeting. So Herr Doktor prepared to go to the man, like a son to a father. Going on his knees, if you could believe it: supplicant now, begging to be saved. For he was indeed drowning. The women were pulling him down like Loreleis, Rhine sirens of the Nibelung, luring him into the rushing waters of love to be swept away forever. As though they both had him in one mind — two cats playing over the same mousie, playing him to death. He was blind to everything but the women, seeing only the tangle of twining limbs and hands, breasts and behinds yielding to him as he plumbed his lust. And in the abysmal, impossible task of choosing one of them forever — he was torn apart. But he confessed none of this to the man in Vienna. Replying merely:

"Subject's treatment has progressed remarkably. Speak of this and other things upon our Wednesday."

It had been the driest summer Vienna had ever known. The lilies in the public flower beds had shriveled in the gray dirt, and the fountains run dry. Even the watering of private gardens had been forbidden by order of His Imperial Majesty's Public Works. Still, a daring handful of uncivic souls watered their flowers by night, and so here and there a spray of color blossomed against the drab stone ledges: the blue of a morning glory, the lavender of iris, a yellow rose . . .

Herr Professor of 19 Berggasse tried to ignore the summer's standstill, but with no sign of green, no dark rain clouds, the blinding whiteness seemed to get inside him, only to be squeezed into the damp of his undershirts. When he slept he dreamt of rooms filled with hissing steam pipes, bubbling boilers, and ticking gauges — only to wake in the middle of the heat-soaked night with nausea and belly cramps. Then later, drifting off again, he saw a flock of sparrows, like those that thronged the ornate cornices of Vienna's buildings, swoop down all at once, splashing into rain as they struck the pavement. Yet every morning he stared at the flat white sky, and all the joy of life's purpose seemed wholly evaporated.

On yet another numberless white-sky day, Fritzi the postman brought young Herr Doktor's letter, tapping it to his forehead in that foolish psychic manner, predicting piously, "Ah, Herr Professor, a young visitor. He is earnest. He seeks help. Your wisdom. And counsel. He is coming one day soon —"

"Give me that!" Herr Professor growled, in no mood for jokes. Upstairs, a patient waited. Damn! He would just have a peek at the letter, just a little glance to satisfy his curiosity. He poked his head in the waiting room.

"Just a minute, Frau —"

Frau who? A complete blank. A stout young woman with a dimpled chin and a deep bosom. Yes, he knew her. Three years in treatment. Frau Blank smiled sweetly. No name came.

"Just give me half a minute," he told her.

"Take your time," Frau Blank answered congenially. And that annoyed him too.

The letter took only a moment to read. The words "progressed remarkably" seared into his brain. The business with the girl unfolded for him like the final acts of a play. They had brought her to the root of it, so she could pursue the paths of a normal life. Her own apartment. Therapy. An education at the university. Perhaps even a job as a waitress in a café. And now the son was coming to the father. . . .

The sky beyond his window had turned a shade darker, with the filmy outlines of yellow clouds. Rain? Well, who cared; he wasn't going out. He was going to spend a dreary five hours from ten to four-thirty with several well-paying patients — all with various troublesome complaints. A part of his mind heard the faraway rumble of thunder. Heat lightning flickered over the walls. All afternoon he felt the gathering storm. Gray clouds streaked with purple came out of nowhere and laced the air with knives. When the last patient had gone for the day, an ominous stillness hung over the consultation room.

Herr Professor toyed with his young friend's letter. A trickle of sweat ran down the inside of his shirt. Once upon a time there was a junior nobody crouching like a toad in the shadows of a great castle. Now, miracle of miracles, the Princess had laid an enchanted kiss upon him. And behold! there arose a great Prince, who raised a mute mummy like Lazarus from the dead. Curing the incurable. Unraveling the mysteries of the soul! He struck Jung's letter with his open palm. Then sprang from the chair with *Hurrah!* on his lips, but his own huge voice was drowned in a crack of thunder. A blast of wind toppled the totems off his desk. The ancient statues lay on his rug like so many dead gods.

The rain had come to Vienna at last.

Torrents exploded on the windowsill. He knelt to rescue his ruins, picking up one fallen god and dropping it, picking up another and dropping that one. All the while muttering, "Ja! My Method cured her. My Method. Mine!"

And when the rain squall finally passed, the soot of the city's streets washed down the drains; the wilted flowers in His Imperial Majesty's gardens drank their fill. And Herr Professor rose from his knees, content at last to set his own gods in order. For each new Believer leaped to his hand like a flaming blade, a brand with which to slay the infidels. And Jung was to be his holiest sword.

Fräulein Schanderein desperately wanted to see him off at Zurich's Central Station. So she planned to find a departure schedule and lie in wait for him on the platform. Ready to melt back into the crowds if Frau Emma came along to say farewell . . .

She lost her temper with an officious clerk in the ticket office. The bureaucratic gnat had flatly refused to give her a printed schedule unless she bought a ticket. Yet she wanted to avoid the public board, as too exposed in the midst of the milling station. During her argument with the unhelpful clerk an irritable line of ticket buyers had backed up behind her; they made noises of protest and consternation. But she snarled them to dumbfounded silence. Then bought a third-class ticket to Holz, a near suburb on the line. "My schedule, please," she insisted. The clerk reluctantly slid it across with her ticket. She snatched the timetable and marched off. Voices called after her; she had left her third-class ticket in the change well of the booth. "Use it yourselves," she cursed the crowd. "You can all go to Holz!"

She chose a spot at the base of a support girder, hidden behind a red-and-white-striped cart selling roasted sugar peanuts. She bought a small bag to hold in front of her face as she ate. But her mind was in two places. Also in Herr Doktor's office. Alone with him, the sounds of the house a dull murmur. Near the open window, a huge furry bumblebee buzzed sleepily against the drawn curtains. Their exchanges of petting and touching and release had gone from soft to hard, sinking gently through the green currents of the deeps, emerging at last, flailing and gasping for air. Fierce in the end, they tore each other's clothes, roughly grabbing breast or thigh. And when it was done, they lay back languidly on the couch, disheveled creatures of the flesh, sunken eyes in flushed faces, hardly stirring — and waited for the sweat to dry so they could arrange themselves again.

More and more she opened herself to him. Their clutching arms, his hurried lips, the dark place down below . . . Fräulein sagged weakly against the towering steel pillar, feeling the strength of it along her warm flank. She kept eating the sugared peanuts, crunching and swallowing them half chewed. Her lips were dusted with sweet crystals. . . . While the longer she waited, welded sideways to the steel beam, the surer she was he would come alone.

"I'm glad you're here."

He stood beside the red-and-white peanut cart, a small suitcase in one hand, his own bag of peanuts in the other. He shoved the bag of peanuts in his coat pocket for later and took her hand. They walked down the concrete platform, passing the empty train. The blue sky beyond the arched glass enclosure showed wisps of floating clouds. Soon they were close enough to the locomotive to feel the huge swelling of the steam in the engine. The humidity suffocating . . . She saw the edge of his shirt collar, dark with sweat. She rubbed the drops from her forehead as they ran into her eyes. He offered his handkerchief and she took it, but didn't mop her face.

She started to laugh, because they both looked so much like when they touched in the dark of his office, smiling damply into each other's feverish eyes. And he laughed too, reading her thoughts.

"Yes, just like that, isn't it? Except we're in public now."

"With nowhere to go!" she cried, clinging to him.

"No, nowhere," he whispered tenderly.

The train whistle blew. He hoisted himself into a vacant compartment and leaned out the open window. She reached for him. Their fingers touched, hers sticky with peanut sugar. The train jolted forward. She kept mouthing their last words as the lumbering cars rolled past. The coaches swayed as they gained speed. The steel wheels sang over the iron rails: *nowhere to go, nowhere to go* . . . Until suddenly the train flew away and Fräulein stood on the platform, alone.

The two men sat in the empty consultation room, the older explaining a totem from his collection. It was a homely lump of coal with slits for eyes, a hole for a mouth, the barest hint of breasts and belly. The younger man's face took on the strangest cast, first doubt, then cold recognition: Mother of Stone.

The goddess frowned in Herr Professor's hand, polished smooth with years of loving finger-worship. Young Herr Doktor looked trapped in his chair. His eyes darted from the black thing to the face of his friend. My God! Where had the clever shaman found it? But Herr Professor did not seem to notice the younger man's anxiety.

"She's the oldest of the old. From the Peloponnese."

"Sparta," the young man said thickly. "Arcadia . . ."

"Here now, you're pale as a ghost. Let me get you a glass of water —"

But before Herr Professor rose, the younger man seized the black goddess from his fingers. Amazed to be holding her in his own two hands. Stroking her, peering intently over her every facet. But still a deep current of rejection flowed through him, a refusal to see the evidence in his grasp: part of him wanted nothing to do with her, or Herr Professor's crazy sex quack theories, stories read God knows where! He shook his head in denial, grappling with the stone as if trying to crush the very token of his lust and treachery. Rambling: "No, no, no! I refuse to believe it. They never did it that way: beating an old man . . . sleeping with each other . . . women going with women . . . They never did those things! I've read Frazer. Pausanias. Hesiod. Ovid! They're all just sensationalists. Pornographers. Writing to shock like those cheap magazines with pictures of Siamese twins joined at the hip, with their wives and children. Just lying writers!"

The younger man fell into an embarrassed silence. He handed the little she-goddess back, not daring to meet his mentor's eyes. The older man seemed ashamed to see young Herr Doktor stricken so. He took the small stone and set her amid a dozen of her later grandchildren. An ugly, unshapely lump, squirreled in between a lithe Egyptian princess and the forbidding figure of an Assyrian warrior king. A dreadful thought crawled into the older man's mind, like a worm swallowed whole, still living as it wriggled down into the pit of his stomach.

My God, he thought. This young man, my colleague, my friend, my best and only hope . . . Concealing himself. Hiding.

Lying.

To . . . me.

Once again, Fräulein stared at her frayed art book, its title still dimly readable across the blue-green cover. She had replaced its gutted insides with bound blank sheets of drawing paper. How many times had the guts of this aching book been cut apart, thrown away, made again from scratch? She flipped past some tentative starts — the lush torso of Lady of the Veils, the swollen serpents of Men with Tails.

She picked up a pencil and sharpened it. Her pencil skated dreamily across the paper.

How disgusting. How shameful. Imagine making the lovely Lady of the Veils do those awful things. Not like drawing her dancing or preening in her pretty nakedness — but this! A picture of the Lady going with the Deer Man. He had his huge man-thing out and was pressing it into the Lady's wet openness . . . gashing her.

And on another page the Lady had torn off his hugeness and was running with it, flaunting it over her head as all the Howlers with shrieking mouths came after — all fighting for a chance to touch the bloody god. And on another page, another shameful drawing, and another! She shut the book and pressed it to her chest.

"I should tear them up," she whispered

Ja, she could tear them up if she wanted. Throw them away if she wanted. Or make another book — with even worse drawings — if she wanted. She chuckled to herself. Bad, naughty girl. Sure! Make drawings twice as bad. Nice drawings. Bad drawings. Filthy awful if she wanted. *Whatever* she wanted. No Sister Nuns. No Little It. No wolf at the door! Her laughter banged about the room. Laughter at being as bad as she wanted. As much as she wanted. Look, everyone, I'm laughing. Laughing!

Chapter 4

Face to the Wall

The Zurich-bound train sped over the tracks, as the wheels clacked *gotta get home, gotta get back.* Herr Doktor bought a bottle of May wine and a pack of expensive cigarettes to keep him company on the ride. The countryside skipped past his window, the full, leafy trees and the stern telegraph poles rushing by in packs.

His head drifted in the rosy glow of evening sun in clouds. How dearly Herr Professor had taken him into the family, setting him at his right hand during dinner. Then coming into his room the next morning, balancing a tray of cocoa and cream. The older man sat on the bed as the younger man drank it in his dressing gown, propped up with pillows.

They had even called a special meeting of the Wednesday Society for Thursday, an evening devoted to his treatment of the Schanderein girl. And as he talked, a deep silence gathered round the table, the cigars and cigarettes went out, the drinks were pushed aside. Ties undone. Cummerbunds unhooked. While time itself seemed to pause, leaving nothing but the words of his tale, tracing out the crooked, crazy path of her deliverance from madness. And when the tale was done, there came an even greater silence. Followed at last by murmurs of approval and tremors of awe, far more profound than any bravo or applause.

Then the questions! Endless! The night wore on . . . talk upon talk. And when every detail was seen from every angle, Herr Doktor felt beaten and sore. While the group of them remained around the table, worn and bleary-eyed like gamblers who had played through the night. Herr Professor rose at last. Gray dawn peeped in at the edges of the curtains.

"Fascinating tale," he said dreamily. He cast a hooded glance in the younger man's direction. How clearly the old man wanted him placed before the rest. To stand alone. A lord among princes. Father and son would join their mighty forces. An alliance sweeping away the old order. Zurich and Vienna. A new power rising, a force to be reckoned with. London. Paris. Rome. Berlin. All ready to fall.

For so many years Herr Professor of 19 Berggasse had held out against the mindless hordes, so heroically, so alone. But now Elder Man and Younger Man were calling out their armies; no mob could stand against them. The rabble of the city-states would either kneel — or burn.

And the train went clackety-clack, *can't wait to get home, can't wait to get back!* Herr Doktor settled down in his seat, his feet propped on the couch opposite. He poured his May wine into a silver traveling cup. Drained it and poured himself another. The fantasy of power shifted to a new one. . . . His time with Fräulein, going on as before, only more so. The girl coming every day to his office, where they analyzed her dreams. And helping her to study for medical school, helping her to become Fräulein *Doktor*. Then their timeless moments together on the couch. It was this last sweet thought he lingered over. Feeling her under her hands, holding her as she unbuttoned herself, undid herself for him.

Then going back to good, fine Emma. The two women seemed to blend in his mind. The plush train compartment came alive, belonging to one woman or the other. The walnut paneling above his head like Fräulein's skin along her arms, the delicate gold filigree like Emma's wide eyes staring at him as he came for her in bed. Tugging at his coat, he heard the girl clutching her own clothes. When he moved his feet on the couch, he felt the rasp of his hand across his wife's smooth spine. The padded armrest under his elbow was the tender curve of Fräulein's thighs, waiting to open. Beneath him, the taut seat cushions were Emma's spread behind as he rose and fell, emptying himself into her. The rush of air along the car was the girl's last sigh . . . while all about, the warm compartment cooed him steadily to sleep. And when the train whistled its lonely whistle across passing fields, he heard the women's wail, calling his name.

Calling him home . . .

But in the short time Herr Doktor had gone abroad, unexpected things had come to pass. In his hospital office he found a white envelope sitting on his desk. With a sinking feeling, he examined the letter. The girl's mother, Frau Schanderein, had plainly addressed it. But with a copy sent to Herr Direktor Bleuler. He read the woman's letter twice. It was strange and cryptic and totally unfathomable.

He went directly to his superior's office. Bleuler waved languidly for him to sit, nodding to himself as though he knew the reason for the visit. "The trip went well, did it? That's good. You can tell me about it later. Had a look at the mother's letter, did you? Came yesterday. What do you think?"

What was he supposed to think? He suppressed the urge to bite his nails. Finally he chose to remain silent and simply shrugged.

"My reaction completely," Bleuler remarked casually. "Thought maybe you'd have some insights I overlooked."

Insights! He suddenly waved the letter and burst out:

"What is this woman accusing me of? She says, quote: I've heard various tales of your behavior with my daughter in compromising private sessions. And then, quote: Have I a history of mistresses and conquests? And then, and *then!* Since I've paid a great share of her daughter's hospital bills, am I expecting additional favors in return? Favors! How many tales of my behavior has she heard? Stories of my dancing in her room? Of blood on my face? Which tales did the damn woman hear?"

"Heavens!" Bleuler implored, raising his hands. "I don't tell tales myself, you know."

"Is it about money, then? Did she know I paid her husband's whore bill from that club in town? Perhaps the mother should know about that too!"

Bleuler quietly pushed back his seat, a look of silent shock in his eyes. His fingers played with a pencil. "Actually, I'm sure she does know," he said flatly.

But Herr Doktor wasn't pacified. "How do I respond to this assault? Shall I resign? When the girl first came here she slobbered like an idiot, wore a ratty sheet instead of clothes. Next month she's to attend Burckhardt's introductory lectures at the medical college." His voice rose to a shout. "How long have we had? Tell me. Nine? Ten? Eleven months! Who cares! Freud does them in five years. Yesterday he told me so!"

Herr Direktor held up his hands in entreaty. "*I'm* not accusing you of anything. You've had remarkable success with the girl. No one's questioning that. I've read the reports; I know what the poor creature's been through. Give me a little credit, please. The mother is obviously deranged. The father — worse than useless. The only question is how do we reply?"

Herr Doktor slumped back in his chair and picked a fallen page off the floor. Yes, of course, how to reply. He shook his head to clear it, but the room shifted. Again, Herr Bleuler's voice coaxed him.

"Let's all be reasonable. The mother's lifetime work was making the poor girl crazy. Then you came along and made her better. *Cured* her, ja? And so that makes young Herr Doktor Siegfried the enemy now. All that remains for us is to . . . ah . . . disarm the mother. Perhaps we — the hospital — can waive the outstanding balance on the girl's bill. Perhaps we can congratulate the damn woman on her daughter's stunning progress. I assume you are presently being compensated for the private sessions? Fräulein is paying you something, isn't she?"

Herr Doktor pressed his fingers to his head. The room turned slowly around. . . . What was the man asking? How was the girl? How was she in private? Bleuler's voice prodded him:

"The girl is paying you something, isn't she?"

"Yes," he said with effort. "She's paying me something. Privately. A private fee . . ."

"Fine," Bleuler said confidently. Herr Direktor seemed so sure of himself, so ready to take the problem in hand. "Now as for the rumors. Ignore them. Who knows why people start rumors? Idle. Jealous. Stupid. People are all those things."

Herr Doktor felt too exhausted to comment. Wearily, he said at last, "I'm not sure I'm capable of replying sensibly to this letter."

"No, but I can. Official stationery and all that. I'll show you a draft before I send it out."

The room stopped turning. Now Herr Doktor focused on the man's face across the desk. "All right . . . if you want." Bleuler seemed pleased, chuckling softly to himself. He had taken on a measure of stature. Impotent during the long months of the girl's treatment, if he helped young Senior Physician in this small way, then he too had contributed to Fräulein's recovery. He began gently bouncing the heavy rubber eraser of his pencil on the desk, bouncing it and catching it deftly between the ends of his fingers on the hop: tap-tap-tap-

tap. "Well, that's that," he said with a thin smile. "Why don't you tell me about your trip?"

She let him spread her open in the quiet dark of his office. She thought of it as his "welcome home." Her days had been un-eventful — no sudden traumas, no frights, no conflicts, nothing to break the steady rhythm of wake, study, eat, sleep, wake again. . . . So there was nothing really for them to talk about. They quietly lapsed into what was simplest for them to do. He had kept his office dark on purpose. She barely said hello; simply entered and walked across the carpet. She led him to the couch. It was so familiar; they knew the rest. The touching. The taking. The sweet finish.

She sensed the trip had gone well, though he hardly spoke of it. She could guess what they talked about mostly. Her. His great success.

Is this what it meant to be his mistress, then? Groping in the dark, then, later, walking out of his house and back to her room? Always in his possession but never properly possessed? And him never really being *hers*?

"What is it?" he asked.

Am I his mistress? she wondered.

People talk. Many were capable of saying it.

Bleuler, Nekken, Bosch, Zeik! They were all capable. Someone joked. Another lied. A cretin who scribbled dirty filth in a back stair-well: the crazy bitch is a doctor's whore. She'd seen a scrawl in the women's toilet. *You're a slut*, it read. *And so are you*, she scribbled back. *With worms in your cunt.*

Then last of all there was Frau Emma.

Wife.

Yet every time they met, the woman showed nothing but polite poise. If she suspected something, wouldn't there be the sharp flint of anger in her eye? A blackness in her smile when she greeted Fräulein at the door or met her coming weakly down the stairs from his office after an hour under her husband's hands? Why cajole the girl into the kitchen for tea? Blushing and a little flattered, Fräulein always came. She loved the way Emma brought out pieces of cake or leftovers from the night before, the way she clucked, "Look at you! Thin as a rail! Don't you eat at home?" While Fräulein, with her mouth

406

too full to talk, devoured everything set in front of her, nodding eagerly when Emma said, "Isn't that soup better the next day?" And hiccuping in laughter as the older woman chased Geschrei from perch to perch, until in frantic desperation the cat hid, hissing, under the stove.

To Fräulein they were like two girls together, talking for an hour about things that made no difference. Like what flavor frosting went best with orange buttermilk cake, or how many ribbons go well in your hair, or how difficult it is to sneeze politely with beef goulash in your mouth . . . The woman's books and private studies were strewn about the kitchen, just like Fräulein's at home. And from her books, Frau Emma showed her pictures and drawings from a time even older than the ancient dream tale. No ladies in veils — but there were deer men with antlers. And in one picture she saw the shape of Mother of Stone carved into the rock of a cave wall.

"I dream of this," Fräulein whispered in confidence.

The older woman did not seem surprised. "So you've seen her too, eh? In a museum? Or a book . . . ?"

What an odd light in Emma's eyes, as though she herself had seen what went on in those strange dreams. Fräulein had the terrible feeling that if she told of what she saw — the village fields, the woods and rushing stream — the spark in Emma's eyes would leap eagerly to flame and she'd cry, "Yes, I saw that too!"

But Fräulein always held her tongue. Was this woman who fed her and sometimes made her laugh, was this the same woman who wrote lies to her mother? Who now touched hands across the table, not with leaden cold fingers but with warm living ones that seemed to speak endless tales of the shadowed man they shared? Frau Emma had more reason than any to write those lies. Saying:

My husband dances lurid dances in your daughter's private room. Saying:

He bought her clothes. Entertaining her at late-night parties. Saying:

He gave her baths. Saying:

He took her out of the hospital so he could have her under the same roof as his wife. So he could have them in the same bed; watching them woman to woman or having both on him. Perhaps Frau Emma was more capable than anyone. . . . Writing this spiteful letter even if it wrecked her husband's future at the Burghölzli. Even if it tore apart the remains of her marriage. For what hope had she? Frau Emma *must* suspect them in her heart. Yes, actually know in that secret wordless way a woman always knows about a man. So if his passion for Fräulein could be defiled, the wife would wait. Circling like a bird of prey over the wasteland, waiting for the shreds of him when all was done.

Fräulein rose abruptly from the cradle of his arm.

"What's the matter?" he asked.

Suddenly the man seemed so callous and transparent. What did really matter? What mere foul-mouthed letter could hurt them? What on God's earth could Mother do to her now that she had not already spent a lifetime doing?

"I'm not a twiddler in the dayroom," Fräulein said out loud. "I'm a person living in my own apartment. Soon I'll go to *school.* And if I still want to be crazy I can do it alone. In private. For my own relief. But not out there for everyone to watch!" She waved her hand to the drawn curtains and the vast world beyond. "When I was a safe little egg, I didn't exist. When I fed my babies to Herr Wolfpants, I was half alive, trying to create the other half. But now I exist. So alive that turd-mouthed people scrawl about me in women's toilet stalls. So important some maggot-eating ghoul writes my mother, telling her how bad I am. Telling her I'm your mistress. Well, nobody asked me — and I'm not your mistress. I'm my own mistress.

"My own!" she shouted.

Herr Doktor sat bolt upright. How did she know?

"Did you think Mother would write just you?" Scorn and pity in her eyes . . . He fell back against the cushions, breathing with his mouth open like a trapped man. "Did you know Father left her?" Herr Doktor shook his head silently no.

"Now Mother says she's coming here to Zurich. She wants to see where I live."

"Oh," he said after a moment. She stared at him for a long time. He appeared blank and confused. Fräulein knew she was going to tell him the final truth of how she wanted things. Ask him to take the last step with her. In life. In death. Forever. Take her by the hand and go into the future as it was meant to be. The words surged out.

"Leave her," Fräulein told him. "Leave Emma. And come to me.

Because of what we've been. And what we are now. For what we're supposed to be. Man. Woman. You . . . and me."

Her words were like the first crack in a wide beam supporting a roof. No sign of mounting stress or impending collapse under the massive weight, but the sudden searing break as the thick wood splintered across the grain.

Herr Doktor looked neither at the girl nor at any object in the room. She saw his reason unraveling inside: eyes that fled inward, losing touch with her, the moment, reality. Dead eyes. Slack mouth. His body drooping with no will — except the fingers of his left hand covering his groin as if it pained him. Fräulein had never seen a *sane* person that way before.

Then with great hesitation he staggered awkwardly across the carpet to his desk, free hand groping for support. He touched the desk, and its solidness seemed to guide him. He shuffled slowly around the edge, coming to a stop. And there he stood, wavering gently like a reed. Is that the way I looked? A broken doll? A dummy head stuffed with sawdust? No wheels moving inside. Just a face to the wall? A sickening, knowing weakness flooded her. Yes, just like that.

Why doesn't he just come to me?

Doesn't he know it's all right?

But Herr Doktor made no sign nor any sound. Yet she waited, as he had waited for her through the endless sick time . . . watching a slim knife of sunlight from a gap in the curtains inch its way across the carpet. And when, at the end of the hour, the man still hadn't stirred, Fräulein gathered herself together and left his office. Shutting the door sadly behind her. While Herr Doktor remained as before.

A face to the wall.

Chapter 5

Dark Passage

The maid knocked, heralding the arrival of the next patient. When Herr Doktor did not answer, the maid peeped cautiously inside. She saw the man slumped against the wall, his head sagged.

"I'm not here," he mumbled. "Can't see anyone. Tell them to go away."

The maid fled. She found Frau Emma. And it was Emma who made the apologies, turning the patient away with: "I'm terribly sorry, Herr Doktor is feeling poorly today. . . . Can you telephone us tomorrow?" The patient said he'd telephone tomorrow.

Emma went back to the office. She tried to comfort him with clumsy words. She petted him; she kissed his dangling hand. She tried to pry him gently from the wall. But he was made of wood. With a dull quaver, Emma noticed a dark article of clothing abandoned on the couch. One of Fräulein's black kid-leather gloves. She picked it up. The kid glove felt warm to the touch. She drew it slowly over her fingers and slipped her hand inside. How appropriate. A perfect fit.

When evening threw its long purple shadows into the office, Frau Emma still sat with her husband as the day wore away. Now he trembled with fatigue, as if at any moment he might fold. Gently Emma went to him once more. "Please, come. Come with me. . . ." The words seemed to rouse a deep echo. Then an imperceptible shiver, like the final crumbling of some private foundation. After what seemed an age, his fingers twitched to life. Hesitantly he searched out hers. His hand was limp and clammy. At length he let himself be led off to the bedroom, docile and unresisting.

410

She undressed him. She said tender words to him, words he did not seem to hear. Dusk darkened into night. He lay in bed a sick man, his inward eyes staring out at nothing.

Whom did he love?

Which one with all his life?

The girl he saved from insanity?

Or his wife of years, the keeper of his bones?

They were players in a play he had written for himself. Players on a stage of good behavior, of life's rules, of work and sacrifice. And upon this barren stage he was frantically groping for an open portal, a way out, a trapdoor. . . . The sounds of the night preyed on him. The dripping of water down a gutter, the whirring of a motorcar on a distant road, the creak of wind against the windows. Next to him, the rhythm of Emma's breathing pounded like a hammer inside his skull. He wished he could take a pillow, press it to her face, and stop her maddening sighs. While across town he thought he heard the girl — her pen scratching across the blank paper of her art book, the sound like the screeching of a rusty weather vane. Setting his teeth on edge.

Which woman?

Which one forever?

He closed his eyes and slipped off into the ancient dream time. . . . But the girl's sacred place was no longer any refuge. Now a loathsome swamp of stench and dread. Bitter sun beat down upon the village fields. The crops had withered to brown, rattling stalks. Birds sat on the orchard's dying branches, pecking at the rotten fruit. A powerful thirst took Herr Doktor, overthrowing his whole mind. But the rushing stream had shrunk to muddy pockets; bleached stones lay in the bed. Clouds of flies and mosquitoes hovered over the stink.

The body of a woman lay sprawled where she had knelt for her last drink in the fetid puddles. She was stripped naked to the waist. Her flesh hung loose, breasts sagging to wrinkled sacs. A green spotted toad had stuck to her tit, drinking the body's water through her skin. She was too weak even to detach it from its sucking. A swarm of gnats covered a swollen, bloated face. Fräulein smiled at him through blistered lips. "Come to me. For what we'll be. Man and woman. You and me."

Herr Doktor awoke in bed. The morning light, airy and golden, slanted in at the window. Sparrows chirped in the trees outside. He quietly moved his eyes about the room. Then to Emma, sleeping peacefully beside him. Good, fine, deep-sleeping Emma. The covers had fallen back from her. He contemplated her long, strong body. Slowly he perceived the lines of Emma's figure had undergone a subtle change. The slimness of her belly gone; and a heavy roundness had come to her breasts. Was it all in his mind? Or had he just noticed her change for the first time? Think back! Seven, eight, nine weeks ago . . . too early to show? A little early. But still, what an undeniable firmness to her skin, a ripening luster. Ja, more than possible. With all the madness between himself and the girl, then going straight to Emma afterward. Never taking any precaution, just spreading her and going in . . . He gently caressed the first swelling. Emma wriggled pleasurably under his hand.

"Feel better?" she asked softly from the pillow.

"Yes, better," he said.

She patted his hand, pressing it to her belly. "I'm so tired," she murmured. "So lazy . . . But I'll get up. Get up in a second. You stay in bed. I'll make breakfast." She sighed into the pillow, dozing off once more.

Was he better?

A few weeks passed in the drowsy limbo of summer's close. Fräulein no longer came for her morning sessions. But this did not strike him as so unusual. She had begun the first semester at the university and had once mentioned something about a waitress job. Had she decided to leave him alone? Was she hoping he would come for her? He gave up the question. Surrendering the struggle for a choice. It seemed far simpler to let Emma speak for him right now. Think for him. Exist for him.

Just at this time another letter arrived from Herr Professor in Vienna. The president of Clark University in Worcester, Massachusetts, America, wanted both of them — elder man and younger man — for a series of lectures in late September. Travel expenses would be forthcoming. Should they leave from Trieste, sailing through the Mediterranean? Herr Professor wondered. Or meet in Bremen, sail down the Weser and out the dreary North Sea? Prepare a lecture, young man!

And prepare for a bit of fame, the letter warned. Bring your tuxedo. There will be newspapermen and photographs taken.

He prepared a lecture, taking some desultory notes from Fräulein's dusty and voluminous case file. He had to force himself through all the pages devoted to her. How lifeless they seemed to him now, how dull. He found it more exciting by far to jot down ideas from the troubles of a new patient, lately come to his office.

He had his tuxedo pressed.

Steamship tickets departing via the Mediterranean were not available on such short notice. So they booked passage on a ship from Bremen. A few members of the Wednesday Society planned a bon voyage party: lunch for seven at the Bremenstadt Musiker Hotel. In the waning months of summer, he concentrated on the fascinating troubles of his new patient.

As for Fräulein, she had not forgotten him, nor let slip one moment of their last hour together. She fretted, as if waiting for an obscure decision from a court of faceless judges. A decision that never came. Yet there were tides of hope — and then tides of despair. Yes, she thought, he was going to leave Emma. He was coming now. Walking from his house, the woman's sobs fading in the wake of his footsteps. He was taking the tram with a single suitcase, hat and coat slung over his arm. She saw so clearly how he crossed the courtyard. How he mounted the stairs, sweat dampening his shirtsleeves. She left her apartment door unlatched, so that when at last he knocked, the door would creak gently aside, inviting him in. . . .

And then the sinking knowledge. Back from a day at the university or an evening at the café, where she took orders all night long — she ran home, pounding up the creaking stairs. In dread that the flat was empty.

She left the door open. But he never came.

In the end she broke down and went groveling to his house. And for the first time in her life she fully understood what it meant to grovel. Not just cower in terror but with a clear mind abase yourself before others. Humiliating yourself by begging for what you want to come true.

Emma let her inside but did not invite her upstairs or into the kitchen. Those times were over, as though they never happened. The woman was pregnant. . . .

413

"You've come for your glove."

"My glove?"

Emma handed over a black kid glove. Fräulein twisted the limp thing in her hand. Wasn't it strange how the word "glove" was made up mostly of the word "love"? For a few seconds Fräulein forgot entirely what she had come to say. Emma stared at her, plainly hoping she would leave. "Can I . . . Can I . . ." Fräulein put the love-glove on her hand, wriggling her fingers into place.

"Can I see him?"

"He's with a patient now."

"Can I come back later?"

She felt the embarrassing urge to twiddle; in fact, the hand dangling by her side began to twitch. God, how hopeless, with Emma barring the way. Fräulein almost told the woman all of it, blurting the truth. You don't want him. You can't please him. You only decided when you saw yourself losing him, getting pregnant just to keep him! But if Fräulein burst out with this, she really would descend into an attack of the twiddles. If only Emma's baby died, if only she could kill it before it grew . . . Somehow she managed to draw off her black glove and shove it in her purse.

"Thank you for saving this for me," she said before she left.

"You're very welcome."

As Fräulein walked down the stone path from the house, she felt Emma's cool eyes upon her. The door latch shut, metallic, cold, and final. The woman had not even said good-bye. A growing blackness like a cloud covered her mind: she had not even managed to *see* him. Must she corner him in the hospital? Catch him on a street corner?

At home she took out fresh white paper and began to draw. The paper slowly filled. The Howling Women, the Deer Man, the Lady of the Veils: she drew as many in a single night as she had in all the years past. And when at last the sparrows sang in the blue-blackness of dawn, she had smudged her writing arm with graphite from wrist to elbow. Still she drew on — until the sun rose redly and her eyes burned. She tossed the pencil aside and fell into bed, a dead thing.

When she awoke the sky outside was white-gray like milk. A shower helped to clear her head. A change of clothes felt even better. She went to the four-franc table and gathered all the drawings she had done. She carried them to the post office under her arm.

There she bought a manila mailer, put the drawings inside, and went over to one of the high oak tables to write out the address.

The address . . .

Fräulein's hand hovered over the envelope. 17 Berggasse? 16 Berggasse? She knew it once, had seen it on a letter or a paper. She tried to recall . . . Number 14? Number 15? Bergasse? Berggasse? Or something-else-strasse? She threw down the pen in disgust and stalked from the post office, the manila envelope clamped under her arm.

Herr Doktor came to his hospital office at the end of the day, a secretary in tow. Bleuler had given him an assistant, a pale, earnest young man with a runny nose and bulging eyes, who followed him about like a lost spaniel. Herr Doktor seemed taken aback to find her sitting behind his door, but only Fräulein noticed, for he calmly controlled his face.

"Leave us for a minute, will you, Frederick?" he asked the secretary. And when they were alone Herr Doktor sat at his desk, putting the big piece of furniture between them both. "I expected you for your daily sessions," he went on quietly. "But you never came. Would you like your regular hour back?"

She stared at him, incredulous. Expected her? And never wrote, never *telephoned?* Her love-glove hand began to twiddle in disbelief. She struck it against her thigh to kill it.

"Oh, here now! You can control that if you want to."

She broke, not trying to hide her twiddle any longer. "You were waiting for me? Emma turned me away! I came to see you, and all I got was this!" She wrung the glove off her twiddling hand and flung it at his head.

"Try and be reasonable. People outside can hear us. You're not crazy anymore, you're —"

"No!" She cut him off. "Not anymore. But who are you? Herr Doktor Touch-Kiss? Do you think they can hear me now?"

"Yes, I'm sure the whole floor knows now."

"They should know. How you used me. How you opened me up and *took* me. Was it because my parents didn't pay my fee? How much do I owe you? How much do you want?"

"Nothing! Nothing! You owe me nothing —"

"But you owe me." Her voice sank dangerously. "You owe *me.*"

Herr Doktor wilted in the chair. "I never promised you anything."

"Curing me was a promise. Buying the dress was a promise. The way you touched me was a promise! You were supposed to be my doctor," she hammered. "My *friend.*"

"I know," he mumbled into his hand.

"You were supposed to know what to do," she sobbed. "Supposed to want what I want too."

"I know." He cowered. "I know. . . ." His contemptible, pathetic cringing set her free. She swept the papers and pencils off his blotter. A crystal paperweight fell to the floor with a crack.

"You saved me and then you used me. You betrayed me and then you raped me. You're nothing but a liar," she choked. "A liar and a coward!"

The man covered his face, arms up about his head. "I know." Someone knocked on his office door. Frederick, the secretary, warning them in a quavering voice that people outside were complaining of the noise.

"Why are they complaining?" Fräulein shouted at the shut door. "They didn't when I was crazy. So why now? Because I'm sane and say what I like. Then I want everyone to know:

"You saved me just to use me.

"You betrayed me and you raped me.

"You're a liar and a coward.

"And I wish I never met you!"

Dead silence beyond the door . . .

Her head felt light, her stomach queasy. She spied a letter fallen from the desk. An inkpot had tipped over it, gurgling its contents onto the carpet. Black drops splattered the letter's white face. A letter from Herr Vienna Professor. She immediately recalled the address.

19 Berggasse.

Fräulein staggered back to her seat, collecting the envelope. The room felt empty. "You should have left me the way you found me," she said to the hollow room.

"The way I was."

Chapter 6

Train of Thought

Herr Professor of 19 Berggasse sat in the deep plush of a private compartment on the Bremen train. On his lap lay the sheaf of the Schanderein girl's drawings. By coincidence they happened to arrive the day he left on his trip to America. In the rush to pack, he had not found the opportunity to look the pictures over. Frankly, he doubted whether he should study them at all. She was Jung's patient, not his own. What was so impossibly urgent that he breach their privacy? Once at the hotel, he told himself, he'd do the proper thing: post the drawings back to Zurich immediately, sealed and intact.

But as he sat on the rumbling Bremen train, a deepening curiosity came over him. A growing sense that these pictures were in some way part of young Herr Doktor's secret trouble. "We've had a falling-out," the young man had written since that Wednesday visit. "I gather she is sending you a list of grievances." What an unhappy word, grievances. A death word.

The stub of a cigar burned between his fingers. Nicotine had stained them yellow, a permanent discoloration, like the taste of ashes that never went away. The mark of a crucial flaw. Most mornings he hated himself for smoking.

Herr Professor suddenly undid the envelope. In each picture the people were naked. In rags or drapes. They reminded him vaguely of ancient Greek vase paintings on cups or vessels. But the Schanderein girl's drawings were stupendously shocking. In one drawing two women played over the dismembered parts of a man's sexual organs. In another, a man wearing the skull of a deer raped the headless body of another man, penetrating the gushing stump of his rival's neck. In yet another, a man squatted in the act of elimination — passing a huge egg out of his behind, and from the egg a woman was being hatched. The woman smiling coyly.

Herr Professor was awed. "My God," he murmured. "This girl is absolutely crazy."

And one more shocking than the rest. A man clad in the pelt of a deer was entering a woman's lavish vagina. His whole body entering. He had penetrated past his head and shoulders, nearly to his elbows. His arms pinned, his hands fluttered impotently at his sides.

And the woman was laughing.

At first Herr Professor felt the powerful urge to deny it. The brutality. The animality. Transgressing in the cave of your mind was one thing. Cunning greed. Desperate lust. Sweet revenge. But to act it out. No, that was no longer *of the mind*. But of the world, of life and death. If young Herr Doktor had actually touched the girl, actually made love to her . . .

Deep perversion.

No! No! No! The devil wouldn't dare! Let these drawings be mere fantasies, misunderstood desires, hopes, and wishes. Sick dreams. But not histories. Not chronicles of their intercourse.

His denial felt like an actual weight, a stone upon his chest. A great weariness fell over him, a terrible exhaustion making him close his eyes to what he had seen and what it meant. Close his eyes and rest, forget and rest, leave the whole problem to someone else and *rest* . . .

The red afternoon sun slanted into the compartment, peaceful and quiet, as if the train had slowed to a halt. The man gazed dreamily out the window. Squinting through the fiery shafts of sunlight on his eyelashes, he glimpsed the queerest faraway place. A wonderland. A sanctuary. Like a miniature stage in a theater in the house of dreams:

He saw a wall of snow-covered mountains. A village huddled in a lower valley. Sun on a patch of pine trees. Water sparkling as it fell from a cleft of a crag. He heard the brass tinkle of sheep's bells on the flocks in the hills above. Yes, he realized, this is where it happened. The things from the crazy girl's drawings. The place of all the young man's troubles. Where it all began . . .

The perfect little images of the village enticed him out the window. The finery of his traveling clothes melted off his limbs. He saw himself clothed in rags. The starry night rose like a temple dome.

Two women were leading him by a rope around his neck, like a bull to slaughter. Emma and the girl, he thought. . . .

By the light of the fire, the women anointed his head with oil. They splashed his legs with wine. Then cloaked him in the flayed hide of a deer, putting the horned skull upon his head. From out of the dark a man appeared. The stranger held a sword. Naked. Faceless . . . The wind moaned over the fluttering fire. Or was it the women?

Herr Professor awoke with the name Pygmalion on his lips. The luxurious train compartment came back to him strongly. He fumbled to gather the girl's drawings. Outside the window he saw the gray steel and concrete pilings of an industrial town. The rusty brick walls of warehouses. The train rattled heavily over the switching tracks of a railyard. The conductor tramped along the corridor, rapping his knuckles on each compartment door. A whistle shrieked. Bells clanged.

They were pulling into Bremen station.

Older man and younger man embraced in the hotel lobby, kissing one cheek and then the other. But the crowded lobby was no place to talk. They escaped to the hotel's glass palm house, where they could stroll along the gravel paths. The plant beds rose in neat terraces around them. At the center stood a wide stone basin with a bronze fountain cast in the shape of a pudgy laughing boy. The little boy was thrusting out his hips and peeing a stream of fountain water back into the pool. The stream splashed on another bronze casting, that of an irate duck, flapping its wings and squawking out of harm's way.

The elder man thought young Herr Doktor seemed outwardly calm; but he sensed the faint acrid whiff of expectation — perhaps distress. "Did you look at the drawings?" he asked at once. "They were drawings, weren't they?"

"Yes, I looked. . . . But I posted them back from the front desk. Should I have kept them so you could see too?"

"Heavens, no!" the younger man said with some alarm. "I think she and I have been to bad enough places enough already."

Odd choice of words, the elder man mused. . . . Been to bad enough places enough already. As if to say, Now enough is enough already! For a fleeting second he saw the mountains in the house of dreams, the leering faces around the fire. Why just then he did not know — but it made the sweat break out across his neck. And he said abruptly:

419

"Your patient's dream is very contagious."

The young man glanced up sharply, as if some dread possibility were coming true. But the older man took him kindly by the arm as they strolled about the palm house.

"You know, my friend, when a patient lays all his hopes and fears upon us, we risk an entanglement. This, as you know, we call the transference. And from start to finish we risk lapses and failures along its stages. One of those lapses is the inevitable and diabolical counter-transference. For there comes a time when each of us hopes for things that cannot be. Hoping for things from our patients and ourselves which we have no right to expect. Or demand. Special favors . . ."

And here he paused. "Even gifts of love —"

"Are you lecturing me?" The young man's eyes flashed. "Do you think I've done something wrong?"

"Have you done something wrong?"

The younger man disengaged his arm. "Haven't *you* ever been accused?"

"Me!" the elder burst out. And he laughed until he sat weakly on the lip of the stone basin in order to catch his breath. "Patients of mine have publicly accused me of many grand feats. Of defecating on one man's head. Of demanding homosexual intercourse with another. Of receiving it in my consultation room under the guiding eye of my wife —"

"And in each case," young Herr Doktor asked sharply, "weren't those patients simply responding to your *unconscious* desires? Things you wanted to see come true?"

The older man pondered this for some time, thoughtfully stroking his face. He left off and caught his friend firmly by the elbow, pulling him down to the stone edge of the basin, where he could whisper the darkest confession:

"Always, Herr Jung! Always! But since my psychoanalytic practice was so slim, I could hardly afford the liberties of such wishes and still meet the rent at the end of the month. So I must admit, I *rarely* acted as often as I wanted upon those perverse desires my patients sensed so sharply in their beloved and esteemed Herr Professor Sex Quack!"

The younger man broke into a slow grin of relief. "Oh, it's good, so good to see you. This thing with her nearly ripped me up, don't you

know? And then when you told me you had her crazy dream too . . .
I thought, well, maybe you were going mad like me. Or worse, some
trick of hers to turn you against me —" He halted as if he'd said something dangerous. Yet Herr Vienna Professor seemed not to notice.

"That I had her crazy dream, as you call it, is easy enough to account for. You wrote about it in your first letter. Then it came up once
more at my house that Thursday evening. Are we not getting together
again today, a few of the very same faces around a table? But you have
to remember, if I went to that old place, I went on the vehicle of my
own dream, not hers. My own dream with its own drives and mo-
tives. Not hers. Because after all, we only put her name on the dream
for convenience. It doesn't belong to her. How can the village I see
in my sleep be the same as yours? Or the mountain you see in your
head be the same one she sees in hers?"

"It can't," Herr Doktor answered. But secretly to himself he said: It
is, the same, the very same.

After a moment the elder man smiled wryly. "Unless, of course,
you're implying the Schanderein girl is sending out her dreams by
mental wireless. First you, then me, then perhaps the emperor's cabinet ministers? Do you think you might use your influence with the
girl to put in a good word for me concerning certain imperial medical appointments?"

His young friend chuckled slyly. "Only on certain terms and conditions. That I am personally entitled to the discovery, the lectures,
the tours, the publications, and so forth. Are we agreed?"

The elder man opened his hands in submission. "The world rights
are yours. . . ." Then rose as their business was concluded. "The front
desk is holding our tickets. I suppose we should claim them."

"I'm a terrible sailor," the younger man admitted sheepishly. "Vomit
continuously, day and night."

"Ah, then I'm sure you will make a charming berth companion.
How are you as a stuffed shirt? Did you remember to bring your dinner jacket?"

Herr Jung's face turned pale. "My God! I forgot. Do you think I
can hire one?"

"You'll have to. Besides, you can't be a genuine stuffed shirt unless
you're stuffed into someone else's cummerbund. I've saved my father's
for all special occasions. The silk is a little threadbare in the back, but

421

then no gentleman takes off his dinner jacket in public, unless it is to revive a faint woman with a flapping noise. Shall we go in to lunch?"

The hotel restaurant was called Die Konzert. The Concert. In keeping with the tale of the Bremen Town Musicians, the hotel of the same name had decorated the restaurant with small black silhouettes illustrating the famous story. The two-dimensional flats stenciled around the dining room walls in a narrative band that retold the tale in pictures. A tale of poor, aged animals cast out of their homes, farms, and occupations.

First, a fly-bitten jackass sitting on a broken millstone. Then a cat purring sleepily beside some playful mice. A dog limping along on bandy legs after a measly bone. A ruffled rooster with drooping feathers perched on an iron cooking pot.

In the first scene, the robbers were feasting grandly at a table laden with food and drink. Then leaping up in fright as all the animals burst in upon them, each on the shoulders of the next: ass, dog, cat, and rooster crowing away on top. Then a silhouette of the animals around the abandoned table, feasting on the spoils of victory. While a short way off a robber tried to sneak up on them, cudgel in hand. Then the riot of the animals: The cat hissing and scratching like a witch. The dog biting the robber's leg. The ass giving him a kick in the arse. The feather-loose rooster clapping over his head as the lout scampered off. And finally a silhouette of the animals sleeping contentedly in a friendly heap.

Herr Professor was so taken with the silhouettes he spent some time wandering around the restaurant, following the path of the story. But his mind was not on the hopeful tale of the animals' fortunate fellowship in their struggle against incontinent old age — no, his mind was consumed with the face and bearing of his young colleague. The younger man's look of vague apprehension at the mention of the girl's drawings. The slight turn of guilt over the "countertransference." And at the words "gifts of love," the flash of anger of one unjustly accused. Then answering every question with a question, as if, yes, Herr Jung himself had once felt the promptings of his own desires. A host of little signs, but not the hint of the bold, daring denial required to pull off a grand deception.

Had the boy slept with her, or not?

Herr Professor paused at the final silhouette of the Bremen Town

Musicians' tale: the animals sleeping together in a heap. Sleeping the earned sleep of the just. The dark-purple circles under young Herr Doktor's eyes meant the trouble had not vanished. And the boy was trying to hide it. Saying nothing. Admitting nothing. Unable to choose between maiden and wife. Letting the women and the world think what they wanted. The young man had stumbled down a sloping path, avoided problems at every turn. And yes, the easy way out was steadily killing him. Feeding off his insides.

Damn you, Herr Professor swore. Why didn't you come to me with this? I've lived longer. Seen more. I know more. I could have helped you. We would have searched for a solution. . . .

Several of his colleagues at their long table called Herr Professor away from his dark thoughts to join them so they might begin. The wine was being served with a herring. The herring mustn't wait.

A small package had been placed in the midst of them like a center-piece. The gift, about the size of a narrow perfume bottle, wrapped in white tissue paper with a black bow at the neck. It had a strangely girlish appearance. "Open it! Open it!" Herr Professor tugged at the ribbon; the tissue fell away. The gift was an ancient bit of reddish rock. A miniature totem symbol, called a herm — unmistakably a phallus.

Herr Professor roared with mirth. "Why, gentlemen, how very thoughtful!" He picked up the stone, examining it more closely. "For the man who's lost everything, I presume!" Hoots of laughter. "Why, it reminds me of my youth." A rustle of applause. "Or of my father. Or both. My father's youth!" More laughter.

Now everyone began talking at once.

"Here, pass him around. I want a look."

"I should get one for a patient."

"A woman, no doubt."

"No, a man. Pass the wine."

"A toast! Master, give us a toast!"

The glasses were filled again as they passed the stone god of man-ness from hand to hand. Herr Professor rose to give a toast. Clinking his wineglass with a spoon for quiet. The table settled down.

"Thank you for arranging this bon voyage lunch for myself and our newest colleague. I propose we drink to a rational sea crossing and to Clark University of Massachusetts, for their portentous surplus of honorary degrees!"

Everyone said, "Prosit!" and drained his glass.

Herr Professor caught his young friend's eye before their glasses were drained. Saying privately across the table, "And may we find our way." To this, Herr Doktor raised his glass, locked eyes with the elder man, and downed his wine in one long swallow.

The stone of the herm finally came to the younger man. Vaguely, he heard the others telling the history of the thing. How the name itself meant cairn or pillar; becoming the object of reverence and worship in the center of a village, stuck in the ground but pointing to heaven. The earliest symbol of the god Hermes. How in the womb of the fertile mother stones the erect herm planted the seed of all life. . . . An odd reluctance came over him to handle the object. It no longer felt like hard dead stone, but warm and pliant, as though flesh and blood. His head buzzed. Why did they talk so loudly around the table?

He looked at the herm and how it seemed somewhat larger in length and breadth, indecently huge like those Japanese drawings. Then he noticed it stealthily growing upward out of his hand. Didn't anyone see? Didn't anyone want it to stop? Any moment he feared it would strike the roof of the dining room.

Then everyone would see. And they'd know.

What he did to the girl.

How he failed her in the end.

"Herr Jung, are you all right?"

"Herr Jung?"

He leaped to his feet. "I'm all right, for God's sake! Can't you see I'm all right!" The herm stone slipped from his grip and fell to the polished wood floor with a horrible crack. The table went silent. Herr Doktor picked up the herm and offered it across the table like a sacrifice. Stammering, "I'm sorry. Terribly sorry."

Chapter 7

The Slayer

Herr Professor's gnarled hands took the two broken pieces of the herm stone in tremulous fingers. "I'm sure it can be mended. . . ." Part of him went far away. A tiny voice said, This must be analyzed. What simple evidence. In the two pieces of a stone phallus, a young man's lust for a girl. Not the gift of love. But a broken promise . . .

He glanced around the table. To his dismay, the dining room had emptied. Colleagues gone. Waiters gone. Only Herr Doktor, staring coolly at him with knowing eyes. Scornful eyes that said: So you think you can judge me, Father? Well, maybe in front of your band of toads . . .

But not in *here*.

Herr Doktor touched a finger to his head. In here, it's just you and me. Which one prevails. No truth. No lies. No place to hide . . .

Night reared up around them. The elder man bolted from the luncheon table into the gaping dark. Vines and tendrils lashed his face. He fought the mounting panic. Don't run! Whom do you fear? A naked stranger in a stranger's dream?

Behind him the leaves crackled in pursuit. The Slayer and his mob. But no matter how hard he tried to run, trees blocked his path. He stumbled on a root and took forever rising to his knees. His leaden feet were stuck in muddy tar. The bloody, wet antler hide dragged him down. He tried to tear the stinking thing away. He ran wildly, blindly, the hide clinging to his head, running for his life.

The rabble caught him at the birthing cave. Their hands ripped him, tearing at his limbs. "I showed him how to cure her!" he howled. "I showed you all the way!" But they snatched the words from his mouth. A cruel blade bit into his belly. He saw his entrails ravel out in lengths. Eager hands plunged into Herr Professor's open cavity.

And god-king Jung held his living guts to the face of the moon.

The elder man came back to the crowded luncheon table. The broken herm lay before him on the white tablecloth. Herr Doktor had apologetically resumed his seat. But the eyes of the younger man stared out through a blank mask, cold and hungry. Ja, Herr Professor thought, he's betrayed his wife. Had the girl. With no intention of taking her forever. Had her like a whore. Even now I can feel his will beating down upon me. Urging me to silence. So he can slit my throat. Steal my work. Make it his. While the life bleeds out my veins and I shrivel into dust . . . And then a single clear, brutal thought overcame all else. A thought of despair and irrevocable tragedy. My God, this Jung will survive me. Live beyond my years. Watch my death and still keep on. Survive me.

Sur—

The company jumped to their feet. Herr Professor had slipped back in his chair, gripping the tablecloth. His wineglass sluiced in a stream. The broken herm rolled off the edge, this time breaking into a dozen unmendable fragments. Restaurant diners gawked.

Orders shouted. No one listening. "Look out, he's fainted! Check his pulse! Hold his head! Don't let it fall!"

Then the voice of authority. "Here, I'll take him." And it was Herr Doktor who lifted the stricken man from the chair. Who helped him to an adjoining room. Who set him on a couch. The other fellows of their party hovered about uselessly.

The elder man's eyes fluttered.

"You've just had a faint. Rest here now." He rose to leave. The old man's hand commanded him to wait.

"Stay!" he croaked.

"Don't try to talk."

Then, with effort, "I understand. About you and her. You and me. We don't have to fight. There's room enough. Time enough."

"Enough for what?"

"For everything," he rasped. "Before I *lose* you."

The younger man sank to his kness, taking the soft, lined monkey's

426

paw of his elder friend. "You'll never lose me. You never will. Let me tell you everything," he begged softly. "All of it. Confess."

Herr Professor shut his eyes in weariness. Insisting, "Not necessary . . . you cured her. After all, Herr Doktor Jung, you *did* cure her."

"She cured herself."

The older man sadly shook his head; that wasn't what he meant. He meant a method doesn't cure a man's soul. Only a person can cure another person. Not a method. Methods were for nincompoops and schoolbooks and blind worms groping, with no minds of their own. "Yes, I know she did," he found the strength to say. "I know. She took your hand and climbed from the pit. In the end she cured herself. But . . ." He drifted, lapsing again.

"Who cures us?"

Chapter 8

The Summons

They boarded ship the next morning, setting sail. The trip went splendidly. Herr Doktor threw up across the Atlantic; and he rented a tuxedo in New York. They had newspaper pictures taken in Worcester, Massachusetts, with Stanley Hall, president of Clark University. Another photo was taken of their group as a memento of their journey, the Master among his disciples: A. A. Brill of New York; Ernest Jones of London, England; Sandor Ferenczi of Budapest, Hungary; C. G. Jung of Küsnacht, Switzerland.

Their audience was lively and attentive, even showing flashes of hostility and rejection. But now they were speaking with one voice, drowning out the howls of the mob. They returned across the ocean triumphant. Each man to his home. Where analytic societies were to be formed in each capital. A disciple at every helm.

Fräulein unpacked her drawings. Herr Professor Freud had included a note with them. "Shall we talk about this upon my return?" Shall we? she wondered. She put the pictures away and did not look at them again. What had they to talk about? Could he put a spell on Herr Doktor, making him forget Frau Emma and fall for her instead? Would he marry Fräulein to her prince in a secret place, where they might live together, have children, and grow old as if nothing came before . . . ?

No, the great man could do none of that. No secret place to go. Not even the dream tale. Nowhere . . .

She swept the floor of her tiny flat and made the bed. She did the dishes in the sink and washed the tile in the bathroom. When she fell asleep that night she dreamt of the wolf, but he seemed vague and tired. White fuzz had grown around his muzzle, and he did not seem particularly interested in devouring anybody. She awoke to the sound of cart bells in the street. Mother was coming today.

Fräulein sat by the window, standing watch over the courtyard. The slow morning hours slipped steadily by. She rose once from her perch to make a cup of tea. That's when she heard the feet on the stairs. Mother had crossed the courtyard and Fräulein hadn't even seen. . . . The teacup clattered to the sink. The teakettle began to sing, but she turned it off.

Shoes on the stairs. The steps creaked with great pauses, as though Mother climbed slowly, inch by inch. . . . Fräulein began to shiver. M-m-m was coming. The Maker of Ninny Blue Toes.

The stairs creaked.

M-m-m, who made her cuckoo.

Owner of the loving brush. Would you like this, darling? I'll let you have it if you show me. Don't you want it now? And snip-snip went the scissors as all Püppchen's hair fell off.

The footsteps stopped outside the door.

Her hand trembled in an awful twiddle, sawing fitfully on her thigh. She leaned weakly against the wall. Mother.

Owner of the broken horses.

Ruler of the Brass.

Someone knocked.

Mother. Who gagged her with the home brew. Little It on one leg, clutching the swollen bag that hung from her behind. Saying, Do you promise not to look at the book? Do you promise not to touch the brush? Promise me. Fräulein clasped her hands to keep them steady. Hissing, "Prumse not to draw the Lady of the Veils. Prumse not the book. Prumse not the brush. Prumse never bad bad bad again." Until the wolf snout jammed in. And the Brass swallowed her whole. And she fell forever as the Beautiful Lady cooed:

We'll be together soon.

Sooon

Soooon

The woman stood in the dark landing. She looked like an ungainly stork who had lost her way. She peered uncertainly about her.

"Hello, Mother," Fräulein said. "Won't you come in?"

The woman stood awkwardly in the light of the room, blowsy and flyblown. Her complexion pale as milk — all the blue veins glowed luminescently through her waxy skin. She poked her nose curiously about the room, then paused at the table laden with books and papers, now neatly stacked. She glanced at the newly made bed. At the row of bright plates in a drying rack over the sink. She stood in the middle of the room, unsure of what her eyes told her and ill at ease before the unfamiliar young woman standing nearby.

"What kind of place is this?" her mother asked in a frail voice.

"It's my home, Mother."

The ungainly woman sank to a chair. "Home . . . ?" as if she no longer knew the meaning of the word. What had happened to her mother, her proud, terrifying mother, in that single year? What had happened to wreck her, to devour her soul? The long, gangly woman began to weep, her hand limply waving at the four walls of the room.

"Why, this is terrible. All this. This place. Terrible. And after such a splendid hospital. Why did you come here? Can't you go back? I didn't raise you to live in a tenement. We had so much better, finer things at home. Bigger rooms. Servants too. Before your father . . ." Her voice trailed off. "Before your father . . ." She halted wanly. "Why, if he saw this now, how you are living, I just know he'd come back. Yes, I'm sure. . . ." Mother fell silent. She gazed into her daughter's face, trying to find that person, that little girl, who no longer existed. "You've changed somehow. When did you change?"

"Mother," Fräulein tried to explain, "you haven't noticed I can *talk*."

The older woman considered this for some time . . . lost in the spell of an elusive feebleness; the inability to grasp the essence of what stood before her. Slowly she took from her purse a dirty scrap of folded paper. Smoothing it over the surface of the table, she read it again, as if for the thousandth time. "It says you're his mistress. That you sleep with his wife. Are you? Do you? Your father left before I could show it to him. Who sent it? Do you know? You're really not his mistress, are you?" The words dribbled from her mouth, weak, pointless.

"You didn't let him do anything, did you?"

Fräulein started the fire under the water once more, and the tea kettle whistled its warning. She poured hot water into cups and dunked a tin tea ball filled with leaves.

"No, Mother," she said evenly. "I didn't let him do anything."

430

This seemed to ease the woman's mind. The dirty scrap of paper fluttered to the floor. Her eyes darted nervously after it, then wandered away. A steaming cup of tea was set before her, and bowls of cream and sugar.

"Oh, how nice," she said mechanically. "You made a tea party for me."

"Yes," Fräulein whispered. "I have a bit of cake too."

Her mother made a motion to reach for her tea, but even this was too much effort. Her hand fell limply to her lap. Fräulein forced herself to look over Mother's body, forced herself to remember how proud and straight it had been. How sharp her glance, how stern her bosom. How beautiful Mother's clothes; how each piece fitted to perfection . . . But now the woman seemed to be faded and frayed, sagging and wrinkled and unkempt. Mother's dark hair had gone gray in streaks. On some impulse, Fräulein found the silver-handled hairbrush and took it up to brush her mother's hair.

The woman held the matching mirror to her face in wonder. "Why, where did you ever find this? I've been looking forever. I thought your father stole it. . . ." She left off as if recalling something cloudy now. The silver brush tugged through her mother's limp tresses. It left slivers of pale scalp through her thinning hair. "Oh, didn't I use to be so beautiful," the old woman mourned sadly, "and now I'm going quite bald. . . ." Mother patted the lackluster waves about her face, smiling with shallow vanity into the silver mirror. Fräulein abruptly put down her brush.

Mother was failing . . . adrift. Lost.

Father had left her just to avoid living with a madwoman. To avoid seeing her decay. Mother held the mirror to her bony features, smiling vacantly into it, as though admiring a face she wished to see. "Mirror, mirror in my hand . . . who is the fairest in the land?" She laughed in hideous cackles. "You said you had a cake. A cake for me?"

Fräulein brought the cake. She sat with Mother while she ate. Sat with her as the afternoon lengthened into evening, the sparrows falling silent in the eaves outside. She sat there until Mother rose to leave.

"Well, I really must be going. I'd like to do some shopping before all the stores close. I have a four o'clock train tomorrow. Shall we have lunch at my hotel before I go? I just came to . . ." She paused, uncertain why she came. "I came because I wanted to . . ." Wanted

431

what? Mother did not remember. She glanced at the floor and saw the scrap of folded paper.

The worrisome letter. But clearly she did not find it so awful any longer, now that her mind had been put at ease, her fears to rest. She made her way to the door, calling back, "What a nice tea party. Well, good-bye for now. Be a good girl while I'm gone." And Fräulein answered, "I will, Mother."

The ungainly woman tiptoed timidly down the stairs. Then the stairs were empty. At last Fräulein whispered words to the vacant hall, speaking the question she had never dared to ask:

"Mother, did you love me? Mother, did you? When I was small? Did you really ever?"

Frau Direktor Schanderein sat in her office of the Rostov clinic watching the strip of wallpaper curl slowly off the wall. Why did it choose that moment, after all those years of staying up, to suddenly come curling down? Why now?

Was it because that single child she could save had gone? How bare the old place felt now . . . without Marie. In this final letter she had mentioned the plight of the child and the two unlikely guardians who spirited her away. Now she addressed it: To Herr C. G. Jung, Bollingen Tower, Bollingen Zee, Switzerland. The wallpaper curled again, slinking down six inches as though it had a mind of its own. How long would her letter take to reach him? she wondered. . . . Would it ever?

They came for her in the afternoon. Voices in the front hall. Not school voices.

"Where now?"

"In the back."

"Wait here."

Frau Direktor Schanderein noticed the dull gleam of his leather coat. He had come into her office without knocking and stood for a moment taking it all in. Its dingy shabbiness. Her place behind the desk. She tried to look at his face, to see what kind of man he was — but gave up after a moment. He had the animal face of a human pig. Soft pouches around the mouth, sullen eyes. The bored expression of a man engaged in empty ceremony. A mere formality. He produced a greasy paper. "Sabina Schanderov, Direktor." At first she did not register the speaking of her given name. . . . Then decided to ignore the Russification of her last one. "It says here you have twelve charges. Two interns. We counted only eleven charges. One intern."

"The paper must be mistaken."

A short silence followed. The greasy paper vanished into the man's overcoat pocket. How many battered rooms had he traveled through today? Was she the first? The last? Without waiting to be told, she collected her coat, her purse, her glasses.

"Come along, then."

No one had bothered to turn on the lights in the main room. One of the children cried out at the sight of the black leather coat.

"Who will stay with them tonight?" Frau Direktor asked.

"They will be collected."

Then silence as the shadow of the man followed her own silent shadow. For some reason she thought of the golden butterfly she'd seen earlier in the day, fluttering vainly against the window in the bitter cold. A butterfly in winter. It must be dead now too. . . . A darkness closed around her head, a gray sinking cloud. The world seemed very empty.

Chapter 9

A Candle in the Wind

Emma found him in the long grass. "You were curled up like a caterpillar," she said. He wondered what the hell she meant by that. But felt too weak to argue. "Help me sit," he ordered her. So she sat him like a rag doll in his chair by the stone window.

"You were holding this."

The girl's crumpled letter with the bold face of Lenin on the Soviet stamp . . . "Yes, give it here!" He snatched the thing from Emma's fingers, glanced at it, then thrust it away. "No, burn it. Put it there." He looked to the dead embers of the hearth; the old letter settled to the cold ashes.

Herr Doktor now stared at his hand resting on the stone windowsill. The fingers moved. See? Good as new. Better than new. Just then he noticed the golden butterfly upon the ledge. It lay on its side, quite dead. Its wings trembled in a sudden breeze; a gust took it and swept it away. His eyes lost the silly insect somewhere in the grass. He wondered what it meant. And then forgot about it.

He rose from the chair, feeling hungry now, famished. He wondered anxiously if there were a few potatoes left in a barrel. He went to the well to draw water for a pot. But when he got back, Emma had still not lit the fire. She was rummaging about in his small cupboard of banished memories, among the fallen mess of papers. "Here now," he told her. "I'll do that. You just start the fire."

"Who are these people?" She showed him a postcard from Paris with a candid snapshot on the front. A favorite of tourists who have their own photos taken, before Montmartre or the Eiffel Tower. This particular photo postcard had been shot in front of Notre Dame. Standing before the doors of the cathedral were a man, woman, and child. The two adults held the young girl's hands as if they were her parents. The man and woman seemed careworn, foreign, like mismatched strangers. But they were smiling. The girl stared hostilely into a middle distance. He could not place the faces, but he felt as if he should know them. The postcard was addressed plainly enough, yet the message meant nothing to him:

> Petra has contacted your friend Dr. (name smudged) at the Neuilly Clinic. Miracle of miracles! She found a maid's position. As for me, I've got work as a *plongeur* at the Hotel Crillon. It's not the Hermitage operating theater — but it's 100 francs a week. Our dear Marie is getting fat on pain au chocolat. Many, many thanks.

The signature was smudged as well. He gathered the snapshot postcard along with all the other spilled papers from the cupboard and tossed them onto the cold ashes of the hearth. "You don't know them?" Emma asked again. But now indifferently, as if the question had little value.

"They're somebody's children," he answered her. "Or grandchildren." He poked about for matches, fumbling over them as he tried to strike a flame. "They're friends of a friend," he muttered. Then, finally:

"Who knows?"

The match head flared; the old papers caught. Emma stood with her back to him, peeling potatoes. His answer already forgotten.